Unfulfilled desires transmit themselves i
ways . . .
- I

A sect of sensual medieval heretics stumbles upon the secrets of quantum entanglement, a centuries-old wanderer thrives on rebellion as well as blood in the ruins of post-WWI Munich. Anti-austerity demonstrations lead to haunting connections with past and parallel events, while quantum computing meets 'welfare reform' in our near-future. Meanwhile, persecuted Jews in early 20th century Russia must decide whether extraterrestrials are allies or the *schnorrers* out of space.

The stories of Rosanne Rabinowitz span the centuries in a remarkable mixture of European history and the familiar world of modern Britain – as well as some all-too-likely near futures. These stories are rooted in the spirit of resistance and rebellion without ever feeling didactic. They are coloured with a sense of the fantastic, the surreal and even the mystical – rubbing shoulders with the reality that arises from every street, every shout of fury or peal of laughter, every dizzying glimpse of human possibilities.

All together as they are here, they weave a cyclical sense of the ebb and flow of power and tyranny and resistance, yet the end result is not hopeless but quite the opposite. Just like so many of the characters in Rosanne's writing, as we read these stories gathered in one volume, we begin to see ourselves as living with echoes of and surrounded by the past. That the struggle is ongoing does not make it seem futile; instead, we are connected, for as one character notes, "what we call time, and history, exists in layers all around us. And I should be able to see every one of them." Reading Rosanne's stories feels like standing in the ruins of a thousand-year-old fortress where you can almost hear the past breathing around you, or in some other liminal place: a magical wood, perhaps, but sometimes the most ordinary of city streets, where you might slip into somewhere else before you realize what's happened.

- From the Introduction by Lynda E. Rucker

I will always raise my voice and write things down so people will know about them. I will never be like a bell without a tongue.

- From The Bells of the Harelle

Resonance & Revolt

by

Rosanne Rabinowitz

Resonance & Revolt
by Rosanne Rabinowitz
ISBN: 978-1-908125-51-4

Publication Date: March 2018

This collection copyright © 2018 by Rosanne Rabinowitz
Introduction copyright © 2018 by Lynda E. Rucker

All stories have been edited for this collection.

Cover Art by David Rix, copyright 2018

EibonVale

www.eibonvalepress.co.uk

Publication Information

In the Pines in *Extended Play: the Elastic Book of Music*, edited by Gary Couzens (Elastic Press) 2006.

Return of the Pikart Posse in *Journeys into Darkness*, edited by Trevor Denyer (Midnight Street) 2014. Originally published in *Midnight Street 4* in 2005 and revised for *Journeys into Darkness*.

Bells of the Harelle in *Tales from the Vatican Vaults*, edited by David V Barrett (Constable & Robinson) 2015.

The Matter of Meroz in *Jews Versus Aliens*, edited by Lavie Tidhar and Rebecca Levene (Jurassic London) 2015. Anthology reprinted in 2016 by Ben Yehuda Press.

Survivor's Guilt first appeared in *Black Static 14* in 2009. Reprinted in *Never Again: Weird Fiction Against Racism and Fascism*, edited by Allyson Bird and Joel Lane (Gray Friar Press) 2010.

These Boots published at www.laurahird.com, 2005.

The Pleasure Garden in *Something Remains*, edited by Peter Coleborn and Pauline E Dungate (Alchemy Press) 2016.

Living in the Vertical World in *Mind Seed*, edited by David Gullen and Gary Couzens (T-Party Publications) 2014.

Lambeth North in *Horror Without Victims*, edited by DF Lewis (Megazanthus Press) 2013.

The Colour of Water *Midnight Street 4* Edited by Trevor Denyer, 2005.

The Peak appears for the first time in this collection.

Pieces of Ourselves in *Horror Uncut: Tales of Social Insecurity and Economic Unease*, edited by Tom Johnstone and Joel Lane (Gray Friar Press) 2014.

Keep Them Rollin' in *We Need to Talk* (Jurassic London) 2015.

The Lady in the Yard in *Soliloquy for Pan*, edited by Mark Beech (Egaeus Press) 2015.

Tasting the Clouds in *Café Olé: Too Hot to Handle*, edited by Sarah Crabtree (Independent Persons Press) 2005.

The Turning Track (a collaboration with Mat Joiner) in *Rustblind and Silverbright*, edited by David Rix (Eibonvale Press) 2013.

CONTENTS

9	*Introduction by Lynda E. Rucker*
13	In the Pines
59	Return of the Pikart Posse
85	Bells of the Harelle
113	The Matter of Meroz
145	Survivor's Guilt
163	These Boots
175	The Pleasure Garden
189	Living in the Vertical World
211	Lambeth North
229	The Colour of Water
243	The Peak
261	Pieces of Ourselves
293	Keep Them Rollin'
301	The Lady in the Yard
329	Tasting the Clouds
343	The Turning Track (*with Mat Joiner*)
373	*Afterword by the Author*

Introduction

by
Lynda E. Rucker

There's something very special about finding a writer whose work speaks to you in a particular way. Usually, you "meet" the work first and then the writer, but in the case of Rosanne Rabinowitz, it was the other way around. I've known Rosanne for a long time, in a manner of speaking – we originally became friends sometime around the turn of the century on an online mailing list run by Andy Cox of TTA Press. It was only quite a bit later that I read any of her fiction, and that was when I was struck by that sense of a kindred soul, someone else who imagined there might be things in the margins and on the periphery and just beyond reach.

There is a deep sense of longing in Rosanne's fiction, for other times, and other places, and a better world. In fact, at the heart of *Resonance & Revolt* is a radical reimagining of what the world could be, both politically and metaphysically. Revolutionaries spill out of its pages, whether they hail from 15th-century Central Europe, the present-day era of austerity in the UK or one of its likely near-futures. All together as they are here, they weave a cyclical sense of the ebb and flow of power and tyranny and resistance, yet the end result is not hopeless but quite the opposite. Just like so many of the characters in Rosanne's writing, as we read these stories gathered in one volume, we begin to see ourselves as living with echoes of and surrounded by the past. That the struggle is ongoing does not make it seem futile; instead, we are connected, for as one character notes, "what we call time, and history, exists in layers all around us. And I should be able to see every one of them." Reading Rosanne's stories feels like standing in the ruins of a thousand-year-old fortress where you can almost hear the past breathing around you, or in some other liminal place: a magical wood, perhaps, but sometimes the most ordinary of city streets, where you might slip into somewhere else before you realize what's happened.

You will find all of those places in here, ruins and enchanted woods and city streets that unexpectedly contain magic, and more besides. This sense, of the permeable nature of time and place, is one of the things I love best in these stories, but there are others as well: the striking characters, artists and misfits and activists, many of them existing on the fringes but all of them tough survivors still engaged with the world around them.

The stories here make you want to look at the world more intently, for it is heaving with possibility if only we know how to look. This is an idea that comes up again and again, the sense that we need to *pay attention*. That there really is a deep mystery at the heart of it all, and it's worth seeking it out.

The collection's evocative opening tale, "In the Pines," signals some of the collection's preoccupations with its vivid portrayals of three different points in place and time over a period of more than 100 years, and an exploration of how they are linked – and all the ways in which we might slip into another reality. In this collection you will also find an alien invasion, an encounter with one of Pan's many incarnations, even a magical nightclub. The influence of Arthur Machen is here, along with the pagan, mystic sensibility of Algernon Blackwood. There is plenty of physicality and sensuality as well, and characters for whom sex guides them to a kind of transcendence.

There are some beautiful sentences in here that so poignantly evoke certain states of being that I found myself writing them down. I want to share them all, but that would be unfair; your experience of this books should be your own, and you should encounter your own favourite parts in the context for which they were intended. Still, there is one more I cannot resist sharing, for if this book has a single theme running through it, it is this:

> *I will always raise my voice and write things down so people will know about them. I will never be like a bell without a tongue.*

This is precisely what Rosanne Rabinowitz has done in these pages, in stories that are deeply political without ever feeling didactic and profoundly mystical without ever sacrificing a gritty, grounded sense of reality.

It often takes a collection for a short story writer to receive the attention she deserves. Showcased in one volume rather than scattered throughout anthologies and magazines, a singular vision can emerge, the exploration and development of themes that is the hallmark of a writer working at a mature level of artistry. I think that's what readers will find in these pages, and I hope that, like me, some of them also come away with a sense of having made that special connection with a writer's imagination that leaves you feeling a little bit less alone in the world.

Lynda E. Rucker
Berlin, Germany
February 2018

In the Pines

1 - The Longest Train
Georgia, 1875

Where is he? Where is he? I still look for the rest of my husband in the wreckage that remains. I only find shiny lumps of coal, a twisted length of iron, a chunk of wood, pieces of machinery.

They wouldn't even let me see Sam's head. It would have been my last sight of him. They told me the head was 'without a scratch'. So why can't I see it?

"You wouldn't want to see the look on his face. He must have seen that crash coming up, and he couldn't stop it."

"It isn't a pretty sight", they said. But he never was pretty. I didn't love him for being pretty.

He was the only one on the train, driving through to Tennessee. He'd had no rest since his last shift, but the company ordered him to do the run anyway. Coal and wood needed hauling. Factory owners up North were waiting for their fuel.

I grew up in a country of trees. I know silver birch. I know the squat branches of old apple trees and the smell of fallen fruit in the sun.

When I walk through the birches and oaks long enough, I feel the change in the air. It turns colder, and it carries a scent that is clean and raw. No more crackle of twigs or crunch of leaves under my feet. The dark pines rise up above me, the ground is covered with their needles. When I was a girl I thought that those needles should be sharp, like sewing needles that go through cloth and draw spots of blood from your fingertips.

But the needles beneath the pines are soft, covering ground where nothing else seems to live.

In the hidden swamplands south of here, the pines were giant cedars that stained the streams red-brown like tea. I've never been there, but my grandma and grandpa told me stories about the place and I can see it in my mind.

Pines stand in the deepest part of the forest, they guard faraway hollows and moist lands. They stay alive even in the winter, the only green when snow coats the ground and everything else is brown and black.

How can they live when everything else dies? I used to think that the pines must take all the green, all the sap from the other trees. Maybe they take their life from the living things that move and struggle beneath their branches.

There are also pines at the top of the hill where Sam is buried. But these are thin trees with half their branches bare. They are bent by the wind, bent by their vigil. I sit under them by his grave, and wait for him to tell me where to find his body. I have done this for days, though I know I have work to do. "This can't go on much longer," his brother told me. It won't.

I can't bear thinking of his head buried there, his body lost without the head. When I look at the headstone and the length of ground in front of it, I laugh with bitterness. There's only a head there, do you need that ground just for a head?

Sam was a big man. When we married we had to make a new bed that would be long enough for him.

"Only the best pine for us," he said.

We went into the deepest woods, where trees grew so close together their branches tangled into a roof above our heads. Two of his brothers came to help us. We chopped and sawed and got a good tree down. The sun came through the hole we'd made in the roof of the forest, falling into moving spots of light that looked alive.

Sam pointed out "rings" on the stump that was left. He said they tell stories about the tree, and maybe they can tell you things about people too. Perhaps there is a forest somewhere with a tree for each of us that tells everything about our lives.

When I looked at the rings inside our tree, I couldn't see where one began and the other ended. They were all of one piece like a rope coiled up in a barn. I kept staring at the ring and I was sure it had a story to tell like Sam said. His brother Tom said he'd been a carpenter for years and he never had a tree say shit to him about anything. Maybe the smell of the sap was going to both of our heads and making us see things.

Later, we turned the stump left by the tree into a seat where we could rest whenever we went walking through those woods. We polished the surface and made it smooth; kept cutting back the weeds and small branches trying to start up again. There was barely enough room for the two of us, but we didn't mind sitting very close.

Later, Tom made Sam's coffin. As I walked behind it, I listened for the sound of something round rolling around in the big empty box.

How many times have I seen that train go by?

I was a little girl the first time I watched it rumble through the pass. This machine bellowing smoke and steam awed me much more than tales of God in Sunday School. Its rhythm was a pounding I could dance to if I dared. Car after car went by. One bearing stacks of logs, the next full of coal. Mysterious cargo covered by burlap, another load hidden in a closed car.

The train snaked its way through the valley. One morning I watched it from beginning to end. Did the first car pass just when the rooster crowed and the birds began singing? Maybe the caboose passed when it was well past breakfast time and I was shouted at for shirking chores. It was worth the shouts and scoldings. I just had to see it.

Later I was filled with pride when Sam started to drive that train, amazed that he could hold that thundering hulk of steel under his control. We were blessed, I thought. What a wonder to ride this power across the valleys instead of going below the ground to dig coal in darkness!

Now, I'm only thankful that we didn't have children.

I start singing to Sam in a tune I must've heard before. I want to tell him how I felt when I was a child watching that train go by. Time takes so long when you are small. How can I say that? There was a post in our hollow to mark six miles from the last town, and I used to stand close enough to feel the train pull at my clothes and hair as it went by. *The longest train I ever saw went down that Georgia line. The engine was at a six-mile post, the cabin never left the town.*

The tune tugs at me in the same way. My uncle played the fiddle, and the banjo too. As if he is standing in front of me, I see how the bow slides across the strings and gets them to make that sound.

When I was little I thought there were strings inside each person that can be pulled and twanged and moved in the same way.

Of course, I knew what insides look like from seeing animals slaughtered. I knew what they felt like to touch as soon as I started to help my ma gut chickens. I saw plenty of folks hurt or killed, like the soldiers I found in a ditch during the war. They were mangled so bad I couldn't tell if their uniforms were blue or grey.

Our insides are soft and squishy, all the shades of red and liquid. I once believed that the strings were hidden in there.

But these days I think there is only an empty place inside me, so empty that there is no end to it. Imagine the whole of the night-time sky held in a body, but there's no stars, no moon. There's nothing at all, just a nothing that goes on forever.

That's what the music makes me see. Yet it also makes me feel the wind, the needles beneath my feet and the grit under my nails from touching Sam's gravestone. There's the train winding through the valley, a train that goes on as long as the empty sky.

The colour of the air changes from dusky grey-blue to deep green night. I smell a whiff of salt and fish that doesn't belong here. But it's gone in a flash, and only the music I'm seeking remains.

The tune brings words to me. Where did I first hear it? From my grandma, or my pa when he worked in the yard? Perhaps I stopped hearing it when he was killed, or when my ma passed away. But it's coming to life again with Sam's death. *Your head was in the driving wheel, your body was never found.*

Would he want to hear this? Yes, because he wouldn't want people to forget.

Finally, I tell him that I'm saying good-bye.

As I leave Sam and walk towards the woods, I remember the tales from our old home in the swamp. Is there another place like it? Some people there had been slaves finding the way to freedom by the stars, but they didn't go all the way north and found a home among the great cedars. Other folk were Cherokee, still others brought as servants from across the sea, Irish and Portuguese. The blood of all these people flows in my veins and their songs fill my ears.

That swamp was drained, or turned into plantations by the lumber companies. My people fled again, this time to live here in the mountains.

Now it's time for me to leave. I can set out north, all the way this time. Or I can walk into the pines, deeper and deeper until I come into the open again. Another old melody goes through my mind as I walk, a song of escape. *"When the sun comes back and the first quail calls, follow the drinking gourd..."*

But here the trees hide the stars, so there's no sign of the drinking gourd or the twins. My grandparents fled like this from the government men who drained their cedar swamp. They had to hide in the woods and mountains and make another life, but they also had each other. I only have a new song that hasn't been finished, a song of sorrow and a place in the sunless and starless heart of the pines where no one can find me.

2 - Jersey Devil
New Jersey, 1973

My girl, my girl don't you lie to me
Where did you sleep last night?
In the pines, in the pines where the sun never shines

Linda tried to find a more comfortable position on the grass and closed her eyes as she listened to the band. Despite her deep gravelly voice, the singer was just another white Jersey girl not much older than Linda herself. No way was she a grizzled blueswoman who'd lived a long life of struggle and grief, or a hillbilly girl drowning her sorrows in a still of moonshine.

But that singer came out with notes that reached inside Linda, grabbed her guts and *squeezed*. Could she be the only one affected that way? Look at those happy families sitting on blankets with the remains of their picnics. Over there, older kids, lucky to be out of high school and having a life. Laughing.

"Hey, there's room on our blanket!"

This guy was talking to her. He was leaning back, his long body stretched out. He held a joint in his hand. His dark hair was tied back in a ponytail, but ends of it came loose around his face. He wore a silver earring, which gave him a kind of pirate look. Maybe he looked a little like that Pentagon Papers guy, Daniel Ellsberg, except younger and cooler. She'd put pictures of Ellsberg on her wall when he got busted a couple years ago for giving the papers to the *New York Times*.

Next to the guy with the joint, an older woman with grey-streaked, curly Afro-style hair nodded with encouragement. She was quite round, but in a pretty way.

"There's plenty of room," the good-looking guy said again. He handed Linda the joint. She took a deep drag on it, passed it back.

She'd only smoked pot twice before with Martine, but it didn't really do anything. Some kids at school smoked it all the time. They cut classes and hung out in the patch of woods near school. Linda cut school too, but hid in the local library instead.

The library people must have thought she was doing a project there. But school projects never involved reading Kurt Vonnegut or Hermann Hesse or poems by Ferlinghetti. No one in her school read books like that.

No one she knew ever read her kind of books, except for Martine.

"Thanks," she stammered as she inched her butt onto their blanket. She kept her eyes on the band. She didn't want to be caught staring at that guy next to her. The fiddle player had a bright red beard and sticking-out red hair. The singer was thin and blonde, with baggy jeans she kept pulling up. Like many women here, she didn't wear a bra. When she stood under the spotlight you could see her little nipples through her thin blouse. Some of the pot-smoking girls at school didn't wear bras either.

No way Linda could get away with that. Even after she'd lost weight she still had big tits. If she went to school without a bra the guys would be singing '*Ug-Ug-Ugly Linda*' all day.

> *In the pines, in the pines*
> *Where the sun don't ever shine*
> *And I shivered the whole night through . . .*

That song was making her shiver too. It made her quiver inside like Jello. It reminded her that she was alone. It made her think of Martine's Mom on the phone last week, telling her that Martine was dead. From an overdose. Then she slammed the phone down, as if Linda had given Martine the drugs and it was all her fault.

Martine had been Linda's only friend, separated by twenty miles of the New Jersey Turnpike. Recently Martine had been very busy with boys. Boys never noticed Linda, unless it was to point and sing *"Ug-Ug-Ug-ly Linda . . ."*

Fuck them. They're just immature jerks, Linda thought. It's not like she's even fat anymore. She hasn't been fat for over two years. So what's their problem? They're just jerks.

"You OK, kid?" It was the curly-haired woman. Linda didn't like being called 'kid' but the woman had a kind face, with warming brown eyes behind little round glasses like John Lennon's.

"Yeah," Linda mumbled. The joint came around again. The pirate-guy's fingers brushed hers this time. *Wheww!* That tingle started in her fingertips and went straight up her arm and everywhere. It twisted like a blade, a good kind of blade. He smelled like fresh tobacco, though there was only grass in the joint.

> *The longest train I ever saw*
> *Went down that Georgia line*
> *The engine passed six o'clock*
> *And the cab passed by at nine*

There goes a harmonica, like the whistle of a departing train. And the fiddle player came in with a sound that was rough and scratchy, but sweet.

"I've seen you before," the guy said. "My name's Phil, and this is my friend Kerry. You've been at Change Your Mind bookshop in Madison. You were with a dark-haired girl . . ."

"Yeah, Martine is – was – her name." Phil didn't notice Linda's change of tense. Good. She didn't want to explain. Not now, though she only came here because of Martine. Linda didn't even like folk music. She preferred David Bowie and Alice Cooper. And the Jefferson Airplane.

Folk music was kids' stuff. Songs they made you sing in school like "This land is your land" (no, it's *not*).

But Martine had loved folk music. She said she'd take Linda to this festival and show her what it's really like. Martine had the same olive skin as Phil, but she wasn't thin like him. She had a graceful, pear-shaped body and green eyes. Martine understood her, and Linda thought she understood Martine. Maybe she didn't do it well enough. Why the fuck did Martine take that shit and leave Linda alone?

And now Linda's here and she's met Phil. She almost felt guilty about meeting this cool guy, with Martine dead. But Martine would *want* it to happen. Martine had worried about her not having friends to hang out with at her crap school full of bigots and junior Republicans.

Martine would be so pleased. But Linda better not think about that too much. Martine *wouldn't* want her bursting into tears and ruining her chances.

Phil was handsome, a really mature guy who must be in his 20s. Maybe he'd like her. People said that Linda looked older because she was tall. Maybe she wasn't pretty, but at least she didn't look like a dim cheerleader type from Fuckwit Township, New Jersey.

Her father had to give her a lift to the bus stop so she could come here. You couldn't do anything without a car. You didn't have *towns* in her part of New Jersey, just town*ships* that were stretches of highway, shopping malls and streets of spread-out houses.

Martine lived closer to New York, where the transport was better. She was able to get on a bus when she wanted, then come home. Her parents were strict Catholics but at least Martine was able to go to a bookshop or listen to folk music in a park without it turning into a federal case. Linda had to promise that she'd get a bus back before midnight and phone from the bus stop. When her brother was her age he never got this hassle. Boys didn't. It wasn't fair.

They say that life isn't fair, but that doesn't mean you can't try to change it.

She can't wait to get away.

New Jersey *sucks*.

> *My man he was a railroad man*
> *Killed a mile and a half from town*
> *His head was found on the driving wheel*
> *His body was never found*

This wasn't kid stuff at all. Where did her man's body go? It was gross about that head, but she wanted to find out more. It was like the woman in the song was tugging at her sleeve needing to tell her story, and Linda needed just as much to hear it.

"Who's that playing? What's the song? They must have been in a bad mood when they wrote it."

"It's an old, old song," said Phil. "That band didn't write it. They're the Raritan Ramblers from New Brunswick. They wouldn't know a pine forest if it smacked 'em in the face."

"No pine forests in Jersey," agreed Linda, "unless you go to the Delaware Water Gap."

"Hey, I can tell you're a North Jersey girl," said Kerry. "Haven't you been to the Pine Barrens?"

"No, it's south of here, isn't it?" Linda sucked at the joint when it came her way again. South Jersey didn't interest her. North was what mattered, north to New York City where her family originally came from, and where she'll return. Now she's sixteen she'll try to get a job at the library, save up money and then *go*.

"I come from South Jersey myself," said Kerry. "Closer to the shore, not really in the Pine Barrens. But I know the area, always found it fascinating compared to all the crap amusement parks and arcades down my way. When I was a kid we used to dare each other to spend a night out there. I was too chickenshit. Then." Kerry grinned. She was missing a couple of teeth.

I asked my captain for the time of day
He said he throwed his watch away

Why would someone *throw* their watch away? She imagined the captain – the conductor? – flinging the watch down on the tracks to be crushed and mangled by the train. Just like . . . No, it didn't bear thinking about.

But that train rumbles on, and on. No watch, no time. The night in the pines lasts forever. Just like poor Billy Pilgrim in *Slaughterhouse-Five*, unstuck in time.

The song itself finished however and people cheered. When the group returned for an encore, the singer explained that they'd run out songs – but they'll do "In the Pines" again.

"I never get tired of hearing that song," said Phil. "It's a classic, whether it's played with a high lonesome sound or low-down and bluesy like Leadbelly. It made me cry the first time I heard it."

Oh! Linda felt herself melting. This guy is really *sensitive*. "I don't know much about folk music, so this was the first time for me. What's it about?"

"It can mean all kinds of things," said Phil. "There are versions from different times and places, so there's no *right* answer. The head could be on, or in or 'neath the driving wheel or driving gear. It has also been found by the firebox door! Sometimes the train isn't in the song, but the guy loses his head all the same. Sometimes it's the girls' father who gets killed – or the girl herself."

"Other versions say 'Black Girl'. Some say it's about a lynching," said Kerry. "But a 'black girl' or 'dark girl' in traditional music can also mean a mysterious brunette who doesn't play the game . . . that probably wasn't what Leadbelly meant."

"Lynching or train wreck, life was hard." said Phil. "And it's still hard in many ways, that's why we listen to those songs."

Linda watched the tops of the trees around the stage sway in the breeze. The chords and notes were turning into ropes twining around her legs, twisting around her body. The trees seemed to sing along. A hoarse refrain came from the earth as if its stones were grinding together and making the music. Her heart beat along with it, much too loud in her ears.

It must be the pot. It had only made her cough before, she never knew it could do *this*. She heard each instrument clear and full, she revelled in the blend as they came together. She felt fragile and small in the music's power. Just like the longest train, it could crash and crush her. It could also take her far away from New Jersey wherever she wanted to go, or drag her to the place she feared the most.

She wondered if Phil and Kerry guessed this was all new to her. What if they asked how old she was? She wouldn't know what to say. But who was asking? They just accepted her.

Who is she anyway? Linda, Linda.

When does Linda start, and where does she end?

Linda stared at her hands in front of her, and flexed her fingers. Did she finish at the tips of her fingers? But she felt the vibration of the singer's throat as if she was stroking it; she could touch the wind in the trees and it was part of her too.

Why would that woman run to such a dark and cold place? Was she hiding, was she scared that her head would end up on a steering wheel too? Was a driving wheel the same as a steering wheel anyway? Who wanted to know where she'd slept last night?

Kerry and Phil passed around great slabs of carrot cake. Linda had tuna sandwiches in her bag, but the cake was more tempting. She ate it crumb by crumb. It was moist and dense, the creamy icing tangy and smooth.

Other acts came on. Phil's mouth was near her ear when he told her who they were, that they were much more famous than the Raritan Ramblers. His breath against her ear made those sparks fly again. Each one fizzed, then melted like a snowflake and formed again when he spoke, when he was close. It could go on and on if they ever did it.

Doesn't pot make you horny? But it's not only that, it's *him*. It's the night, it's the mournful music making her want to draw him close.

She shivered again as that plaintive chorus of *"In the pines"* kept coming back to her while the famous people were singing other songs.

Linda had no idea what the time was, but she had a horrible feeling it was time to leave. She stood up and brushed off grass and crumbs. "I better go catch my bus home. It was great talking to you guys. Maybe I'll see you again."

"Are you sure you can get your bus? It's almost midnight," said Kerry.

"Shit! It didn't seem that late. Shit!"

"Hey, don't worry. I know it's hard if you don't have a car around here." Phil patted her arm. "You can stay at our place in Madison if you want."

"Oh, are you roommates?"

Kerry and Phil exchanged glances like they were sharing a joke. Then Phil winked at her, letting her know the joke wasn't about her.

"Well, it's more like a commune," said Kerry. "A group of us live there."

"I didn't know there were communes in New Jersey. I thought you have to go to New York for that."

"There are communes everywhere," said Phil. "Even here. There's more to Jersey than meets the eye."

Linda was pleased with the day's second invitation. Then she remembered that her parents were waiting for her to phone from the bus stop. "Yeah, Phil, that sounds great about staying at your place. But I've got to call . . ."

No way can she talk about *parents*. "I've got to phone my friend who's expecting me back tonight. You know, my roommate. Can I phone from your place?"

"We're not going there straight away," said Kerry. "First stop's a little party out in the Pine Barrens. But we can find a phone booth on the way to this party. It'll be friends of friends I knew from college. I just went to Glassboro State, while some of these guys come from Princeton. But they're different. Science guys who like weird experiments, loud music and parties."

"I'm – I was – crap at science," said Linda.

"I don't think you need to know much science to party with them."

She told her parents that she'd met a friend at the festival – from the bookshop over in Madison remember? First it was: who is this friend? What's her name, where does she live, what's her telephone number? But still, she had another *friend* for once. And this *friend* had other friends who were students from *Princeton*.

Princeton boys? Her Mom was over the moon. Of course you can go.

Linda folded herself into the backseat of an ancient two-door sports car bearing a bumper sticker: "Don't blame me, I'm from Massachusetts".

She'd been the only kid at school who was against Nixon last year, so she might as well be from Massachusetts too.

Maybe she'll head *there* after high school.

Linda peered out the window as they drove. The road signs flashed names she'd never seen in family trips to the shore. *Mount Misery Road. Ong's Hat.*

"That's a funny name. Ong's Hat!"

"Oh, there's a story to that," said Kerry "This guy called Jacob Ong flung his hat in the air, and it didn't come down. Some say it got stuck in a tree, but others say it went into another dimension. That kind of thing often happens in the Pines – allegedly."

"Yeah, sure!" Linda snickered. They were passing a bar, marked by a sign showing a grinning red devil with an overflowing mug of beer in his hand and the legend 'I partied with the Jersey Devil'.

"That's the second bar we've passed called the Jersey Devil," Linda observed.

"There's a dozen bars round here with that name. He's South Jersey's most famous resident," said Phil.

"Never heard of him!"

"What? I thought even North Jersey people know about JD!" Kerry seemed truly shocked. "We're heading towards his native habitat, maybe you'll get to meet him!"

"Kerry's just pulling your leg. Ain't no such thing!"

"I believe in JD! It's a good old story anyway."

"Tell me about it." Linda was getting to like Kerry's tales.

"Some poor woman in the eighteenth century had twelve kids, see. When she was pregnant with her thirteenth she cursed the child and said, 'let this child be the devil'. And first he looked like a normal boy baby, but he grew horns, tail, got wings, the works. And he hangs out in the Pines. But some people say he's an evolutionary throwback from an isolated bog."

"Like the Loch Ness monster?"

"Maybe, but Nessie stays in her lake and doesn't go flying about and getting into mischief," said Kerry. "JD's a winged reptilian creature. He makes a lot of noise. Some say he attacks travellers, others have him going through peoples' garbage and stealing chickens. In 1906 he got bored in the Pines and rampaged around Trenton and Philadelphia, where he attacked a streetcar. It was in the papers."

"That means it must be true, eh?" Linda giggled.

The car made another turn, the road thumping and bumping beneath the wheels. They were driving through a forest of stunted, twisted pines. White sand between the mini-pines gleamed in the headlights. Another turn, back on a road between oaks with wide-spreading branches that scratched at the sides of the car.

Phil turned the radio on to a station coming from Philadelphia, and sang along with another quivery, bluesy song: *"Let him go, God bless him, Wherever he may be, He can travel this whole world over, and never find another girl like me."*

She always liked the mournful melodies the most, and it seemed Phil did too. Maybe he was sad, like her. Perhaps he had a friend who died, or maybe he had that sad bit inside him that didn't seem to come from anywhere.

They pulled into a clearing with a scattering of trailers, cabins and shacks and those big tee-pee things. There were chicken coops, but they didn't appear to house chickens. A few children crawled out of one and waved fizzing sparklers.

"Here we are," announced Kerry. "Here's the party!"

People gathered around a big campfire. Strings of Christmas tree lights glowed between the trailers, speakers were placed around the clearing as well. As they got closer to the group Linda heard "Ohio", that song about student demonstrators shot by the National Guard. Though it was an angry song, its defiance and rhythm also made her want to dance. But everyone was just sitting around and talking.

"C'mon, Linda. Let's go near the fire," suggested Kerry. "Oh, here's Sunny and Joel!" A short woman in a long Indian dress came over, along with someone who looked like a bigger version of Cousin Itt from *The Addams Family*.

Kerry gave Sunny a hug and explained: "We went to Glassboro together, but Sunny went on to bigger and better things as Princeton's token Piney."

"*Ex*-token Piney," Sunny corrected. "They've called our thesis 'seditious nonsense' and we're out on our asses! But they haven't come up with a replacement. After all, you can't get any Piney-er than me. I'm even a descendant of the woman who gave birth to the Jersey Devil."

Kerry nudged Linda. "I'm part Scottish, so maybe I'm related to Nessie."

Joel looked up from under his heap of hair. "Yeah, the resemblance is obvious. Check the profile!"

He did speak a little slower than Cousin Itt, in a strong Brooklyn accent. He chuckled briefly, then lapsed into silence and stared at the ground.

"Don't mind Joel," said Sunny. "He overdid the weed. You know the kind of things he worries about when he gets paranoid."

"Hey, Joel, you always make me think of that joke," said Phil. "How do you know when a mathematician is being outgoing? He looks at the other guy's feet!"

"I object to that," said Joel. "I'm a *physicist*, and I've got a joke for you. An engineer, physicist and mathematician go to a motel . . ."

Science kids at school were really straight, Linda thought. Always peering into a microscope or a test tube, not caring about what happened around them. Sucking up to teachers so they can go to a college with fancier telescopes. Can you really be a scientist *and* a hippy? Linda pushed her hair behind her ears, as if it would let her hear and understand all the chatter buzzing around her.

". . . connecting between two or more resonant spaces –"

"– multiple realities in the same spatial location, but slightly out of phase."

". . . dissonant symmetry."

She felt more than slightly out of phase herself. The words echoed in her head until they meant even less than she thought.

". . . our skin is a boundary but so much can cross it."

Who said that? She stroked her arm, imagining what she wanted to cross the barrier of her skin.

Meanwhile Sunny was saying something to Kerry about "quantum voodoo".

"You always were an intense chick, Sun." Kerry was laughing.

Are these people too busy talking shop at parties to do any dancing?

And Joel was finishing his story ". . . and the mathematician said 'a solution exists' and went back to sleep!"

Linda was getting tired of standing so she went to sit on a log near the fire. When Joel slumped down next to her, she was surprised but pleased.

29

"Hi there," he said. "I've not seen you before. So you're a friend of Phil's?"

"Well, I just met him tonight. At the folk festival."

"Good old Phil. He's always meeting people and bringing them round. He's a great guy. I've known him for years. Kind of a charmer, but he means well."

Charmer. Is he warning her? Does that mean he *knows*?

The idea that anyone could *know* mortified Linda.

Better change the subject so she doesn't look so keen.

"Sunny said you get paranoid," she said quickly. "So do I! What do you worry about then?"

Joel looked at her and blinked. "It's not paranoia. It's facing the truth. The universe will freeze, though the sun might swallow us up first. We have no escape. At the most we can delay our miserable end by a few million years. Unless . . . There may be one way out, but *they* –"

"Is Joel bending your ear? He's always such a big laugh at parties." Phil ruffled Joel's great volume of hair and sat down next to Linda.

Kerry and Sunny joined them on the log too, now talking about pals from college. As Kerry chatted with her friend, she took hold of Phil's hand. It startled Linda. But she held Phil's hand in a loose kind of way, as if they were just good friends. Phil did introduce Kerry as his *friend*.

Martine used to hold Linda's hand sometimes. It first felt weird. Then she realised it must have something to do with being French. Kerry looked like she might be partly Italian, and maybe that's how Italians do things too. She wished she could be French or Jewish or Italian. *Something*, not just a boring American Twinkie-eating WASP.

She started shifting back and forth on the log. She looked around. Two women were dancing together – to a slow song. Were they . . .

Whatever you do, don't stare. But where will she look instead? It would be worse if she got caught staring at Phil.

Martine always knew her way around places like this. The first time Linda went to Change Your Mind, people were sitting around the desk, talking about going to an anti-war demonstration in New York. Linda wanted to join in, but there wasn't any room left to sit there. Martine was in that group too.

So Linda went to look at magazines. She picked up one with a cartoon on the cover showing a man in a suit running around with a butterfly net outside a school. He was trying to catch the kids who were running free all over the place. That must be why the magazine was called *Outside the Net*.

Inside was a poem by a high school junior who later committed suicide. This kid drew to express the things that pushed inside, he wanted to carve it in stone or write it in the sky. At school he had to sit in a square brown desk, but he thought it should be red. He hated to hold the pencil with his arms stiff and his feet flat on the floor, the teacher watching. He drew a yellow picture, and it was the way he felt about morning.

But the teacher said he should draw pictures like the other boys. So he wore a tie and drew rocket ships and airplanes. But he was messed up by it.

Linda later read that poem over and over and knew those last lines by heart:

> *He was square inside and brown*
> *And his hands were stiff*
> *And he was like everyone else*
> *And the things inside him that needed saying*
> *Didn't need it anymore*
> *It had stopped pushing*
> *It was crushed*
> *Stiff*
> *Like everything else.*

"Hey Linda, can I get you a drink?" Phil pointed to the biggest trailer. "There's lots of cold beer in there."

While Phil was getting the beer Kerry gave her some brownies – hash brownies, she said. Linda ate half of one, and put the rest in her bag. When Phil came back with their beer he sat down next to her and asked if she was OK.

"You seemed quiet. Hope you don't feel left out. I know what it's like being a stranger." He smiled that crooked smile.

She wanted to tell him everything now. She *had* to.

"You know that girl I was with at the bookshop?"

"Yeah, Martine."

"She was my best friend and now she's dead."

Those words sounded so short, so final. *Now she's dead.*

"Hey, I'm sorry to hear that. Really sorry."

"She OD'd. Her parents blame it on her friends. They hung up after they told me on the phone. Well, they did give Martine shit about going to church, being Catholic and going out with boys. Sometimes they drove her crazy with that stuff and it got her down. But they'd been OK in their way. They invited me to supper and made French food. They're French, though Martine was born here. And all the time I'm wondering what happened, why it happened. It must've been an accident but what led up to it? And I keep wondering if I could have done something to stop it."

Phil put his arm around her. "That must be terrible."

Linda was trying not to cry. Sometimes, it was harder when people were nice to you.

It had been like that the first time she met Martine in the bookshop.

Crushed. Stiff. Like everything else.

First, a single tear rolled down her cheek.

She sniffed and wiped it away. But tears just kept coming. She always knew there was something wrong with her. This was it.

Square inside. Everything in you just scooped out.

Then Martine came and asked her if she was OK. Linda felt like a fool. But Martine took her into a little room with lots of comfy cushions. They ended up talking all afternoon.

Linda didn't want to cry this time. Her voice was shaking but at least she was able to keep talking. Phil held her and stroked her hand and even though she was so sad, she felt wonderful. He leaned forward and his lips just brushed her cheek, though her hair was in the way.

Talking to Phil made everything feel lighter. Soon she was telling how Martine had helped her with her French homework and then taught her the best French swear words.

Phil seemed to enjoy her collection of French curses. He stopped giggling and taught her some things in German.

She knew she can be a laugh sometimes, and maybe that was why he liked her too. It made her feel warm and oozy to think of that. He really did like her. He didn't treat her like she was just a kid.

"Hey, I'm getting hungry now, are you? There's food in the trailer too. I'll be back!"

Linda waited for Phil to return, but he was taking a while. She needed to find a toilet. Could there be one in the silver trailer with the beer?

The trailer was crowded with people who probably needed the bathroom too, so she kept walking up the path. There was a light twinkling in the woods. Perhaps that was a cabin or an outhouse. The music from the party filtered through the trees and she heard the Jefferson Airplane singing about how people will rise up against the government in 1975. Only two years to go!

Maybe she'll go back and dance, especially if they play 'Volunteers'. Maybe Phil will dance with her.

The thought made her stride ahead into the moonlit woods.

She heard rustling and murmuring from the trees on her right. She was about to avert her eyes to the path in front of her and walk on, then she recognised one of the voices. Phil? He'd gone for food, but that trailer must've been crowded for him too. But who was with him?

He had his arms around someone; they swayed together.

A quick sickness stabbed Linda in the stomach. He'd liked her. Remember those fingertips brushing, that quick squeeze. How he hugged her as she told him about Martine.

She should have walked on. But she was rooted just like those crazy stunted trees they passed in the car.

She heard a low chuckle. *Kerry?* Phil and Kerry were together? She'd thought they were just friends. She'd thought Phil liked *her*.

Linda stepped forward to flee, but made a loud *crack* when she put her foot down. The couple separated.

"Hey Linda! You OK?" Kerry emerged from behind Phil. Her hair was sticking out, looking even greyer in the moonlight.

She wished she could dissolve in a puddle like the wicked witch of the fucking West. Melt away, after being caught out. But Kerry was smiling at her.

Phil grinned and gave her a thumb's up.

"You lost?"

"Yeah, I was looking for a bathroom, but the trailer was packed and I couldn't wait. I saw a light and thought there might be an outhouse or something."

"That's an old clubhouse they use. There might be a toilet. But they keep a lot of stuff there so it's probably locked. You just might have to use the natural facilities."

"Yeah, I remember how to do that. Cover your shit with leaves. Fucking Girl Scouts!" Linda couldn't stop herself from talking nonsense.

"I went to Scouts too," said Kerry, "but it was a long long time ago."

"I hated Girl Scouts," said Linda. "My parents made me go 'cause they thought it would be good for me and I'd stop being 'negative'."

The two of them were being *too* cool about it. Phil must think she was just some kid he could pat on the back when she cried. It didn't even occur to him that she'd be upset to find him with Kerry like this.

"I gotta go," said Linda.

"See you later," said Phil. "Let us know when you want to leave."

She started to walk, but she couldn't stop herself from looking back. They were hidden by trees now, but seeing nothing was worse. Then she ran.

On each side of the path the columns of pines didn't move a needle, though the breeze moved strands of hair into her face. She walked towards the light and found it. A single bare bulb surrounded by moths and gnats above the door of a single-level building. It didn't look like it would have electricity, but those hippies had managed to wire something up. A faded sign said it was a 'Rod and Gun Club'.

"Phil's a charmer, but he means well." Joel must've seen *it* in her, all her thoughts and desires. She'd been making a fool out of herself.

She knocked, then banged at the door. It's locked, fucking *locked*. With a final bang she ran again, further into the woods.

As the path narrowed, the trees on each side reached over to each other to make a tunnel. Where did it lead? Not back to the party, to failure and humiliation. They all must be laughing at her now, that silly lump of a girl who took a shine to Phil. They were nice to her, but it was only because they felt sorry for her.

So people are scared to stay out in the Pines at night?

She wasn't scared. She'd put on insect repellent at the festival. She's got sandwiches left. And hash brownies.

Why did that woman in the song run into pines?

She was beginning to understand.

Linda thought she'd been following a path. But now she made her way through random spaces between the trees.

Soon she heard a stream, and she moved towards the sound. The trees were so close together, like bars on a prison. Some were half-bare, limbs twisted like pretzels.

No leaves rustled, no animals scampered. Silence filled the forest.

She was getting hungry. She took out a sandwich and took bites out of it as she walked. The mayonnaise in the tuna salad had turned the bread soggy.

The ground was also getting mushy. Little puddles formed between her footfalls. Then a space showed between the trees. She walked through it to a clearing where she found the stream, widening into a broad patch of water like a pond.

She rested at the edge, and took another bite. Here there were white birches, pale like skeletons with pines among them. Some of the pines had no branches at all, only clumps of needles sticking out from the trunk. They made her think of pictures of thalidomide children she'd seen in *Newsweek*. There was a patch of ground in the middle of the pond covered with the white birch-bones and one single twisted pine tree. On the grassy bank opposite, tall dark ranks of pines extended to the places she couldn't see.

She never thought she'd be eating a tuna sandwich alone in the woods at night. She always ate her lunch alone at school. It was what she knew. But she never knew what it's like to look at the sky and see no one else under it, no one at all. She finally found a place behind a tree and squatted. It sure would be easier doing this in a long hippy skirt.

Linda felt like she was being watched. Not by a person, not even by an animal. It was the place itself, poised and waiting. She listened for a breeze, for anything. She began humming. *"In the pines, in the pines where the sun never shines . . ."* She thought of her only friend Martine, slumped dead over the desk in her room, stretched out on the bed or lost somewhere . . .

She walked along the side of the pond, slow through boggy land. Good thing she had hiking boots on. She wore them everywhere because she liked the way they looked.

The thalidomide trees gave way to cedars as wide as barrels. Their branches arched and looped over dark water. A flowerpot was hanging from a branch of the biggest one, but there was nothing left growing in it.

A clean spicy wood smell filled the air. She knew they were cedars from that smell, because Martine used to burn cedar-scented incense. The fragrance went to her head and her humming turned into the song itself.

People used to say she had a good voice. Her parents urged her to try out for the school choir. Made her. She got in. But her singing never blended in with the school anthem, the national anthem and or any other stinking anthem. She quit before the Christmas assembly because she hated the carols, especially those warbling high notes in the 'Gloria' choruses.

'In the pines' was a song that went low. She pushed those low notes out with deep breaths, and the high ones came piercing and forlorn. *"My girl, my girl, where will you go? I'm going where the cold winds blow . . ."*

The emptiness of the forest gathered her notes, and waited.

Out of the sky came another voice if it could be called a voice, another note weaving between and below her song. It was soft at first, a thread of dissonance. But it rose, and kept rising into a shriek. It was distress, it was a threat. It wasn't human, and it wasn't like any animal she'd ever heard. She's seen films. She's been to the zoo. So she knew what a lot of animals sounded like, and this wasn't one of them.

It could have started from many throats, but came out of only one mouth.

It came from far away, but it was getting closer.

It was here, with a beat of wings cracking the branches above her.

It landed in front of her, under a cedar tree.

It had a face like a horse, but without the attentive expression of a horse. It was a blank face, made of two flat planes of bone on a long thick neck. It had curved ram-like horns, a long body covered with scales. They gleamed in a liquid but murky way, like the puddles between the trees. It had hooves on its back legs and claws on its forelegs, long leathery wings like a big bat's. It reared up on its back legs and held up two short front legs, with claws extended.

It let loose its cry again, starting with piercing mournful notes and subsiding into a low and hoarse rumble.

Fuck! This must be the Jersey Devil. It's *real*. And it's not holding a beer and inviting her to party either.

What can she do? Where can she hide? Her heart was banging, she could hardly draw her breath in and out. It hurt her ribs. But –

She didn't believe in devils, so it must be an animal. And wild animals don't usually attack people unless they're cornered or scared.

Can't you talk to animals to calm them down?

"Hi, are you the guy called the Jersey Devil?" She made her voice low and soothing, the way she used to talk to the dog at Martine's. Their huge Airedale was always in a huff, but he was soon wagging his tail whenever Linda came round. Martine's Mom thought Linda had a way with animals. She sure hoped so.

"Where do you come from? Oh, what am I saying? Of course, you live here. Sorry if I disturbed you."

Just keep talking. Anything. Animals don't understand what you say, but they'll listen to the sound. It'll hear that you don't mean any harm. Or is it a 'he'? According to Kerry's story, JD was born as a human boy. She wasn't sure about *that*. Male or female didn't seem to apply here.

"I guess I wouldn't be happy if someone came crashing into my home, making lots of noise. Was my singing that bad?" Her heart was slowing down. At least this blabbering was calming *her* down. She must *not* panic, or the clawed creature will smell it. "Or maybe you didn't care for the song . . . You know, the one I was singing . . . '*In the pines in the pines where the sun never shines*'

The creature cocked its head to the side and let out another yelp that climbed into a crescendo. Just listening made a pressure form in her chest. It made her feel sick. Everything about this creature seemed so *wrong*, as if it was put together to fit another place.

It lunged.

Linda stepped back and her foot got stuck in the soft ground. She put out an arm to break her fall and her sandwich flew from her hand. She cowered on the ground in the shadow of its wings as it stepped forward.

A clawed foreleg reached out for a piece of sandwich.

The creature sat back on its haunches as it quickly disposed of it. Then, it grabbed the other half.

Thank fucking goodness it found that sandwich more appetising than me, Linda thought.

"Liked that didn't you? Here's another one," She reached into her bag and threw her remaining sandwich towards the beast. "And look, here are some cakes."

There go the hash brownies. Maybe it'll get good and stoned.

When all the food was gone, it began to make a barking sound.

"No, sorry that's all I've got. I'll bring more next time. Maybe I should just be getting on my way. Thanks for your time, mm, uh, do you mind when people call you Jersey Devil? I mean, I don't like it when people call me Ug-ug-ugly Linda. You know, like that sappy Paul McCartney song? It's crap, that song. Everyone knows John's the only old Beatle who writes good songs now. My favourite is 'Working Class Hero', but you never get to hear it unless you have the album. All the radio stations banned it 'cause he says *fuck*."

She was starting to feel like someone else, someone who knew what to do. It was like swimming to the top of a huge wave and riding on top of it.

But where does the wave go?

Just keep talking. Pretend this scaly thing's just a grumpy Airedale.

"Even WNEW banned the song, and they pretend they're *so* cool. But John's right. We get stuck in schools where you don't learn anything except how to conform. They only prepare you to take orders in some crap job or fight wars for corrupt politicians. They brainwash you with religion, TV and bullshit . . ."

Then the creature howled. It seemed as if each howl floated to a place so desolate it could never be seen.

"OK, OK, sorry, so you're not a John Lennon fan! I thought you came to tell me to shut up when you flew over here, but maybe you really like 'In the pines'.

She began to sing that song again.

"*My girl, my girl don't you lie to me, where did you sleep last night?*"

She didn't remember all the words. But didn't Phil say that people made up their own words as they went along? "*Her body was on the driving wheel, her mind was never found. Martine, Martine why'd do you die on me?*"

Every sound the Jersey Devil made clashed with her singing. It would have given the choir teacher a heart attack. It didn't make her feel that well either.

Yet the sounds belonged together.

It was singing of its own loss too. It was singing about being lost, of fleeing to darkness – the only place it could ever make its home. Light was for other people. Not for Linda. Not for the Jersey Devil.

The creature keened. She felt as though something was about to split in her chest. Notes floated from the trees like needles, like leaves. The minor chords tugged and unravelled her. The pines were full of voices. The noise released them, as if they had been trapped in ice and amber now melting.

Sound waves never die. She remembered that much from science, taught by greasy Mr Gerber. So where do they go, when the person making the sound is dead?

When the creature came closer, this time she wasn't afraid. It stretched out, now resting on its front legs. It lowered a wing, and looked at her with eyes too big for its face. They were flat, yet facets below the surface shifted. She was sure those eyes were meant to see another kind of light, and the Jersey Devil was trying to find it. And it seemed to want her to sit on its back.

"No, no I'm too heavy," Linda protested. "I don't think it'll work!"

But it waited, and barked with impatience. It wasn't going to give up.

When she sat astride its back, she was overwhelmed with the smell of swamp. Yet there was a clear sky scent too that must have clung to it when it flew. Its scales were surprisingly warm and dry. She tried to find something to grasp on its narrow back. She wasn't aware of lifting into the air. The lurching movement didn't come as a result of flapping wings, or putting one foot ahead of another. She wasn't aware of going *up* or *down* or *sideways*. Yet they moved.

The air was full of angles and curves, suffused with a green light as if she looked up through a pool of water covered with lilies. Branches surrounded her and pine needles pressed against her, each one bringing a stab, a spark. Each needle falling off made a *ping*, a ring like a glass singing before it broke. Everything smelled of sap and wood. The pines spread below her feet, an ocean of trees cut with the shine of waters, fringed on the horizon by a darkness that might be the Atlantic.

Then they angled in a direction that could have been 'down', for the trees were coming close again. "Where are we going?" Linda whispered to the Jersey Devil.

It didn't reply. Even if it spoke to its own kind, it didn't know her language.

But she could guess the answer.

In the pines, in the pines where the sun never shines.

3 - High Lonesome Frequency
Cornwall, 2015

Look, two blokes in brand new hiking gear. Poking about, but trying not to appear that way. Too studiously casual to be officials or property developers. They're not tourists – too sombre, too intent.

This isn't actually our land so I can't tell them to fuck off.

I don't want them to see me. I walk faster down the hill. I have work to do, so I'll just ignore them.

I only need to duck down a little at the entrance of the cave, stepping through the fringe of bluebells, ferns and foxgloves that grow around it. The afternoon sun throws light into the passage, showing fractal patterns of moss and lichen over the dry-stone walls and the stone slabs that make up its roof.

"Alright, mate?" I nod at the figure carved into a boulder near the opening, a man with long hair and raised arms, the left side of his face flecked away. Some heritage people from Penzance come to look after him, but he's showing his age – a good 2000 years or so.

I follow the passage as it curves deeper into the earth and I turn on my torch. As I descend the sounds of buzzing bees and squawking birds fade away with the light.

In the main chamber I sit down with my back against the wall. I take my laptop out of my rucksack and let it boot up.

There's plenty of time before our interview tonight so I open a page of equations that have been pissing me off for days. The light my computer sheds on the walls of the cave is not at all harsh or out-of-place. I've found yet one more use for something that was obviously built to last. This iron-age hideaway might have been used for rituals or to store grain. Smugglers and wreckers took advantage of its protection. There are stories of Saxon massacres and witches' sabbats here, though if a coven consists of thirteen then those parties must have been standing-room only.

"Resonance, resonance . . ." I mutter, as if simply repeating the word will achieve something. Maybe the Celts chanted a lot down here, but it obviously didn't do them much good. I had a semi-mystical phase myself. But it only went so far, like everything else.

A few days ago I gave another set of equations to the musicians. The only result was a headache when I ventured into their studio. Let's see, if two people have headaches with the exact pattern of pounding pain, can they share their thoughts? Try that for an experiment!

I scan the figures and symbols again, but I see no completion. Something's missing. I sigh and close my eyes. I try to imagine vibrating strings tied up in knots and how I can put that in numbers; and the ways I can translate and express those numbers in music and in colour. But my surroundings fill my mind instead.

So far I've not seen any ghosts of witches, smugglers or Celtic warriors down here. Ghosts don't interest me anyway. But often I sense a shifting in the stillness of this place. It's like I'm sat in a traffic island that's deadly quiet at the centre, but there are vehicles whizzing around it. I'm trying to hitch a lift but no one's stopped. I can't even see the cars but feel the breeze and smell their 'exhaust' as they go by.

What I really smell is earth and stone, damp dirt and dry dust together. It's a scent of time passing. There is rot and decay, fresh growth that extends roots from the ground above; the lichen and moss as it clings and penetrates the walls. Particles of stone falling off and crumbling. There's something else, a clean almost-medicinal smell like pine. I breath deeper, let it fill me, let it expand. The space around me also expands as I breathe, my confined room opening up until I'm in the centre of a hub that spirals out in countless roads and paths.

I still can't catch what passes by, or where the roads go.

Then there is someone, just walking in a place where everything else moves so fast. A tall strapping woman with curly dark hair, a smile with a promise of mischief. Her sights are set ahead. I'm afraid she'll get knocked down by the traffic. Though I can't see it, the traffic must be dangerous because I feel its sucking undertow as it goes by. But she walks forward, calm and set on her goal.

Except for the silver in her hair, she looks just like me. I dye mine these days.

I know her name. *Esther*.

I'm hit by sadness, feeling a loss that came before all others. It wells up uncontrollably, a hidden spring of salt water.

Then I'm staring at my screensaver, a photo of our big black cat Schrody.

When I emerge outside, the sun is already setting.

"Briony, you were down that fuckin' *fogou* again." Deb doesn't usually swear, but in this case she can't resist a bit of alliteration.

She's already working her way through a pile of washing up. "I know when you've been down that hole. You're always late."

"Sorry, I just lost track of time. It happens there. But I get ideas too."

"What idea did you get this time?"

"Oh, I'll tell you later." This isn't the time to tell her I saw my twin sister – who had died shortly after birth. I don't know if it's a vision – my unconscious grasping something that could be there, but hidden – or simply a wistful dream. I've never told Deb about Esther. Why should I? I was just born, what would I remember? I only heard stories from my parents and I used to wonder about her. Then I stopped thinking about it when I became interested in mathematics and boys.

Perhaps stress brought it on. This interview, maybe.

I used to be good at interviews. I'd made presentations, sweet-talked grants committees, appeared on talk shows and gone on book tours. I admit I enjoyed the attention. I was full of *chutzpah* and I knew the *craiq* too. I got that much from my Jewish *and* Irish Catholic background, along with a great multicultural helping of guilt and repression.

The woman who's interviewing us – Linda Brooks – used to be famous too. Years ago she was a top war correspondent. She went missing in action; then she was found. Now she only writes occasional articles about health and mental health and women who do unusual things. Deb said that Linda's last article was an excellent piece on services for torture survivors. So Linda should be very worthy. No headlines like "Curvy quantum cutie" from her. I shouldn't worry.

Deb is playing some of my old music, *Nirvana Unplugged*. It always amazes me when young people listen to music I loved when I was even younger and full of angst. I'd just moved to London and started university. I was living in a grotty bedsit with one ring for cooking my baked beans, etcetera etcetera – the whole scene.

Despite her taste in depressive 1990s rock, Deb's always been upbeat. Somehow, she skipped the miserable phase. People like that seem to come from another planet – bless 'em.

"Oh hi, I guess I'm early! I was afraid of getting lost and I *hate* being late." A bright gee-whiz American voice chimes at the door.

This must be Linda: a tall blonde woman in a brand new Goretex outdoor jacket – trendier than the stuff worn by the maybe-spooks I spotted this afternoon. I can smell the newness of the jacket from here. My eyes are drawn to her lime green knee-high wellies.

Who let her in without warning us? I'm not ready.

Deb holds up her plastic-gloved hands. "Oh hi you caught us by surprise! Sorry about the mess, but we weren't expecting you until later. Just let me turn the music off."

Linda is clearly shocked at the state of our kitchen. The clutter, cupboards open, plates and cups still in need of washing. What did she expect? A laboratory?

Linda isn't what I expected either, kitted out in full retro-cool London-luvvie-roughing-it mode. But what did I expect – a flak jacket?

"Never mind," I say. "Have a seat." I point to the armchair by the bay window. But it's still occupied by Schrody, who often gets mistaken for a cushion. I scoop her up and onto the floor. She lets out an indignant *miaou* and stalks off.

Linda looks likely to do the same as she scrutinises the chair.

"Sorry Linda, are you allergic to cats?" I ask

"No, I'm not allergic, just . . ." Linda brushes at the cushion and finally lowers herself into it. "It's OK."

This woman fussing about a few cat hairs was once dodging bullets? But then, that was years ago and I've changed too. She must be older than me, somewhere in her fifties but seems younger. With her jacket off, she has that raw, incomplete look that large-boned people have when they're too thin.

"Perhaps we can get started." She's all business, leaving out the introductory remarks about the weather, her guesthouse accommodation and the long journey from London. We don't even have time to offer a cup of tea before she takes out her phone and sets it to record, placing it on the table.

"So Ms . . . Dr . . ."

"Call me Briony. And this is Debjani," I add. "A physicist working on our project. She also co-authored the second book."

Linda gives Deb a big smile with teeth gleaming like piano keys, but her eyes are only on me as she gets her machine going. "As you know, *The Review* wants a human interest rather than a technical angle. I'm not a specialist myself, but I did find your books fascinating and liked the fact they were written for a lay audience. Your work on time travel, alternate universes and dimensions sparked a lot of debate. Then you disappeared . . . What have been up to in the last eight years or so?"

"Well . . ." I find myself staring at the contents of a teacup that had escaped the washing up. Get a grip! You're not telling the woman's fortune. "Well, I needed a change. Being a celebrity scientist was getting in the way of the real science. And I was thinking beyond pure mathematics, and wanted to explore other symbolic systems and other disciplines that embrace all the senses. Abstract formulas showed the way, they gave me the bones, but where was the flesh?"

Is that a snort of suppressed laughter coming from Deb at 'flesh'? No doubt she's thinking about some earlier 'experiments' I told her about. I'm reminded of our age difference in moments like this. I give her a discreet nudge with my foot and carry on: "It's been said that the separation between science, art and music is relatively recent. But we wanted to take these connections further and see how 'art' can actively aid scientific exploration, particularly in areas that are new and a bit strange. So we got together with artists and musicians and settled here. I was drawn to this place on my first visit, and blew the advance from the second book on a rundown old wreck. But we did a lot work. Not bad, is it?"

I point to the bay window and its view of the valley, a lush swathe cut into arid cliffs and windswept fields.

"It's lovely," says Linda, "But wouldn't you find it isolated after being at the centre of things? You were at the top of your profession at a relatively young age. Why did you suddenly withdraw and give up your academic position in London?"

"I could ask *you* a similar question!" I snap back without thinking.

"Briony just needed more space to do her work. We all did." Diplomatic Deb jumps in. "We just wanted to get on with things, working as a group. There are about 20 of us coming and going. Some of us still teach or do research or other part-time jobs, but what we do here is our main interest."

I will give Deb credit for *not* mentioning that some of our lot still sign on.

And I'm also thinking that it's time to stop. I can see my spiel getting disjointed and my ill-temper taking over. I've fallen out of practice, I really have. It won't be fair on Deb to get stuck with playing good cop to my bad one.

I want to talk about the work we do together, now that I've done my job as a formerly famous person by drawing attention to it. But with the way that silly cow's been ignoring Deb, I don't know how much good it will do. I really don't trust this woman.

Maybe I'm just getting to be an old cynic. I shouldn't ruin it for the others. *Try* to be nice.

"Linda, maybe we can show you around." I suggest. "And our musicians are playing in the local tonight. You might find that more illuminating than listening to me! You're here for the weekend, so we can go into more detail later. Let's have a break and a cuppa," I put on the kettle and get some mugs onto the table.

Linda picks up a mug and furtively examines the rim. "What music were you playing when I came in?"

"Just Nirvana," I say.

Linda shrugs. "I have big gaps in my musical knowledge, since I was . . . *away* for a lot of the 90s. Some old stuff is really new to me. It sounded OK."

"You like it? I'll play my favourite song from that album." Deb puts the music on, then goes foraging for biscuits while Kurt Cobain begins to rasp and wail that old song about headless bodies and hiding in the pines where the sun never shines.

Linda stops her inspection of the mug, putting it down with a thump. She looks like she's just been punched in the face. She's shaking. She slumps forward, puts her hand over her eyes.

Deb runs to her rescue. "Linda, you alright?"

Linda doesn't respond, except to hide her face more.

"Maybe you need something stronger than tea," I suggest. "Would some whisky suit you better?" I take a bottle of Jameson's from the cupboard and pour a healthy amount into a glass.

Linda reaches for the whisky, with a muffled 'thanks'. Suddenly she takes her hand away from her face. She tips her head back to swallow it, fast. Her face is white, her eyes reddened but otherwise she is still in control.

"I never heard that before," she says in a flat voice.

"Eh?"

"That version of "In the Pines". I've not heard that song for years, so it took me by surprise. It brings back memories, not good ones. Don't get me wrong, it's a good song though. Y'know, I used to collect recordings of it. In high school. I worked part-time in a library and spent my wages on old records instead of saving for college. This was before YouTube and all that. You had to go out and get records, actual records. And there's hundreds of recordings of that song – Bill Munroe, Hank Williams, Joan Baez, Leadbelly, Dolly Parton, Bob Dylan . . . I was so obsessed, I got ill. Ended up in the hospital.

"But I got better," she adds quickly. "Completed my high school equivalency. Went to college, grad school, became a journalist. I pulled through."

"It's an intense song," I comment. "I've heard Marianne Faithfull singing it, and Hole. But Cobain's version is just . . . You hear it and think: he sounds like he's really going to do it."

Maybe that wasn't the right thing to say, because Linda looks even more disturbed. "I'm really sorry about this," she says. "It's not really professional, is it?"

"Don't worry," says Deb. "Maybe we're not so professional either."

"I first heard that song at a folk festival when I was sixteen and met people who took me to a party in the Pine Barrens. It's like another world there, though you're only a couple of hours from New York and

Philadelphia. We visited a bunch of hippies living in yurts and trailers. They were into science and weird physics, some Princeton dropouts who took too much acid. I was . . . a friend had just died and I got upset with the people I came with and ran off. It was almost like the song, someone I loved had died and I spent the night in the pines."

"I had a friend who died when I was a teenager," I say, pouring a whisky for me and Deb and another for Linda. "She got killed in an accident at work. Another crashed when he was joyriding. Bad things seem to affect you even more at that age."

Linda's now keen to tell more about her teenage nervous breakdown. "The shrinks said I was a classic obsessive-compulsive. Keeping order was a way to stop things from *slipping*. But I snap out of it in the face of danger, real danger. Everything's clear then. That's why I was good on the frontline. But then it stopped working . . ."

Like many Americans, Linda seems to enjoy revealing highlights from an extensive back catalogue of therapy sessions. But she still doesn't say what happened in the Pine Barrens.

After another round of whisky we head to the pub. On our way I point out the art building, dwellings and music studio. "We have the studio heavily soundproofed. The music boys – and they usually seem to be boys – have a band called the M-Theories. Like the M-People, geddit? The landlord invited them to play when he heard them talking about music, but I'm not sure how they'll go down at the local."

"Briony's tastes are a little old-fashioned. *I* think they're good," said Deb.

I shine a torch on the path ahead as we go deeper into the valley, surrounded by rhododendrons gone feral, clusters of ferns that stand higher than our heads. A few designer houses with angled window-covered wings perch on the ridge above us, looking like giant dragonflies. In their way they are beautiful, but not a good sign of things to come.

"When we bought this land, this was a deserted valley among the rocks far from a town or railway line," I tell Linda. "Only a few fishermen and some old hippies lived here, and the fishermen were getting fed up. Later came some low-key guesthouses and holiday cottages. But now developers want something big. We've got police looking for drugs every other night, and the developers have people in the council making up planning violations as we speak. There's also been tapping on the phone, suspicious people lurking about. We suspect that it's not only our prime real estate drawing unwanted attention, but also what we're doing."

"A couple of centuries ago, this valley was a hide-out for brigands and smugglers," Deb adds as we come down to the stream. "I like to think that in our geekish fashion we've been carrying on the tradition!"

If only, I think. If only the authorities really had something to worry about! They might believe we're onto some great subversive free-for-all dimension-bending science they have to stop, control or use for their own purposes. But we're not getting closer. Still, it's better we tell people what we're *trying* to do, rather than the wrong people find out and keep it to themselves.

We stop for a while at the bridge across the stream, look down at water rushing around moss-coated stones. If you follow the stream a mile to the sea, it swells and tumbles down the cliffs in a noisy multi-tiered waterfall. Even here, mist and spray wafting from the bubbling, bashing water casts a layer of pearl over the green. I shine my torch on it, searching for a rainbow from a spectrum I've never seen.

I caution Linda to avoid hitting her head at the entrance of the building. "It's a very old pub, 18th century I think. But like a lot of people around here, the landlord's family dates from the 1960s."

Linda is very impressed with the house brew, beer of an amber-honey colour with a head that's pure voluptuous cream. I let it slip down my throat as we watch the band setting up.

It's not the main session night, so our M-Theories won't face the usual rowdy lot here for Irish music, fiddle tunes and jigs. Still, people arrive from isolated cottages where fishermen and tin miners once lived. A few punters get off the bus that stops here twice each day.

There's old Jake with his dog, an alarming Rotweiller-Doberman cross that's really the soppiest animal outside of a Disney cartoon. A few of the session regulars, old-timers and the more settled incomers like me and Deb.

There isn't really a stage, simply a space at the front. It's all very cheek-by-jowl at sessions where fifteen musicians might materialise out of the woods. Tonight, there's a keyboard player, electric violins and two standing basses. There's a drummer whose kit gleams with extra gadgets, surfaces and snares. Someone else twiddles two dials and flips switches back and forth on a big black box while alternately twanging a tuning fork. I hope there'll be some improvement with the new equations, despite their flaws.

Ben, who plays standing bass, introduces a song. "While we're getting the dimensional resonator tuned I'll tell you a little about us."

"A what?" Linda frowns, then pulls a notebook out of her bag.

"I guess we're different from what you usually see here!" Ben continues. "We aim to pluck more than guitar strings, though guitar strings help. The strings we're plucking and the membranes we're hitting exist in ten and eleven-dimensional space. We want to twist them, braid them and roll 'em into a ball! This song gets into the heavy stuff – we call it "Dark Matter!"

Then it starts. Ear-splitting waves, poundings, electronic burps, gurgles and screeches piling onto each other. It has an effect like a massive hunk of chalk dragged across a slate that might be called 'Earth'. Deb is nodding and grooving to the din, but Linda is looking truly stricken. Then she seems bored. She plays with a packet of crisps, as if the rattle of crumpled paper is more pleasing to her ear.

The dog starts howling. Ben must be taking that as a compliment, because he grins and whacks the strings of his standing bass with even more enthusiasm.

Then Linda laughs. It's the first time I've heard a proper laugh from her. "What a bunch of hippy shit!" She's laughing so hard she almost falls into the sawdust on the floor.

Despite my own reservations, I feel compelled to defend our lads. "Look, they're weaving physics into music, trying to cross dimensions with chordal structures, frequencies and harmonics." I raise my voice so she can hear.

"You're bullshitting me. I don't care what dimension they're from, it sounds like shit."

I give up. "OK, they do. But it's an experiment. And maybe they should keep their experiments in the laboratory or the studio, and not torture that poor dog with them. But sometimes you have to get things wrong before you get them right."

"But it's elitist rubbish to assume that the more obscure, tuneless and annoying you get, the more revolutionary and provocative you are!"

"They're not trying to annoy anyone. Most people writing seriously about parallel universes talk about great machines and particle colliders and messing about with massive charges, energies and black holes. But what about other methods of finding a way through, of achieving resonance? All that hardware at the LHC is impressive but maybe there are things we can do in our own garden shed with materials we have at hand, using our imaginations, voices, visions and simple musical instruments. Our approach is very DIY but the results might not be something you can sing along to."

"Why the fuck not?"

I don't have an answer to the question. *So why the fuck not?*

I'm mulling this over when Linda gets up and returns with more drinks. She takes a long draught of her beer, emerging with a foamy moustache. She wipes it off with the back of her sleeve. She's definitely not the same woman who walked into our house today.

The M-Theories are lurching through another discordant composition. Someone's trying to calm the dog.

"Why don't you play a goddamn tune!" Linda bellows, brandishing her pint.

"Linda, no!" Deb lays a light restraining hand on Linda's arm. "Shh-shh."

"Shhsh yourself Deb," I tell her. "I know you enjoy this stuff, but is it going anywhere? Just another bunch of geeks pissing about! Maybe our musicians need to be challenged."

Ben and the others are still twiddling their strings. They relish a bit of opposition, a bit of negative energy they can transform. Perhaps they're hoping the dog will howl again. The drummer stops. The guy on the dimensional resonator carries on. I can't hear what comes out of it, but the dog certainly does.

"Yeah, play some tunes!" I call.

"Alright," Ben agrees. "Maybe the music of the spheres isn't right for a night down the pub after all. Anyone know some tunes? Grab an instrument and join us."

One of the regulars rises to the occasion and picks up a violin. "Requests?"

I get an idea. "In the Pines?"

I make my suggestion a question, not sure what Linda will think. Does she get upset *every* time she hears it?

Linda glances at me, then down into her pint before another big swallow. "Yeah, why not? It's a beautiful song, it only took me by surprise before." She raises her voice again, shouting to the musicians. "Yeah, play 'In the Pines'!"

"Right." He begins scraping out the song. He plays it rough, torn from the belly of the instrument. There is discord in this too, but at its heart lies the melody.

> *My girl, my girl don't you lie to me,*
> *Where did you sleep last night?*

When he gets to the chorus, Linda is already singing along. Her voice is surprisingly strong and tuneful, however slurred her words. A hush falls. The barman leans on his elbows, just listening. The dog's ears prick up, but he stays quiet.

Before I know it I'm singing too. My voice is off-key and hesitant, but it fits in. The music blends with the rush of the stream beneath the bridge, the world outside becomes another instrument.

I've heard that song many times, usually the Nirvana version. But this is the first time I feel it. The electrified violin and standing bass, our own physicist-designed drum kits bring a new rhythm to it that beats beneath the soles of my feet and makes the bottles at the bar rattle. The dimensional resonator must be doing something in the background, though I don't know exactly what.

As the chords change there is a shift in me too, a bittersweet taste in my mouth. The bitterness stings. The sweetness makes me ache, ache to hear more of it. I am sucked into the darkest blue oscillation. I reverberate inside it, every cell pitched to that high and lonesome frequency that I am sharing with so many unknown others. My heart vibrates at a perfect pitch. The pitch is answered; it's found its match. I close my eyes and I see . . .

Scrawny pines at the top of a hill, bent by the wind. A woman sitting beneath them, facing a grave. *Where is he?* Twisted trees you can hide yourself in, staining the waters of a swamp.

The song cracks an egg open, letting everything out. *Where is he?* Where are my friends who died before they reached eighteen? I think of a would-be boyfriend blown up on a bus on his way to our second date. Lives never lived, potential not realised. Parts of me are missing, like the husband's body that was never found. *Where is he?*

Where is she? Where is Esther, the twin who shared everything with me long ago? I only know now how much I can still miss her.

Does sorrow have a frequency, does longing and pain? It is a strong one.

> *I asked my captain for the time of day*
> *He said he throwed his watch away*

I've not heard that line before, not from Nirvana or Leadbelly. It makes me shiver. That damn conductor throwing away time. But isn't that what we're *trying* to do? The dizziness I felt in that fogou comes back to me. No time, all times. Happening at once. Take care in the traffic.

The sound of the stream is louder, almost a roar. Am I still in the pub? Deb sits across from me but doesn't seem to notice me. No, I'm not in the pub. Yes, I am. But the pub has expanded, and it contains a forest. It contains a world. Dark rolling hills, the pines. Someone once wrote that each human creates from birth to death a double furrow of light and sounds; so do music, events and movement. I am falling into a furrow now.

I'm sitting on a seat formed from the stump of a tree. When I get up, I run my hands over a smooth, polished surface. The polishing brings out the pattern in the wood, a spiral instead of concentric rings. I run my finger around the spiral; the end of it loops back to the centre and begins again. I can't tell the age of this tree.

I realise I have company. Linda, lime wellies and all. Christ, Linda. She must be freaking out.

But she's only pulling her hood up as if going for a stroll. She seems very much at home though her cheeks glisten with tears. She gives a sigh of something that sounds like resignation.

Maybe she's stunned. I should explain what's happening, even if I'm a bit dazed myself. I want to skip and cheer. What a brilliant discovery. But I'm also tuned to the frequencies of loss, ready to cry. I have to keep it together.

I try to be reassuring as we walk along a path. "It's alright. We just need to stay calm. We never left the pub, but that pub shares space with another place, or many places coincide in the same place as the pub. Think of radio waves. We are surrounded by them, but you can only tune to one frequency. But what if we have more than one radio on? After so much faffing it took a simple folk song to achieve this . . . this resonant coupling, this connection! Brilliant, brilliant – Jesus Christ! What the fuck is *that*?"

There's a flash of grey and green wings through the upper branches of the trees, an eerie cry rising and descending scales not meant to be heard by human ears. Something lands in front of us, a very badly designed dragon with a head like a horse with bone disease. It spreads its wings and shrieks and glares with red eyes.

"What the . . ." I stutter. Take a deep breath, try to listen to something other than my heart in my ears. Curiosity should win over fear.

Those eyes transfix me. They have another colour besides the red. I don't recognise it. More than one colour there, but they don't blend. They are just *in the same place*. Maybe the creature isn't glaring after all. But what is it looking for?

Linda pats my arm. "Don't panic, it's only the Jersey Devil. I've met it once before. It'll be fine if you give it something, you know, make friends. The poor thing's just lost. I don't know why it stays stuck."

The poor thing is making a racket far, far worse than Ben's first few numbers.

"Good thing I still have some crisps." Linda opens a packet and tosses them towards the noisy monster squatting yards away from us.

The Jersey Devil snaps up the crisps, devouring the packet along with the crisps. It flies away, disturbing branches above us and shaking a shower of pine needles loose.

I'm beginning to understand more, the part Linda didn't talk about. "Is this where you went that night in the Pine Barrens? And it was just by accident? You seem so relaxed about it now." I look at her with new respect.

"I'm not so worried *now* because it'll wear off and we'll be back. I know I really lost it back in the kitchen. But now that we're here . . ." Linda shrugs. "The hard part is after you come home and try to live a normal life. That was my undoing both times. You think you're on a sidewalk, but something shifts and you feel it rocking like an ocean swells beneath it and huge waves are about to crack through. You suspect everything, see a different form flexing beneath every surface. Sometimes it even felt like there's another person in the same space as me. The second time I got caught was in Bosnia. But in the short term, we'll be OK."

"Deb must be worried about us!"

"She might not even notice we've been gone. On the other hand, it might be weeks to her. We can't think about that now."

Linda puts her fingers to her lips and whispers. "If you listen to the trees, you'll hear the song in so many ways. Not all in English, but you'll understand them."

There's a high, silver hum from the needles. Each one a spark of light, a membrane of someone's universe ending. The needles fall over us as we walk, they hum beneath our feet. Slivers of strings form minute melodies. Each one is a high lonesome frequency, cutting into you like a diamond.

Even now, I'm thinking: *You must observe. You must collect samples, you must collect data.*

But the rest of me is full of the song, and the sorrow that formed it.

A rhythm underlying our steps and our breath becomes louder, until it swells outside of us and fills the air. We walk faster, as the sound comes faster too. The trees are so close together we have to struggle our way through them, as if the fragrant pines had turned into a cage. But there is light ahead, moonlight, starlight showing through the trees.

What would the stars look like here? I must get into a clearing to have a good look.

"Don't run," cautions Linda.

But already I see where ground drops in front of us, and we come to the edge of a steep valley. I expect to see the stream, or the sea pounding down below, but there is only a railway track. And then we hear the vast noise of the engine.

Below, an ancient steam train makes its way, clouds of smoke reflecting back the silver light. The metal moves with a groan, as if the machine protests. Some cargo cars are covered, others carry gleaming heaps of black anthracite. Carriage after carriage passes. There is still more of the train beyond the horizon.

Linda recites softly: "*The longest train I ever saw, Went down that Georgia line, The engine passed six o'clock, And the cab passed by at nine*"

All the windows are covered, no lights on. Faster and faster, the clack-clack swells. There is always more of this train. Perhaps it will loop back on itself with no end, ever.

Linda is watching, her face unreadable. Has she seen this before?

"Briony, I believe you," she finally says. "When you told me that the song put us in synch with signals and waves elsewhere, I believed that. Why do you think I wanted to I interview you? I wanted to find an explanation, and hoped you had one. But tell me – can't we do the same thing with a happy song? Imagine how wonderful that could be."

Wonderful, yes. But I remember the kind of music that clutches at you and hangs on. I think of how it takes a high lonesome sound to reverberate through a void and bring you to the other side of it. I think of a bass that thunders in sorrow. That is where the power lies.

"Sorry Linda, but I think that minor keys are the only ones that *work*."

Return of the Pikart Posse

Unfulfilled desires transmit themselves across the years in unfathomable ways . . .
- Greil Marcus, Lipstick Traces

"I'll have the 'Pot for a Hungry Hussite', please." Evelyn spoke to the waitress in rusty Czech while eyeing the long hooked blade of a weapon hanging on the wall. She sipped her pint of *pivo* and started to feel better. She leaned back, then jerked upright when she realised she was just about to rest her head on two crossed cudgels studded with nine-inch spikes.

As she opened her rucksack, a ripe fruit-laden scent engulfed her. She breathed it in. Peaches. She'd bought them earlier, now they must be close to fermentation. The aroma went to her head, making her forget for a moment why she had opened her bag in the first place. All she wanted was that sweet juice filling her mouth.

No, not yet. Leave it for dessert. She was looking for her notes, wasn't she?

She found the folder and a sheaf of papers tumbled out. After rummaging, she found what she was looking for. *"Let loose your prisoner! Give me your soul and receive mine!"* The passage made her laugh out loud all over again.

What a chat-up line! Students in her "Introduction to Medieval Dissent" session would have a giggle at that. But Evelyn stopped laughing when she remembered that her days teaching that class might be numbered. Drops of moisture spotted her papers, and she had to wipe her forehead with a serviette. Though it was evening, it was still very hot. Her light cotton dress felt like heavy armour against her skin.

The waitress came with a huge bowl of stew. Evelyn shoved her notes aside to make room for the food. But just as she lifted her spoon, her mobile rang out with the bass riff from "Guns of Brixton".

"Hi Gerry," she answered, phone against her shoulder as she took a mouthful.

"What's wrong?" Gerry asked. "You don't sound yourself."

"Nah, I'm OK. But I've had a disappointment. That professor I'm working with had an emergency. Her mother's ill. So I'm fending for myself and staying at a guesthouse. We spoke on the phone and we'll meet another time, but it's still disappointing. The museum's closed now, but I can't look at the new material until she's there anyway. Of course, I'm sorry about her mum . . ."

Silence. There'd been a lot of silences between them lately, and this was a particularly expensive one. She imagined him stretched out on the sofa, with the phone in one hand and perhaps a beer in the other. He'd *love* the beer over here.

"Evelyn, why don't you come home?" Gerry hesitated. "Maybe this situation is telling you something . . . You even said your professor told you that your Adamites would be hard to research. So maybe a bunch of medieval shaggers and pissheads isn't the thing to study anyway!"

"Hah, we could learn something from them," Evelyn replied, deciding to take his remark for a joke. "Did you know that when an Adamite woman fancied a lad, she'd tear open his breeches or reach under his tunic, and say *'Let loose your prisoner!'* Maybe I should try it when I get back! It's been a while . . ."

"Evelyn, I don't wear *breeches* and certainly not a tunic! And it would be a real turn-off if you groped me like that."

Evelyn almost dropped her phone into the stew. At one time, he would've said something wonderfully rude in reply.

"Gerry, where's your sense of humour? And . . . everything else?" *That* just burst out. "But we can't talk about this on the phone," she added. "Why don't you come here? Get a cheap last-minute flight. Tábor's only an hour from Prague."

"Why don't you come back to London now that your plans have fallen through?"

"Because I'm here and I want to do what I can."

"It just looks like you're making things difficult for yourself again. I worry about you, you know I do. With all your work and studying, you're still so insecure, still struggling. You need to be more realistic."

"Gerry, I'll be fine. This trip hasn't turned out how I expected but I'll make the best of it. And what *do* you want me to do, drop everything to become a computer programmer like you? How can I? I'm crap at maths and besides, programmers are made redundant too . . ."

The argument heated up until Gerry finally shouted down the phone: "Do something useful with your life!"

Evelyn tried to go through more notes. She read the same section over and over. *"No longer should there be a ruling king or ruling lord: for there should be servitude no longer . . . Now you will not pay rents to the lords anymore, nor will be subject to them, but will freely and undisturbedly possess their villages, fish ponds, meadows, forests and all their domains."*

She just couldn't concentrate.

The formidable Alžběta Morosova had warned that her topic it would be difficult: "Little is known about the lives of commoners, and less about your Pikarts", she had written. *Pikart* rather than *Adamite* was the preferred term. "Most were illiterate peasants and artisans who took their secrets into the battles and the flames that consumed them. All that is left are myths and allegations."

But Evelyn was used to warnings like that. Then she would dig and dig and extract the truth. Despite the discouraging words, Dr Morosova must have recognised that. Not only did she invite Evelyn to stay at her home, she offered her a look at fragments of a manuscript found recently in a remote part of Greece and shipped to Tábor's museum. It *might* have been written by a refugee from Bohemia, who referred to a woman leader of the Adamites called Maria.

Did the threat to Evelyn's job start with the spoutings of the reigning education secretary? Medieval history courses were 'ornamental' and 'dodgy', according to him. Just a waste of public money.

After this official pronouncement, Evelyn's boss Robert had called her in to tell her that her position – an 'adjunct lecturer studentship' – could be scrapped. Corners must be cut, and medieval history was not a priority area.

Robert had actually lived in the same squat as Evelyn some fifteen years ago. Occasionally he used her old nickname, Evo. He liked to remind her a lot about those days, especially when he was about to make her redundant.

However, he told her she might be in with a chance for another position if she did something 'sexy' for her PhD. Something publishable and controversial.

"You know what I'm working on," she told him. "How much sexier can you get than that?"

"You'll need to come up with the goods fast, *Evo*."

The goods. And this was the guy who used to accuse anything that moved of 'selling out'.

You expect problems from a boss, Evelyn thought, but what do you do when a lover you've lived with for eight years tells you to give up? It brought back the panic that plagued her when she first returned from her extended travels in the early 90s. A stretch of teaching English in Prague didn't do her much good in getting work, and then the Job Centre was getting on her back . . .

Gerry's words made her doubt herself.

Maybe she is wasting her time, she thought. She'll end up carting all her possessions about in a shopping trolley, muttering 'spare some change' in Latin and medieval Czech. A bit of old French and Flemish thrown in.

But think of Maria, she told herself. Remember the woman you want to bring to life in your work. Would Maria sit in a tavern and sulk after she argued with her mate Rohan? No. Maria was a woman of action.

Maria didn't read or write, but she must have moved people with her voice. Perhaps she savoured every word on her tongue as she spoke, then passed it into the mouth of each person who heard her. It must have been like making love with everyone who listened.

Maria, tell me. Was love really that free for you, didn't anyone get jealous? Tell me who you really were, because all that is known about you is your name.

Evelyn ordered another beer, staring at the weapons displayed on the walls. She'd love to use that long twisty-hooked thing or that spiky cudgel on Mr Secretary of Education. "Ornamental", he said. She downed the beer, and ordered another.

Yeah, she could show him something 'ornamental'.

Evelyn lurched about Tábor's old section, down narrow streets that wound around and crossed each other. Designed to confuse attacking armies, the streets would confuse her too if she cared where she was going. She passed pavement cafés filled with laughing young people; there was the click of glasses, the hiss of cappuccino machines. Hungry Hussite stew and pints of *pivo* sloshed inside her with each step.

In the central square, she squinted at whitewashed buildings with flower-petal facades, gawked at the pastel lattices and gilded curlicues, lace spun from plaster that framed windows and softened the peaks of roofs.

This town displays its past in every street, window and rooftop. But the past has many layers, Evelyn thought. Look past this baroque splendour to an earlier century when Tábor took root, starting as an encampment in the shell of a fortress. First there were tents, then rough cabins and cottages made from logs or planks.

The first cooling breeze of the evening ruffled Evelyn's hair as she imagined people flooding in from the countryside and from the towns, throwing everything they had into communal barrels. People marching off to take what was denied them by the gentry and the Church to fill those barrels once more.

And there was another kind of sharing, the Adamite love feasts. They could have happened in those cottages, in tents or perhaps fields just outside the town walls. Under the shadow of the old fortress of Příběnice, later surrounded by the waters of the Nežárka River on the Isle of Hamr. *Nameless Wildness, untrammelled freedom.* But some of the *wildness* did have a name; Maria.

Unfulfilled desires transmit themselves across the years. Those desires were reaching her now . . .

A woman is stretched out on the flat stones along a river bank, her nude body half-submerged. She is tall for her time and thin, but with broad hips and strong legs. Her dark hair fans out, drifting in the water. A man leans over her.

The woman's eyes are closed against the sun, as his fingers run up the tender inside of her arm. It is one of the few soft parts left of her, when her limbs are hard from fighting and running, her scars showing in streaks of silver and white. He loves those scars because they are part of her and speak of what they share. He draws his tongue along them.

Then he finds the other soft places too. The hidden, inner skin of her thigh . . . *Rohan, slide against me, fill me.* A woman joins them, another man.

Evelyn sat down on the side of a fountain, suddenly breathless. She could have been there herself, stretched in the afternoon's heat, cooling in the water as the current nudged her. She was languorous, opening to the touch of many lovers.

Maria, who are you? Where did you come from?

Maria would have left the countryside. Living among the dispossessed of Prague, Maria would have heard tales of peasants rebelling and of others cut down. Of weavers smashing their looms and burning churches. An inquisitor mysteriously murdered; brethren escaping the inquisitors of Tournai to seek freedom in Bohemia. She heard fugitive Lollards preaching in their strange English tongue. She joined them all in storming the New Town Hall, casting the corrupt councillors out the window.

Then Maria came here, to Tábor.

The expanse of white cobbles and well-preserved gingerbread façades blurred with the pang of that young woman's desires – and Evelyn's own. *I'm listening. Tell me as I walk through the streets of the town you helped build, the town that turned against you. Put your long-forgotten words into my mouth. Let me lick them.*

When Evelyn looked up towards the clock tower across the square, she saw it only had one hand. It seemed to have a message for her, though she didn't understand it yet. Perhaps that one hand pointed the way.

Evelyn staggered forward with new purpose. She must follow her hunches, no matter how bizarre. It had worked with her "groundbreaking" MA on the Tournai heretics. All that remained of them were a few documents left by the Inquisition, and a chronicler's account of the jeering lyrics sung by angry crowds as they followed inquisitors in the streets. But she unearthed much more, acting only on hints, fragments and a dream she had almost forgotten.

Think again: the end of time, nothing is measured, untrammelled freedom . . .

Straight into a great heavy chain; it hit her across the knees. She recovered her balance and faced the statue that the chain was protecting. Old Jan Žižka himself, the one-eyed general who led the armies of fifteenth-century Tábor. What a huge droopy 'tache he had, extending beyond his chin in two thick brushes made of stone. Žižka wielded a cudgel and wore what looked like a 1970s-style sheepskin coat over his chain mail.

"*Make my skin into a drum for the Hussite cause,*" had been his dying words.

"And throw a few Adamites on the fire while you're at it," Evelyn shouted at the statue. Gripping his weapon, Žižka remained frozen in the same step forward and didn't take one bit of notice.

"That's right, you kinky old bastard! Repressed and repressive, but really as camp as a row of tents, moustache and all . . ."

A tall slender man with cropped black hair stopped to listen. His smile lit up a narrow, intense face, along with the glint of a ring in his eyebrow. Evelyn grinned back. Did this smiling guy know what she was talking about?

"Hello. But what do you have against Mr Žižka?"

He didn't sound like a native English-speaker. Just a little too precise, with a hint of American. Was he German, perhaps?

"Well, he massacred the Adamites, though they fought back several times. Or Pikarts, since the term 'Adamite' comes from the eighteenth century."

The young man nodded. Evelyn took that as encouragement to go on.

"And you know why Žižka decided to attack the Pikarts at Příběnice? He objected to the behaviour of the women! A repressed kind of guy. But hey, I'm kind of pissed. I don't usually go around talking to statues. I was in a pub, a Hussite theme pub with flails dangling from the walls."

"A Hussite theme pub? That's new."

"Perhaps the heritage hype is mild by Western standards, but I did eat something called a 'pot for a hungry Hussite'. Maybe there's another theme pub in Klokoty serving Frisky Adamite Fries and Pikart Crispies. Oh, Klokoty's where JZ burned about seventy Adamites at the stake," Evelyn explained, hoping he didn't mind her joke. Gallows humour came naturally in the historian's trade. "And the Adamites were called Pikarts because they'd been hanging out with these refugee heretics from Northern France, you see, and people thought they all came from Picardy . . ."

He put his hand up. "You don't need to explain *everything*. I grew up here, though I've lived in Germany for years."

"Oh . . . sorry if I'm being arrogant and talking shite. You didn't sound Czech."

"No problem. Mind you, my knowledge of local history might be limited. When I was growing up, it was just boring propaganda at school. In the Middle Ages we had the world's first Communist state in Tábor, so they said. And I didn't want to know. But when I mention my home town to my German friends, sometimes I found a surprising reaction. 'Wow, do you still walk around in the nude?'"

"That wouldn't be a bad idea in this heat!" Evelyn laughed, very aware of her dress sticking to her thighs. To let the evening air cool her skin, as she stretched out near a river or somewhere deep in the forest . . .

"But what did these Adamite women do to annoy the good general?"

"If they fancied a guy . . ." Then Evelyn remembered Gerry's reaction. "Well, they were very *assertive*."

"You'll have to tell me more. As I said, I have only heard the official version." Then he offered her a hand to shake. "I'm Jan. I was going to meet friends at a gig, which marks the end of a festival. There's a group here that organises international events. It should be good, and you're welcome to come."

"I'm Evelyn. Or Evo, my friends used to call me."

Only two musos were making all that noise. A woman whammed the drums in a funky-punky rhythm and it swung too. The bass player thundered and thudded. They sang in French-accented English and something Slavic but not Czech.

Evelyn had been dancing and dancing. It could have been hours, and maybe she has only just started. There was only one moment of movement and music, a moment that expanded until it swallowed every other moment. She couldn't move without touching or entangling with someone. But they all smiled, Jan's friends and total strangers. The sound of many tongues mixed with the music, turning into another melody. The rhythm changed and shifted, and compelled her along with it.

Jan's dancing was loping and graceful. She drew closer to him and mirrored his movement, until someone else lured her into another dance. A voluptuous red-haired woman, a short guy with blond hair and rosy cheeks. A tall French bloke with wavy dark hair took her hand and twirled her around like they were line-dancing, then he got twirled in turn.

She finished her beer. Another drink was passed around, a tall glass filled with water and a layer of the beautiful but bitter green of absinthe. A woman with long grey hair came from behind the bar and tossed two pint glasses of water on the dancers.

Evelyn let the drops of welcome wetness fall on her. The French man lifted up her hair and planted a kiss on the back of her neck and they were dancing too, his eyes fixed on hers, arms and hips moving to urge her on. Legs touching, between hers. Big bass vibrating beneath her feet, travelling up her legs, stroking deep. He kissed her again, this time on her lips.

The big red-headed woman came close to Evelyn, and took her by the hand. Water drops rolled down her face and gleamed between her breasts, on the pale flesh spilling over her bustiére. Her rounded belly and full bosom cushioned Evelyn as her French friend put his arms around her from behind.

A last drop of water trembled on the woman's upper lip. Evelyn wiped the water off with her fingertip and suddenly pressed her lips against hers. They parted and let Evelyn in. It was a kiss that kept opening like a flower, a core of petals unfolding.

The woman ended it by smiling, and taking the absinthe. After drinking she gave the glass back to Evelyn with another kiss, this one bitter-flavoured but more delicious. *There is always bitterness underneath. This is the pleasure of paradise, but the Earth is the only possible place to taste it.* Underneath, underneath. The room flowed in front of her eyes, and for a second it wasn't a room. Evelyn was dancing under a deep black sky where the stars blazed.

She drank again, and again. Sweat rolled off her, as if the atmosphere itself was water and she swam in it. She had to come up for air.

As she made her way out of the club, she found Jan near the bar. "How's things?" she asked him. He seemed subdued, or worried about something.

"Not bad, but very drunk." He leaned towards her. "And thinking too much."

"I'm much more than drunk. I'm . . ."

"You're what?" Jan put his arm against a ledge behind Evelyn, almost touching her. His presence stirred the air, and he reached her through it. The shock of his presence shot heat to her centre, and another beat began. He had dark blue-grey eyes, slatey and deep. Evelyn moved closer to him and the power increased. She felt it in her fingertips, urging her to slide them down the side of his face or the neck of his t-shirt.

She thought of the red-haired woman. This power grew from that kiss shared with a stranger, an extension of the wild dancing.

"I'm . . ." *The black sky that is our roof, the blazing stars. The summer breeze on hot skin.*

Had she been whispering of the black sky and stars, of pleasures enveloping her like a sweet-stinging swarm of bees?

"Jan, let's go outside."

"Yeah, good idea. The music's good but it's too hot here."

Evelyn didn't really want to leave everyone else behind, but she also needed to be somewhere else. *Under the black sky.*

Outside the club, two stocky men played guitars and one sang a ballad. He said it was an old Kurdish song. She didn't have a clue what it was about. But it made her remember how she felt sitting alone on the square listening for the voice of a long-dead peasant girl turned revolutionary.

The two Kurds moved on to a livelier song and a woman got up and swayed in a belly-dance. It wasn't a familiar dance, but Evelyn joined the woman and discovered a set of muscles she had never known about. Others joined in and the celebration spilled into the main street. It was spreading beyond the boundaries of this street, this town. Jan danced behind her. His hands rested on her hips as she moved them in a slow figure-eight. Just like that she began to lean against him.

A police van drove up the road and started to slow down. Jan tensed up and stopped dancing.

"The police are here!" Evelyn heard people saying in Czech, then repeated in other languages. *Get inside until the cops are gone.*

69

Jan released her. "Evelyn, it's too hot to go inside again. Let's have a walk instead. There's something I know you'll want to see."

They walked along a ridge above the Lužnice River. They passed a piece of the medieval wall, and the only remaining gate to the old city – Bechyňská, flanked by the Kotnov Tower. At the bottom of the valley, the river was small and far away.

A breeze lifted from the valley, as if greeting her. It let her know that the town on the hill and the dark slopes below it will give up their secrets, and the knowledge she sought won't be found in museums or in old manuscripts.

"Be careful, Evelyn, or did you say Evo? I know this shortcut well but it's easy to lose your footing after a few drinks. Slowly now . . ."

She grasped the broken banister as she made her way down the stone steps cut into the hill. Jan held Evelyn's other hand and squeezed it. "I said slowly, don't want you to fall! Oh! You alright?" When she stumbled against him, he put his arm around her. She remembered his hands on her hips, and how she fell back against him and moved.

She straightened up, suddenly gawky and shy. She hadn't been with anyone besides Gerry for eight years. Jan must be a good ten years younger than her.

"Yeah, I'm fine," she said as she stepped onto level ground.

They walked past an old house, through a field into the woods. A creek bubbled over rocks and gurgled in a little waterfall, where discarded plastic bags tumbled in the moonlight. A rank sewage smell hit her nose. Next to the creek, a sign pointed the way towards Klokoty and Příběnice. On the other side of the creek stood a tree with five thick branches rising from a massive trunk. It looked like a hand with fingers reaching towards the sky.

They crossed the bridge and walked up a wide forest path bordered with slim candlestick trees. Deep shadows . . . a movement and whisper of pine needles surrounded them. Touch you everywhere.

The desire in those whispers seemed to fill the air and seep from the ground itself.

Did Jan hear it too? Did he feel it the way she did?

He was very quiet, and a trace of a frown wrinkled his forehead.

"Are you alright Jan? You seemed worried in the club."

"Did I look worried? I've been enjoying myself at last after going through some heavy shit. But sometimes the heavy shit catches up in my thoughts."

"What happened?"

"A few weeks ago, in Thessaloniki at the G8 demonstrations. I got a bad beating, but at least I ran away in the end. My friend didn't get away so fast. He's in Prague now, but he still isn't well."

Evelyn didn't even know that anything had been going on in Thessaloniki. "Sorry to hear that. About you getting beaten up. And about your friend."

He shrugged. "The cops are there to beat people up, that's their job. And I could only do my best to help my friend. But I was more disturbed by the fighting between demonstrators, and a lot of the action just didn't go anywhere. It also made me think about what I'm doing in Germany, which isn't a lot except working, then travelling to counter-summits. So I've come here to rest, and figure out what to do next. Were you in Thessaloniki?"

"Noooo . . ." Evelyn said, embarrassed to be so out of touch. "I did think about going to Prague a few years ago, in 2000. But I didn't because I had to finish my MA. I'm doing my PhD now. On the Adamites, if you didn't guess."

"I'd never take you for an academic!"

"No? Is that a compliment or what?"

"Academics don't go around shouting at statues! But maybe I don't look like a plumber, which is what I do. So why did you become an academic?"

"Same reason you became a plumber," she answered "But then, you probably don't get obsessed with your pipes, the way I do with my subjects. I get so convinced that what we call time, and history, exists in layers all around us. And I *should* be able to see every one of them . . ."

"Like clicking on the layers in Photoshop? Not that I'm an expert..."

Evelyn laughed. "Now that you mention it, yeah... kind of like that."

"You're right I don't get obsessed with plumbing, though I make very sure anything I do works. It's a way to make a living. I started my training in the 1990s."

"And I started mine in the 90s too, when I read a book called *Lipstick Traces*."

"Just what kind of training do you call *that*?"

"At the time, I thought I was just reading a totally bonkers book, with this bloke called Greil Marcus ranting about medieval heresies, punk, surrealism, all sorts... He claims that Marguerite Porete, a French heretic burned at the stake in 1310, *could* have written the lyrics to 'Anarchy in the UK'."

Jan laughed. "I don't see Comrade Žižka enjoying that song."

"Of course not. But Marguerite, that's another thing... The idea made me laugh, then I wanted to find out more. So I took evening classes in medieval history. I did Open University, then a degree. This was when they still gave grants. It came just in time to save me from a crap Job Centre scheme working for nothing."

"I've been on those. They weren't schemes, they were just called work. I don't do badly as a plumber in Germany though. But you want more than that, don't you?"

"Yes, you do want more. Now... I might be made redundant. But even if I keep my job, I need to make other changes."

Evelyn thought about Gerry. If she'd been at home, they might have gone to a film. They'd come back to the flat, go to bed and have sex. She could hear the silence surrounding them as they did it. The two of them would eat breakfast in the morning, read the papers and not say much again. Maybe they'd go out with friends, also in couples. But at the end of the night, it would be just the two of them again.

They certainly wouldn't go for a walk in the woods at night. Gerry was mad about keeping fit, but that meant going to the gym or swimming back and forth in the council pool. But a walk in the woods? He'd worry about catching Lyme's Disease from a tick.

An anguished face on a stone monument made Evelyn stop short.

But it was only one of the Stations of the Cross leading to the monastery up the hill. Strands of light filtering through the trees revealed more paintings and carvings on stones, within miniature chapels along the path.

Jan slowed down for her. "Are you checking this out for your research?"

"Let's carry on. Jan. This stuff isn't my century. I don't do the eighteenth!"

"I'm still curious why you study the fifteenth. Here, history matters because different regimes use their own versions of it. So I understand how views of the past affect the present. But the Middle Ages, even the late Middle Ages, seem so distant."

"No offence, but you sound like my old advisor. He didn't approve of my specialisation either. People with my *interests* usually go for British social history. You know, Chartists, clogs worn by Lancashire mill workers . . ."

Jan shot her a puzzled glance, as if he'd never heard of clogs.

"I'll explain. My advisor really meant: 'Medieval history is the exclusive turf of ex-public school toffs, hobbit-fanciers born with leather patches on their elbows and pipes in their mouth."

Evelyn had to take a breath as old resentments washed over her, heightening more recent fears for her livelihood. "We're talking about the kind of people who were learning Latin since they were in short trousers. Medieval history is *not* for the spawn of Essex comprehensives whose closest encounter with Latin is giggling at 'Biggus Dickus' in *The Life of Brian*. Stubborn cow that I am, it only made me more committed to my era of choice!"

Jan laughed again. "*The Life of Brian*, yes, I like that film too."

"Well, I know more than Biggus Dickus in Latin now! When I look back, I didn't mind the work and the catching up I had to do. The hard part was trying to fit in. I went along with it so I could do what I loved. There's a line in *Lipstick Traces* that goes: '*Unfulfilled desires transmit themselves across the years in unfathomable ways . . .*' So I set out to decipher all those unfulfilled desires as they hurtled across the centuries."

"But do you only want to 'decipher'? What about taking action and realising those desires?"

"What about it? What kind of action can we take?"

They walked past a cluster of domes and steeples, the monastery that tourists came to see. But that couldn't be what Jan wanted to show her.

At the edge of Klokoty the pastel plaster on the houses was faded and cracked, the flowers in the front gardens drooped. One place was boarded and abandoned, though ornate carving around the windows peeked from behind the boards. Further up the road was a 1960s-era housing estate with five-storey blocks.

"That's where I'm from." Jan gestured towards the estate. "But I really wanted to show you this." He took her to a great boulder, a sculpture set on a mound at the centre of a tiny park, little more than a traffic island with grass and a few trees. The monument was dated 1996. A plaque on a wrought-iron stand explained in German, Czech and oddly-translated English:

> *To the radicals of Tábor – the monument of the Hussite Movement violation. Here in the spring of 1421, there were put to death by fire members of the 'Pikarts', refusing the obedience and standards of the Hussite village of Tábor, out of which they rose themselves.*

She came closer to look at a carving, which showed some bearded men. One held a stick. Could it be a weapon? She didn't get the connection. Perhaps she expected to see Maria. Maria and Rohan the blacksmith, a group of people dancing. But she was touched all the same to see any marker at all.

Lines of paving stones ran like spokes from the monument, and around the spokes was a circle of paving stones. Thought and care had gone into the design. Yet weeds grew between the stones. Several crisp packets dotted the grass.

"Evo, is something wrong?"

Evelyn cleared her throat, and tried to wipe her eyes unobtrusively. "It mystifies me, but it's also moving. I assume my obsessions are obscure to most people. Now I see that those women and men who rebelled so long ago – and died for it – are remembered. But *that* wasn't just erected by some local nutters with the proceeds of a jumble sale! It must've been a proper city council job . . . official dedication, reception with wine and cheese, the lot. Who put it up?"

"I wasn't here at the time." Jan said. "But I can guess. After '89, history was rewritten again. So someone's tried to rehabilitate your poor old Pikarts as good anti-Communist dissidents! My mother was a dissident, though she was not such an activist. She just spoke up if she thought something was wrong. She'd been a doctor, but got 'demoted' after '68 and worked as a chambermaid at a hotel. That's where she met my father. He's a waiter."

"Did she get to be a doctor again?"

"Yes, in 1990. But they're making cuts at the clinic where she works so she might lose her job again."

"That's me and your mum both!" Evelyn suddenly felt tired. "Let's have a rest, there on that bench."

As they sat together, Evelyn looked across the valley. "Did you know they were burned on this hill so they could see Tábor as they died?"

"I know nothing about that, though I've walked here so many times," Jan said. "When I was little I once saw some hippies leaving flowers where the monument is now. I didn't know what it was about."

"Didn't you ever wonder? Imagine you were taken here in chains. And the last thing you saw was the town you built, the commons that you had fought for. And now you are cast out and about to die."

Evelyn pointed towards Tábor. Only the lit-up church steeple and the very edge of Kotnov Tower was visible now, even with the moon out and the sky brightening at the horizon.

"I had other things to worry about," said Jan. "Getting by. Hanging out with my friends and getting into trouble. But I'm interested now. Sometimes, it takes a stranger to show you a different side of a familiar place. Perhaps I'll visit you and show you something new about London."

He touched her knee, and rested his hand on her thigh. Warmth spread from under it, reaching within her. Again, she remembered his close presence at the party: drops of water running between the red-haired woman's breasts. The French man lifting her hair. All those desires, where could they go? Across the years, in unfathomable ways. She closed her eyes as those desires found her.

Cool fingers stroked the back of her neck, with the lightest of touches. *Jan?* They drew sparks in their wake that made her open her eyes again . . . to a different Tábor.

The old walls now wound completely around the town. The full fortifications formed a grim terrace halfway down to the river. And where was the monastery, and the tall buildings that had blocked the view?

Lights across the sky, the drone of a plane.

Smoke filled the valley. The towers and walls of Tábor blurred and shimmered, sifted through a hot haze of dust and ash. *That smell.*

For just a second: unimaginable, unendurable pain. But when she looked beyond the town, the pain stopped. The smoke blew back as if reeled in fast-motion, and a lone woman spoke from within it: *I didn't burn here, but I sometimes visit and sit here too. I didn't die at Hamr either, but everything else did.*

"Evo, what are you thinking of?" Jan's voice cut through the last wisp of smoke. The view across the valley now appeared as before, though the sky grew lighter. A raucous dawn chorus of birds had already started, but it didn't reassure her.

For the first time, she was frightened. When Jan put his arm around her, she clung to him. He was solid, he was really there. But where was she?

"I also felt strange," he said, "for a short time, things didn't look right, but not all wrong. And . . ." His lips were close to her ear, she felt them move as he spoke.

Evelyn turned her head, going the vast distance to kiss him. First, a simple touch of lips; a sharing of breath that expanded and filled her. As his arms tightened around her, she felt it fill him too. She wrapped herself around him, felt his long lean body and where he was hard, pushing against her.

He released her, only to stroke her belly between the buttons of her dress. The sensation from it grew and radiated under his fingers.

She had to follow it. But where? The shadow of a ruined castle. The island, where a woman with dark hair basked in the sun and closed her eyes with pleasure.

"Let's get away from here. We must go to where they had the feasts and festivals. In Příběnice and Hamr."

He nodded, as if he understood exactly why. "Příběnice . . . it will take a while but we can walk. I used to go there when I was young, to get away and . . ."

"What? Smoke dope and drink beer with your mates and get off with girls?"

"Yes. And at this time it will be very quiet."

They passed through deep pine-scented forest where the dawn didn't show yet. Then sudden clearings full of the misty light. They walked through stands of silver birch where the leaves rustled with a sound like chimes. Was this what Maria heard in these woods? Tell me, Evelyn thought, tell me what it was like.

We needed to leave Tábor. Their God judged from above, ours dwelled within and led us to pleasure. With the spring, we shed our toil-stained garb. At last, I let the air touch me everywhere.

Touch me everywhere.

"What are you thinking about?" Jan asked. "You're in another world! Tell me about it. I'm interested because I'm not sure what world I want to be in, and it's not as simple as whether I end up living in Prague or Berlin again."

I was thinking about a woman who's been dead for 600 years talking to me about taking off her clothes.

How could she say that?

"Jan, sometimes I feel like I'm somewhere else. I've been told there's very little documentation on what I'm looking for. But imagination helps me find those things. So I'm trying to picture these people. And there was a woman, Maria. Since I've been in Tábor, I hear her. But not enough."

The conversation stopped. Evelyn was sure her indrawn breath must be much louder than the twigs breaking under their feet.

"Your passion for the past fascinates me," Jan said at last. "And maybe it comes from passion for much more than that. So I'll try to hear Maria too."

"Will you? Perhaps it takes the two of us to listen."

They slowed down in their walking, and they kissed again. "*Evo*," he said. "That is more like you, than 'Evelyn'. You know, my girlfriend split up with me, I didn't think I'd want anyone else. But when I saw this crazy English woman talking to a statue, with her creamy skin that makes you want to see and touch it all, and smiling green eyes . . . Yes!"

Sometimes it takes a stranger to show you a different side of a familiar place.

And Evelyn realised it doesn't even have to be a place.

She didn't know how long they'd been walking. They held hands so their fingers caressed and entangled and moved against each other, as if making love. And so slowly . . . it took hours for the thrill of his fingers between hers to travel and bloom.

Then other things moved fast. The thoughts in her mind. Her breath. The placid Lužnice turning active at a weir, churning white over rocks.

They travelled through a field filled with the lace of elderflowers and a flash of goldenrod, plunged into another deep forest. Crimson berries in the undergrowth burned bright.

Jan talked about his life in Berlin, the massive international gatherings and confrontations. Prague, Genoa, Evian. *Taking action to make those desires real.* But it sounded most unreal to her. She had looked for this kind of action when she was young, and she had abandoned that for a life, a job, a flat, a boyfriend.

A cliff face rose straight from the river. As they went along a walkway built on stilts around the cliff, Evelyn felt as if they were floating in the air, and there was a fall and touch of frigid icewater.

But when they stepped off the platform back onto the grass, it wasn't winter and it wasn't spring. There was only the familiar warmth of summer. The water was calm again, muddy as it flowed past a clearing and the remains of an ancient stone house.

Beyond the woods, towards a road, she saw signs of a construction site, fences and stalled machines. But up the hill were stone ruins and a pale sky behind the lace of branches and leaves.

Before tackling the hill, Evelyn knelt at the edge of the river. She splashed water on herself. It was cool, but not cold as it ran down her face. She splashed more on her chest. "I hope this isn't polluted too."

But the water running through her fingers looked clear enough, and the air only had a bright and clean morning scent spiced with pine.

She splashed at Jan, who laughed and took his shirt off. She traced the tattoo on his chest with her finger tip; it looked like a rising sun. His skin was smooth, except for a line of dark hair trailing from his navel and into his jeans. She ran her finger along this line, down to the zip. Inside the jeans, just a little. She leaned down, to kiss his stomach. His hands were in her hair; he scooped a handful of water and let it run down her back. His hands followed, then found her breasts. Then he stopped.

"Didn't you want to see Příběnice?" he teased. "We still have that hill to climb! There's not much left of the castle, though. It was already empty when the Táborites seized it from a local lord. I remember that much from a school walking trip."

"So, the Adamites had *squatted* it!" Evelyn said. "Imagine kids running through the corridors; peasants, common people walking in and out of a castle like they owned it. Having great big parties. Love feasts." When they stood up, she put Jan's shirt in her rucksack, next to the bag of very ripe peaches.

As they walked up the hill, they passed a wall with grass growing between the stones. There was a hole that might have been a window. Thick patches of weeds and birch saplings found footholds in the earth on top of the walls, subduing them.

She drew deep breaths as the walk got steeper. She hooked a hand in Jan's back pocket, gave him a squeeze. I'm not usually this . . . *assertive*, Evelyn thought.

She put her hands in his pockets again and pulled him close, standing on tip-toe so she could feel him against her in just the right place. *Here, in our clothes, standing up.* She gripped his hips, and pushed against him. He lifted her up and she curved a leg around him, put one hand on a tree to balance and moved against him as if trying to pass through, reaching for a rhythm . . .

Then he put her down. "We'll get to a good place very soon. Let's continue?"

He led her ever-upwards on the path. As they rounded the hill, she looked down on the riverside clearing where they'd been. She imagined people there, feeding and pleasuring each other, cries and sighs reaching them in the shell of the castle.

"Here," Jan said, showing her where walls formed a rough corner, partly enclosing and screening them. There was grass to sit on, and the remains of a recent campfire at one end. "I've had some good times here," he said with a wink, and patted the ground next to him.

Evelyn settled against him, then took out a peach. "Jan, did they tell you about the love feasts in your school history classes?"

"Hmmm, I think they were just 'depraved orgies', if they were mentioned at all. Tell me more. You're a lecturer, so give me a lecture!"

She bit the peach. The ripe pulp of the fruit burst from the skin. She held the peach out to Jan. "A lecture you want? Right, so you probably know that the Hussites insisted everyone had the right to have wine as well as wafers at communion."

Jan didn't take the peach from her but ate from her hand, his lips touching her and his tongue flicking between her fingers. The pulse in her throat and the pounding of her heart made it difficult to speak. Then Jan took his mouth away from her hand and the remains of the peach, waiting. "Yes?"

"That's no big deal now, but then it was an attack on the privileges of the clergy." Evelyn went on, her voice unsteady. "But . . . the Pikarts went much further. There was nothing divine in a dry thin wafer or a mere sip of wine. Instead, all food could become sacred because it sustains our fleshly beings; and our bodies and our senses are the gateway to the 'pleasures of paradise'."

"That's a beautiful expression, *love feast*. Here, have another peach." He held it out to her. She took a bite as he pulled the shoulder of her dress down. Then he rubbed the peach over her breasts. The fruit pulp still felt warm from yesterday's sun. It fell from the stone, releasing more of its rich scent. He licked, gently biting and sucking. His short hair against her skin tickled. She squirmed and laughed.

"Yes . . . it is beautiful. Love feast. It's like . . . ahhh, feasting on love, filling yourself up with food, feeding bonds of passion and comradeship and feasting on that too. Oh, I don't usually talk like this. What am I saying?"

Jan was drawing a circle with his tongue, then he looked up. "You were saying a lot about love feasts. Tell me more!"

"It was a feast for all the appetites. A tart mouthful of wine, the sweetness of fruit, savoury shreds of meat," she said. Yes, she could taste those words.

His kissing and savouring punctuated the most delicious words. She arched her back and spread her legs, needing his touch.

"You're making me very hungry. But go on," he said.

"Not much more. About food. We only have peaches. Often the Adamites didn't have much either. They could hunt or fish, or raid a noble's estate. But there are other ways to feast."

"I'm sure there are." He stroked the inside of her thigh with his long fingers, then up under her knickers and he pulled them off. With his other hand, he helped her shed her dress. Just the early sun and the light breeze on her skin was enough to make her shake, about to brim over.

The air touched me everywhere. And so did Jan, very slowly as they fed each other the remaining peaches. He sucked her fingers long after the juice had been licked off. He kissed her belly, stroked behind her knees when she sat astride him. Each time Jan kissed her, she relished the flavours of the feast in his mouth. Wine and beer, and meat charred on an open fire. The juice of ripe fruit, and spices seized from a lord's larder. And a flavour very much his own.

Then he pushed beneath her. A shaft of light shot through her and fountained into streams that reached her fingertips and even the ends of her hair. Her desire bent the world around her, until there wasn't a straight line left. Everything was curved, everything flowed and pulsed. The colours of the world brightened; the moving and changing greens of the trees, even the khaki colour of the Lužnice below them and the grey stone and moss of the castle ruins.

"Wait," said Jan. "I really wasn't expecting this, but I always carry one with me." He pulled a little foil packet out of his pocket.

Evelyn chuckled. "Let loose your prisoner!" She tugged at the zip of his jeans. It was difficult to get it down.

Evelyn wanted to speak. *Jan, do you feel the air like it's another lover, touching you everywhere?* But this was no time for speaking, only hungry and deep kisses as he moved inside her.

She could keep opening forever . . . ready to embrace the world that contained her lover. The strength of this unfolding shocked her. It could stop the clocks, crack panes of glass. Unruly like resilient weeds, it made castle walls crumble. She had to close her eyes. Behind her lids burst rhythmic colours of rich yellow, dripping and delicious like hot butter. The clock on the tower, with no hands at all, dissolving in yellow. Something gave way, a wall; a pane of glass, the heaviness that trapped her in a single layer of time. *Let loose your prisoner.*

Evelyn felt a gaze like sun, like honey. *Jan, do you know she's here? I feel her now, stroking my back.* Maria's hands were calloused, but their touch tender.

She opened her eyes, and opened her mouth to kiss the naked woman beside her. Maria smelt of woodsmoke and crackling fire, the murky river and the pines. She tasted of the feast, salty, bitter and sweet.

Though she was young, the lines on Maria's face had already set. Cold wind and the sun's glare had put them there. Maria looked at them both with steady grey eyes used to visions, close to silver against her sun-darkened skin. They lit up Evelyn as they settled upon her, drawing her out and sharing those visions. *Give me your soul and receive mine.*

Maria's hair was tied back with a ragged piece of purple velvet, a colour forbidden to a peasant. Her full lips lifted in a smile that was shy at first. Then it broadened to show the dimples in her cheeks and the gap in her teeth.

Evelyn stroked Maria's thigh. She was no ghost. There was the rough ridge of a scar, then tender skin. *Maria, I know your soft places too. The inside of your arm, where you are still pale. Between your breasts, underneath. The very inner skin of your thigh . . . Let me find you.*

Maria sighed as she stroked the curve of Evelyn's hip, and leaned over to kiss Jan. Their murmurs of discovery were insistent tongues.

Evelyn buried her face in Maria's hair, now loose from its fastening. How many unfathomable centuries has this woman crossed? Now her heart beat under her hand.

Maria, Jan, surround me like the air and the water.

Jan's eyes were closed, his breath quick. *What colours do you see, Jan?* He moved deeper, faster. Time stopped, and began again.

On the grass near the river, others were celebrating. Feasting and filling themselves up, filling each other up. Evelyn felt many hands exploring and seeking, entering, smoothing; many hearts pounding. A world shifted within her, exploding into a million points of light.

And all the prisoners were let loose.

Bells of the Harelle

When King Charles's troops entered Rouen to put down the rebellion, the Harelle, the first thing they did was strip the tongues from the city's bells. I listened as they did so, hidden in the belfry tower with my two lovers, Christophe and Adrian.

The troops entered the building. They were heading straight to the top, to the bells. To us.

Christophe put his finger to his lips and pointed to the wall and the faint outline of a door. He opened it; the three of us squeezed in among the pots of polish and cleaning fluids. Their scent went to my head and filled my lungs. Perhaps it had an intoxicating effect like liquor, and influenced Christophe's later behaviour.

I was sure the soldiers would open the door and find us. But they passed by many times. I saw shadows moving in the crack below the door and the floor, the soles of soldiers' boots.

A creak of something heavy being moved . . . ascending steps, up to the bells themselves. Much cursing came from above, a clanging and wrenching. A great cheer and round of applause.

Slow steps coming down, a heavy object hit the floor. "We will melt this down and make the damned rebels drink it, as they did in Aragon."

"The only good idea to come from the Spanish!"

We crouched there, well after the last soldierly steps and a slam of the door.

Finally, we emerged from our hidey-hole. Shading our eyes from the winter sun funnelling down from the belfry, we saw that the bells were still there. But the soldiers had taken away the tongues.

"Damn!" Christophe clenched his fists, trembling. "They take the voice from our city, steal the voice from the people. Damn them! I will ring those bells anyway."

He went to the bell ropes. "We have no tongues, but we still have a voice!"

Do we? I wondered.

But Christophe had no doubt. He pulled on the ropes and the bells swung, with only a creaking. But *something* rang out. A vibration started in my core, and set off a ringing in my ears. It was a protest, a lamentation, a cry of warning and defiance. The silent but powerful noise shouted out our hopes, the delirium and joy and the fear of the past days.

Adrian and I went to help, pulling on the ropes with Christophe, lending our combined strength and fervour to his efforts.

When we stopped ringing the tongueless bells, the three of us embraced.

I decided then I will always raise my voice and write things down so people will know about them. I will never be like a bell without a tongue.

That is why I've been writing these accounts and I continue to write them, here in Bohemia. I am now in bed, doing my best to wake up, with the help of Hans and Josef and Jehanne . . . fine young people who would help an old woman and listen to her stories.

Did I dream of those blasted bells again? I must have dreamed of Christophe's wild carillons, or Adrian's account of a cloth workers' meeting where they plotted to put the world to rights.

Josef gives me a piece of bread. I nibble at it.

Meanwhile, my young friends gaze at me with some expectation, so I feel I should make a point.

I hold up the bread. "This is sustenance for the body! This is not a symbol consecrated by a priest to become the body of a man who is long dead. This bread sustains the physical body, which is ours for celebrating life." I return to the subject that has set Prague alight for a good few years. "Communion of *both* kinds . . . pah! We seek communion of *all* kinds!"

"Seraphine, you must eat before you preach," says Hans, speaking to me in Flemish. The son of a Flemish bricklayer who built some of Prague's great structures, he knows how I prefer the sounds of French or Flemish in the morning.

"And you should have a drink," he adds, "Someone's gone to get water."

"Water? Who knows what's been swimming in the water here! *Someone* get beer from Vaclav. That should be clean. Would do me good too."

"You want to hear some preaching," Hans says. "Go to Our Lady of the Snows and listen to Zelivsky. They'll be marching from there for the prisoners."

Processions have been forbidden in Prague, but people continue to defy the ban.

"I don't like that man Zelivsky." I tear off another chunk of bread and offer the rest. "He wants power as much as any petty inquisitor, and there are enough fools who will give it to him. But take me to the Snows. If there's trouble, that's where I'll go."

My strength tends to wax and wane. In the mornings I find it hard to move. But once the day gets underway, I revive. What I feel in mind is not always what I feel in body, but on such days I can certainly progress at a good clip with my cane.

We share more bread, but I'm finding it hard to eat. I'm on edge. In Prague, heretics preach from pulpits, market squares and taverns. Processions and clashes in the street happen daily. Is today any different?

Why were the bells of the Harelle ringing in my dreams? Do I hear their echo now?

"Let's go," I urge as I get out of bed.

So I won't be a bell without a tongue. But I must also remember that the bells Christophe rang were the voice of a commune. Therefore, I don't only write for myself. I must relate the dreams of those who shouldn't be silenced . . . A young man suggesting that our universe started with an explosion, who disappeared forever. Young women trying to make lives for themselves without husbands. Artisans and paupers calling for the end of a tax and an end to oppression.

And what of those sensual and far-working bonds that form between us, extending over distances? That is still a mystery to me.

When I was a young woman towards the end of the last century, the uprisings of cloth workers broke out in Ghent. The rebellion spread to other cities in Flanders. My family, French woollen merchants, naturally viewed these events with alarm.

But I only wanted to find out more. Fortunately, my old nurse had taught me Flemish when I was growing up, along with empathy for those whose lives were different from mine. She came to visit and told me that the people rioted over taxes, tithes and poor wages.

Despite my comfortable background, I sympathised with those on the streets. I was unhappy, and their agitation seemed to address a cause of my own discontent. I'd been sold off in marriage to an older man, a nobleman with not much left but his title. My father could offer a tidy dowry. So it was a marriage made in heaven, or hell as far as I was concerned.

My husband was not overtly cruel. He didn't beat me. But he was indifferent, and grumbled when I couldn't give him a child. He never let me forget that he owned me. His idea of pleasure in the bed was a quick thrust and grunt and then he rolled over. I submitted.

I was sure he had mistresses or visited prostitutes, yet he insisted on this ordeal for reasons of procreation.

In my mind, I went elsewhere. A boat trip with my nurse along the canals where trees arched overhead, letting loose flowers that spotted my cloak with pink and white. A hidden garden, the comforting trickle of a fountain.

During the troubles of 1381, I was told not to go out on my own. Instead, I should send a servant out to conduct my business.

I couldn't take this confinement for long. Finally, I put on my plainest garments and snuck out. When I heard the noise of an angry procession, I went straight there. I was scared, though. Maybe I'd be spotted as one of the enemy, a pampered rich brat, and set upon immediately. I'd heard many times that the 'Jakes' and the 'merdaille' were wild beasts who would attack a well-bred lady.

But no one paid any attention to me. They had other things on their minds.

Standing on a crate was a hunched and thin man who appeared blind in one eye. He must have been more than sixty. He spoke in Flemish about unfair laws, burdensome taxes and the impositions of privilege. He was, he declared, a weaver of cloth who could barely afford to clothe himself.

"Perhaps I will be naked next time I speak to you, while the cloth I've woven will cover the backs of burghers, knights and lords."

Everyone laughed, but it was a bitter laughter. Though my own father was a merchant of cloth to those burghers and knights, this man spoke for me. His words were angry and sweet and made me see, for the first time, something much bigger than myself. I later learned this man was called Nicolas, and he was famed throughout Europe as an orator of the streets.

Then another speaker mounted the improvised platform. He spoke in Flemish, and then in French. He was a patrician like myself, yet he also spoke of injustice and rebellion. Though he denounced the French king's oppression of Flanders, he cautioned us to remember that people in the French towns were also restless, and shouted "*vive Gand*" when they took to the streets. He bore the common English people no ill will either. "The poor of England have risen up, and we will do the same."

Again, his speech inspired the crowd. They responded with cheers and took their first steps towards the Town Hall. And I went with them.

As we marched, I spoke with the second man. He seemed approachable because he'd spoken in French. And though he had the bearing of someone who came from comfort, he had already set out on the course I wanted to take.

I just blurted out everything that was on my mind.

"If you believe in justice, there are ways you can help," he said. He explained that I could raise funds for the rebels. I could also communicate their goals to those who only speak French. And if I am able to read and write, I could work with an order of beguines to teach these skills to others.

I nodded, taking the advice to heart, already planning my escape.

My husband quickly became angered by my new activities and associates. I argued with him constantly; I argued with the owners I came across, urging them to pay their workers more. Meanwhile, I stashed coins, notes, jewellery and anything I could sell once I struck out on my own.

It didn't take long before my husband petitioned for an annulment.

Though I had little religious vocation, I joined a small group of beguines who devoted themselves more to worldly good deeds and less to holy devotions. Beguine houses were not tightly controlled by the Church or any order of monks. They were also open to women from humble backgrounds, who didn't offer the dowries required by established religious orders.

These sisters did foreswear marriage, but I was happy with that. I had no desire to marry again. They shared a small house in the city, supporting their work with spinning, tapestry production, needlework and scribing. I became a scribe, which I still do from time to time. It is a better trade than selling fish, which is what I did when I first came to Bohemia.

About a year later, we received news of agitation in Rouen. King Charles VI the Mad had levied a tax on staples, a *gabelle*, to finance his unending war. I volunteered to travel to Rouen to bring funds and support from Ghent, accompanied by a beguine who wanted to visit some sisters nearby.

I arranged to meet with a cloth worker called Adrian in the market. He arrived with another young man, Christophe.

Adrian had straight fair hair, Christophe had dark curly hair. Their eyes were the same deep brown and they appeared to be good friends. I met both pairs of brown eyes with a sense of recognition. The moment stopped, and everything in that market became almost too vivid. The scents of horse dung and roasting nuts, fish sizzling on grills, sweetened bread fried and dusted with sugar.

And there was the noise . . .

"*Haro! Haro!*" The streets of Rouen rang with this cry, an appeal for help and a demand for justice.

"*Haro!* We need more people to secure the Town Hall. Help!"

"*Haro!* Seize the city's gates and close them."

Christophe nodded at us both and hurried away.

"*Haro!* We'll end this tax. We work too hard and eat too little."

The bells of the city's commune began tolling. It was nothing like the measured sounds of an ordinary day, or the peels of the church bells. Its cadence called: *Haro! Haro!*

Adrian pointed towards the bell tower. "That's Christophe's work!" He beamed with a pride that warmed me too.

More people poured into the city centre, answering the call.

A man emerged from a draper's shop to urge the crowd. "Destroy records of rents, lawsuits, debts and privileges! A good ripping or a few fires, and we're free of those things!"

All afternoon we rampaged through the streets, building bonfires of transactions and demands. We vented our fury on the churches, whose prelates lived in luxury while tithing the hard-pressed people.

I was surfacing after a life spent half-asleep, awake at last. *Haro, haro!* I rubbed my eyes, as if ridding them of sleep's last residue. Without thinking, I reached for Adrian's hand as we turned a corner.

We found people breaking into the residences of nobles. Some emerged with arms full of food and drink, which they shared among the crowds. Adrian passed something to me that tasted of aniseed and clove.

Faces glowed with the light of stained-glass saints as people ate forbidden cheese and fruit, even when their mouths were smeared with sauce and jam.

I didn't see anyone killed – the rage was vented against the property of our rulers, against the bonds made of parchment. There was smoke and flame, and laughter too, as we set them alight.

As night set in, Christophe left his bell-ringing post and rejoined us. We stepped into one of the noble houses and heard the noise of revelry coming from the wine cellar. The owners had deserted the house in fear of the crowd.

In the house where I grew up, we had a wine cellar like this.

I went downstairs where people were sampling the delights. I held up a bottle, one of my husband's favourite vintages. "This is excellent wine. Will you join me?"

"Of course, Seraphine," said Christophe. "With a bottle of wine and a name like that, you must be an angel!"

"Or perhaps a devil," added Adrian.

"I am none of those things. I'm only me."

Fingers brushed as we passed the bottle. Shall we sit down? Yes, here's a place. Thigh to thigh in an alcove, sweet grape fumes and damp earth.

Since I left my husband, I'd been happy to spend time with female companions from the beguinage. Sometimes I admired suitable men from afar, but remained aloof.

But I didn't feel aloof then. I liked both of these men, and they made it clear that they liked me. I didn't consider choosing one over the other. They didn't compete. To this day I still don't understand quite how it happened. Invisible strings grew taut between us, pulling us closer into an inevitable embrace. I just couldn't bear not to touch them, not to exchange breath with them. Anything else was unthinkable. Ordinary worries and caution fled.

We found a room upstairs. It was not overly ornate. But the carpets, the bed and the blankets had the feel and scent of comfort. Laughter rose up through the floorboards. Glass still shattered outside. People still called for help at their tasks, others shouted greetings and threats. Someone played a fiddle, raucous voices joined in an unfamiliar tune.

"I've only been with my husband," I said suddenly.

"And who is your husband?" Adrian asked.

"It doesn't matter," I decided. "We're finished with all that." *Finished with all that.* I was thinking of much more than my marriage.

Adrian's lips tasted of aniseed, Christophe's only of wine. Each touch showed me something new. I felt Adrian's wonder as he learned to read, taught by a beguine. I heard Christophe when he hummed during the lesson, and got sent outside.

But the hum stayed with me, deepening as he stroked my back and I kissed Adrian again, searching for the flavours of more spice. I stretched out between my lovers, our thoughts and limbs entwining.

If I closed my eyes, I saw colours. Adrian: midnight blue and dawn grey. Christophe: blazing yellow. Their colours filled me and I showed them a hidden garden where lilies floated in a fountain and the purple glimmer of violets drew me into dark corners. I invited them in with me.

Later, we talked more. I didn't question how we had shared thoughts. It was too new and strange. But I now welcomed the simplicity of talking, the vibration of a voice under my fingers.

"We've known each other for years," said Adrian, as he stroked Christophe's hair. "Our families shared the same premises. We had our pallets in the same corner. Now we argue sometimes. Christophe only cares about his bells and making music, while I worry about the troubles of the world. But we're very close."

"You will make me jealous," I said. They looked at me in surprise; why would a woman like me wish for the lot of two labourers?

"You have a lifetime of friendship, while I had to cut myself off from my family in order to be free."

I saw the sympathy flicker across their faces, a visible change. "You have us now," Christophe said.

I had no idea how long we would be together or what could happen next. But it was enough to sustain me when both boys put their arms around me. Everything was soft and gentle, contrasting with the battle outside. Though I used to have physical relations with my husband, this was the first time I truly made love.

You have us now.

And I saw that they also had each other, in a different way than before.

The only Holy Trinity is *this*, I said. My companions laughed.

We woke at daybreak. With morning, some caution returned and I decided to disguise myself by putting on a tunic, along with breeches and hose that I found in the house. We emerged to join a passing procession, composed mostly of journeymen.

"A king! A king! We will find a king!" People at the head of the procession pushed a large cart with an empty armchair placed upon it.

I nudged Adrian. "What do we need a king for? We still have to fight off the current one."

"I think it's a joke," said Adrian.

Our procession turned a corner into a side street, which must have been overlooked by last night's rioters. We interrupted a portly gentleman trying to move a well-padded commode out of his house. He turned with a start, his red face draining to white.

The chair-bearers gave whoops of delight. "Don't run! We will make you king!"

Before he could object a group placed him on the chair.

"You're our great king Mr Fatso, you are!"

We paraded him through the city as the new monarch. More people came out to cheer, pelting the anointed king with looted flowers and fruit. People bowed and scraped and displayed their bottoms as the throne went by.

He looked about, bewildered. "Put me down," he commanded. But he seemed even more terrified when his 'throne' was set down in the market square.

The draper who had called for the destruction of public records arrived with a scroll of parchment. "We were up all night drafting this. Now our new king will sign it."

He began reading: all the unfair taxes that burdened artisans and workers must be repealed. All debts cancelled in the spirit of Jubilee.

"Go on, sign it! Sign it, your great big royal highness!"

King Fatso did as he was told.

A procession of petitioners asked his advice. "Should I tie up my master until he raises my pay?"

"Do it, do it," the king said, prodded into assent by a playful poke in the back.

The draper stepped forward. "Shall we attack the abbey of St-Ouen, which has been granted royal privileges over our city and robs us with its tithes?"

"Do it, do it," advised King Fatso.

We will, we will! We marched off to the abbey. We broke in and destroyed the gallows, ripped the monastery's charters to shreds, stripped the abbot of his vestments, and forced him to sign a new charter that took away the abbey's royal privileges over the town and granted rights to the workers of Rouen.

After that, I wanted to return to 'our' house, the three of us, but there was too much to do. We had to secure more barricades, ensure supplies of food and water, organise defence.

We eventually fell asleep, tangled together among cushions on the floor of an upper chamber in the Town Hall.

After the initial celebration, the city was tense. We expected the army, expected a fight. No one came.

After a few days, two messengers arrived to tell us about the revolt of the hammer-men, the Maillotins, in Paris.

The king and his troops had set out for Rouen, but when the troubles broke out in Paris he turned his army around to go there.

We carried on. Leaders of the guilds sat in the Town Hall. Bakers baked, produce-sellers made arrangements with farmers and weavers kept on weaving.

As for myself and my lovers, we had to be discreet once the euphoria of the first few days departed. We didn't even make love again, but that one time bound us. Christophe and Adrian both had jobs to do, yet I felt they were always with me. I heard the chime of the bells as I walked. I heard the clack of looms. Other thoughts tugged my heart and mind, and I revelled in their richness.

When we came together, we barely needed to speak.

Some beguines had spoken of ecstasy, of connection to God or a universal spirit. But my connection to anything close to that came with two other human beings, through flesh and human passions.

This is the real Holy Trinity. I had laughed when I said that, but maybe it frightened me too.

Then news came of the bloody massacre of the Parisians, of hundreds hung and burned and beheaded. It wouldn't be long before the king's troops would turn around again, and come for us in Rouen.

Now I am close to the age of that half-blind rabble-rouser Nicolas, who first set me on my path. I live in a strange city, which resounds to the followers of Jan Hus. He was burned as a heretic, prosecuted by Pierre d'Ailly, the same inquisitor who would later persecute us in Brussels. Surely that bound Brussels and Prague together, as surely as the Harelle created the trinity of myself, Adrian and Christophe.

When I first arrived in Prague, I saw a strange wall on the other side of the river, running up Petrin Hill. It didn't appear to serve any defensive purpose and its top was jagged, like teeth.

"That is the Hungry Wall," Hans explained later. In the past century, when there was no work, a king gave the poor of Prague tools to build that wall. He also gave them scraps of food while they worked but he didn't pay them. When the wall neared completion he ordered the workers to make the top uneven to look like teeth, as a reminder that the good king had given bread for the poor to chew.

When I see that wall, I don't think of the largesse of a king who didn't pay his labourers, but the most generous monarch of all.

And I hear the clink of glasses, as Adrian and Christophe join me in a toast to King Fatso.

But I never knew what happened to them. While the army came down hard on the rebels of Paris, Rouen negotiated a surrender and suffered less. Ten leaders of the revolt had been hanged, but others were treated more lightly.

"You must go," Adrian told me, when we were still in the bell tower. "It's still possible to escape."

"And *we* must stay and keep our heads down. We'll put in pleas for clemency. This is our city and we will not leave it," said Christophe.

"I know of places where you can go," said Adrian. "My brothers among the cloth workers and the beghards can help you."

Perhaps their pleas were accepted. Perhaps they lived to marry and have children. They still speak to me, but I'm never sure where their voices come from.

I set off alone, heading back to Flanders. In Rouen we had fought and we had lost. But I felt haunted by my experience there, for better or worse.

Perhaps study and contemplation could help me understand why I kept hearing those bells. And why, if I let my mind wander, I'd start tasting passionate kisses full of wine, aniseed and cloves.

On the way, I found Adrian's associates, who directed me to a suitable beguinage.

One of the women who welcomed me laughed at my name. "Seraphine! You should fit in here because we devote ourselves to spiritual liberty and seraphic love, as described by our great teacher Bloemardine."

She lowered her voice. "Be aware, that what we say among ourselves and what we tell the priests and bishops are two different things."

"More like three or four things," added another sister.

The beguinage was a large building set within woods on the edge of Brussels, along with a chapel and bell tower. It was old and run-down, but I felt at home there. I settled into my routine of reading, prayer, meditation and discussion, work in the gardens and grounds. My early training in needlework proved useful in the tapestry workshops.

I absorbed the work of Bloemardine, especially when I read: *Love's most intimate union is through eating, tasting and seeing from within.* The body, according to Bloemardine, serves as a connection to divinity . . . and divinity itself can be human.

"Love came and embraced me, and I came out of the spirit and remained lying until late in the day, drunk with unspeakable wonders."

I lifted a glass of wine to that!

When I meditated, I listened for Adrian and Christophe. *Ring the bells,* Christophe said. *Finish what we started.* Adrian spoke above his loom, urging me to study more.

And we spoke in both our languages, with words that sent insistent tongues between my thighs, around the tips of my breasts.

I established the bell tower as my place to meditate. There I could look out over the woodland on one side, towards the city of Brussels on the other. Over the horizon, to the south, I imagined the place where my lovers could be, touching me from afar. I reached towards them, hoping they would also feel my touch and share my delight.

When presented with a choice of communal tasks, I immediately chose bell-ringing. Christophe's dedication to that vocation became mine. I improvised as I tried to capture the chimes of the Harelle on this simple set of bells.

Think of the cry for justice and for action . . . *Haro! Haro!* I shouted it as I rang. Think of the draper calling people into the streets, the closure of the city gates, merriment in the mansion basements.

Haro! Haro!

Some sisters complained about my discordant bell-ringing, while others praised it for keeping them alert.

But something was missing, a beat or a cadence. Could it be the carnal element between me and the two young men, which brought on the rough music and the bonding?

For this, a few beguines had turned to their sisters, and I tried this too.

> *It happens sometimes that one never finds two creatures who are of one spirit in one realm, but when it happens by chance that these two creatures find each other, and cannot hide themselves, and if they then want to do so, they cannot . . . Such people have a great need to be on their guard . . .*

This passage from Margeurite Porete jarred me every time I read it. Porete was a favourite among the sisters, coming close to Bloemardine.

But while Bloemardine died of natural causes in 1336 at an advanced age, Marguerite Porete burned at the stake. She was an educated woman who wandered about, expounded heretical views, published a book of them and got into trouble.

I shivered when I saw the similarities to myself. Could I meet the same end? Beguines have faced persecution, with mass burnings at Narbonne. Then they've been tolerated, and persecuted again.

Though I had no intention of producing a screed like Marguerite's, I was already writing accounts of my travels and travails and thoughts. I would not be a bell without a tongue.

Marguerite seemed a peaceful soul. While she refused to withdraw to a beguinage, she never took part in disorderly multitudes. I believed that I'd left that turbulent life behind as well.

When I read Porete's passage about the two souls who are bound together, a word came to me: *entwined*. I thought immediately of my two young men. Could more than two souls become entwined?

Now I had a name for what had happened. How could such an *entwinement* persist over distance?

If Adrian and Christophe were alive, could they still haunt me? If they were indeed dead, did I feel their ghosts? When I heard their thoughts and felt them entwined with me, did it mean we found each other on another plane of existence?

I spoke to other beguines about this, leaving out the details of our first night together. One suggested this bonding can be forged in 'turbulent and tender times'.

But she cautioned me. "Beware . . . Your soul can be captured in hatred as well as love. This has happened to me." She added, "I came here to escape it."

But I came here to seek it.

I watched seasons pass over the landscape from my vantage point in the bell tower. Even in the winter, I stayed up there, wrapped myself in blankets. My reveries warmed me more than my flasks of hot infusions.

I was drifting in a boat down the canals of Ghent with Christophe and Adrian as white blossoms fell upon us. We found the hidden garden, where we knew entwinement again.

Like the sisters in Ghent, we also taught reading and writing among the city's poor. Our lessons were basic, our words scratched on slates or wax tablets, but we incorporated philosophy and debate into them. We urged our pupils, young and old, to think for themselves.

Bloemardine had the status of a local heroine in Brussels, and several groups had sprung up to engage with the ideas of this long-dead mystic. They appealed to people of all stations.

During the Harelle, the poor stood up for themselves, taking direction from no one. They were neither stupid animals nor voracious wild beasts, as members of my family believed. And now I found myself among artisans, weavers and street hawkers as they considered the implications of 'seraphic love'. With so little love and pleasure in their own world, these ideas offered an inspiration the Church could never approach.

This attracted the attention of the Inquisition, which launched attacks on 'Bloemardine's heresy'. They came poking about our beguinage, and stuck their snouts about the streets of Brussels.

When I went into the town to teach lessons, I saw the inquisitors striding forth, expecting everyone to quiver with fear.

Instead, children threw rocks at them. Old folks and working men and mothers also followed them, singing songs and laughing.

Then Pierre d'Ailly, the Bishop of Cambrai, ordered our house closed down and the property handed to Dominicans. Other beguinages met a similar fate.

We dismantled our tapestry workshops and transported the materials and tools elsewhere. I would have burned the whole place down in order to keep it out of the greedy grasp of the Dominicans. I raged and raged, and my memories of the Harelle became strong again.

I had turned to mysticism when I believed it impossible to change the world. I aimed to increase my knowledge and live a simple life. But as long as the Church and its Inquisition reigned, the spiritual life will offer no way out.

Some women accepted transfer to an approved nunnery. Others went back to their families, perhaps making meagre livelihoods as spinsters. But I had no real family.

Yet help came from those who possessed very little. The artisans and weavers we had been tutoring helped some of us in turn. They took us into their homes. And we helped by bringing our looms and valuable tapestries with us, which aided their trade.

I joined Henryk and Adele and their three children, the little darlings who had been at the centre of the stone-throwing gangs that followed the inquisitors. I had been accustomed to my austere but solitary room at the beguinage, so I needed to adjust to some extremely close companionship.

My hosts introduced me to spiritual groups that were meeting in the city. I met the man known as Giles of Canter, who had formed a group called *Homines Intelligentiae* or Men of Understanding, along with William of Hildernissen. And this group included *women* of understanding.

Our teacher Giles preached of an age of the Holy Spirit, where the Scriptures will lose their relevance and the conventional 'truths' proved false. The Church's doctrines of poverty, chastity and obedience belonged to the old Dark Age.

"Farewell to virtues", as Margeurite Porete wrote.

While my life as a beguine had been devoted to simplicity and 'voluntary poverty', these people had no time for that.

"We already live in poverty," said Adele, a petite sharp-tongued woman. "There is nothing *voluntary* about it. We have no need for purification and self-denial to become close to God; anyone who is poor is already close as can be. We claim our spiritual liberty now. The only purgatory is the poverty we live in."

As for Giles . . . he was a peculiar man. He once ran down a road, completely naked, while carrying a plate of meat on his head to give to a pauper. He liked his wine, and when he had enough of that he would also take his clothes off.

I got tired of it, I must admit. "Giles, please! I have seen enough of you."

But another time when our group had enjoyed drink and stimulating discussion together, we *all* took our clothes off. It just felt like the right thing to do.

Many women in the group first fell in love with Giles, though I have to say he wasn't much to look at. He had a way of making love that he claimed was like Adam and Eve. Pah! I don't know about that. He was very good at it though, and knew how to give a woman pleasure. It went on and on, without him spending himself, and there was no need to worry about pregnancy if it wasn't desired.

But Giles was at least sixty and it wasn't long before he died. This forced us to change. We were, after all, seeking our own illumination, not following one man. The other founder, William of Hildernissen, a less flamboyant sort, did not want to inherit Giles' role. He proposed that we take it in turn to prepare a talk for each meeting.

We met outside the city walls of Brussels in a tower belonging to an alderman. This meeting room was much more comfortable than Giles' hovel. On a clear night we could see the stars through the windows. Our host placed cushions about on the floor, and we lounged on those rather than sitting in chairs. It was the 'eastern fashion', he claimed.

At this time, new members were arriving, younger people who would have grown restless listening to Giles preach. There was Matthys, a headstrong youth who constantly demanded 'action' as well as contemplation. Sometimes I wanted to slap him, but I grew fond of him as well. I met Jehanne, a young woman from the south who had worked in the vineyards and spent time in prison for some sexual indiscretion.

Such 'indiscretions' became an important topic. Giles had spoken about the sexual act as 'the pleasure of Paradise', a fleshly way to embrace the divine. We spoke frankly about this. Finally, I told everyone about my adventures in the Harelle with Adrian and Christophe, which resulted in my only experience of mystical union.

I suggested that spiritual love could not exist without carnal love, just as we could not exist without eating and drinking. Such pleasures bring us into a union with all that is alive. God resides in the pleasures of nature, not in the authority that condemns them. These sentiments weren't far from what Bloemardine's imagery expressed, but we meant it much more concretely.

"Sensual pleasure should take the place of baptism," said Adele, and we lifted glasses to that. Time to become drunk with 'unspeakable wonders'.

Discussion turned towards public affairs and the price of bread as often as spiritual matters. We mocked and disparaged all authority. I started to feel as if I had come in a circle back to the concerns of the Harelle.

As we made ourselves comfortable on the alderman's cushions, talk turned to banter and ultimately to more touch, invoking my 'Holy Trinity' with Christophe and Adrian. With the erotic explorations of the group in full swing, I tried to repeat that experience in various combinations.

Sometimes the invisible cords that bound me to the two men from my past pulled tighter, and I felt their vital pulse. Something had to happen, something I needed to do . . . But always, I fell short of that.

When it was my turn to give a lecture, my talk naturally centred on 'entwinement'. I suggested that bonds may be forged in the heat of battle, the light of pleasure, or even in anger. We become entwined in ways we don't understand, and feel the effect of each other's actions in mysterious ways.

"Notes from afar reverberate in my ears, in my heart. It is a breath, a motion which I yearn to complete. It's a sensual impetus that works from a distance. Maybe this happens more than we realise, but the possibilities pass us by unless we become conscious of it and strengthen its effects."

Stefan, a reserved man new to the group, spoke up for the first time. "Perhaps we can draw on this capacity to enable us to communicate over long distances."

"Yes," I agreed. Could there be a practical use for such a mysterious process? "It took so long to find out what was happening in Paris during the Harelle. Most of the time we didn't know what anyone was doing. We could use this *entwinement* to communicate."

Matthys, who often dismissed our more inward-looking concerns, perked up. "We can use this to outwit the Inquisition, and smash it once and for all."

This sent Stefan into a long dissertation. He recounted an exposition called *De Luce* . . . 'On Light'. Written by a monk called Grosseteste, this study proposed that the universe started with a big explosion. "If the fabric of the universe originated in this explosion, we are all cut from the same cloth," he said. "We only need to uncover our common threads."

"Porete has written about a similar idea," I suggested. "She described how two souls that are united on one plane will recognise each other on another, and they can't hide from each other."

"We wouldn't have 'common threads' with *everybody*," objected Matthys. "Not with the people who persecute us!"

William listened to all this quietly, then said: "To say the universe originated with an explosion contradicts the precept that God created the universe."

"So what if it does?" Stefan stood up and paced about. "And why say there is only one universe? There could be many universes. That's not even a new idea. It was banned by the Pope over a century ago, which is all the more reason why we should talk about it now."

A dozen arguments exploded. Even among the heretics, you will find more heresy. We talked and contemplated, debated and pontificated. Our discussion ranged to alchemy and attempts to grasp the physical universe. Both the sensual and mystical dimension flowed from this as normally as water runs downhill in a stream.

Then the Inquisition arrested William and took him to Cambrai to appear before Henri of Selles. Pierre d'Ailly was continuing his mission to 'extirpate the remains of the nefarious heresy' and he had appointed Henri to investigate our group.

I was astonished to hear that William would be on trial alongside Giles, a dead man. Giles would've found that funny.

But there was nothing to laugh at when they took Adele and Henryk to Cambrai. I was left with the children. To them I became known as Grandmother Seraphine, though their own grandparents were long dead.

I wondered why the Inquisition didn't take me, while they took my hosts. Perhaps the inquisitors decided that leaving me with the children would be punishment enough. I'd been a decent teacher for the little devils. I could indeed sit them down and teach them letters for an hour or so. But to pay attention to their constant mischief all day and night was another thing entirely.

Fortunately, others in our group helped. Matthys showed a surprising talent for entertaining children and getting them to do what they should. Jehanne finally made arrangements for the children to stay with Adele's relatives in Tournai and accompanied them on their journey.

Then the house was quiet, save for Matthys sitting around with a flask of mead, muttering darkly.

"We wait for them to take us, too. We have to do more. The Inquisition has held people in thrall for years. We must break their power, show they're vulnerable."

"And how are they vulnerable?"

"They are human. They want us to believe they represent the divine when they trample it under their boots. But an inquisitor can die like any human being. When they come sniffing around here again, they'll get the reception they deserve. And I don't mean a few pebbles thrown by children."

I didn't see Matthys for a while. Word came later from Cambrai that William had recanted. This earned him a relatively mild sentence: three years in prison, followed by banishment from Brussels.

I always liked William, though he was more sedate than the rest of us. I didn't want to think he could betray us. I hated the thought that I could do the same under torture, so I asked a wise woman to concoct a poison to take if I was seized.

I still have this tiny vial of poison though I hope I will never have to use it, now that we live in Bohemia.

Perhaps William offered a long account of Giles' habits. That would have given the inquisitors a lot to chew on, and they couldn't harm a corpse.

A sister called around, an old beguine who had associates in Cambrai. She told us that Henri of Selles had been seen on the road to Brussels.

Then they took me. I was at the market. And silly fool that I was, I'd left my poison at home.

I don't like to think about those days now. But if I close my eyes they could be with me in an instant.

They kept me alone in a cell. Would they remember me from the Harelle? Did William say anything about me?

If they questioned me, I could tell them more about Giles running about with a plate of meat on his head. Tell them how he slept with every woman in the group, and every man too.

I waited to be tortured. Yes, I'd say it was all Giles doing. He claimed to be a prophet and he bewitched us. Giles would be proud. I would quote at length from Bloemardine. Her books have been passed around Brussels for over a century and they haven't even been banned.

I journeyed inwards to find Adrian and Christophe, and the parts of myself still entwined with them. I heard the chiming bells that called for freedom, and the steady clicking of looms that cautioned me to stay patient and think. I tried to sleep. Memories of Rouen filled my dreams . . .

The scent of grilled fish at the market on an overcast summer day. Adrian in discussion with a beghard preacher, Christophe laughing at them both. A young blond boy, who looked like Adrian.

Then the three of us gliding down the canal in Ghent; autumn leaves fall past my face, a yellow one settles on Adrian's hair.

That was where I tried to keep my thoughts, and myself.

The inquisitors didn't always seem sure what to do with me. They brought food. They would ask questions. Do you regard the sex act as a sinless 'pleasure of Paradise'? What *is* your concept of sin . . . do you deny the authority of the Church? What infernal methods do you have of spreading your beliefs?

I gave them lengthy, rambling and ultimately harmless comments about Giles and Bloemardine. As I spoke, I listened again for Christophe's riotous carillon. *Infernal methods.* Mere thoughts would betray me as much as any words. They would show on my face. Exploding universes, entwinement . . . desire and designs smeared across boundaries in a heightening of heresy.

No, no . . . let the mad clang of bells drive all that from my mind as I talked and talked about absolute nonsense.

Then they asked about Stefan.

He's not from Brussels, I told them. He only came to a couple of meetings. He said he'd heard about us in a tavern. Is that where you heard about us too?

Then they'd be called from my cell, and I was left for another day.

They didn't appear at all for some uncountable time. I was parched with thirst, empty with hunger. The worst was when I actually welcomed the sight of my gaoler.

I was told to go. There would be no trial, but I was banished from Brussels.

So I eventually made my way to Tournai to join Jehanne and the children.

Adele and Henryk had been released too. I found them in Tournai. They seemed shrunken and subdued, but still determined. I was confused by our relative good fortune, once they had dealt with William. Perhaps our alderman had intervened, or the authorities wanted to avoid an outbreak of disturbances in Brussels. Perhaps.

"Have you heard anything from Matthys? Did they arrest him too?"

"Matthys has disappeared," said Henryk. "And we've heard that someone tried to kill Henri of Selles as he crossed a ford. *Unsuccessfully*, I'd add. Whether the two have any connection, I can't say."

Matthys, an assassin? He seemed to be more mouth than anything else, but perhaps I was wrong.

"And what of the others? What about that odd Stefan, with his theories of the universe? The inquisitors were very interested in him."

No sign of him either.

We tried to find out more. None of our 'spies' picked up anything. Not Hilde the baker who had a shop near the Cambrai court and prison, nor the man who washes the floors at the Brussels gaol. The alderman could provide no information.

I spent a lot of time walking about Tournai, through the streets and the marketplace. I was happy to be living in a French-speaking town, though they spoke a confusing Picard dialect. The Czechs didn't understand much of it either when we came to Bohemia, which was why they called us Pikarts.

Though many beguinages had closed, there were a still a few small houses where unmarried women worked on tapestries or taught a mixture of rich and poor students. A dissident family here or there . . . Like-minded people lived in this city too. A new city, a new life. We tried to make the best of it.

But then, in my wanderings I sensed people following me. A movement as I turned, an unknown face that appeared with too much regularity.

No friendly aldermen offered meeting places where we could see the stars. New groups formed, meeting in the woods. Always, we were looking over our shoulders. No, we weren't in Brussels any more.

If the Inquisition prosecuted us again, we would face the stake as unrepentant heretics. Chimes rang in my ears, warning chimes. The sound of looms urged me: go, go, go.

Then the word came, passed from traveller to traveller, to the dissenters of Tournai. Matthys had fled to Prague, a place where reform livened the air.

His message: join me in Bohemia.

A tongueless bell should not make a noise, but I could swear its ringing enters my heart, with much more power than mere sound. It reaches inside and squeezes. I hear it with my entire body.

My morning lethargy dissolves in its wake. Finally I'm out, walking with my friends. The streets are quiet, too quiet. Vaclav's tavern is still closed. Less activity at the Horse Market.

Soon we approach our Lady of the Snows.

No one is around there now.

"Zelivsky must be spreading rumours to get more people to his sermons," I say. But look, the courtyard and the surrounding roads are littered with debris, the leavings of struggle and scuffle. A ripped piece of parchment. A child's boot, an officer's cudgel. And a battle-flail, a short club with a chain and a spiked striking head. Many of these have been appearing around the city in the past months.

I pick up the parchment. There are only a few marks on it. I could use it.

I point to the flail. "One of you should take this . . ."

Then I laugh. "Sign of my advanced years, eh? I take a piece of parchment, and leave the flail to the likes of you."

Now I hear distant noise. From the Horse Market, and the New Town Hall. Random shouts of commotion. A cheer.

People are running towards us. "We need help at the New Town Hall! Go there! Our prisoners are free. The king's councillors have been thrown out the window!"

"Who? Out the window . . ." I pick up my cane and get ready to move again.

It's happening, I think, it's happening!

Then a deep tolling sounds from the empty church. It's so loud and sudden my companions jump. I jump as best as I can, with joy. The tolling quickens. The rhythms stop, start and increase, a dam of sound bursting open. They make music I've never heard from Our Lady of Snows, I haven't heard this cadence in Bohemia and I haven't heard it since 1382, when the humble people proclaimed their triumph in Rouen.

"We have to go in," I say to my companions.

"Seraphine, no . . ." Though they are startled by the sudden ringing, my friends have other things on their minds. Of course, I'd feel the same way.

"Yes, you go on to the Town Hall. I'll join you. Whatever's happening will happen, regardless of what an old woman like me does."

I make a shooing motion with my hands. "Go! I'll be fine. I can look after myself."

With a glance backwards, they hurry away. Then I go inside and ascend the steps.

How long did Christophe pull on those ropes, ringing his composition into the silent air? Now its tumult carries over the distance, and over the years. *Entwinement.*

I clutch the banister as I make my way up the steps. The cadence vibrates through my arm. The notes radiate from my core, pushing me upwards.

I make it to the top of the bell tower. Yes, the empty ropes are swinging. The bells continue ringing, their notes rising and rising, a cross-rhythm starts. It's enough to dance to, enough to make me cry.

"Adrian . . . Christophe . . ." Their names entwine with my tongue.

Is it a peal of triumph, or a warning that the king's army has entered our city again? Perhaps it is both. I look out over Prague as the bell sings in my head. I see the crowds around the New Town Hall. Is that splash of colour the robe of a councillor on the ground, one of the men installed by the king, gaolers of our prisoners in the dungeon?

I try to see more, see if troops are moving. I look over the river, find the jagged teeth of the Hungry Wall. I shake my fist at the wall and laugh.

When the bells start to subside, the presence of my two lovers still animates the air. They will always be with me. We are entwined.

I turn and make my way down the stairs. Slow, but methodical, I'm soon on solid ground. I get my cane going double-time as I head to the New Town Hall, ready to join my comrades and see what I can find.

The Matter of Meroz

Samuel's mind is ablaze from tzaddik Avrom's lecture.

He nudges his friend Lev. "Bet they didn't teach you anything about *that* at yeshiva!"

An old fellow in the front row turns around to glower at the boys. Then with a fury of phlegmatic throat-clearing, he opens the discussion.

"Tzaddik, will you explain just how beings from other worlds could have souls? Hashem bestowed the Torah on Man. There is only one Torah as there is only one God. And we are the only creatures who have been granted free will by Hashem."

The tzaddik counters: "But each congregation has its own Torah, so why shouldn't each world have its version of the sacred scrolls?"

He runs his fingers through his ginger and grey beard as he thinks. "Look at the Book of Judges, where the prophetess Deborah curses the inhabitants of a place called Meroz for not helping the Israelites in their fight the Canaanite general Sisera. But where is a place called Meroz? No one knows, though there are references to stars. So the Talmud concludes that Meroz must be a star or planet. So wouldn't this curse recognise that the inhabitants of Meroz have the ability to think, to choose between good and evil?"

"But . . ." Samuel starts. Everyone turns to look at him and he wants to shrivel to a speck of dirt on the floor. How dare he, a smooth-faced outsider, speak up?

The tzaddik smiles and nods at him.

He clears his throat. "So how can someone from our world curse those who live upon another world? How does a curse travel over such a long distance?"

"If a curse punishes the ungodly, surely Hashem makes the curse effective," comments the surly denizen of the front row. "Do you doubt the power of the Lord?"

"No, Dov. This young man asks a good question," says the tzaddik. "Yes, the Almighty is the supreme power in the universe. He has also endowed his favoured creatures with free will *and* a capacity to overcome physical obstacles, such as vast distances. For example, Rashi explains how the road folded itself up for Jacob when he travelled from Beersheba to Haran, so he was able to complete his journeys in an instant. This manner of travel is described as the leaping of the road, *kefitzat haderech*."

"What did he say about a road?" Lev whispers to Samuel.

"*Shush!*"

"Deborah and other adepts could make the roads 'leap', thus shortening the distance they had to travel between two places. They could also instigate *the crumpling of the sky*, which allows travel between the stars. Then they made the sky smooth again and restored the distances."

Samuel has never read *that* in the Talmud. Maybe he missed something. "Where do you learn how to do these things?" he asks.

Now the tzaddik frowns. "This isn't something to do in your home! It is dangerous, and it is forbidden."

"But you're telling everyone about it. How forbidden is that?"

"My son, it is one thing to know *about* this. It is our history, our birthright. But to know *how* to do this . . ." The tzaddik shakes his head. "This knowledge is handed down to one person in each generation. There may be a time when we have to use it. But that time isn't now."

It hurts Samuel's head to imagine that such things could be true. But it's a pleasant ache, like the one he gets when he tries to imagine the 'unseen colours' from his favourite section in the Zohar: *There are colours that are seen, and colours that are not seen.* When he walks around the village, and the mud is grey and brown beneath his feet, he imagines those unseen colours, dazzling behind the muck. And what unknown colour lurks behind the dreary ledgers at the tailors' shop where he works? He hopes to discover it someday.

After more discussion, the tzaddik calls a halt. "Now it is time to dance." He gestures and the klezmorim take their places on the platform.

They begin their tune, slowly. Samuel stays in his seat next to Lev.

He remembers warnings that the Hasidim seek to convert other Jews. Though he enjoyed the discussion, he has no intention of joining their sect.

Soon wine is passed to Samuel and Lev. They drink and clink glasses, and the music is too catchy. They just have to join in. Legs kicking, the boys clasp hands on each other's shoulders, song vibrating in their throats and rising to their lips.

In the dancing, Samuel feels his heart expand until it becomes part of a much greater heart that beats at the centre of the universe.

The two boys head home across the fields, a good hour's walk. "I wish the road could rise up to meet us now," Samuel says.

"Your head's more likely to hit it first, after all the wine you drank," answers Lev.

"No, my eyes are on the stars!" Samuel giggles.

"But the tzaddik didn't talk about golems," Lev goes on to kvetch. "I was hoping for advice on that. I still don't understand why our formula hasn't worked."

"Feh! Golem, shmolem . . . Your mind's in the mud – look at the sky instead!"

It's a clear night, and the stars are hypnotic. So many and so far, they appear as mist across the heavens. And each of them surrounded by worlds! Samuel reaches up to the sky, spreading his fingers then closing his hand into a fist. Is this how you crumple the sky? But there is nothing in his hand.

"Samuel? Look where you're going!"

Drek. A huge cowpat.

Samuel wipes his boot on the grass.

Lev watches. "A fitting end to the evening," he observes. "The tzaddik did say some interesting things. And these Hassidim enjoy a dance and so do I. But what's the point of dancing if there are no girls?"

Samuel swipes his boot one last time. "You sound like my meshugge socialist sister, though she would ask that question for different reasons."

And now his crazy sister will be coming home from Odessa.

Raizl swings a suitcase in each hand. Samuel is supposed to meet her train, but where is he? Maybe it's just as well she didn't bring her favourite weapon, the pole with spikes. She would have wrapped it in burlap and schlepped it here along with her two suitcases filled with schmattes, but Arkady talked her out of it.

But she'd brought her revolver. After the last pogrom in Odessa, trouble is expected everywhere, even in sleepy old Fekedynka.

At least there's a newly formed group of comrades here. She looks forward to meeting them. She's brought them a gift from her group – a megaphone. But she really ought to try it out first and make sure it works.

She holds her head high, sure she is observed. Here comes the Odessa mama! Back home, are you? Still not married? *Of course not.*

Home. The place where she was born stopped being home long before she left it at fourteen. She's only just off the train and already she misses Arkady. She misses Odessa, though not all its memories are good.

Drying pools of blood in the gutter. She catches her breath. A memory. It's only a memory. This village doesn't even have gutters, only dirt roads.

"Raizl!"

So now Samuel is here. "What time do you call this, schmattekopf? Never mind, don't worry about helping me with my luggage. I'm a strong girl."

"Ah, Raizl, I see you haven't changed."

"Why should I?"

In the deepening dusk, crows rise from the fields, flying over the village. It has spread out since she was last here, two years ago when her father died. Now it's almost a town.

As they walk, Raizl hears the Odessa-bound train pulling into the station, then letting out a blast of its whistle as it leaves. A part of her wants to be on it.

When they arrive, Raizl's mother Feygele emerges from her last-minute packing, preparing for her journey to Vilna to live with Raizl's eldest sister.

She actually looks younger than last time; it must be the anticipation of this new life and the growing brood of grandchildren awaiting her. She's got rid of her sheitel and has let her own hair grow again, lightly covered by a scarf. Raizl is glad for her choice of present, a lovely embroidered scarf from Smyrna. Mother doesn't have to know that it fell off a boat in Odessa harbour and into Raizl's hands before it hit the water.

Feygele brings out the samovar, along with a plate of rugelach. Raizl has fond memories of those buttery bites tasting of nuts, raisins and cinnamon. But they are dry in her mouth now.

Siblings, relatives and neighbours drop by to bid Feygele goodbye. Some glare at Raizl, the wayward daughter packed off to the Odessa cousins. Raizl smiles back. She doesn't care what they think.

Sister Hannah and her husband arrive with their twins. Those warm milky bundles are quickly parked on Raizl's lap, one on each thigh.

She does like babies, provided they aren't her own.

Once the guests depart, the table is cleared and Feygele retired, Raizl takes a bottle of vodka out of her bag and pours two generous portions.

"You're better off with this than the kosher wine, Samuel." They raise their glasses to each other, then knock back their drinks.

Raizl clears her throat. "So, Samuel . . . You know that mother wouldn't leave unless I promised to 'look after' you. So I'll tell you now what that means. I'm here if you need me, but I won't be your servant. In Odessa, living with my comrades, we eat and cook together and share all tasks. That's what will happen here."

"But . . . I have to work and study."

"So will I. How do you think we'll eat?"

"I can't cook. And everyone will laugh."

"Ha! Let 'everyone' learn to cook too! You don't do your part, I go on strike. But maybe you'll see sense with more vodka. And what do you study? Just what is so important that you can't cook a meal?"

Samuel looks away from Raizl. "Kabbalah, that's what we study. Me and Lev. Lev shares his yeshiva books, but we go our own way with them."

"Oy Samuel. You once wanted to learn *science*. You liked to learn about animals and plants and look at the stars. So what's this?"

"But I still look at the stars. We went to a lecture about them by a tzaddik. He believes that beings from other worlds have visited the earth. It's in the Talmud."

"So if it's in the Talmud, does that make it true? A smart boy like you, believing in bupkes," Raizl says. "And what are these other worlds? Mars? I read a book about an invasion from Mars. *War of the Worlds*. In English. I've been studying English at a workers' institute and they had it in the library. The librarian told me that HG Wells is an important socialist and this is a book about the British class struggle!"

Samuel snorts. "I've never heard of it."

"It's just a story. Our librarian doesn't know English. My English wasn't so good then, but I improved it by reading this book. I might try to find pupils for English here."

"Most people here don't even speak Russian."

She shrugs. "So I teach Russian. Even here in Fekedynka the new twentieth century starts! Parents will want more for their children than superstitious chazzerai from the cheder."

Raizl pours herself another vodka. "But you know, farshtunken Fekedynka is still a miserable excuse for a village. You should come back to Odessa with me. Even with the quotas against Jews, you can study with your circle of friends, then pass your exams. You can become a scientist. My friend Leah . . ."

Raizl stops. When the pogrom started, comrades divided into groups to defend certain areas. It was only by chance that Leah ended up in the group that met with a massacre. Raizl had originally volunteered for that group, then Leah said she preferred it because she had family in that area.

Raizl shudders with guilt for surviving, sorrow for the friend she lost.

Samuel is waiting for her to finish the sentence.

"My friend studied science. But she was killed."

"So you want me to go there and get killed too? What a great sister you are!"

"Yes, it's dangerous in Odessa. But it's dangerous everywhere. All it takes is one incident, one accusation . . . Maybe you need to raise your head up from your books and your crazy Kabbalah davening."

"You call me crazy but anyone might say the same thing about you."

Maybe I am, Raizl thinks. She knows she should lie low, when revolutionaries and activists in the self-defence groups are likely to face arrest. But how low can she lie if the trouble comes here? She's already been invited to speak to the local comrades and help with their self-defence practice.

"So, Raizl, how's it going with your shaygetz, your Russian fancy-boy?" Samuel lowers his voice, even though he can hear their mother snoring above their heads.

They both raise their eyes to the ceiling, and Raizl answers in an even lower voice. "Arkady? As well as expected. I hope you'll meet him one day."

They drink a last glass of vodka. The conversation lightens, turning to visits from the matchmaker and tips on foiling plans for unwanted marriages.

Finally, it's time to sleep. Samuel goes up to his room, while Raizl takes the pallet down and covers it with blankets. She undresses and stretches out, still warm with the heat from the fire left burning in the grate.

Raizl drifts into sleep. She sees flames and desolation, a home levelled to rubble. A tree-lined street near the sea, glittering glass on the road and blood drying in puddles.

Samuel and Lev make their way across the fields on Sunday afternoon, hoping they will be able talk to the tzaddik alone in the study house.

"This tzaddik is meshugge for the stars and he's not much good on golems. But I like him after all," says Lev. "More fun than our rebbe, eh?"

"I told Raizl about him, but she said go to Odessa and learn real science."

"What does she know? She hasn't heard Avrom. And women wouldn't be allowed in such a meeting."

"They can study science, though. Raizl's friend in Odessa did."

The one who was killed, Samuel reminds himself.

"So," says Lev. "That doesn't say much for science!"

They stop at some woodland near a stream, planning to relieve themselves before moving on.

Samuel undoes his trousers. While he attends to his business he closes his eyes as he recites a prayer. Commentators in the Midrash spoke of becoming close to God during the most humble activities. They said nothing about activities as humble as this, but shouldn't they be celebrated? To take in nourishment and excrete it is part of living. It is Hashem's plan.

When he opens his eyes, he notices a dark shape on the other side of the stream. A touch of white to the indistinct darkness of the shape, a little blue?

He steps over the stones, across the stream to investigate. As he comes closer, a clenching in the pit of his stomach tells him what his eyes still refuse to see. A pale hand, blue and white fringed cloth, a tallis.

The tallis is covering the man's face. Samuel reaches out, lifting it away to reveal bruise-coloured skin, bulging eyes. Hair and beard, red and white.

The tzaddik.

Samuel screams.

His friend runs over. At the sight of the tzaddik, Lev joins Samuel's lamentation.

"We have to go tell them," Lev finally says.

"Go. I'll stay with the tzaddik."

"You can't stay. It isn't safe. What if . . ."

"What if? We can't leave the tzaddik's body alone. *Go!*"

Lev doesn't argue again, seeing Samuel's determination.

Now that he's alone with the tzaddik, Samuel pulls up the tallis to cover the dead man's face, this time with reverence. He sees the dark straps bound tight around his throat. The man was strangled with his own tefillin.

Samuel falls back as if this horror has just punched him in the gut. His hand thrusts into leaves, touches a soft fabric. He finds a square velvet bag. It is a plain deep green, worn in places.

Inside he finds a brass cylinder with four retractable sections, leather covering the largest section. A telescope, an instrument for looking at the sky!

There is also a book, a very old one. There's no title on the cover so he has to look inside. *The Book of Deborah* – the prophetess Deborah who could make the sky fold and crumple.

He says a kaddish for the tzaddik while clasping the book and telescope tight in his hands.

He hears shouts, people responding to the alarm raised by his friend. Who will come? The Hasidic burial society, the tzaddik's students, or the police? *Hey hey daloy politsey*, as his sister likes to sing over the washing. *Down with the police, down with the Czar.* A better tune than that dirge droned by her crowd, all about being hated and driven away. Of course you'll be hated and driven away if you sing that drek.

He puts the precious objects back into the velvet bag and slips it under his shirt, under his tallis, and waits.

When Raizl was growing up in this village, she believed she was alone in her desire for a better world. There were rich people, and poor people. Among the poor people you found poor Russians, and poor Jews. The two groups fought each other rather than those who kept them poor. She was only a child, but she knew this wasn't right.

And here in farshtunken Fekedynka, she is now meeting a small but active group affiliated to the General Jewish Labour Bund. There are fresh-faced gymnasium students from the better-off homes, as well as youngsters from poor homes like hers. A few older people, like Mordecai the blacksmith. He says he joined after Jew-haters vandalised his smithy. His daughter, a sharp-faced girl called Sheindl, had recruited him.

They are meeting in the woods for some short talks, then shooting practice. Though it's a chilly day, they are sheltered by the trees and the slope of the valley.

She'd been invited to talk about events in Odessa. But these now fill her with despair after all the hopes of a near-revolution – the strikes and rallies, crowds gathering at the harbour to support the Potemkin mutiny.

Being here makes her think of Arkady, though he obviously didn't attend Bund meetings. He had questioned the need for a separate group of Jewish activists, and they still argue about it. To her, it's practical when Jews usually live and work separately from goyim, and even speak their own language. But Arkady's group of anarchists often worked with the Bund, helping especially with the self-defence.

So that's what they have to do now, defend themselves, rather than build a new world. It's a grim thought, yet these comrades lift Raizl's heart. These are boys and girls with dreams and hopes. She envies them for their confidence, something she lacked at their age. She'd been a shy girl, though she'd had her moments of boldness.

She had heard about a boy in the village called Yankel who shared her views, and she just had to speak to him. He could become her soul mate, a true comrade . . . perhaps more. She decided to call on him to talk about their mutual interests.

When she knocked on his door, his mother opened it and Raizl explained that she wanted to meet her son. Yankel's mother slammed the door in Raizl's face. Later, she was denounced as a girl of loose morals and a disgrace to her family. But this led to a new life when she was sent off to stay with her cousins.

That same boy is here, asking her about Odessa.

"We've heard about your bravery in the revolution and fighting the pogromists," says Yankel.

She's an Odessa mama again!

Revolution? It had only gone halfway.

Brave? Years ago, Raizl had been terrified just to knock on this young man's door. And how brave had she been in Odessa?

She remembers a Jewish woman with wild hair running up to their group, throwing a stone at their banner. At the time, they were marching in response to the Czar's reform manifesto. This woman didn't think they were brave.

"You bastards! They are chopping people up over there and here you are taking a little stroll. Your banners mean less than bupkes."

So they rushed over to the woman's neighbourhood and stopped the attacks. They did save lives on that street. But they were too late or too few to stop other crimes.

A mother hung upside down by her legs, with the bodies of her six children arranged in a circle below.

A baby thrown out of a window.

It would've been much worse if we hadn't acted, Raizl tells herself.

Raizl tries to share what she knows, though it doesn't seem to be enough. She tells them that non-Jewish workers helped by forming self-defence groups and supporting pogrom victims. Railway workers, metal workers, sailors . . . But others? Maybe it was a worker who had thrown that baby out of the window.

Yankel says they have support from a socialist doctor called Oleg, plus other local activists. Some peasants are sympathetic, especially those who've been working or trading with Jewish families. But many others don't have these ties.

Then they get on to shooting practice. Only a few have guns. Most are very old: something a father kept from conscript days. A few have Bulldog guns like hers. No rifles or bayonets.

"A comrade from Odessa will try to bring more arms. In the meantime, we can practise with what we have. And remember, we can do a lot with an iron pole, especially if our blacksmith modifies it with spikes," says Raizl.

Those who know how to shoot show the newer recruits, aiming first for the lower tree branches. Yankel suggests that the best thing for target practice would be a portrait of the Czar, but who would have such a thing?

Someone shoots a partridge. This is met with cheers. Then they begin shooting at other birds. There'll be a good meal after the practice, even if it's not kosher. Matzo balls might not go well with partridge soup, but their catch should make a good stew.

Raizl concentrates on instructing the girls. She takes Sheindl aside, holds her arm and warns her to prepare for the recoil.

Then there's a crashing in the undergrowth.

Thank goodness no one has a jumpy trigger finger, because it's only Samuel.

"How did you know we were here?" She's pleased, thinking he wants to join them.

"We heard you! We're not deaf!"

Raizl nods, and introduces Samuel to her comrades. "My brother."

"The tzaddik is dead," says Samuel. His eyes are red as if he's been crying. "He's been murdered. And the Hasids are asking for all of you to guard the funeral."

"Tzaddik Avrom only wanted to look at the stars. That's what the rebbe said. He went out walking to look at the stars, and they killed him."

Raizl tries to console Samuel. She doesn't think she has anything left for that while she mourns Leah, but she is surprised how grief lightens when it is shared.

She is also surprised that the Hasidic community asked the Bund for help. Jewish elders usually petition the authorities for protection, but they must have seen indifference from the police when they reported the murder of an itinerant tzaddik.

Their group will stand guard outside the synagogue, then flank the procession to the cemetery.

The Bundists arrive well before the mourners with about forty in their group, including sympathisers from other parties. All have guns or poles, prepared for trouble.

A clot of people are already standing near the Hasidic synagogue. Raizl recognises a few faces. A local landowner, a horse merchant, some young labourers. All these people glare and swear when their group arrives.

But she catches nervous glances among the Jew-haters. Perhaps they don't expect resistance from Hasidic funeral-goers.

Could the murderer be among this crowd, or is he lurking further in the shadows?

"Mamzers," mutters Sheindl. "Surprised to see us, are they? Think we'll go like lambs to the slaughter . . ."

"Mamzers they are, but you don't shoot now," says Raizl. She can see that Sheindl's on edge, her hand clutched around the gun in her pocket.

There's nudging from the other side, and one of them shouts out as if on a dare: "What are you doing here? Not a beard among you. Are you Jews or just Jew lovers?"

Sheindl has to shout back: "And what are you, if you have nothing better to do than hang around here?"

"I used to have a job but a Jew took it away."

Now the mourners are arriving. They hesitate at the sight of the hostile bunch. A woman holds her hands up in supplication.

"Bugger off to Japan or Palestine!"

The Bundists surround the mourners, creating a protective corridor so they can file into the temple. Most of them weep. But Raizl is dry-eyed. She has no tears to spare for a man she's never met, but she will defend those who mourn him.

"One Jew down, too many to go."

The man who calls that out gets too close and receives a warning poke with a pole. "Think you're tough with your little sticks," he sneers as he backs off. "You won't do so well next time."

But with the mourners all in the synagogue, the Jew-haters start to get bored and drift away.

The young Bundists grin at each other. By standing together, they've seen the trouble off. The funeral prayers wafting from the synagogue do little to dim their enthusiasm. *Yisgadal, v'yisgadal*... the mourners' kaddish.

Last time Raizl heard that was at her father's funeral.

Now the mourners file out of the temple with the coffin. Their Hasidic garments make a ribbon of black against the brown and grey fields, heading to the cemetery.

As they march out with the mourners, Raizl sees dark figures at the top of the hill. These are not the departing louts, but gentlemen who sit like officers on their horses. Watching. And waiting, she fears.

On her way home, Raizl sees Samuel and Lev disappearing into the woods. The boys are up to something. She follows them.

"Hello, little brother. What are you doing?"

They react with shrugging and shuffling. Then Samuel replies, "We're just talking. We know there's going to be trouble. We have to do something."

"You should have joined our shooting practice."

"But will a few more shooters hold off the Black Hundreds and their friends in the army? You said that yourself the other day," argues Samuel.

For a kid whose head is filled with mystical nonsense, sometimes Samuel asks the right questions. The sad ones.

"So you are right. Like a broken clock, one second in a day. But what do you suggest?"

The three look at each other. "We've only started to talk," says Samuel.

"I know! We can raise a golem," says Lev.

"A *golem*! Something out of fairy tales. Are you mad?"

"I think I've worked out what went wrong with our formula last year," continues Lev.

"Last year indeed!" Samuel's contempt for the idea matches Raizl's. "Golems! You are lost in the sixteenth century! What good is a man of clay and stone when our enemies can blow it up? Boom! We need more than a golem. And the answer could be in here."

He pulls a book from out of the inner pocket of his coat. "*The Book of Deborah*. I . . . found it on the ground near the tzaddik, along with a telescope."

He looks around as if expecting condemnation. "It was meant to be," he adds.

"I don't know about what was meant and what was not, and I know nothing about this book. It might be drek," says Raizl. "But you did the right thing. The village police could have stolen it. You know what that schmuck of a constable is like."

"This book is *not* drek," Samuel shouts. "It contains the words of the prophetess Deborah, and her instructions on how to contact other worlds. These are worlds beyond Mars, beyond our own star. This is a world circling the star Meroz."

"*A curse on Meroz and all its inhabitants,*" quotes Lev. "Deborah cursed these creatures. So who needs them now?"

"And how will we bring them here?" Raizl considers *War of the Worlds*. "And why? Maybe they won't be our friends. They could be worse than the Cossacks. Did you think of that?"

"No, no . . . Deborah cursed them for what they *didn't* do. They wouldn't help the Israelites and she cursed them by closing the passage point. But in this book, she says she regretted this action. She believes there may be ways to stir them to action, and future generations might need to reopen the point of passage. She also believed it can be a source of knowledge."

"So what's this 'passage point'? Not an airship or flying machine?"

"No ships or machinery are involved, only the principles of "kefitzat haderech", making the roads leap," says Samuel. "It creates the passageway that enables you to move from one place to another in an instant. Except it involves the sky, and bending the substance of space."

"*Pah!*"

"It's like this." Samuel takes off his tallis, spreads it on a rock and puts his fingers on either side of the rock. "Think of this tallis as space, as the distance you need to travel. So you close the space like this . . ." He draws his fingers together, folding the material, until his fingertips are touching. "The crumpling of the sky!"

"Very clever. So this book tells you how to do that? Can I see it?"

Samuel places the book in her hands.

It isn't very big. If it contained such extensive secrets, Deborah must have made her points quickly. Now, if only Marx had done the same.

Raizl opens it to pages of Hebrew. She knows a smattering of Hebrew from synagogue, but it's a 'sacred' language and not meant for women. Hebrew was never a language of food, love, work and life for her. Yiddish is her mother tongue, her mame loshen.

But the Hebrew in this book would have been Deborah's mame loshen.

The illustrations in the book are simple line drawings, but they are striking. They compel her eyes to see something more than what's there. This book must have historical value, even if it's only a made-up story like *War of the Worlds*.

Raizl tries to keep an open mind as they prepare. Ritual has its place for unbelievers as well as the devout. After Bund meetings, they link arms and sing 'In Struggle', 'The Oath' and the 'Internationale'.

And of course, they have a meal.

The boys take turns reading from Deborah's book.

> *There are other worlds around other stars, but this is the only path I was able to open. It may be due to the celestial creatures' nature, and ours. Perhaps the other worlds cannot be reached for good reasons.*
>
> *I say 'celestial' and not 'divine'. Celestial pertains to the stars and the sky. They are part of the natural order made by our creator; they do not stand above it.*

"Creator?" Raizl interrupts. "There is no creator."

"Shut up," says Samuel. "Do you want to hear this or not?"

"This is why we don't allow women to take part in rituals," says Lev, stroking his barely sprouted beard.

"Deborah was a woman," Raizl points out.

"Raizl has a point, Lev. Deborah *was* a woman. She communicated with celestial beings and had the power to open and close the gate to them."

"Your sister is no prophetess," argues Lev.

"You bet your tuches I'm not. And what's with 'prophecy' when we have 'free will'? How free can we be with some big zayde in the sky?"

Lev is about to retort when Samuel holds his hand up. "Stop! We can discuss this later. This isn't a Talmudic talking shop, we need to plan something."

A few lines in the Talmud, a secret book from a dead tzaddik. Yet scientists and socialists like Mr Wells have also speculated about life beyond the earth.

So how do these other-worlders live? In these worlds, do some prosper while others grow poor? Do they have social and economic classes?

Now that makes sense, Raizl thinks. We will ask the workers from another planet to join in solidarity in our fight against the police, the Czar and pogromists.

"Let's do it," says Raizl. "But we do it along with other self-defence efforts."

"Whatever you want, sister," says Samuel, as he opens the book to another section. "This part is called 'Preparing the Table'. Now, Deborah says there are variations. There's a sequence that worked for her, but many things can affect the contact. She says these beings are volatile."

"Volatile! Sounds like what we need," says Raizl. "So let's be clear: there's no fasting or mortifying our flesh? I won't be having that."

"No fasting. No mortifying – only fortifying. But it's more than that. Deborah says that "celestial sustenance" can connect the worlds."

"Well, well, a universal nosh! But how do you know what these beings *like*? Deborah's people ate differently from us, I'm sure."

"That doesn't matter. It's most important that the banquet is enjoyed by those who prepare it."

"You mean it's *me* doing the preparing."

The two boys look at each other and shuffle about in that abashed-boy way.

"That's not how it will be," Raizl insists. "You'll have to make yourself useful in the kitchen. Both of you."

Carrot tzimmes with honey and raisins, potato kugel and sweet noodle kugel. Hunks of barley bread to mop up the juices. Soup from the remains of Friday's chicken.

"You better get grating and chopping. Down to the knuckle, boys."

"Ha, you're as bad as Chaim the tailor."

"No, this is cooperative work. See, I get my hands dirty too, alongside you. And they're *your* guests anyway."

Raizl starts singing 'In Struggle', a favourite workers' anthem, as she mashes fish and crumbs together. "*We are the hated and driven, Tortured and persecuted, even to blood . . . 'Tis because we love the poor, The masses of mankind, who starve for food.*"

Raizl chuckles to think that she's preparing food while singing a song about the starving masses. But she's learned how to make a little go far: lots of matzo meal and seasoning. Short of revolution and expropriation, this helps fill the belly.

"*We are shot down, and on the gallows hanged, Robbed of our lives and freedom without ruth –*"

"Stop it!" Samuel complains. "Yes, we all suffer. But do we have to suffer more? At least the Hasids play tunes that are good for dancing."

"I'll think about changing the music after you do some work."

Samuel shrugs, then closes the shutters.

"And what's that for? How do we make the sky crumple when we can't see it?"

Samuel opens Deborah's book and reads: *"The sky is space, and space is everywhere even when it is enclosed."*

"Space, schmace!" Raizl carries on with the preparations. But in keeping with the theme, she shapes the rugelach like stars.

When everything's bubbling on the stove, the boys spread a bed sheet out on the floor and begin drawing diagrams with charcoal and pens.

What are they doing to that sheet? These scholars will have to learn to do the washing too.

Samuel labels eight places at the table, and several in the middle. He adds lines around it, a vortex of rings around the centre, plus other figures.

"It's the Tree of Life," says Samuel.

"Whatever you say, little brother."

He draws lines linking the circles together, creating pathways and a central vortex. "And the food goes here."

So the table is set, and they place the food on the sheet following the symbols and geometrical figures from the Book of Deborah.

Finally, the rugelach is ready, warm and fragrant from the oven. Raizl hovers with the plate, then plonks it down on the trunk of the Tree of Life, in the centre.

"Tiptheret!" exclaims Lev. "It stands for beauty. And it's where the synthesis of opposites meet."

"Well, it's where we find a plate of rugelach, our mother's best recipe. I put poppy seed in them and . . ."

The boys begin davening and genuflecting towards the food.

"Stop it. Eat!" orders Raizl as she picks up her knife and fork.

She is tasting every piece of gefilte fish she ever ate in this mouthful.

Then the carrot tsimmes is sweet and savoury at once. With nourishment from the chicken soup flowing into her veins, the symbols on their improvised tablecloth begin to make sense. That one there, under the plate of rugelach, does indeed look like an opening, a tunnel.

"Look, we've fortified ourselves. Now we carry on the ritual," says Lev.

The boys start to chant what sounds like a series of numbers, pronounced in many languages as well as Hebrew. It puzzles Raizl. Singing the 'Internationale' might be a ritual too, but she knows what it means. It inspires her. But this?

"Raizl, you look confused. The chanting frees our awareness to travel and open the path," says Samuel.

"So tell me, how do we chant and eat at the same time?"

"Stop with your squabbles," interrupts Lev. "We have a road to make rise, and a sky to crumple! Or have you two forgotten?"

"But I'm asking a perfectly good question."

"So here's a perfectly good answer. The chanting is a kind of verbal alchemy. By forming these words, then changing their letters, we can change the nature of reality – or in our case, the distance between two worlds."

"Alchemy, you say? So maybe food is an alchemy of the stomach. An alchemy of taste and scent as well as words and sound. They say the way to a man's heart is through his stomach." How she hated that phrase when she was growing up. On the other hand, her home cooking did impress Arkady and all her comrades.

"So, boychiks, the way through the centre of the universe and out again is through the stomach too! What did Deborah have to say about that? Maybe we eat rugelach now, before you start making noise again."

So Raizl eats a pastry crumb by crumb, the taste of poppy seeds, raisins and cinnamon lingering on her tongue. Then she starts on one she made with almonds and dates.

As the pile of rugelach on the plate diminishes, Samuel keeps rearranging the remaining pastries into a pattern. This pattern begins to make sense too. And then they begin chanting again. It starts a buzz in her ears, between her ears.

The pattern of pastries converges at Tiptherah, a point of beauty and synthesis. She takes another, this one with sweet cheese curds and dried apricots from Odessa. A blaze of flavour at the point of her tongue, taking her far beyond that city. At the vortex of the star-formed pastry is a tunnel, and there is *something* at the end of it. Light, colours rippling through an utterly new spectrum.

Other tunnels branch from the one they travel. Are there other worlds at each end? Maybe *these* are the worlds that will show solidarity. She takes a look . . .

It's only Fekedynka. But the dirt roads are paved, full of odd sleek automobiles.

At another tunnel she sees Fekedynka's synagogue in flames.

As a young girl she would have gladly burned that place down herself. Samuel would have no great love for it either after so many beatings at the cheder.

But this smoke fills the tunnel, catching in her throat and infecting her with fear. The fumes flood her with a taste of iron and meat. It makes her gag. Ominous outlines begin to reveal themselves through the smoke. A tower?

No no, leave this place . . .

She's afraid at first to look into other tunnels, but she hears music that tempts her. Like klezmer, though it's not very good. A fat man sings a song against a backdrop of a village like hers, while people wearing furs applaud.

She moves on to another tunnel lit by kaleidoscopic blocks of colour that warm her even more than chicken soup. The kaleidoscope turns to a living scene. Her farshtunken village again: but here's she's walking hand in hand with Arkady in the market. Everything is still lit by the colours of the kaleidoscope. She feels peace. She thinks she's happy.

But then a deep noise wells beneath her feet and wrenching bass vibrations churn her stomach and rattle her teeth, threatening to undo her. Shake her into pieces, breaking everything down . . .

"Raizl, stay with us!" A rough hand on her shoulder, Samuel shaking her. "We bring them to us, you don't want to be going to them!"

The deep bass carries on, but now she feels anchored against it. Something shrill spills out of an opening in the floor along with it, a column of light that hurts her eyes, noise approaching melody.

The colours scream with the sound, and she has to close her eyes against them. Something breaks. Plates? The ceiling above her head? She grips Samuel's hand, and remembers how he once gripped hers when he was much smaller.

Then it's quiet. So quiet. And a strange man's voice addresses them in something that sounds like Hebrew.

Raizl opens her eyes. Two men and a woman sit at their 'table', clad in Arabian-style robes and sandals. It must be cold for them, even with the room warmed by cooking.

A lot of plates are broken, but someone has moved the rugelach aside. That plate is still intact and the leftover pastries have retained a somewhat shaken pattern.

Raizl takes a deep breath, picks up the rugelach and offers it to their guests.

These beings speak Hebrew, Samuel thinks. Not the devotional Hebrew he knows best, but it's close to the Hebrew of Deborah's book. In a moment their old house was filled with eye-blasting light and colour and gut-wrenching noise. He forced himself to look, even if it shattered him.

These creatures are composed of noise, and they weave their unseen colours with it.

And now they sit here in robes and sandals, accepting Raizl's offer of rugelach.

Then in a blink they're wearing warm clothes. They must have assembled the substance from the air, the vapours of the food, anything around them. From this they create their flesh and blood, their clothes. Some would consider them gods, but Samuel knows there are no other gods before Hashem. They are God's creatures just like he, his friends and his sister and the beasts of the field.

Yet jealousy stirs in his mind. Hashem created Man above all other creatures, yet here are creatures far more powerful. Perhaps the Lord was not pleased with what Man has become.

"We're speaking the right language?" The first word from the woman grates like a rusty hinge. Then the next ones soften. Each word makes her voice more like a woman's, a human that God created.

Samuel tries to stifle his envious and selfish thoughts. He answers, while his friends are still stunned. "You're close. We use a similar language for prayer, and something else for every day."

"Yiddish," adds Raizl, still offering food. For all her revolutionary Odessa ways, Raizl can be so much like their mother. Perhaps he should become more like that too. In the end, he did enjoy the cooking.

"We tried to change to your form as soon as we entered, so we're sorry if we hurt your eyes and ears," says one of the men at their table.

They're very polite for accursed inhabitants, thinks Samuel. But he can't bear to be polite himself. He needs to know so much.

What did they want with Earth and the ancient Israelites and why didn't they help? Samuel is not sure what to ask first.

The three new human-like beings look about. "The stories we've heard of your world tell us of heat and light, and a very bossy woman," says the woman.

"Have something to eat. You've travelled a long way. Rugelach isn't enough. We can talk later," says Raizl.

"Eat?" one of the male aliens says.

The woman jabs him with her elbow. "Food, remember? You put it in your mouth. That's the stuff that drew us here, where there are so many senses to experience."

Raizl is thoughtful. "Three strangers will attract attention in a village full of yentas. We need stories for them. Arkady can get papers. Our guests are students from the yeshiva, yes? And one of you is a sister of a student."

"What is a sister?"

"A pain in the tuches, that's a sister," replies Samuel. "But my sister speaks sense when she says *eat*."

So that's what they do. The alien woman takes a piece of gefilte fish with her fingers. After a small mouthful she seems to glow with pleasure in the food, as if a light has flickered on under her skin.

Lev clears his throat. "It might be easier if you were all yeshiva students. Friends from a town not too close. But one of you will have to, um, change yourself, if you can do that."

"I expect that will be me," says the female. And then her face and form seems to melt. Now Samuel does look away. When he sees her again, she has become a brown-haired boy.

Remember, they are only creatures like me. They do things we cannot do. Maybe they can help us. But they are not God.

Finally he speaks up. "Do you go around visiting other worlds?"

"When we can, though it's hard to get through. We need help from the other side. We like to sample things and study them. We create sound-scores to enjoy at home," the first young man from space explains. "Yours is the only world we've found where beings are so different from us, and produce such a wonderful and strange variety of sounds: some sweet, some harsh. We all heard stories about a visit, then access was denied. Some woman wanted us to fight in a war. We don't do wars."

Samuel translates this into Yiddish for Raizl.

And Raizl answers, "Neither do we, me and my comrades. Our only war is the class war –"

Lev interrupts, and soon they are talking about points and pathways and how these beings arrived. They pick up each other's Hebrew idioms quickly.

Raizl recognises some of the Hebrew words, but most of the time she watches. She sees how a light flickers in their faces as they enjoy their food.

The three look so ordinary now, but Raizl remembers the dazzle of their light and their pulsing waves of sound.

So these creatures of sound and light enjoy a vacation in the flesh. They change their size, they change their shape to look like us. They *seem* harmless, compared to the kind of human tyrants she has dedicated herself to overturning.

They talk like people now. But she is sure she hears an echo in their voices, as if they come from across empty spaces. And their talk is empty too, empty of feeling.

It's like people going to the Black Sea to swim and eat ice creams. But this is no time to kibitz, no time to fool around. Not in Deborah's time when a wicked king held the Jews as slaves, and no time for kibitzing now.

So they want a vacation, they only want to schmooze and eat and drink and make 'sound-scores'. Raizl remembers what she saw at the end of a tunnel: the fat man singing on a stage, making an entertainment of someone's poor life.

They've assumed their bodies of flesh and blood for momentary pleasures, while that is all we have.

The three guests pick up their Yiddish quickly. Raizl puts them upstairs in the room she's taken over from her mother, so they'll be out of the way. She goes back to the pallet in the kitchen. It's warm there, and it's where she slept as a child.

If the visitors broke a few dishes on arrival, they are now the tidiest of guests. They've been given names: Hymie, Yaakov and Herschel.

They spend a lot of time in Samuel's room. She hears chanting and talking. They go out at night and look at the stars with the tzaddik's telescope.

Then they go to Odessa for a look around. It's just as well they're away, before they get a visit from the matchmaker urging them to marry someone's daughter.

When the guests return, they say how much they like Fekedynka. Especially the food. They're not so interested in fine things, but in strong tastes and aromas and sounds.

Raizl cooks another meal, more chicken soup for the schnorrers out of space.

Of course, she did try to get them to help in the kitchen. Yaakov-from-Meroz obliged. Not for him grating potatoes or any hard graft; he created something that looks very much like gefilte fish out of nothing, or 'emanations' as Samuel likes to say. But she didn't see anything emanating there, just some gefilte fish.

Then she took a bite. It tasted like damp sawdust. An imitation.

She remembers when she took Samuel on walks where they'd find flowers, collect them and look them up in a big book, their father's treasure. She should have tried harder to convince him to study this kind of science. He could have done something useful, instead of *this* . . .

Get rid of them, she's about to hiss at Samuel, who is now chopping onions. He has the book, he must know the curse to send them back. But she has also seen how the aliens flicker when something affects them. She remembers those bone-rattling notes, the unmaking chords at their heart. Surely the goniffs could be good for something. Even Deborah thought so.

Meanwhile, she tutors her pupils in Russian. At the end of it, a few coins. She goes to help sister Hannah with her babies, and tells her that Samuel has guests. Better say that, before the chitchat goes around.

Hannah has other concerns. "There's been trouble," she says. "Drunk boys in the market mouthing off about a pogrom. They called it a cleansing, though they're dirty schmucks themselves. They were throwing rocks, while soldiers supplied vodka."

On her way home, Raizl calls in on Mordecai. At his smithy the windows are boarded up and glass still glitters on the ground beneath them. He shows her a collection of spiked poles. Is that enough? Oleg said that he expects more arms to arrive, but they're overdue.

Raizl runs home. She goes up to Samuel's room, where the three guests would be. She flings the door open. "Listen! Do you want to experience real life on this Earth? Soon you'll see it in all its horror. Life isn't just a bowl of chicken soup."

They're all crowded around the open window. A cold wind blows through the room. Samuel turns around, holding his telescope. "Ssh! They're showing me the stars with inhabited planets."

Raizl is lost for a response. Then she goes downstairs and gets the megaphone she brought from Odessa. Time to try it out at last.

Back in Samuel's room, she shouts through it: "Wake up, you schlubs!"

Alien guests and humans alike jump at the sound.

And maybe the creatures of sound and light jump a little more.

Doctor Oleg passes on the bad news. Comrades in Odessa have been arrested and the arms were seized.

Faces of her friends flash before Raizl's eyes, but she doesn't have time to worry. Without these arms, they need other help. They knock on doors, get promises of a loan of a horse or cart. A few pistols are donated; the blacksmith will work overtime. They enlist the support of the Jewish toughs who hang about the market: these goniffs don't give a shit about politics but they'll pile in if a fight breaks out.

Raizl is at home, writing out a chart of Yiddish and Russian words. Then the blast of a shofar from the village synagogue interrupts her train of thought.

Since it isn't a holiday, that only means one thing.

It probably started in the market. It usually does. And that's where Raizl's group will go, while others patrol elsewhere.

Raizl shouts for Samuel, then gets herself ready. Heavy coat and scarf over her face, her stoutest pair of boots, her pistol in one hand and an iron stave in another. She picks up the megaphone and slings it across her chest with its strap. Though she doesn't expect to make speeches, they might need to communicate.

"And what are you going to do, boys?" Raizl turns towards Samuel and Lev. "Cast some more spells?"

"No, we're going out! We'll defend the synagogue."

She nods at her brother. "There'll be a group heading there now. And where are your guests?"

"They went out to do some . . . *recording*, they called it."

A curse on Meroz and all its inhabitants.

In Odessa, Raizl was able to dodge and run through the streets, shelter in buildings and alleys and emerge again.

But this is a village of ramshackle shops and dirt roads, exposed in a valley to an enemy that comes from all sides. From other villages, from the towns and even the cities, their enemies prepare to sweep through any place that stands after October's pogroms.

Some of these attackers are peasants, armed with pitchforks and scythes. But there are also soldiers among them, officers and Cossacks too.

She wants to vomit. Did Yankel speak of bravery? She'd flee if there was anywhere to go. The enemy will sweep them aside as easily as dust off a wooden floor, then go on to the next village.

She has her pistol. She'll take a few of them out of action, out of life before they kill her. But she doesn't want to die.

Then their *guests* appear in the crowd. Just behind her. Swathed in coats and scarves, like everyone else. Hymie, Yaakov and Herschel, the yeshiva boys from Meroz. They are pressed up close to her, and even though they just look like boys, it makes her shudder. They make noises to each other that bear no relation to a human language.

They don't write anything down, but they look at each other, look at the scene in front of them as if comparing notes.

Then there is a gunshot. Bayonets extended, swords and clubs raised, the Black Hundreds spill into the village.

There are screams from the front – are people getting trampled?

"Let's go," Raizl shouts. "We have to move forward."

Pogromists come straight into the market, horsemen in front. Closer they come, then Raizl runs forward and shoots. The first horseman rears and falls. Yankel and Sheindl start a volley at the other horsemen, but not before other shots ring out.

Comrades scatter, but one ducks into the butcher's to emerge with a meat hook, showing a clear intention to use it.

The Bundists keep shooting, but in a flash they're surrounded and pushed back against the tavern. A Jewish thug called Mendel comes out of the tavern and starts throwing rocks. Someone starts shooting from the upstairs windows, just missing a Cossack but bringing down his horse.

But they're only a handful cornered here, plus the schnorrers out of space.

"*A curse on Meroz!*" Raizl echoes the prophetess Deborah.

She knows it's the end. She has chosen to live the life of a rebel, and she did the best she could. Now it's over but she'll make a good exit. She shoots and shoots. When she runs out of bullets, she's prepared to use a pole and then kick and punch if she loses that.

And she'll sing. This song will be the last thing in her ears, not the curses of the Black Hundreds. "*We are the hated and driven,*" Raizl begins, lifting the megaphone to her lips.

Mordecai's bass voice booms out. Sheindl and Yankel, everyone joins in. "*Hated are we, and driven from our homes, Tortured and persecuted, even to blood; And wherefore? 'Tis because we love the poor . . .*"

Yaakov-from-Meroz visibly shudders. Raizl can feel it move through him and convulse him. "That . . . that . . . that terrible tune. Those words," he complains in Yiddish, pulling his hat tighter over his ears. "Farshtunken! Miserable!"

They sing louder. Then Raizl pulls his hat off, exposing his ears. "Put that in your sound-score, you putz!"

Luminescence moves through his face, similar to the glow excited by the pleasure of good Jewish food. But now it expresses pain, shown by the way his too-human features contort. The light is stronger. And Raizl understands. Soon he will lose control, and stop being Yaakov.

Yes . . . Sound affects these creatures most, for that is what they are made of.

She sings through the megaphone. "*We are shot down, and on the gallows hanged, Robbed of our lives and freedom without ruth, Because for the enslaved and for the poor, We are demanding liberty and truth.*"

The alien's body swells. And the other one gives a cry, worse than a fox in heat or a cat meeting its end.

"Sing louder, sing!" Raizl urges her friends. She kicks Mendel. "Sing, goddammit!"

And Mendel sings.

The aliens burst out of their clothes; their flesh comes apart in shreds of light and patches of darkness.

The pogromists back off, frightened by what they see and hear.

"But we will not be frightened from our path, By darksome prisons or by tyranny . . ."

The alien fleshly form dissolves into a tangle of waves that boom in pain, deep dissolving throbs that makes the horses bare their teeth, shriek and turn and bolt.

Meanwhile, other Jews emerge from defensive posts around the village. They move forward with sticks and guns ready to finish the job, even if they've had to share some of their enemy's pain.

Oleg and a few others tend to the injured on the ground.

Have the aliens fled, taking their sound-score with them? Maybe they've decided this world is not a suitable place for their holidays after all.

Or they could still be here in some form, lingering like the scent of a fish gone bad.

The tavern keeper emerges with flasks of wine. "The mamzers have run away!"

Samuel and Lev arrive with others from the synagogue, followed by a beaming rebbe.

"It's God's doing, like the horns of Jericho," intones the rebbe, accepting the offer of wine after a brief blessing.

But Raizl shakes her head and passes her wine to someone else. She remembers what she saw in the tunnel, the place where the sky crumpled and let in the alien light. Now she knows where Deborah's gift of prophecy came from. When she opened the pathway, those other corridors showed her what-could-be. Deborah did not predict *the* future, but she was able to look into possible futures.

Raizl can't forget the burning synagogue, the smoke that must hide a horror more brutal than any pogrom. But how will she speak of this to others? Who will listen? She understands now that Deborah might have been much more accursed than the inhabitants of Meroz. And so is she.

While the others toast and celebrate a victory, Raizl cannot join them.

Survivor's Guilt

As I enter the meeting hall near the Thames, I breathe in the scent of tobacco and wet clothing, perfume mingled with fried fish, the malt and yeast of beer flowing freely. Strains of Spanish guitar are already wafting from the auditorium.

Two fresh-faced students are taking tickets. But there are also Yiddish-speaking East Enders hawking *Frei Arbeter Stimme*, as well as a few of the more moneyed Marxists copiously donating into the collection bucket. There's a bunch of literary folk whispering over well-thumbed books. I hear people speaking many languages: Polish and Spanish, Russian and German, as well as several varieties of English.

I feel at home, though my original language is so obscure and ancient there's no chance of hearing it even in this glorious babel.

I peer through the crowd, though I'm not sure who I'm looking for. Even under the best of circumstances, Gunther won't be here in person.

I used to believe that he had died in Munich, shot by the Freikorps. Now I'm not so sure, and tonight I hope to discover the truth.

"Hi Mara," someone greets me. I nod at people I've worked with in the Freedom group and the Anti-fascist Welfare Committee, a few from the Independent Labour Party. But I keep to myself, too anxious to socialise. I have my notebook and pen with me, ready in case I want to pass on a message. I haven't written anything yet. Gunther was the writer, not me.

On stage are two guitarists, a trombonist and a stocky woman who looks like she could also throw a few good punches as she belts out the tunes. "... *La luchamos contra los moros, mercenarios y fascistas. Aye, Manuela,*" she proclaims in a ringing contralto while the guys "*rumbala rumbala*" behind her.

People clap and stomp. "*Vive le quince brigada! rumbala rumbala*"

The music rattles at the doors of my mind and I let them swing open, just a little. In come the images, snatches of thought. For a moment, I'm with the people making the music.

I'm where those songs come from. I see:

The narrow streets of Barcelona hung with banners: *No Pasaran*.

Wind, smoke, explosions among olive groves.

Women wrenching up cobblestones from the streets for barricades.

And there is the fresh sting of defeat, filling my mouth with dirt.

But that only makes me want to raise a clenched fist and storm the nearest barricade, though there are none on the streets of London tonight. This song summons the music of my early childhood, the music of bloodsuckers, godless mountain-demons and monsters. We have our own songs of persecution, our songs of battle. No matter that the songs of my dwindling tribe are about defending some far-flung pile of rocks none of us would want to live on now. And even though they're sung in a language unknown to humans, I hear those songs in the chords of many struggles, far beyond Spain.

"Want a programme?" A child tugs at my dress. "Take one and make a donation. It'll help the refugees." Other children are underfoot or helping out. A while ago you wouldn't see so many. People were wary of attacks from fascists, but since we routed Mosley's crew at Cable Street a few years ago, physical attacks have been rare.

I hand the boy some coins and take a programme from him. The bill includes music hall performers, a jazz group, a classical violinist and a Basque dance troupe. And sandwiched at the beginning is a reading of new work by the elusive writer Arto Westman – by his agent.

Can this agent be trusted if I want to pass on a message? I worry that I might write something that could give either of us away.

The singer is asking for requests.

"*A las Barricadas!*" Shouts for a Spanish anarchist anthem don't go down well with some Communist Party members, who grumble and mutter.

But one of the guitarists grins and strums the opening chords.

"*Negras tormentas agitan los aires . . .*"

"Would you like to buy a copy of *Cloudforests*? Special edition with the Left Book Club, authorised by Arto Westman to aid the fight against fascism!"

This time the vendor is a woman in her twenties.

"No thanks, I have my own copy." I take the book out of my pocket and show her an earlier German edition. "I have all of Westman's books. But this is my favourite."

Cloudforests evokes the lives of workers on a coffee plantation in the mountains of Chiapas, southern Mexico. The author uses a mixture of Spanish, English and a smattering of native languages, but makes every word understandable by context. It is a book about resistance and dreams. It is full of colour and light and the sensations of walking among the clouds.

Yet a cadence to some phrases connects this distant place to more familiar city streets, as if that part of Mexico isn't so far from Munich after all.

Another Westman book, a collection of stories about a general strike in Seattle, has also made me think of Gunther. Though the stories take place in the wet and windy Northwest of America, I find lines of dialogue we could have uttered to each other after some turbulent beer-soaked meeting in Munich where workers also set about transforming a city.

I'm not the only one who sees this connection. There are rumours that Arto Westman is a German who fled the repression of the Bavarian workers' councils in 1919. Like many refugees deemed too dangerous to stay in England or the US, he lives in Mexico. He avoids any personal attention. There are rumours he is a man I believed to be dead. *Gunther.*

I remember teaching English and Spanish to Gunther, how quickly he learned and his love for language. He said he wished he could be fluent in every language in the world, a true internationalist. I wondered if I could ever risk teaching him mine.

Meanwhile, he taught me how to run a printing press and forge documents. Perhaps he also showed me how you can keep changing your name, yet stay true to yourself.

After an amnesty in the twenties, many spoke freely about the Bavarian uprising, but others stayed in the shadows. Erich Mühsam had written: *You are no longer a fugitive, Gunther. Let us know if you're still alive. Now we can let the truth be known.* But Erich was later tortured and murdered in the Oranienburg concentration camp.

Let me know if you're still alive, Gunther. Have you wondered the same about me?

Or were you sure it was the end when you heard those shots on the road behind you?

"*Black storms shake the sky, dark clouds blind us . . .*"

There were many dark clouds in the skies twenty years ago. There are dark clouds gathering now that will do more than shake the sky. They will drench the earth with the kind of blood that will never sustain life.

But in 1919 there were also moments of hope, and we drew together in the middle of one.

"*Alza la bandera revolucionaria que llevará al pueblo a la emancipación . . .*"

I'm humming the tune as I make my way to a seat closer to the front. I have my notebook ready. All I have to do is write a short note to his agent to pass on. I'll let Gunther know I'm alive and give my address. Then he can write back. If he wants to.

A stout man gets on the stage, fidgeting in his tight suit as he introduces himself as Jack from the dockers' union. "We'll have more music after a reading on behalf of Arto Westman, a writer known for keeping a low profile. But he's standing up to be counted in his own way. His agent and close friend will read some new work."

I let loose a gasp when I see who is getting on the stage. Then I come close to laughing out loud.

It is Gunther himself, now a robust man in his forties. His skin is tanned and weathered. The grooves down his cheeks and along his mouth are deep, put there by a life lived outdoors. Now his hair is grey instead of blonde, but the contrast of his dark eyes is just as startling.

Does he really think he can get away with posing as his own agent? It's ridiculous, but I can't stop grinning. He always was a cheeky guy! Then, many of the people likely to recognise him after twenty years are already dead.

I look down quickly. Exchanging letters over thousands of miles is one thing, letting him see me is another. I have my own reasons to stay in the shadows.

In those days, I cut my hair short and wore modern straight-cut dresses without a corset, as radical women did. We were denounced as 'mannish', but I doubt I earned that particular epithetic with my plump figure.

Now my hair is long and curly again. I wear a full dress cinched at the waist in the current style. But those changes are only superficial. If I had prepared for this I could have applied cosmetics to appear older. Worn glasses to obscure distinctively green and tilted eyes. Gunther said they had attracted him when we first met, though we argued constantly.

I make do with letting my hair fall in a veil in front of my face, as I did when I was a child shielding myself from the nuns meant to be caring for me. Those strands of hair had to hide the hunger that surely showed there. Then I would sneak out a window at night and run through the woods and finally feed myself. For a while I was free from black-garbed figures and the muttering of prayers, free from those who would burn me if they knew.

I never thought I'd repeat that gesture here. I raise my programme and peer over it through my hair. It must look odd, but I wouldn't be the only eccentric in this audience.

"I'm sorry that Artie can't be here," Gunther says. "He really doesn't travel. He's much more at home in the mountains and the forest, or at home learning to play piano with his beloved Lucia, and of course typing away at his next book. And by his own admission he's *lousy* at speaking to an audience anyway, so he won't inflict such an ordeal on you."

Gunther, you don't fool me with that American accent! I still hear hints of German, traces from other places too.

The groove along the side of his face deepens for a moment, like a wink. "Artie hasn't been on this side of the Atlantic for a very long time. OK, maybe in the early days he'd been tempted to return to his native Finland for the sake of a good sauna. But then he discovered the traditional Mayan sweat bath, which he recommends highly. Mexico is now his home and he doesn't like to leave it. So he sent me instead to read something he wrote very recently, together with an introduction and message of solidarity."

Native Finland! Not only am I trying not to be seen, I have to work harder not to giggle again. Already the man in the next seat is looking at me with the expression of one of those nuns about to *shush* me in church.

Of course, I've come up with some far-fetched stories in my own time.

I wish we could sit together and laugh at all our disguises over a glass of schnapps.

Now I can't resist. I touch his mind, in a way I've only done once or twice before.

Even then there was so much static on its surface, so many layers and contradictory thoughts. There were words, already in several languages, words assembled for newspapers, leaflets and proclamations. Most of this was submerged by a dense layer of fear as heavy steps thundered above our heads, or when our guards cursed and the lorry rattled as it brought us to our execution. That was just before I kicked open the door . . .

Now his mind is layered with another twenty years. It is dense with subterfuge, meanings hidden in other meanings, more jokes that make me smile. And I find a feeling that I don't recognise at all. It is calm but purposeful. Warm, with an edge that can turn white-hot.

Gunther clears his throat: "Artie writes: 'This is new and very rough. Maybe I won't ever put it in print. But I want it to be read. I've denied much of the past out of necessity, but it's now necessary that this past doesn't get buried. As our comrades rose up in Spain, we had an uprising in Germany twenty years ago. The Nazis – and all those in power – try to bury that history, and we have to bring it into the light. This is dedicated to a comrade I knew and loved in those days.'"

A woman sits in the front row, watching with pride. Lucia. She stands out from the crowd with her green open-work shawl and dangling earrings. Her hair is long and dark, with flashes of white at the temples. She gives him a brief nod of encouragement.

Arto – Gunther – begins to read.

"You went by many names. So did I. Though we were lovers you didn't tell me everything. When we had to hide. I thought you whispered 'be still' in my ear though your lips didn't move."

No! I expected stories about coffee-bean pickers, strikers in Seattle, rebellious oil field workers and adventures riding the rails across America. Not *this*, even after his introduction.

He doesn't mention the name I used. But then, he knows enough not to do that, being an old player of the name-game himself.

Now that he's slipping out of his role as agent for 'Artie', he leads me back to Munich.

He writes about the cold, the comfort and camaraderie. Twenty inches of snow fell at the beginning of April that year. As I listen to him, I could be in the room we shared in the noble's villa we helped occupy. Homeless families had moved into the many rooms upstairs, and we converted the front room into an office that housed Gunther's printing presses. Travelling comrades came to stay, sharing news of unrest in Augsberg, Vienna, Berlin and Budapest.

We slept next to the office. It was a comfortable room, its great windows framed in gilt. But with the shortage of fuel it was very cold, and snow seeped through cracks in the ornate frames. I wasn't really affected by the cold, but I often felt him shivering next to me. Then I'd move closer, and we'd make love.

"Our secrets were never shared but they bound us together," Gunther reads.

Yes, there were things we never found out about each other. It didn't matter. Gunther was already used to fleeing, changing identities. It was only right that I kept my secrets too.

Like him I was absorbed in revolution and art, though I worked in a hat shop at the time and didn't do anything overtly artistic. But art was not just for artists, it was for everyone.

On the day the Räterepublik was proclaimed, crowds of jubilant workers decked out in their best clothes promenaded and conspired in the most fashionable avenues. Soldiers had turned against the war and ran through the streets, tearing epaulettes from their officers' shoulders. The red flag streamed over the Wittelsbach Palace, where typists leaned out from the silk-curtained windows of the former Queen's bedroom to cheer the crowds below. We walked hand-in-hand into the palace where vast rooms filled with the tread of workers, farmers and revolutionary soldiers. We also heard some heavy snoring as exhausted comrades recovered from days of turmoil on the plush palace sofas.

But we raced up the stairs, urged forward by our exhilaration. While curious citizens and countless new committees and councils were occupying most of the palace, it was quiet up there. We found an empty room and sat on a divan. I started to think about storming another mansion over a century earlier, near Manchester. Blood from a mill owner, the pent-in motion of his struggle making its flavour sharp. The fruity fumes of fine wine looted from the pantry, a boy devouring handfuls of red preserves. Flames moving through each shattered window and licking out the hole that had been the front door, great hollow groans as the central beams collapsed.

"The first time I did this . . ." I started to say.

"Did what? Take over a palace?" Gunther stretched out on the divan, his head on my lap. His voice was muffled, sleepy. His eyes were only half open, barely visible behind his lashes. Perhaps he needed rest too.

The intoxication of revolt was loosening my tongue. It also made me hungry.

I stroked his hair, and leaned over to kiss his neck. "Do you want to know more? I'm older than you think . . ."

He cut me off with an affectionate laugh. "I didn't think you were vain about your age! None of that matters. The past doesn't matter when everything is about to change. There's too much to take in. Don't you see more at times like this? Look out the window. It's just a grey day in November, but even that grey is beautiful."

"Yes, it is," I agree. The clouds were slate grey, edged with pearl where the sun struggled through. So what do old names and places matter while we're looking at this?

"Art is bread," someone once said. Does that mean poems can be potatoes, and ballads can be blood? While we grappled with ending a potato shortage, we also pondered poetry.

Europe must be rebuilt from the ruins of the Great War, its foundations laid anew. How could we create architecture, painting and drama to imagine and remake this world? Writers, artists and actors even formed their own councils to do this.

As I listen to Gunther read, I remember another meeting. It was in the open air, with thousands thronging the streets. I see his friend Ernst Toller proclaiming a poem in memory of Kurt Eisner, a leader of the Räterepublik. Eisner's assassin had explained: "He is a Jew, he is not a German. He betrays the Fatherland."

Ernst Toller was still in his twenties, dark and intense and persuasive. People responded to his eulogy with tears; others called for arms. Then we moved off to the ordnance depot to get them, along with soldiers and sailors with red flags. The workers and poets of Munich rose again.

Who says words can't change things?

Later, our comrade Gustav Landauer drew up plans for a people's theatre and a free school system that encouraged children to truly experiment and learn.

Landauer came to a bad end with all of his fine plans, beaten to death by the Freikorps paramilitaries. This could have happened to me. But being who I am, I escaped.

And for the very first time, it's clear that Gunther did too.

I look at him, a healthy man who had escaped and survived, and remember the one time I tasted his blood.

We were hiding in the narrow space under the floorboards of a house just outside Munich. We'd been speaking to members of the farmers' union about distributing food. Then the Freikorps unleashed its attack through the region.

Gunther reads more, and I remember . . .

Splinters brushed my face. Feet pounded above us, sending tremors through the wood.

Words from every language I knew merged in my mind. Were those men searching for witches? Or Reds?

I knew how to hide. I was hiding in a cave when the local dignitaries shackled and burned my family in 1703, on the side of a mountain facing the Bay of Tivat in Montenegro.

"They're worse than Turks. They are witches, vampires, unnatural women."

We can live forever, my mother had told me. But she didn't. She died in agony. We don't die very often, but when we do it takes much longer.

"You must live and bring down the people who do this to us," I heard her whispering in my mind. I've tried, I wanted to tell her. I'm trying now, and I will try again.

When I was young, I heard of those who rebel against the nobles and the churches, against all exploiters. It didn't matter that these people were not like me, or that others of my kind urged me to stay out of human troubles.

Later I took to the streets of different cities, in different times. I thrived on that as much as blood. I fed on freedom as their control unravelled, turning to strands of orange, bright against the darkness that is my ally.

But I'm still not prepared when it comes to *this*.

The floor vibrated against the side of my face. Things were falling, breaking. I imagine a mirror, a picture of a woman I glimpsed before we closed the floor over us. Drawers pulled out, a rip of fabric.

Do the men making the floor shake above us wear black robes or uniforms? Do they carry pikes and bayonets, or machine guns? Of course, they speak in German. They're the Freikorps, sent by the social democratic government to crush the workers' councils of Bavaria as they did in Berlin. They couldn't get regular soldiers to do this.

Gunther's human scent is sweatier and saltier than mine. Warmth spreads from the points where our bodies touch. I move my thigh closer so we connect there too. He laces his fingers between mine. Our fingers slip and slide, clasp and unclasp against each other. His smothered gasps make me hunger more.

Once I believed I couldn't be close to a lover without the blood. I always had to get under my lover's skin. I wanted the red stuff that kept them alive to sustain me too. For a long time I didn't need that with Gunther. I didn't even touch his mind.

But I have to do it now. His blood will give me strength to fight if it comes to it. And he needs something from me.

What can I offer to help him live through this? Give him calm, give him dreams. He keeps his secrets close. But I might have to reveal some of mine.

Do you hear me? We can't talk, but I'm speaking to you. We have to be calm. We have to slow down. There isn't much air.

I turn my head so my lips are at his throat, watch his eyes close.

I came so close to doing this as we watched the sky from a window in the palace. Now everything has changed again.

His blood tastes of adrenaline, with a whiff of earth. It carries fear and anger. The anger tastes good. Bubbles of it explode and tickle my tongue. It gives me power and clarity, but I can only take a little.

What do I give him? I surround him with my most treasured memories. *Smell the sea and the great rosemary bush near the cottage. And look . . .* The mountains in front are blue with patches of brown and green. Those between them are solid blue, and beyond them the mountains turn to smudges of pale grey and silver.

I used to dream about what lay behind the mountains that I couldn't see. To think of another world waiting to be discovered there always made me happy.

I also show him a woman gathering stones; then potatoes, bread and cheese as market stalls are overturned. I show the crash of machinery and breaking chains – and then I'm barging into a forbidden room full of light and mirrors.

Afterwards, I saw the question in his eyes. I felt it grow in his mind. But Gunther was always discreet, and ready to find a rational answer: *I was faint, I was crazed and half-conscious.*

We never had a chance to talk about it. Though we survived that search, the Freikorps picked us up in Munich shortly afterwards.

There's a gust of laughter from the bar next door, but everyone in this room is very quiet. Maybe it's the quiet that brings me back to the meeting hall.

Gunther has paused, then he starts again. "You showed me scenes from some other life, a world that takes on colour after luminous colour, colours veiled by shadows that hint of far away. Seeing them was like listening to music full of defiance, made all the more powerful by notes of loss and melancholy. I still hear the echo of those notes.

"Now that I write to you after keeping silent so long, I wish you were here to tell me where those colours came from. And after you saved my life, I still wonder if I could have saved yours."

No, Gunther! I had to kick you out of that lorry. I *made* you leave me behind, while I tried to help the other prisoners. That was the only way.

He seems to be a happy man, but perhaps a worm gnaws at the core of that happiness. Being in Europe again has unsettled him. Being here in London, where we first met at a conference to stop the coming war, has prodded that slumbering worm of guilt.

Gunther is reading an intimate letter, a direct and clumsy appeal to someone he believes is no longer able to answer. But I can, I can!

I don't have to look far into his mind to see that he wrote this in his hotel room last night. He was pacing and scribbling, Lucia first urged him to get into bed. Then he read to her, and she urged him to finish it. Her generosity shines from her as she listens. *You are here with me now because of her.*

"After so many years, I miss you as if the loss is new." The paper shakes in his hands. "I want to show you all I've seen since, the colours of cloudforests and of desert. Perhaps visions and dreams won't stop the onslaught to come, but they may be all we have left."

He pauses and looks over the audience. And I look downwards, hold my programme higher and think about what I should do. Leave him to his guilt and pain, or reveal myself?

"Sometimes I think you were fortunate," Gunther reads. "You didn't live to see how the men of the Freikorps made Germany what it is today. You didn't see the defeat in Spain and the rise of Hitler. You never lived with the despair that took our comrade Ernst Toller."

A month ago Ernst was found strung up by the waist cord of his bathrobe in his hotel room in New York, three days after Franco held his victory parade in Madrid. He was 48. Ernst had donated the last of his money to help Spanish refugees. Before he killed himself, he'd heard that his family in Germany had been sent to a camp.

Had he been suffering from the guilt of a survivor? A well-known playwright, Ernst had spent five years in prison for his part in the uprising while others had been beaten to death or executed.

But if you live while others die, you can only go on writing and fighting and doing your best. Perhaps he gave up even on that when he heard about his family.

I could have emerged from my own 'death' to talk to Ernst about living with survivor's guilt – over 200 years of it.

"You stayed pure in your defiance."

Now you're talking nonsense, Gunther. Pure is the last thing I am.

"You spoke to me in my thoughts, though it could have been a delirious dream. I don't believe in God. I don't believe in angels. But you didn't seem to belong on this earth."

I'm not human, but that doesn't mean I don't belong here. That doesn't mean I'm pure.

Tell them how we clashed when we first met at that conference.

You can even talk about our housekeeping arguments in Munich. Or when you tried to stop me from going out at night by myself. Your current lover has shown herself to be much less possessive than you.

157

Tell them how arrogant you could be.

And why don't you tell them how arrogant I can be. It would only be fair.

Lucia leads the clapping. Bravo!

She had encouraged this hurried eulogy. But what if the dead woman suddenly proved to be alive? I understand she's Gunther's editor and friend as well as lover. She runs a crafts shop in San Cristobal de las Casas and also illustrates books. She works hard and enjoys what she does, she believes in Gunther and herself.

Now I know what was strange about recent thoughts I grasped in his mind, a flavour I'd taste in his blood now if I tried it.

They expressed contentment without complacency. A contentment that doesn't diminish the will to fight but imparts the strength to do it. In over 200 years of life, I don't think I've ever felt that.

Will I destroy their happiness if I come forward? Will it disrupt Gunther's view of reality – even his grip on it?

He steps down from the stage. He's not far from me. I can reach out and touch him. Or I can sit here and leave him in the closest thing there can be to peace. Lucia should be able to talk him out of survivor's guilt: *You did what you could.* Perhaps working on this new story will lift the burden.

Jack, master of ceremonies, returns. "We have more music..."

A sharp *crack* against one of the high windows along the auditorium interrupts him. Jack hesitates. When there's no further sound he begins again. "We'll have some performers who made their name in the music halls..."

Another *crack*. It could be nothing, but someone goes to investigate. The musicians start to set up.

Now there's a rumbling from outside, there are voices. Something else hits the window, spreading a spider web of breakage. A boy cries out.

A broad-shouldered muscle-bound bloke runs in from outside and takes the microphone. He doesn't look like he's about to sing 'Doing the Lambeth Walk'.

"Attention! There are fascists outside trying to disrupt this event, but there are more than enough of us to see them off! All those who want to fight go to the door and grab some ammo! And those who can't fight, remember there's no shame in that. Stay here and enjoy the music. Let's show them we won't be intimidated, and let the show go on! *No pasaran!*"

People start shepherding children towards the stage, furthest from the door and away from the windows. Others draw up close as a singer in braces and a fake handlebar moustache bounds onto the stage along with three women in spangled swimsuits. *"When trade is very rocky and you has to take the nocky,"* he sings. *"It's best to face the music like a brick."*

The pianist begins playing. Then he pauses and listens, as if wondering whether to join the fight. But Lucia signals from the audience that she'll take his place, and he leaves. She positions herself on the piano stool with the poise of a dancer, and launches into a jazz-inflected accompaniment.

While the moustached man urges those near the stage to clap along, everyone else scrambles towards the door. Veterans of Cable Street and Aragon, wily ghetto guerrillas escaped from the Continent, East End dockers and liberal doctors ready for first aiding, progressive students, the burly contralto and her bandmates . . .

And then there's me.

I'm spurred as echoes of slogans reach the auditorium. *"No Jews and Reds . . . No immigration!"*

The cracked glass gives way. As I come closer I hear the impact of punches, hits and kicks from outside. The performers continue with a frantic gaiety, as if it's their duty to keep the captive part of the audience entertained. Moustache man bellows: *"If your creditors come down on you for everything you owe, you must bash 'em on the crumpet with a stick!"*

I pick up a chair and snap its leg off. I know from experience it will prove an effective and flexible weapon, especially with my extra strength. The chair itself will do as a shield.

Just as the wood crunches and I pull the leg free, I find myself looking straight into Gunther's eyes as he joins the surge to the door. He jolts with the connection as if it's a physical shock, scattering shards of guilt and longing through the air. *Have I conjured a ghost with my reading?*

Before he says anything, I break another leg off the chair and hand it to him.

These Boots

"You must be absolutely ruthless," says Janice. "You're gonna have a lot less space. You have to downsize."

She is lying on her stomach on the bed, skirt hiked to the top of her long legs as she swings them back and forth. Her eyes follow my motions as I chuck things out of a hulking old wardrobe.

I hold up a pair of crimpers. "Look what I found!

"They should've *stayed* lost."

The flex is caught. When I give the crimpers another tug, a whole edifice of shoes loses its foundation. Out they tumble. Khaki Converse, a pair of pointy-toed red pumps adorned with fabric roses; purple eight-eyelet DMs.

I can't remember when I wore the pumps with the roses. I tweak one of the flowers, which results in a puzzling puff of fine brown grit that doesn't belong to the wardrobe. Did it come from a dirt road or parkland path? I hold a shoe in each hand, disturbed to find them surrounded by so much blank space in my mind.

"Go on Yvonne, we have a lot to go through."

"Do you remember these shoes?"

But Janice isn't looking at the rose-y shoes. She is gazing at the purple Docs with an expression of great fondness. "I remember *those*."

So do I. I was wearing them – along with shiny black leggings and a tutu – when I met Janice at a Bikini Kill gig. Those leggings are long gone, eroded by the great thigh-rubbing unravelling process. The tutu, however, was only thrown away yesterday.

"Now why haven't I worn those?" I ask. "They still look OK. Why *don't* we wear Docs anymore? They were great. They last much longer than trainers, they have more *oomph*."

Then I look closer. Heels worn to concavity, only the edges of the inner soles remain. A spatter of deep pink gloss paint at the bulbous end of one toe.

Janice takes a deep breath and opens her mouth. If she says I should keep the Docs, I'll do it in an instant. But instead she points at the crimpers and the shoes with the wobbly roses. "Out! Into the bin! And what's that?" She points to a square of faded black fabric carefully folded and placed on top of a pile of things to take with me. "What the hell is that rag for? Out!" She jerks her finger towards the bag for rubbish.

"No! Not that! It's important! It's a scarf. I uh, I wore it at the Poll Tax riot."

"The Poll Tax riot?" Janice exclaims, as if I was talking about the Battle of Hastings. "How long ago was *that*? Honestly, Yvonne. And those purple docs, they go too. You can't even walk in them! If you haven't worn something in the past year, get rid of it."

I sigh. "They go then, alright? But it'd be nice if you helped instead of just giving orders."

"I *am* helping. In an advisory capacity, as well as a dinner-cooking and tea-making one. I can't pack for you, but I can keep an eye on you. Otherwise, you'd be too soft. Isn't that what exes are for?"

"You're lucky I don't regard my exes the same way as these old boots. 'Oh, I haven't slept with her for ten years. Guess I'll put 'er in the rubbish!'"

"Yes, I'm lucky." Janice grins. "And so are you. And you're so fucking lucky I'll pack the computer stuff for you and then I'll make another cuppa."

While Janice is in the kitchen, I find something else I had long forgotten.

The pink patent-leather knee-high boots had been shoved far inside, under everything where the dust couldn't reach them. I used to wear them for special occasions only. They are smooth and gleaming as I pull them out, with only a few scuffs near the heel. Why didn't I see them, lighting the wardrobe from inside, not far from where I sleep? Like the pumps with the wobbly roses, they had simply stopped existing for a while.

Glimmers of blue and green merge and dance on the pink patent leather as I turn the boots in the waning shafts of late-afternoon sun, which make their way through a peculiar window in the wall between my bedroom and the front room. I'd only removed the piece of velvet covering that window this afternoon.

An earlier tenant had painted flowers, multi-coloured fish with big smiles and a rising sun on the glass. My room might have been a child's room, the window painted by devoted parents. Maybe they told the kid they were in the next room, *see our light shining through the window.* And the child, feeling safe, must have fallen asleep watching the fish.

But it isn't always so safe. Fifteen years I stayed in this flat. Along with neighbours, I fought the council's attempts to remove us, seeking solid ground in our limbo between tenancies and a shady status as 'licensed' squatters who happen to pay rent. Most of us had won a rehousing settlement, but what will be lost when this street is left to the developers? And how will I pay my new rent and still be able to work part-time?

When I popped into the shop round the corner to ask for some empty boxes, the guy greeted me with: "Funny, there are lots of people from your street looking for boxes. What's happening, are you all giving up and moving?"

No, no, I swore I'd never give up! I clutch the heel of a boot in my fist as tears sting my eyes. The sunset coming into the room, the translucent fish and the magenta-pink boot I'm holding start to blur beautifully. I almost forget to be sad. When the edges of things run together like this, I just keep looking and imagine slipping between them. And it seems like it would be too easy to get trapped there, just like the grinning fish suspended in a pane of glass.

Don't start with that. I don't have time for this. I have work to do. Madam will get grumpy if she catches me daydreaming. But why don't I hear movement and cursing from the computer room as Janice untangles the wires and takes things apart to put away? It's too quiet.

I leave the boots next to my bed and go to investigate.

I find Janice just standing in the tiny room that I've used as a study. She is stroking the scanner as she looks out the window. There is not much to see, with the window facing straight on to a wall. Only stand-by lights on the equipment illuminate the room.

I join her, listening to the flat. Everything sounds different with the place emptied into boxes, even the background hum that is normally called 'silence'. We share the silence. Then Janice puts her arm around me. When I touch her I'm surprised at how thin her waist feels. It must be that job of hers. Too much work to eat properly.

"It *is* sad that you're moving from this flat," Janice says. "Imagine, we were still together when you first moved here!"

"Yes, you helped a lot with the painting."

"That purple and turquoise woodwork in the front room looked really good then."

"Nothing beats that good old squattish patchwork! 'Squatter', 'short-life tenant' or 'licensee', call it what you will – the paint's the same. Bits from every tin of paint your mates bring round from squats long past. And each tin's got inches of plastic skin you need a pickaxe to get through."

"And all that pink," Janice adds. "In the bathroom and in the corridor. But I actually *bought* that."

When Janice and her girlfriend – oh, her *partner* – purchased their own flat a few years ago, they *employed* someone else to paint it tasteful shades of beige.

Now she looks around at our past handiwork with the same misty eyes inspired by the sight of my old purple Docs. She prods me gently. "Sort out the rest of your things while I put the computer away. But you know, it is really old. You can't run any up-to-date software on *that*. Maybe . . ."

"Janice, don't even think of it! It's not like I can get another one."

I go to the front room to see if anything's left in there to pack. Stacks of boxes loom. Everything's changed. Only the blinking light from the construction site over the road is the same, while the building itself remains in a state of flux. It used to be a Victorian mansion block like mine, housing 'proper' council tenants and low-rent licensees. Then the council sold it and a developer is converting the flats for sale at over £300,000 each.

"What's all this for, then?" Janice laughs as we position our cups of tea on a kitchen table piled with broccoli and spinach, red onions, fresh tarragon and dill from the Portuguese deli, chillies – long mellow red ones, those small ivy-green ones that are the most fiery. Olives, both green and black. Lemons and limes in all the shades of yellow and green. Black-speckled bananas. It would make a great still-life.

"For tonight – and tomorrow. Brunch, remember? I make the food, and you lot help me move."

"You won't cook all that, Yvonne."

"We'll take it with us when we move. There's no good market in Kennington. Or Waterloo." I'm still not really sure whether my new home is in Kennington or Waterloo – it's somewhere between.

"What? Brixton market is just a couple of miles down the road on the 159."

"There's the 3 and the 59 too," I corrected.

"Exactly. You can always come back and shop there. But anyway, I got some things from *Borough* Market for lunch tomorrow. I might as well give them to you now. You can look forward to walking to Borough Market from your new place. That will put you in a more positive frame of mind."

Janice reaches into a bag and takes her goodies out. Smoked salmon, not just any old salmon but *hot* smoked *wild* salmon caught on a beechwood-smoked organic fishing line somewhere or other. A jar of *truffle*-infused olive oil! Beautiful stuff I can't afford, especially now. But I don't mention that, because that could lead to unwanted advice to find a career instead of my three days a week at a homeless shelter. She's always at me to look for other work – she thinks I should be doing a more glamorous job at my age. With her job as 'development officer' at an AIDS charity, she gets to be both worthy and high-flying. And she can afford things like truffle oil.

"Thanks Janice, that's great. Excellent fuel for the big move. We'll all enjoy it."

"Who's coming tomorrow? Your boyfriends?"

"Yeah, both of them. And John's other girlfriend. And Jenny, and Andy and Jill and . . . well, a bunch of people"

Janice shakes her head. "I first took the piss that you needed two guys to replace me, but it's lasted a long time. I have to admit to a certain admiration, like you're the last practising non-monogamists left from the sixties and it's kind of brave . . ."

"Fuck that!" I interrupt. "It's got nothing to do with the sixties. That was even before *my* time! And it would've been a disaster if either John or Richard advised me today. They'd tell me to ditch everything, while you only told me to ditch five-sixths. Maybe John would've let me keep the Poll Tax riot scarf. Really, you have been pretty patient. Even now, I started wondering again if I'm doing the right thing. Maybe I should stay and fight it out, in the courts or behind the barricades or both!"

"Yvonne, we've been through that. You were always so bad at choosing and making decisions. Moving will be good for you. It could get you out of all your negative entrenched patterns."

"Oh go make another cup of tea before you start with the psychobabble," I tell her. "For all that, you're one of the most stressed-out people I know. How's the irritable bowel syndrome doing these days?"

Janice sputters into the last of her tea as she laughs. "What'll I do with you, Yvonne?"

"Make me another cuppa, that's what!"

The banter is well-worn, but so comfortable. I'm stricken with an urge to hug Janice, for this is the last time we'll sit in this kitchen together having this kind of conversation.

Before she leaves, Janice goes to the bedroom to get her jacket. I hear a scream that brings me running. Has a box fallen on her?

She is backed against a wall, pointing at the pink patent leather boots. "You're *not* keeping those! Throw them out!"

"I like them. I'm glad I found them."

"Have you worn them at all in the past year?"

"No, but that's because I forgot about them."

"Where would you wear them now?"

"I'll find somewhere."

"You *promised*. If you haven't worn it, it goes."

Janice puts on her jacket, then stands there with her arms crossed and *waits*. Times like this remind me why I left her years ago, but also why I still like to have her around annoying me too. All her bossiness just goes along with the caring.

"OK." I pick up the boots and put them into the charity shop bag. With a flourish I twist the top closed over them.

With Janice gone, my steps are even louder in the emptiness. Tomorrow this flat will be full of friends helping me heft boxes around, but tonight I chose to be alone. I wander through the rooms. I feel like a ghost preparing to haunt a scene of desolation: the block lying empty for months, then gutted before the flats are replaced by expensive broom-cupboards.

But if new people squat the emptied flats, it might not have to happen at all. Maybe someone will find a way in here and make it their home – as I had for so many years. I write in marking pen on a big mirror propped against the wall in the front room: "WELCOME". Then I unscrew the locks at the window that shares a balcony with the flat next door. My neighbour moved in too recently to be rehoused, so she'll be there to let someone in.

I step back. Now those locks look *too* open. The housing officer might spot it. So I twist them so they *look* locked – but are they loose enough so people can still get in from the balcony? I deliberate, screwing and unscrewing the locks to various positions.

I *am* too indecisive. Sometimes when I'm very worried, things around me look different. I see the outlines of what-could-be, what-might-have-been right there. I am paralyzed as I peer at the outlines and shadows. And beyond them I sometimes see other planes that are familiar, but full of elements that are out of place and out of sync. I'm afraid to look closer. I'm out-of-sync enough already.

I'd better stop faffing. What's left? My thoughts turn to the bags in the bedroom. The boots.

Janice really is right. I have to get my act together. *You must be ruthless.* But before I leave, I need to put them on just one more time . . .

I remove my trainers, take the boots from the bag. When they are released, they light up the evening as it approaches. As I put them on, I already feel less burdened. I still need to lace them, though. There are seven holes, plus twelve hooks. Maybe the hooks go a bit quicker, but it's still a slow job. The slowness of unlacing them can be even more agonising.

The boots bring memories, but they are becoming new as my feet settle into them. It was such a long time since I wore them that now I might be a different person. I look at reflections of myself on the surfaces as I lace up. My hair is a different colour these days, but it doesn't matter now because everything becomes a kind of shadow over pink and rose.

I get up and walk. I look down at my feet, bright against a floor now bare of rugs. Though I am already tall, the chunky heels on the boots make me feel even bigger. They urge me to strut. I twirl in front of a mirror, but I'm not pleased with what I see. My boots look garish and unreal with my jeans. That's not right. I take them off again, then the jeans. In my t-shirt and knickers, I look through the charity and throw-away bags for the outfits I once wore with the boots. There's that black lace dress. Black lace went so well with them.

The dress is too tight, now worn and frumpy next to the boots. What about the white stretch jeans with a black lattice design on them? I used to wear them rolled up to the tops of the knee-high pink boots.

No, the inner thigh is ripped. That's why they're in the throw-away bag.

In a bag bound for the new flat there's a straight black skirt, more jeans, a long green velvet skirt, a denim skirt. No, the shine of my old/new boots will turn *all* those clothes dull and faded.

I take off my t-shirt. Pause. Then the knickers go. Too many washes have turned them that special shade of grey that all old knickers become.

The draught on my bared skin is startling. I walk, then twirl fast to feel more air against me. I squint at my reflection and concentrate on the magenta and rose streaks cut by my boots in the mirror as I move. The motion and colour take over. The room starts to spin too so I lie down on the lumpy futon sofa.

I find a still point at the centre in the intricate ceiling rose above me. A Celtic knot, an ancient blinking eye. The painted fish on the glass between the rooms swim in a sea lit by a faded red sun and the blinking orange light on the scaffolding over the road. I raise my legs with the pink boots at the end of them. I cross my legs this way and that. A rhythm comes into my mind, made of all the rhythms I used to dance to and a tune I've never heard before. Outside the window the sky is deepening to violet.

Something pulls me towards that sky, as if my edges have softened and curled back so I can flow up to meet it. The brightness pulls me up, and it travels through me in sparks. A rushing and light, and a *pop*.

I'm looking into the room where a woman wearing nothing but her boots dreams on an old futon. Sudden panic sends shocks after the sparks. My centre isn't holding, will I get pulled apart by the sparks? Will I be trapped in the space-between? But I still wear the same boots as the woman sprawled on the futon. I'm safe with my boots on. I *can* go back, but now that I've lost my fear I'm ready to go forward in a running dance.

Below my pointed patent-leather toes, I see mountains. They are distant purple and pink. This is a dusty pink, night-time pink cut with stones and shadows. Beyond that, a watery expanse, a sea.

I plunge down again, swooping like an evening bird and I'm on my feet. I walk over a hill covered with soft foliage, cushions of undergrowth. My feet sink in and I feel the contrast of their deep pink against shades of green: moss, forest fir, silver-shaded willow. The greens spread on the hillside before me hint at the quieter colours I've painted in the new flat. I don't see an end to the hills and I wonder where I'm going. Then my heels are striking stone beneath the deep growth.

I want to keep exploring, but my feet are starting to hurt.

These boots may be made for walking, but not too far. They may be made for dancing, but not hiking.

The meadow thins out. I'm walking on pavement again. I don't regret it. The city is my home. I'm not sure which city this could be. It is like London, but the angles are different, the colours brighter.

My boots take me further into the city. People rush by on all sides. They don't notice that I'm naked. I've had dreams like this. Everyone does. This time I don't care what people see. I'm not cold.

Now someone *is* looking. But it's only at my feet, and she nods.

I nod back, and walk across a bridge. I know where I am now. Lambeth Bridge. The river is now dark, the wheel of the London Eye bright and spinning.

I have to go home and I'm hovering, confused about where that is.

I decide to follow the road, which takes me from the bridge straight to where I'll move tomorrow – a structure of black-and-white Lego pieces thrown down to create three towers of jagged heights and jutting angles. Stainless steel gargoyles grin between the towers. With their smooth, sharp features and elongated eyes, they are nothing like the gargoyles found in old cathedrals. They stare down at the road, with a coldness more forbidding than the old-time demonic scowls and grimaces. One of them has very pointed breasts.

But she seems to be winking at me, so I wave.

Where did you come from? I ask her. *You weren't here before.*

Neither were you. In fact, you're not here yet! Go back, there's something you forgot!

So I keep walking along the road to Brixton, listen to the rustle of the trees clustered around the red-bricked arches of the old estate next door. Despite the busy traffic, it feels peaceful and out-of-the-way so I'm not prepared for the close crush of shoppers as I enter

Brixton. Sounds of reggae and rap come out of shops. In the market I'm drawn by the greens of avocados, coriander and dill: the scarlet ranks of capsicums. It's too late for the market to be open, but very open it is. I reach the road where I've lived for fifteen years, and enter the flat the same way that I left.

Soon I'm in the front room, foggy-headed and blinking.

The first thing I do is put the boots into a rucksack I'll take with me tomorrow. It's full of the things I treasure the most.

I think of how the boots will warm the place between my shoulder blades as I walk into my new home. I think also of friends and lovers who will come tomorrow to help me make the new flat a home.

You must be absolutely ruthless.

I will be.

So I'll keep those boots. But I'll get some new clothes to go with them.

The Pleasure Garden

It's Daniel's first day back at Cornmarket Publishing since the company moved. He now has a walk to Vauxhall followed by a half-hour train journey to the new office in Teddington. It could be worse for travel time, he thinks, but it's out in the sticks of zone fucking six. More money to pay out just to work.

Though it's not far from his home in Kennington, he's not been around Vauxhall station for ages. Years ago, he actually lived in this area, squatting in a square off Harleyford Road. There was no Vauxhall bus station then, and nothing like that bizarre steel wedding cake of a building near it.

As the train pulls away from Vauxhall, he sees that the old New Covent Garden market has been completely torn down. His household used to raid the bins there for the vegetables they cooked in the community cafe. He used to go clubbing around there too, mainly at the Vauxhall Pleasure Garden just near the market. What a dive!

Thinking about the years he lived around here kindles a warm yet sad feeling. Gigs and parties at the house on the corner, new friends, an opening of his world. That was when he started to think of himself as gay. He met the first man that he really fancied and wanted. Jon was a sensitive guy who liked poetry, too.

This must be what nostalgia feels like, he thinks, but he resists its pull. He's doing okay now, isn't he? Freelance work is varied but steady, and he has his own flat. Well, a shared ownership flat at the edge of a 'regenerated' council estate, advertised as 'cutting edge', which might refer to the poorly finished worktops in the kitchen. Everything was falling apart, even when it was brand new. But hey, he can afford it, it's close to central London and the light is good.

No, the good old days weren't all rosy. Getting evicted was never fun. Being skint wasn't much fun either. And he didn't expect to feel isolated within an 'alternative' society where straight coupling was still the norm beneath the decorative tattoos and weird big hair. Much of that time he was nursing a broken heart, then getting out of his head and into someone's trousers to forget it.

Sometimes, he just had to get away. That was when he crossed the Vauxhall roundabout to get to the Pleasure Garden. It was a passage into another world.

The morning has taken on a crumpled, soiled feeling. It's the end of winter or the beginning of spring. The sun shines but it's a watery excuse for sunlight that never fulfils its promise. His unopened *Metro* lies on his lap as he continues to look out the window.

Then he's not sure where he is at all. The train is passing between two huge building sites. On both sides, unfinished buildings rise, one after another in a jagged skyline of cranes and hoardings. Builders in orange jackets scurry through the site, cranes hoist their loads. Battersea power station is surrounded by another spidery network of cranes, and it's missing one tower.

Could this be where he used to walk every day? And where the fuck has the Pleasure Garden gone?

Duh, of course it's been torn down along with the market. He begins to think about that 'dive' with regret now that he knows it's lost forever.

"Dubai on Thames . . ." he hears a bloke in front of him say to his friend, who is wired up with earphones. They both nod.

The morning sun flickers in bars through the girders of incomplete buildings. The effect disturbs Daniel, the sort of thing likely to trigger the strobe-lit ocular migraines that bother him when he works on computers too long. He starts to look away but then sees someone on the top floor of the unfinished block nearest to the track, loping along the framework. No orange jacket, no builders' protective gear. A slender man in jeans and a white t-shirt, cropped steel-grey hair but youthful face and stance.

Daniel thinks he knows that man . . .

From the Pleasure Garden, almost thirty years ago. But the man looks the same.

Then the train stops. Daniel is aware of a distant beat. For a moment he thinks it's music, then he realises that it's the building works.

"Shit, not again," someone says. "How long are we stuck this time?"

But Daniel is glad for the pause. The man outside has kept pace with the train and now pauses in his peculiar morning run. He leans against a vertical girder, one long leg hooked around it. He frowns as he surveys the landscape in front of him.

Then he meets Daniel's gaze, and returns it with a half-smile. His lips are parted slightly, and he extends his hand – just as he had done years ago.

A jolt of arousal hits Daniel as the memories wash over him.

He places his hand on the window, fighting an urge to pound and shatter it.

The train starts up again, leaving the man behind.

As his train lurches towards Teddington, Daniel remembers the back room at the Pleasure Garden. A grotty club with crap music transformed into its antithesis: a place lit by embers of touch and truth.

Daniel had been dreading the commute to Teddington but when he arrives he is also horrified to discover that the company has imposed a 'hot desk' regime. One of those stupid ideas imported from the US, along with the habit of turning nouns into adjectives and vice versa. As a regular freelancer, he would normally return to the same desk where he had his own drawer. But that's all over. No drawers at all. No place for his mug, photos, bags of Hot Java Lava or sachets of herbal teas. *Nada*.

Daniel also discovers that his favourite editor has been made redundant.

He's given a whole supplement on waste electronic and electrical equipment to copy-edit and lay out, which has to be ready for tomorrow.

But he can't concentrate on *WEEE*. Not when he's remembering the man from this morning and what happened at the Pleasure Garden decades ago. The past floods into the present, filling his head like the drugs he used to take . . .

Strong arms hold him from behind and he's being taken. Others are there, watching. But watching isn't only passive. It can be active, it can be a caress. He looks into strange faces as they witness his gratification. It's like gazing into a well. The water below could satisfy his thirst – or it could drown him.

A shadow falls on Daniel as someone new draws near. Calm determined eyes meet his. The man extends his hand and opens it.

Daniel clasps it. The man behind him tightens his arms, kisses his neck with surprising tenderness. The steady look of the man in front of him touches his skin, spreading its warmth deep. The man doesn't speak but Daniel sees the offer he makes in his eyes and his parted lips, feels it in the grip of his hand and the movement of fingers around his. We will give you pleasure and delight. We can take away your pain . . . for a while.

Then a door opens. The face in front of him is shocked by light, then lost in shadow. Other people push in front of Daniel. There's a fight, or perhaps it's the police.

They still raided gay clubs in those days. The police wore gloves, 'protection from AIDS'. Fools. He once saw a copper wearing washing-up gloves. Couldn't the Met even give its minions proper gloves? No, it wasn't all peachy then.

Daniel goes through his tasks on autopilot as memories and daydreams jostle for his attention. His heart hammers when he yields to fantasy: go back to Vauxhall to find the man and feel that strong hand in his again, and then . . .

Right, find another photo of old fridges. Lots of them, chucked in landfill somewhere. Then clean up those multiple clauses.

Autopilot does its job very well. His first completed pages need only a few corrections after they've been to the production editor.

He goes out for lunch, finding a bench on the riverside path. All he hears now is the rushing water of Teddington Lock but his mind plays a pounding counterpart, full of monotonous pre-techno beats and plastic vocals.

They played that 'hi-energy' disco shit all the time at the Pleasure Garden. Just because he was gay didn't mean he had to like it. Punk and indie was what got him dancing. He used to love going to the Bell in Kings Cross, where gay guys and girls went to dance, flirt and shag. They were young, they were poor . . . and determined to have a good time. They liked the pub prices and DJs that spun a playlist of punk and glam, laced with soul and hip-hop.

One night the DJ put on Joy Division's 'Love Will Tear Us Apart' as the closing number. It was probably a joke on her part but it brought Daniel together with Jon.

But Daniel fell much too hard for him. Some would call it 'love' but it was just an illness, worsened by its moments of elation. When the relationship finished, he just couldn't bear to be in the same place as Jon. He tried to have fun dancing with friends but Jon would walk in with someone else and all enjoyment drained from the night.

So he went to the Pleasure Garden, which wasn't the kind of place where people passed out leaflets for lesbians and gays to support the miners or demonstrate against Clause 28. It was just a place for guys to come and dance and fuck other guys. There was a back room for the latter. People went at it in the Bell, too, but having a room set aside for sex changed the whole game.

He'd been going to the Pleasure Garden for months before he dared open the door to the back room.

And once he was in there, he didn't think about Jon at all . . . for a while.

He's been with others since, but no one else moved him in the same way – unless you count that nameless man from the back room. The same man he thought he saw this morning, dancing high above the ground. Youthful, but not young. Just as he appeared decades ago.

Did anyone else on the train clock the guy? He doesn't know because he was looking out the window. But he's sure that man is as real as the river in front of him and the bench he sits on.

He has a tentative plan to meet his friend Barbara tonight. Perhaps she'll fancy a drink and a nose around their old stomping grounds. He met her on a job several years ago and discovered that they had both lived in the square at different times.

He suggests a Vauxhall-based drink in a text message, hinting he might have a prospect to check out. He's been the token Dutch boy by her side on many nights while she cruised some dyke bar, so it's her turn to be a fag hag of sorts. He chuckles as he clicks 'send'.

Then he closes his eyes. Imagine finding *him*. His strong hand, opening in his. That feels more tangible than the work waiting for him.

He finishes his sandwich and heads back.

On his return, he finds someone else occupying his desk. A brash young thing with an elaborate three-pointed beard and three laptops spread out in front of him. Daniel's notes and printouts have been pushed aside.

"Sorry, mate," the hipster boy says. "But it's finders, keepers round here. Morning, lunchtime, whenever."

"I'm not your mate," Daniel snarls as he struggles to retrieve his things.

Then he pauses. For all he knows, this wanker could be the half-price replacement for his redundant editor. "Sorry. I mean, I apologise for snapping at you but I left my work on the desk and I'm not used to the new system."

Three-Beards spreads his hands in a kind of shrug before he turns his attention back to the four machines on his desk.

The Pleasure Garden

There's a lot more to get through on the *WEEE* supplement so Daniel ends up working late. But finally he's out of there.

The train goes over the river and the reaches of Richmond Park, stopping at a string of semi-suburban stations, until it reaches Clapham Junction. Daniel stares into the deepening evening as the train makes its passage through the Nine Elms corridor.

The cranes stand still and silent now, neon-lit company names suspended in the sky. Ruddy stars mark the heights, forming constellations. To the east, the red construction lights at Elephant & Castle also gather. He thinks of master-builders from beyond the stars descending on the humble roads of South London.

Barbara's not responded yet but he decides not to go home. He walks away from the busy train station for a look around his old square. Every corner and pavement outpost is now covered with greenery, the rickety schoolyard play equipment in the middle replaced by another community garden – back in the day, the squatters were planting the first garden on a wasteground just off the square. It's all looking good now. Perhaps he should have stayed here but he needed to move at the time.

On his way to the site he finds a pleasant little pub with real ale.

Barbara finally rings, asking him about work and his new office.

"I spent all day writing about *WEEE*!" He draws out that triple E.

"You poor thing!"

"It could be worse. I could be writing about *shit*. Anyway, why don't you come south for a pint? I've just stopped off at a pub in Vauxhall and it's okay."

"Never mind the pub. Who's this guy you're after?"

"I met him at the Pleasure Garden years ago. In the back room. Then I saw him . . . near Vauxhall Station on my way to work."

"The Pleasure Garden? I haven't been there in years. I have so many fond memories . . . Women's night on Mondays, and a women's fetish night once a month."

"It's all gone, the whole place has been torn down. It's no Pleasure Garden where I am, just a pub on a side street between South Lambeth and Wandsworth roads. Good beer though."

He remembers posters about the fetish night. It's hard to imagine a leather-clad Barbara cracking a whip but then people always laughed at photos of him when he wore a Mohican.

"What a shame about the Pleasure Garden," she says. "Even though I've not been for ages I always imagine it's there for me if I fancy a night out."

"I felt that way, sort of. It's a long shot about that guy. Really, I just felt inspired to have a drink in the area after passing through it this morning."

That odd regretful feeling that is *almost* pleasant. Not nostalgia, really.

"I had some great times there," Barbara says. "And it was handy for staggering home. I wonder what it looks like now. I hate the way places just disappear and you forget them so easily."

Then he has an idea. He's not sure why he didn't think of it before.

"Tell you what . . . we've both raided those big bins at the market, even if it wasn't at the same time. We know what it's like to crack a squat. How about doing something like that now? Let's get into the site and find some Pleasure Garden memorabilia since we both have warm and fuzzy feelings about the gaff. There might be something in the rubble. Or we can take photos."

"That's *mad*. I like it. But I'm too tired after work to come down from Hackney and climb over walls tonight."

"Fair enough," says Daniel. He has a feeling he'll end up exploring alone. Maybe it's for the best.

They talk about meeting another time. Daniel orders another pint. He turns off his phone, though he's not sure why.

He was good at breaking into places when he was young, especially when they made it more difficult to get to the bins. This time, though, he's looking for much more than free fruit and veg or even bits and pieces of Pleasure Garden.

There must be extensive security for such a high-profile building project. But a vast and sprawling site like this will also have weak spots and places to get in. He knows how it's done.

The Pleasure Garden

After he leaves the pub he walks along the walls bordering the site, trying to remember where the Pleasure Garden used to stand. So much has changed. Even then, the Pleasure Garden had been an ugly 1970s-style place.

It wasn't a quaint old gaff like the Vauxhall Tavern across the roundabout on ground once occupied by the real Vauxhall Pleasure Gardens in the eighteenth and nineteenth centuries. But the Pleasure Garden pub seemed to mark some true down-and-dirty realm of revelry bang in the middle of the industrial zone.

He pulls his hood up and starts to walk the perimeter. At last he finds a place where there's a gap between boards. One is loose. Perhaps some other vandal has been working it free. He moves the board aside without much noise.

He's wary of security guards but doesn't see their hut or HQ. He picks his way past stilled machinery, foundations and skeletal structures. More of them rise in the distance, markers of a ghost town not yet built. Bare unborn boulevards, networks of girders underneath crane constellations, red lights bright now that the night has advanced. He blinks and the red stars form a pattern. Something behind the pattern seems to move . . .

Then a piece of placard on top of a pile of junk in a skip catches his eye. Hot pink and gold, lettering in a familiar black font. That tacky Remedy Double. He picks it up. Yes, it's a piece of signage with only part of a word: '. . . hall'.

He has doubts. Are those the colours? Would the Vauxhall Pleasure Garden really use Remedy Double in its sign? Memory, which seemed so clear, turns muddy. He can only try to recapture the perception of a young man, full of desire but ridden by doubt, walking across the roundabout and seeing the name.

He picks up the fragment and holds it close to his chest. It *could* be it. He bends forward to peer into the tip, only to find himself considering potential building-waste disposal violations. Damn, the autopilot mode that got him through the day now intrudes on his evening.

Some undefined noise makes him look up. His first impulse is to hide or flee, but when he hears nothing else he decides to keep walking. He isn't sure what he's walking towards until he sees lights shining out of a half-dug foundation. Security? But those moving rainbow colours won't come from a guard's torch.

When he's standing at the edge of a hole, he laughs and laughs.

At the bottom, a disco ball revolves on a makeshift plinth. It must be rigged up to a power line.

He stumbles down the slope towards the light.

After he reaches the bottom, he lies on his back so he can look up and watch the disco lights play among the ruby stars.

Then a tall slim man is looking down at him from the rim of the pit. Long legs in faded jeans, a white t-shirt . . . just like this morning. The thrill of recognition hits like a sledgehammer in Daniel's chest. He never thought he'd see that face again or feel the gaze of those thoughtful eyes as they stoked his pleasure.

The man climbs down the side of the hole, loose-limbed and agile, looking like he's about to spring and break into flight. He doesn't seem to mind the night-time chill. Then he's next to Daniel.

His touch is cold, distilled from steel. His eyes are the colour of steel, too, his grey hair still startling above a face so bare of lines.

Daniel finally asks, "Who are you?"

The man smiles but a molten core lights the steel of his eyes.

"Look at this ravished district and you'll understand." The melodic quality of his voice surprises Daniel. With that the tall man touches his lips to Daniel's. The taste is metallic, yet exciting.

He wants to keep kissing this familiar stranger but also wants to hear him speak. He asks the question again, with a slight change. "*What* are you?"

His companion seems to prefer that formulation. He slips his hand under Daniel's jacket, finding the bare skin under his shirt.

"I'm the mind of the old market, and much more. The distilled desires of dumpster divers and bondage queens meet within me. I'm the roots beneath the old Pleasure Gardens and I arise from breathless couplings on hidden paths above them while the band plays Handel. I'm the dust on the streets and the weeds growing in cracks. I'm mud oozing between your toes, the cry of birds fleeing from the reeds. I bring the scents of the marsh, the fumes of exhaust, a sprinkling of sweat and perfume."

He strokes Daniel's chest as he croons, "Vauxhall, Vauxhall, where the hammer will fall . . ."

Daniel imagines an auctioneer's hammer, or perhaps the hammer of a worker pounding metal. Whether it is for building or demolition, he isn't sure. He runs his hands over the cropped hair of his grey-eyed companion. He touches the man's throat as the words vibrate within it.

"Some haunt abandoned ruins but I also haunt places that have yet to be."

"You talk about the market and the Pleasure Gardens. What came before that? And what came after?"

"Real gardens that fed London once grew here. Later came factories and workshops, and the people that worked in them. There were fleeting kisses during tea-time, the flowering of many desires."

"And before the farms and the factories?"

"This land was once held within two arms of the Effra. Another river flowed into the Thames from the other side. They all clashed in a whirl of waters that created an island. You can still find the ancient posts from the bridge to that island. Lives were given to the river – these machines will claim more. But there are other ways to make your offering."

The man kisses him with a tongue that tastes of iron. His hands move over his skin, drawing out his heat in the chilly night. "Fuck us," he says, his voice next to Daniel's ear.

Fuck us, rather than *fuck me*.

This strange man, full of the flavours of iron and steel, grows pliable as they join together. He's only a man, Daniel thinks. But he is also all the things he says he is.

It's over faster than Daniel would have wanted. Already he's needing more as the clean-limbed figure lies quiet underneath him. Will there be another time? Does he have a name? He's afraid to ask for it, as if being named will diminish him.

He slides out from under Daniel, zips up his jeans but leaves the snap undone as if he intends to remove them again very soon.

He points to the ground nearby. There is growth where their bodies have touched the earth, where their fluids have moistened it. The smallest shoot of ivy, a minute leaf unfurling.

"This will crack the foundations . . . in time," he says to Daniel.

The being stands up and holds out his hand for Daniel to join him.

"The others are arriving now. Many have known me in different ways. Their touch makes me stronger and sows the seed."

He looks upwards, the lights playing over his face. "Look . . ."

Daniel only sees the disco lights at first, embers of colour moving around the sides of the foundation. They flow faster, spinning to no audible music but the pulse in his ears.

Then Daniel sees others along the sides of the pit, men and women, their faces illuminated. Some seem uncertain while others grin. That night in the back room, he felt like he was looking down into a well. Now he's looking up at strange faces from the bottom of it.

The new arrivals clamber down the sides. Daniel sees that one of the newcomers wears a security uniform, the jacket disarranged and half-open.

Someone is calling to him.

"You all right, Daniel?" It's Barbara, making her stumbling way down the slope until she reaches him. "I changed my mind about going out. I thought I'd be able to find you. And I did – you and your friends. I found the pub and followed the lights."

She keeps her voice low, watching as more people descend into the foundation hole. Someone she sees makes her smile, then she is looking past them at the horizon. "Lights! More of them . . . Look at all those fucking lights."

Daniel nods, holding onto the hand of his old acquaintance. As that hand slips out of his, he is sure the crane constellation is forming a clearer pattern. He's still not sure what it is but if he looks longer, perhaps he'll understand.

Strong arms hold him from behind. He looks up to the sky again and now he thinks he gets it – tower after tower, sliding to the ground.

Living in the Vertical World

Lenore has to sit down on the bench at the riverside path to get her bearings. She turns sideways so she can look at the tower block set back on the other side of the road. It rears up, its walls spattered with many colours, deep olive mixed with brown, a paler green that might be a herb. Bright floral touches from the balconies, could be rhododendron or buddleia – those bushes are stubborn bastards, big beautiful weeds in fancy dress. In a strip running down the side, solar panels reflect the setting sun.

This is nothing like the computer-generated imaginings shown to her at a seminar fifteen years ago. The growth on those pristine towers were a uniform greeney-green. She'd seen beauty in them, but those images gave her the creeps too. The thought of walking about or sitting in that imagined 'vertical forest' and enjoying 'nature' from such a distance up, looking down, made her stomach contract and her toes curl.

Would you hear the wind rustle in the trees? At such a height, that wind would be more like a gale than anything that rustled.

Towards the top, the colour shading could indicate a tough grass or moss, grown for insulation rather than food. Plants that can weather the wind . . . so Peter and his pals did learn something since their clever vertical forest and farm presentation. Still, there is a fringe of trees on the roof, peeking over a high parapet.

How will those trees survive in the wind? Who's gonna do the actual work in this vertical vision of yours?

Those had been her first objections as smarty-arty Peter showed off his marvellous scheme. That guy was an architect who only left the city for holidays, certainly not a farmer.

So what would she call herself now? No longer a farmer. Not a student either, or the combination of the two that she'd been for a while.

Now she sees movement along the green walls of the tower, the small figures of climbers moving from one balcony to another, or dangling along the wall. Is this how they harvest their stuff? Or perhaps they're doing it just for fun.

She's heard of people disappearing into this tower's labyrinth, a rare place of disputed ownership, disputed boundaries and undocumented comings and goings.

And she must go *somewhere* to escape the debtor's labour regime. So far she's been sleeping on a friend's sofa, a distant friend she knew from her short stint at a London university.

When she had to leave home, she'd emailed Peter.

Not only did he remember her, he didn't seem surprised to hear from her. Should he be?

She leaves the riverside path, crosses the main road and walks along the drive going into the estate. Lights are now blinking on in windows, though some are almost hidden behind the vines and shrubs fringing the balconies.

She kicks stones away on the drive. The wind presses the overgrown grass in waves.

As she comes closer, she sees that people are pulling netting up from the balconies, no doubt used to protect their outdoor crops from the birds. But now, all is revealed. Perhaps it's a curtain-raiser for the party celebrating the occupation of the tower over ten years ago. *A good time to visit*, Peter said. Maybe.

The wind bears green smells and brown smells, the scent of grass and leaves, an aroma like water and soil.

While waiting for Peter at the entrance, she watches people go in and out. She's completely among strangers now, a change from knowing everyone in the village. Maybe it's exciting this way.

Then a white-haired woman in a leather jacket glares at Lenore. Oh shit, Lenore thinks, I must be gawking.

A few others hover at the entrance as if they're security personnel, though they don't stop anyone. Then of course, it's open house tonight.

A couple approaches a could-be security guy. The man has a rucksack and shaggy student-like hair. The slight dark-haired, purple-jacketed woman is busy texting on her phone.

"We have invites," the man announces, waving the flyer with an eager grin.

"So does everyone else tonight." The security guy nods towards the entrance.

Instead of going straight in, the two visitors approach Lenore. "You look a bit lost. You visiting too?"

The woman smiles and it's like the energy collected from the solar panels have been beamed into that smile. This encourages Lenore to answer, despite her resentment at being counted as a fellow tourist. "Yes . . ."

But she's visiting with a purpose. "It's part of my course," she adds.

No matter that it's been years since she went on that 'Innovative Agriculture' programme, run by Totnes techies and ex-hippies. It looked like a good thing to do when she decided to stay on after her parents' death and work the farm, but the course was cut before she finished it.

"See you round, then." The visiting couple disappear inside, followed by a bunch of noisy children who obviously belong here. They joke among themselves, laugh in a way Lenore doesn't remember doing when she was a child, living miles away from anyone.

Lenore looks at her watch. Almost.

Back then, that first time, Peter was late to his own talk. And he might be late to meet her now, so why not have a closer look at some of the crops?

She touches the vines twisting from the ground up the trellised wall of the tower. She can see the purple of aubergine, the dotting of cherry tomatoes and curved snouts of squash.

She nods to those low-key security people. They nod back, but don't seem concerned about what she does, as long as she doesn't damage anything.

She leans against the side of the building, puts her face close to the wall, next to a vine. She closes her eyes. She can feel the structure underneath it, a lattice laid on the concrete. But the grass against her cheek is damp and springy.

Yet it seems wrong. Land belongs underfoot, crops don't belong on a *wall*.

She remembers what it was like to lie upon the ground in her old farm. Real ground, not 'biological concrete' or mixtures of soil, agri-felt and hydro-membranes. But this grass feels the same, and it almost *smells* the same. When she opens her eyes, she notices other items on the vine besides the beans and squash.

Ribbons, cloth, a shine of silver or gold. Containers with paper inside, ribbon strung through a notch to attach them to the vines. Photos.

Offerings? People here must have their peculiar traditions, like anywhere else. But those who tend vertical gardens aren't real farming people, not with their crops growing in the sky the wrong side up. Their heads must be in the sky too, except the sky would be on their right or left, not above their heads.

So what could she put there? It could be the summons and payment demands from Agricentro for patent breaches, numerous legal papers or one of her boots with mud from the old farm stuck on the soles.

She could attach a token of her new identity, which she keeps forgetting.

Or something quite old . . . She opens her bag and takes out a photo, which she's kept with her since she left. She keeps meaning to scan this in. She really should because that paper will just deteriorate.

But she also likes the way the physical photo itself shows the passage of time.

She's about five, standing among plants laden with ripe beefsteak tomatoes. She is biting into one, and its pulp has smeared across her face like blood. She's not aware of that. She's simply enjoying that tomato.

Her parents are looking on. Her mother is a tall woman with short red hair, her father is looking down as he samples a tomato himself.

Before she gets sentimental, Lenore reminds herself that the little girl in the photo looks out far beyond the field. She didn't want to spend her whole life among vegetables in the middle of nowhere, so she left. And returned, when both her parents died in an accident.

Her family had worked that farm for generations, they used to tell her.

In the end, she couldn't let the farm go. She hadn't been doing much in London anyway, only nebulous studies and indulging in varieties of angst.

She keeps telling herself that she did the right thing after her parents died. She did what they would have wanted, but in her own way

Losing the farm has made her think of losing them all over again – and the times they clashed. Her parents used to speak of 'the land' as if it was sacred, and those who didn't work on it were aliens or superfluous at best.

Bigots. She puts the photo back in her bag. She still misses her parents, but she never could have kept living with them. And it's now her turn to be an alien.

A rustle above her head prompts her to look up, and up. A climber in a harness, reaching the journey's end. Watching this gives her the same feeling she had when looking at Peter's renderings of the 'vertical forest'.

When she had to repair the wind turbine on her farm, she just got on and did it, with a bit of help. So she isn't phobic about heights, but . . .

The climber finally drops down nearby with a clatter of equipment. He takes off his woolly hat and nods before he strides off, no doubt pleased with himself. She's relieved that this isn't Peter, choosing a dramatic way to come to their appointment.

"Great to see you again, Lenore."

When she turns around she first doesn't recognise the man in front of her, though she knows who he is. Peter had been slender when she met him; now he is gaunt. That obnoxiously bright-eyed face is furrowed. Now he looks like anyone else struggling to get by.

Perhaps that's why he didn't express any surprise when she first emailed him, she thinks. When you've been knocked about, you retrace your steps if there's nowhere else to go. That's what she's doing, and maybe he's done the same himself.

"Same here. Like I said in my email, I've come to do my part of the exchange, though I'm a bit late. Maybe fifteen years late!"

That had been the deal on the course, 'an exchange of views' between urban and rural agriculturalists. Peter gave a talk and stayed on a local farm, and she volunteered to host because she was always keen to meet new people. Her move back to the farm didn't mean she would stop doing that.

Peter had been annoying and incompetent, though he did offer some useful suggestions on modernising one of her barns. It had been full of junk after she sold her parents' livestock. Eventually she turned it into a greenhouse.

Does he guess that she's after more than a week of looking about, taking notes and saying 'how interesting'?

"I guess you didn't get that funding from Agricentro you talked about at the seminar," she says.

"Of course not." He gives a short laugh. "In fact, they've been sniffing around here. Turned up with some document. We said it was irrelevant and told them to fuck off."

"Maybe I should've said that!"

Peter raises his eyebrow. "Eh?"

"The bastards have my farm now," she continues. "Agricentro did one of their sneaky inspections, claimed my crops had DNA from their creations, and the courts decided in their favour. I appealed and lost again."

"Sorry to hear that," he says, all laughter gone.

Lenore isn't yet ready to talk more about what had happened and what she needs to do. "So why don't you show me around," she suggests.

A broad staircase spirals up from the middle of the lobby, with strings of light blinking under the banisters. "This is a lot grander than I expected." But she wonders if those lights would pass on health and safety.

Peter shrugs. "This was originally built for the hoi-polloi. After they pulled down a council estate to make way for this lot, the developers expected a lot of high-level occupants, especially when the US embassy moved south of the river. This staircase goes as far as the tenth floor, then you have to use the smaller one around the back."

This might have once been an exclusive block, but now Lenore sees the uneven surface of the walls, signs of repeated layers of plasterings, mendings and paint. It makes her think of a favourite pair of jeans that gets patched so many times the jeans consist more of the patches and darning than the original material.

Though there's a lift, most people are going up and down the staircase. Some wear fancy dress, though Lenore's not sure what they're meant to be. Many wave glowsticks and sparklers.

"This set-up looks much messier than what you showed in your presentation," she says.

"Of course it's messy. There's no technocratic fix, no easy answers anywhere." He scratches his head. "I was sacked from that job, the one I was doing when I came to see you. They thought I wasn't drawing enough investors to the project."

"Investors like Agricentro?"

"Yes, I must've put them right off despite my best efforts."

"Giving lectures to a bunch of scruffy south-western micro-farmers probably didn't help your career."

"That's right . . . and I don't regret it. And now I'm happy to show you more of the mess."

They walk down a corridor on the first floor. "Most of the rooms on the lower floors were offices or light industrial spaces," he says. "We were living on this floor before we got the electricity going and lifts repaired. We all lived in these offices together. You could imagine. Fun at first for some, then hellish. We used the open-plan partitions as walls, but you still had to put up with hundreds of people snoring or farting at night."

"I couldn't have that," says Lenore. "I'm used to living on my own."

"But people moved into their own flats here when the community became more permanent. Then we used the big rooms for communal areas. And some of these old offices made good growing rooms, especially those with floor-to-ceiling windows."

Lenore peers through the windows of a growing room. It looks very odd to her eye, a brightly lit forest of cylinders sprouting vegetation. The growth is impressive, though. Strawberry plants, showing red fruit.

"We modified old drainage pipes for that, and then we built growing towers out of plastic bottles when we ran out of the pipes." Peter says. "And plain garden hoses are good enough to keep the plants irrigated in our hydroponic system."

"Huh, must use a lot of water."

"Much less water than in traditional agriculture, because we recycle the water and load it with nutrients again."

That know-it-all tone is creeping back into Peter's voice, just a little.

This makes Lenore even more sceptical, but she's also curious. "Can I have a look?"

"Sure." He rummages in his pockets, bringing out a ring full of keys.

"Lotta keys there," she observes.

"Got to lock the growing rooms, otherwise some of the kids mess about."

As soon as he opens the door, a stale damp odour rolls out. It's fishy, like an algae-choked pond or flowers left too long in a vase after they've died.

"That smells horrible!"

She's reluctant to go in. But that's silly. It's not like she's the squeamish type.

"Sorry about that, someone must've turned off or broken the ozone generator. That usually deals with the odour."

Lenore is still wrinkling her nose and breathing through her mouth.

Peter smiles. "Don't 'normal' farms reek of manure or fertiliser? Your old gaff didn't always smell like rose."

"That's different. At least there was air, at least it was in the open."

But Peter isn't listening to her. He's mumbling about what he'll do to the 'fuckwit' who turned off the ozone generator.

Lenore leaves the growing room in a rush, forgetting about the strawberries. Then she waits for Peter as he locks up.

"Sorry, but that smell made me gag," she says to Peter.

And there's more than just an iffy whiff to it, Lenore thinks. There's something just *not right* about growing things that way.

"Well, we do other things besides hydroponics. You might prefer the roof garden, where the party's headed."

They walk past a gym and a room where people stretch out on sofas and stand in groups, eating, talking and drinking. Children run around another room full of soft furnishings and a bouncy castle. It's big enough for that.

The next room is still an office of some sort, with shelves of books and software packages. A few people type away at computers or peer at screens. A large group carries on a heated discussion in a circle at the far end.

"Then they'll have us out," a woman with lank turquoise hair is declaring.

"Like fuck they will," someone argues. "We get those letters every year. Then they argue over who really owns the place and who's responsible for getting us out."

"We can't rely on their incompetence forever. We have to work out how to defend – oh hi Peter . . ."

"Speaking of incompetence, do you know what's happened to the ozone generator?"

"It broke down the other day, and we decided it's not a priority to repair it just now."

"Who the fuck is *'we'*?"

Someone else chimes in. "Hydro is crap anyway. Whenever I smoke grass grown by hydro, it gives me nightmares. I don't think those strawberries are up to much either."

So I'm not the only one who doesn't like hydroponics, thinks Lenore.

"Never mind the strawberries!" A young man comes crashing into the room, waving a bottle of vodka. "You're a bunch of boring fuckers. There's a party on!"

"Yes, Jamie, there's a party on but you know, someone had to organise that party," says the turquoise-haired woman. "And we have more to talk about and organise now. If you don't want to take part that's your call, but don't interrupt us."

"Join the party!" Jamie waves the bottle of vodka again.

Now several individuals are offering to escort Jamie out of the room.

"Meetings are one thing we never run short of around here," says Peter. "Any time of the day or night, you can be sure there's a meeting. Now let's move on before we're stuck in some silly brawl."

So they go up a floor, and walk through another office where a jazz band plays. The jazz clashes with the hip-hop tune that comes from the stairway.

"Is it noisy like this everywhere? I mean, the idea of a jazz band playing in a former office is appealing, but what if someone has stuff to do?"

"There are quiet rooms too. In a place this size, there's something for everyone."

Even for me? Lenore wonders.

On the next floor Peter takes her along a corridor. Doors to flats are flung open, windows fashioned in walls to create shop fronts.

Lenore smells bleach and the throat-tickling scent of hair relaxer as she passes a flat that now serves as a hairdressing shop. Inside, a woman closes her eyes as blue peroxide solution is painted onto her hair, while a bloke gets his head shaved.

Next is a food storeroom or exchange. People bring fruit and veg in and others take it away.

She peeks into another place where old computers and computer parts line the shelves. Then, a bookshop and café, which appears to be two flats knocked together. "Let's stop here," Lenore urges, ducking through a beaded curtain.

She stops to look at the books on the nearest shelf, expecting something informative, perhaps technical. But the reading material here matches the kitsch curtains, reminding her of cottage bookshelves that received the worst of everyone's holiday reading. A friend from her course ran a holiday cottage, and Lenore used to help out there when she needed extra money.

She picks up a book called *Seventy-Two Virgins*. She recognises the author, Boris Johnson, as a minor politician from years gone by. She flings the book down with a laugh and a kind of snort, which vibrates in her nose, almost as if she's about to cry.

When she was little, she used to cry when she was angry. That must be why she's blinking rapidly, and her throat feels tight with the sick feeling of grief.

But when Peter asks her if she's alright, she says "of course".

They leave the bookshop and carry on walking, up and up and up. Lenore feels winded and tells Peter she wants to stop and rest. He assures her there's no hurry. They lean on the bannister over the stairwell, looking down all the way into the lobby.

"We did this walk all the time when we first moved into the tower, before we got the lifts working properly. People had to bring all their belongings up the stairs. That's why we have these processions, to remember when it was more difficult to live here and honour those who made our home a reality."

"So where did you get the money for all this?"

"Crowd-funding, among other things. Some people also had jobs and contributed from their wages. It was a mixed bunch, climbers as well as urban farmers on board. As you can imagine, it was cut-and-paste and precarious. It still is."

The noise from below swells and the crowd thickens. Cheers ring out amid the music and murmurings. Then two women and a few children are lugging an armchair up the stairs. Other pieces of furniture follow, there's even a fridge. Random people from the crowd are helping with the move.

Lenore watches them. A strange feeling that could be envy tugs at her. She wants what they have, though it might not be much.

"So someone's moving in now . . . without the lift. Is that for this festival? So how do you decide who moves in?"

"Sometimes people apply, or we advertise if we need particular skills and interests. Some of the flats are kept for guests and temporary residents. It might just happen if you know someone, like anywhere else."

"The place seems popular now, and there's lots of homeless people about."

"Just because people come for a party doesn't mean they want to stay here. A lot of people hate heights, or don't want to live in this kind of community. Or *can't*. On the other hand, people who do join us get very attached to the place. We survive by being open and reaching out to people, but we don't stand for interference either."

A dog is following the new family up the stairs. It barks in a rhythm, punctuating the efforts with the fridge.

She turns towards Peter, spurred by the sight of those people moving in. "As you might guess from what I said earlier, I owe a lot of money. Even though they confiscated my property, with the new laws I still have to pay back the debts. I'd be indentured to Agricentro or put in a camp."

"Don't we all owe money?" says Peter. "Or used to."

"Used to? Are you saying you can just un-owe money? That's what I want to do. I'll be blunt. I need somewhere to stay. I have to disappear, and this looks like a good place to disappear in. I have skills. Some of the stuff you do doesn't make sense to me. But I'll try to help and learn."

"It won't be like having your own farm. I had to adjust when I first came here. I wasn't the boss, I wasn't the whiz kid designer. That was a blow. I just had to muck in." He pauses. "There is space if you want to stay. After all, you showed me hospitality. And I know I was probably insufferable."

She doesn't offer polite denials, even to say his ideas for the old barn worked well.

"But there's a trial period if you want to join us, of negotiable length. We also have . . . an initiation, you might call it."

"What do I have to do? Climb the tower?"

"Some people do that, but it's not for everybody. We have old people here, and folks who use wheelchairs. We're not all climbers. I'm not."

Out of the corner of her eye, Lenore sees someone waving from below. She meets the eyes of the two people she met at the entrance. They both have sparklers, and the smiley woman grins.

Meanwhile more people with instruments are joining the procession . . . guitars, trumpets and trombones, bodhráns. Their harsh melodies echo, making a rough music. Then Peter introduces some of his friends. A dreadlocked woman called Lisa, red-haired Elmer, trumpet-tooting Anjuli.

The names and faces come and go. Just before Lenore left home, she only saw a lot of lawyers.

Great to meet you. Want to join us, you say?

She can't hear much more conversation amid the music, a mixture of familiar popular songs twisted around, and stuff she's never heard before.

It sounds like ska . . . lilting, jumping, with a distortion and echo that gives it a far-away sound. The music comes bouncing into her brain and starts her toes tapping.

She used to listen to old Two-Tone recordings. Her one boyfriend in London during her university year had a collection that his mum had given him. But this is harsher, yet more uplifting for it. It makes her think of everything she lost, everything she wants but can't have. Then it gives her something new in return.

It loosens her tongue. Now she tells her story to anyone who listens, how she lost her farm, the people from Agricentro who trespassed to collect 'evidence'. She's shouting as if she's drunk.

Lisa is nodding, then tells Lenore that she's always been a London girl, and she lost her home in the second crash. She'd been respectable, working hard at a job that bored her, then she lost it all anyway.

"Welcome to the well-battered tower of Battersea," she adds.

"Don't welcome me too soon," Lenore laughs. "I've not moved in yet. Peter says there's a trial period. And an initiation."

"Don't worry, you'll do fine. I can tell you belong here."

I have to. Lenore thinks.

"It's different for everyone. I did the climb," she said. "Or part of it. I ended up on Elmer's balcony and he opened his door to let me in. It didn't matter if I climbed all the way, I finished where I wanted. Sometimes I miss my old life, but I'll fight like fuck if anyone tried to take *this* away."

Peter is trying to tell her about how he got interested in architecture, something about an abandoned building he visited as a child. A tree growing in the middle . . . it was haunted. Or thought to be haunted.

"Bow wow . . ." he seems to be saying. Bow wow? No no, it's *Bauhaus.*

"I really can't hear you!" she shouts at him.

"OK, let's get to the roof garden . . . less noise."

Conversation quiets down after that. There's only the stairs, the crowds and the music. The moving-in family continues on their upward journey, fridge and all. But they have plenty of help. Moving in would be a piece of piss for Lenore compared to that, since most of her possessions have been impounded by Agricentro.

But she must ask Peter to tell her more about this 'initiation'.

Then they reach the end of the winding staircase, and take the smaller staircase up the back. They have to hug the wall to let others pass. The musicians quieten down here.

Then a little girl behind them complains: "I'm tired . . . why do we have to walk up the stairs when we can take the lift?"

"It's the custom to do that today, that's why," the girl's mother says.

"But we don't *have* to."

Lenore chuckles. That little girl sounds like her when she was young. So how long does it take for customs and traditions to form, and for some people to resent them?

Finally, they come to a door, open it and step out onto the roof. Yes, it is quiet here. Many scents hit her. Soil, real soil. There's water. It smells just a little like home. She can hear the wind blowing, but the garden provides shelter. Trees and trellises, a living wall. Lights blink on a trellis where decorative and edible plants mingle. Behind all this, a substantial stone wall, built up around the original parapet.

And in the middle of this wall, she sees another door. A heavy wooden door with a big keyhole and knocker, just about visible behind the ivy. She would expect this kind of door to open into an old house rather than a sheer drop off the roof of a tower.

"What's this door for?"

"To go out, of course." Peter takes her arm and points in another direction, towards an open expanse of roof. "I'll show you the helipad now."

He tells her that business bods used it when they flew in for big meetings. "Then the firm went bust in the second crash. When we first occupied the tower, we already had the beginning of a green roof up here. Weeds were growing in the cracks, buddleia trees sprouting near the parapets."

The buddleia is still there, as expected. But so is an old helicopter, with cream and pink hydrangea flowers spilling out the open windows. Fairy lights are strung around it and Boston ivy blazes red around its rotors.

"When we discovered this helicopter, someone checked it out and confirmed it didn't work, and the owners had just junked it. But we decided to keep it. Pretty, eh?"

They walk across the former landing pad, which is now bracketed by basketball hoops. There's also a sound system with stacks of speakers at one end, plus a young woman stirring a bowl of punch on a table. She looks a bit bored.

Lenore feels exposed on this well-lit, still sparsely populated expanse and she's glad when they head back to the more sheltered areas.

And it is there she feels at home. She's far from the earth, yet real trees grow well in their planters . . . pear trees, apple trees full of nearly ripe fruit. Vines curl around trellises and arches, climbing the walls. Though Lenore grew up cultivating fields and loving open spaces, she's now drawn to these enclosed places. Has her new life as a fugitive turned her agoraphobic?

There's that door again. She walks up to it, touches the thick and sturdy wood, puts the tip of her finger in the keyhole. The door fascinates her, as if she really would want to open it to the sky... But the lock's cold metal sends chills from her fingertip through her body.

She turns away from the wall and walks through an arch of autumn clematis, breathing in its vanilla scent. This kind of clematis flowered around the old house on the farm. The scent always made her think of beginnings, a new term at school, and harvests to come. It signalled hard work, but it also meant parties and visits from far-flung family and neighbours.

The term at school usually turned out little different from the last, but that autumnal excitement never died out.

And now it comes on strong as ever. Autumn. A new life.

Peter had been walking behind her, but he's no longer there. She's glad to be alone for just a little while. She can stop and think. She had doubts about this place before, balking at the thought of crops growing on walls, or feeding on smelly solutions of water and 'nutrients'. But she'd love to work on this roof garden. This is where she could help.

There's another bower, which forms a tunnel. More squash grows here, and these vines also bear photos and keepsakes.

She looks at one: friends standing in front of the river embankment, holding cans of beer. Three young women, two lads. They have their arms draped over each other's' shoulders, buildings on the opposite river bank form a backdrop. City kids, like those children running into the block downstairs.

This photo shows the signs of waterings, earth or 'growing medium' mingling in the paper. She still has her own photo in her bag. Should she attach that to one of the vines?

Her parents had believed strongly in 'the land', something that means much more than a piece of earth. But land could be anywhere you make it, and roots don't need the ground to grow after all.

With these thoughts, Lenore takes out her old photo. She finds a paper clip among the debris in her bag and attaches the photo to the trellis arch, almost hidden among the clematis blossoms. This is the right time to do that. She can always scan the photo later, after she moves in.

If she moves in here. After a trial period, an *initiation*?

Lenore mulls this over as she passes through another arch, a tunnel of vines. She stops at a patch of fennel flowers, then an area given over to those small, green and very tasty tomatillos. She used to love them fried or in green chilli tomatillo soup.

Someone is hunched over the tomatillos, a plastic toolbox next to him. It's that guy she spoke to while waiting for Peter. He and the smiling woman had been behind them on the stairs, but must've caught up. Perhaps they cheated and took the lift.

The woman is taking photos and pausing to tap in notes on a tablet.

Lenore has used a similar toolbox before. It has lots of compartments and it's very useful for storing seeds and samples of plants.

And it's likely the people from Agricentro used such a box when they trespassed on her farm.

"What are you doing?" Lenore isn't aware of raising her voice. But in this quiet area, she sounds very loud. Shrill.

The man looks up. "We're doing nothing wrong. 'Everyone welcome', said the circulars for this event. And we're part of everyone, and we will certainly leave this place as we found it. You do seed exchange, yes? So we're helping ourselves."

"Oh . . . if it's a seed exchange, maybe you can give me some of yours." She opens her handbag. "Let's exchange."

They ignore her, and carry on. Not so friendly now, not so smiley either.

"You come from a company. Propably Agricentro," Lenore accuses. "Testing for your patents. Aren't you?" She draws in a breath. "You were invited to a party. You weren't invited to steal and vandalise property here."

"Oh, you're so concerned about property, now? I thought this was some kind of socialist commune here." The man smiled.

"I don't know anything about that. People just get on with things."

"Your concern for the property of this collective is fair enough," the woman says. "I understand that. Our employers are protecting their property, too. But there's much more involved. Agricentro invests money into research that will make life better for everyone. We won't let anyone jeopardise this by stealing our products."

"It's not stealing when the wind blows different ways, and bees see fit to fly where they want."

But she knows that argument about bees didn't do her any good in court, and perhaps it's not much use here.

She's alone with these two. They're really private cops. They could have guns. And where the hell did Peter go?

The man moves on to examine the fennel. Though she should be wary, she can't control her aggravation at that. This time she doesn't cry.

"And what the fuck do you want with the fennel? Fennel is a weed, you can pick it anywhere. Are you trying to patent weeds too?"

The woman with the tablet keeps tapping away.

Are they photographing this? Lenore draws her scarf around her face, remembering how she's meant to 'disappear' to avoid debts claimed by the company. She doesn't know what records it keeps on all their cases, and how it pursues individuals. But she obviously *sucks* at 'disappearing'.

Then more people arrive, pushing branches out of their way.

"What's up? I heard shouting."

"Lenore, there you are! I was looking all over . . ." Peter appears at last.

"These people are taking samples. They're from Agricentro. They admitted it."

Lenore is trembling, full of anger. Already she's prepared to defend this place.

"Are they now? Even *they* are welcome at our open house, as long as they're respectful."

"Didn't look too respectful to me," says Lenore.

More people surround Lenore and the Agricentro inspectors. For a moment Lenore is afraid that she is also a target. But when Lisa and Elmer turn up, they give her a friendly nod. They talk between themselves and nod at her again.

Along with Elmer comes the punch-bowl girl, carrying the bowl and a bag of paper cups, which are passed around.

A tart fruity smell comes from the bowl. Lenore accepts a cup.

"We did invite everyone to a party. So here's punch made with fruit from our garden, grown on our walls, balconies and roofs, flourishing in rooms that used to be offices," Peter tells the two interlopers. He also pours punch into Lenore's cup.

Did this come from that foul-smelling grow room? But she drinks. The punch is fizzy and red, and it tastes as it smells, fruity but not overly sweet. Strawberries, raspberries . . . lightly fermented. It tastes fine.

The crowd in the rooftop orchard swells, filling the clearing, effectively holding the inspectors captive. Peter offers punch to them, too. They accept, exchanging glances, raising eyebrows. The two lift cups first to each other and then everyone else in a sweeping gesture.

"Cheers," the woman proclaims, smile at the ready again. "It's great to see some cooperation . . . We *are* interested in the same things, after all. And this is a wonderful party."

"Wonderful? I'll show you something wonderful." Lisa grabs their box, turns it over and shakes the contents out. Then she throws the box to the ground.

Others snatch away the duo's other equipment.

The interlopers draw closer together. They seem stunned that anyone would dare to oppose them.

Lenore's heart is beating fast. If she had caught the Agricentro inspectors on her farm, she would have stood by helplessly, then found a lawyer. She wouldn't have the guts to confront them like this.

But she was alone then . . . she isn't now.

The woman is no longer smiling. She tosses her hair back and faces the crowd. "We'll add that equipment to our bill if it's damaged, but you can avoid that if you return it now and we won't even prosecute your attempted theft."

"Theft, you said?" Lenore hears her voice wobble as she speaks up. "You've stolen much more."

"You can always buy our produce," Lisa adds. "So why go to all this trouble to sneak about on the roof?"

"We're here to observe as well as gather samples. And we've observed plenty."

"And after you've *observed*, just *who* will you sue for breach of patent?"

"How will you tell?"

"It will be all of us or none."

"All of us or none!"

This turns into a chant . . . almost, then the bouncy music comes on the sound system.

"But the fact is, you're here," says Peter. "So now we have to decide what to do with you. Some of us have suffered from your company's actions. We all will, in the long term." Though Peter says 'we' and 'us', he looks at Lenore.

Then the other people of the tower, collecting on the roof, turn towards Lenore, waiting for her to speak. Lisa hands her a big key, a solid brass key that feels good and heavy across her palm.

Now Lenore understands what her test will be. And there could be several right answers to it, and just as many wrong ones.

Lambeth North

Three middle-aged women walked along Black Prince Road towards the Albert Embankment. After a pint or two in one pub they weren't drunk, but they were certainly having a good laugh.

Their exuberance turned people's heads. Perhaps Diane's knee-high purple patent leather boots, which contrasted with her dark clothes, drew attention too. Or it could have been Eileen's long copper-gold hair, the result of using chestnut henna on white. Perhaps Ria's liking for a touch of green glitter in her cropped hair was brightening up the overcast day for a few people.

Diane stalked slightly ahead of the other two, pulling her coat tightly around herself. Though it was officially spring, she was walking into a faceache-inducing cold wind as she surveyed her new surroundings. She was celebrating a welcome move into a secure council flat after years of unstable housing. But somehow she felt more precarious than ever. She felt downright *unstuck*.

"Let's take a side street back to my place and look around the area," she suggested. "I've been too busy with DIY to have a proper wander. I need to look around more and get my bearings."

She stopped, waving for the others to take a right turning. Then she noticed a row of decorative glazed tiles under the windows of the corner building. She'd never seen anything like them. One tile showed a spiky olive-green star with a central flower like an eye. The next one featured a plump blue star surrounded by stylised leaves. The tiles were glossy despite the dust from the street. Long-dead craftsmen must have chiselled and embossed these figures and applied glazes that kept the colours lustrous for over a century.

The more she looked, the more she found to see. Bronze moulding twisted around the windows, showing wheat and rye bound by ivy. The stonework also displayed patterns of leaves, ivy, flowers and stars.

Years ago, she lived nearby in Vauxhall but she'd never noticed this place.

"What's there to look at? We're in South London," Eileen was saying. "Such an *unshaped* part of London. It has no character." She was teasing, of course, dipping into a long-running current of banter between the friends. Eileen had always taken a strong interest in old records, local history and obscure London byways, but those byways tended to end on the north bank of the Thames.

"No character? So *what* is this?" Diane pointed to the tiles and the moulding. She walked over to the front entrance of the building on the corner and gazed at a sculptural frieze above the door. A woman in a long dress was painting a vase, while bewhiskered men displayed and discussed more vases. A guy with a flat cap seemed to be balancing a board with four vases on his head.

Pillars decorated with oak leaves framed the door, and above it rose tiers of leaf patterns that supported a three-storey turret angling towards the street. Graceful arches framed windows with porthole-shaped panes.

Diane waved her hand at all the architectural finery. "If *that's* not character, I don't know what is."

"Hah! It takes more than one fussy Victorian heap to make South London interesting!"

"Yeah, so what about the Tottenham superstores? That's all great stuff," Ria interrupted. She was a South Londoner too. But while Diane made her move a couple of miles up the road, Ria remained rooted in Brixton. She was indeed sceptical about this northerly end of Lambeth, but she knew where her loyalties belonged when faced with such North London chauvinism.

"Abney Park cemetery," countered Eileen.

"If you're talking cemeteries, nothing beats Nunhead," said Ria.

But the traditional north versus south London debate passed Diane by. Instead, she was looking up at the building, imagining what it would be like to stand in one of those tower rooms with light coming in on all sides.

This must be an office building now, she thought. A bit disappointing, but there's nothing to stop anyone looking at it from the outside.

She walked around the corner and found more tiles. She touched one, drawn by the deep blue flower at its centre. The colour reminded her of the sea in Greece where she swam some years before, but it was also a blue that belonged to London. The petals opened out in a leaf-like pattern, spokes around an ivory wheel with green inlays.

She discovered a clover of midnight blue outlined in copper, gold and copper leaves against radiating lattices of blue and green . . . purple spirals of ivy around star-like leaves.

And another tile featured a three-pointed figure at the centre. A star, or a flower, bound within an ivy design of interlocking leaves and curves.

This one was less colourful than the others, yet it attracted her most. The figure was near-black, with touches of copper, purple and blue. Perhaps it was the way the design conveyed motion. If she stood back a bit, the colours moved with a subtle sparkle.

It reminded her of *something*. She just had to look and look.

When had she seen this design before? Maybe it was in a book. And the purple touches were the same colour as her boots. That must be it. She peered close again. And as she stared, the terracotta leaves and ivy began to turn and twist around each other, the star-flower opened its petals more.

Shit. But it's beautiful. She took off her glove to trace the linking of flower, star and vine. The surface was smooth and cold. A sharp longing washed over her; she needed to understand what this figure represented.

Then more patterns flowed from her fingertips, as if she was painting them. She'll get paint on her hands but never mind. It'll come off . . .

There was the clip-clop of a horse on the road behind her. A *horse?*

Ria touched her shoulder. "Diane, are you OK? And why did you take your glove off? Your fingers are positively blue . . ."

Blue? From the paint? Diane looked at her fingers. No, blue from the cold. They were getting kind of numb.

"I was just looking at these tiles," explained Diane. "They're really something. *This* one especially."

"They certainly are but you know, it really is getting cold. Let's walk back to your place."

So where are we? Diane looked up at the street sign near the first-floor tower room to find out: Lambeth High Street. She squinted to make sure that really was the name. Such a narrow road. It seemed to lead nowhere, with few people walking on it.

"We might as well go down the high street," she suggested.

"High street? What high street?"

Eileen ran her fingers through her copper hair as she looked around. "I reckon this must be an *ex*-high street. It's very quiet."

So there was a carpark and an office building shut for the weekend and a narrow tower with gaping windows, which looked like it had lost the rest of its building. She remembered a dream about moving into a flat with no glass in the windows, just holes where people looked in at her.

As they walked, Diane saw a fringe of trees up the street that could belong to a square or park. And just across from them was a little pub called the Windmill. Hanging flower pots and window boxes added touches of green, though these flowers had yet to bloom; a welcoming glow shone in the windows. The pub's sign advertised home-cooked food and fine ales as well as free WiFi. A few people huddled on benches just outside, smoking fags.

With no need for discussion, the trio crossed the road and headed for the pub.

An old guy was enjoying a solitary game of pool, while younger people sat around a table playing with their mobiles. There was a TV screen, but it remained blank. The pub had the somewhat tatty but comfy feel of a traditional local boozer.

They got their pints at the bar and made themselves at home in the empty semi-circle of armchairs near the fire.

After shrugging off her coat, Ria leaned forward, revealing the tattoo nestled just over her cleavage: *"Je ne regret rien"*.

"I always liked that tattoo on you," said Eileen. "I never got around to getting any tattoos myself. But maybe I'm more of a butterfly-on-the-ankle sort of girl anyway."

"It's never too late . . . for butterflies or whatever else you fancy," said Ria, tugging at her pullover so she could also examine the tattoo.

"If I got a tattoo, I'd go for a design from the tiles down the road," declared Diane. "That three-pointed star. There really was something about that thing . . . I'd like to know more about it, and the building it's on." *Like to know.* An understatement, she thought, remembering the feeling that had come over her.

"Make sure any tattoo is what you want," said Ria. "A few years back, I was even thinking of getting rid of my *je ne regret*."

Eileen laughed. "Contradicts its message, kind of."

"Definitely . . . And I was put off by the prospect of pain, which is far more for *removing* a tattoo. But now that I'm older, I'm fine with it again."

"*Je ne regret rien*," repeated Diane. "I hope I'll have the same thoughts about this move," she said. "Even though I always liked the area. You remember, when I started seeing Steven, he liked to go to the Imperial War Museum to see the tanks."

Ria looked upwards and rolled her eyes.

"Oh Ria, I know he's not your favourite. But some of *your* exes had peculiar hobbies too. Remember Josie the herbalist, who nearly poisoned us all?"

"Tell me about it," Ria admitted. "But *tanks* . . ."

"It wasn't only tanks. We sometimes went to see the more worthy exhibits. You know, about people who went to fight fascists in the Spanish Civil War, or conscientious objectors during World War I. Afterwards we ate at a Turkish restaurant at the end of the Cut. So coming round here used to be a good day out, but now that I *live* here I'm already missing Brixton. Even though my last place was a short-life tenancy, it *was* in Brixton and it did last for years."

"Yeah, while facing an eviction threat each of those years . . . Oh, you will miss Brixton for a while, I'm sure," said Ria. "But Brixton's changing for the worse. OK, I do like the piazza in the centre now . . . Windrush Square. Better than the manky old used car place that used to be there. But the rest . . . Nowadays, where can you see bands for a few quid or for free even? Remember the pub on Brixton Hill where my band used to play? They're trying to turn it into a Tesco."

"That's happening everywhere," said Eileen. "But fuck knows what could have happened on this so-called high street. And we're just over the bridge from the West End, but it's nowhere."

"I don't call it nowhere," Diane interrupted. "It's *somewhere*, like those little squares and parks you take us to, hidden between Holborn, Clerkenwell and Islington."

"Yes, between the boundaries of the known places you find other places, special ones," said Elaine. "But I doubt if you'll find them *here*."

"Why not? My new place is between Kennington, Waterloo and the Elephant. And it looks like there's one of those surprising little parks near this pub. We can go there after our drink."

"Maybe," Eileen conceded. Then she got up and bought a round of whiskies.

They all took sips and clinked their glasses. "To your new home! Even if it isn't in Brixton," said Ria.

"And even if it's south of the river," said Eileen.

Diane nudged her. "North . . . south . . . what does it matter? Like you said, everywhere is changing. The first day I was painting my flat, I went looking for a deli I used to know on Kennington Road. Thought I'd get a sandwich there . . . And found that it's now an estate agent. An estate agent! There's too many estate agents on Kennington

Road. At least five of them. But who has money to buy houses now? And later, I went to register in the surgery. Then I had one of those weird *déjà vu* feelings."

That was happened when she was looking at the tiles. *Déjà vu.* Happens all the time.

"So I was sitting in the surgery, thinking *what the fuck* . . . Then I realised I really had been there years ago . . . doing my laundry. That was when I lived over in Vauxhall at Bonnington Square. The square was all squatted back then, now it gets write-ups as a *des res* in *The Guardian*. Anyway, when I went to do my laundry . . ." Diane paused, allowing her friends time to shudder as they recalled bygone times when they didn't own a washing machine and were forced to make use of launderettes.

"I used to walk down Vauxhall Street and Lambeth Walk, and go to the council laundry with a full rucksack," Diane continued. "Then for £2 I could use the washers and driers, all the equipment. Mangles, bizarre machines hissing out steam, drying racks you pushed into a wall. It was much more interesting than a regular launderette. I usually went for a cuppa in an Italian café on Kennington Road and bought a few nice things from that deli next door. So now it's a surgery. I wondered if they used some of the old laundry equipment for medical procedures."

"Yeah, I remember Bonnington Square, but nothing to do with laundry. I went to some cracking parties there," said Ria. "I remember one with lots of bands; it was a fundraiser for Stop the City. Funny to think we could've been at the same parties but didn't know each other."

"Yes, I remember that gig. I was there!"

"I ended up on the roof, watching the sunrise. I've seen sunrises before, but this time I felt such *wonder* as I watched the earth enter a new day. Those punky-reggae beats were coming up under my feet from the party below, which got my thoughts moving too.

"Those grubby streets looked like another place entirely as the rising sun began to fill them with its light. I was sure those streets could change to something else – oh, dunno, canals filled with that light if I looked longer and willed it. I've only felt something close to that when I'm drumming and I'm caught up with the music and beats and hitting those drums to make a world-bending noise. But I still don't know what came over me then. Maybe it was the speed talking. Or maybe not."

"Look at how we're talking now, without any substances," said Diane.

And when she touched the tile and saw stuff . . . No drugs involved then either.

"I haven't taken speed for over fifteen years," said Eileen. "When you get to a certain age . . . It's been a long time since I partied until dawn. And I certainly try to avoid getting *up* that early."

"I woke up before dawn all the time when I was on shift work," said Diane, "and I hope I won't ever have to do it again!"

Just the thought of it made her feel tired. She leaned back and closed her eyes. And she saw the three-pronged pattern that was a flower or a star, the network of lines and leaves that bound the three figures together. All the talk of old times seemed to make it more vivid in her mind.

"Open your eyes, Diane. Look what I brought." Eileen took out a pack of photos. "I took these at your old place, remember? Since I used to be an archivist, I suppose that's my job." She laid the photos out as if setting up a Tarot reading.

"Remember this party? Must be almost 20 years ago."

"Is that *me*?" Diane was gobsmacked. She actually was good-looking then. She hadn't thought so at the time. But in those photos, she looked just *fine*. That Mohican haircut suited her, and so did that tutu.

And here was their friend Sarah, who had died from cancer last year. Sarah looked at the camera with the brightest eyes, the most vivid anticipation for a future she wouldn't be sharing with them.

Diane kept staring at Sarah's smile, just as she'd been transfixed by the tiles on the old building.

"Weren't the 1990s wonderful?" commented Eileen. "Grown women actually went about wearing tutus. And some grown men too."

Each photo sparked more talk about other times, places and parties as more whiskies were bought. The air in the pub seemed thick with the smoke of bonfires; words read or uttered that changed their lives; music from bands that hadn't played in years.

"Remember those massive gigs at the squatted ambulance station on the Old Kent Road?" said Diane. "Poison Girls played there all the time."

"Dammit, I had such a crush on that singer," said Ria.

"Who didn't?" Diane chuckled. "Even us straight girls did, going all gooey when she sang "I've Seen It All Before". And I kept thinking there's a hell of a lot I haven't seen yet. I still feel that way. What would it be like if we could take photos that show us the things we haven't seen yet, as well as the past?"

Eileen reshuffled her photos, and spread them out again with some new additions. "I can't promise that, but do I have plenty of photos. Here's one from my old place in the far north. Stoke Newington, remember? The house I shared with about a dozen friends."

Far more than a dozen people were sprawled on blankets in the garden, a clearing with a fire pit surrounded by a wilderness of honeysuckle and buddleia in every shade of purple. Eating, drinking, chatting . . . just as they were doing now and hoped to do in years to come.

Eileen sighed. "I do miss my old job in the local archives. It was much more hands-on, more interesting than shuffling about a database all day. When I used to find a cache of old photos or drawings, it was like uncovering layers of time. I never thought I'd have that feeling about my own photos."

But any talk of work led to less pleasant subjects . . . to bad bosses and sackings, and the continuing horror of team-building exercises. Ria and Diane faced wage cuts at the old peoples' day centre where they worked; Eileen had to reapply for her own job in a torturous fortnight-long process. Nothing was certain.

But they were sure they'd live through their current difficulties as they had in the past. For they were friends who looked after each other.

Meanwhile, the pub's windows were showing a certain orange tint, as if the sun had come out just for a moment before it set. They decided it was time to go; they could carry on up the mighty Lambeth High Street and look about the park before it got dark. They lurched into the street again, their voices echoing in the deserted square.

They were entering the Lambeth High Street Recreation Grounds according to the plaque at the entrance. A grand name for this patch of land.

Trees lined the paths that criss-crossed the park. A sprinkling of yellow showed where daffodils made their first hesitant appearance. A birch still bare of leaves gleamed a stark, startling white. These colours had a clarity that punched Diane in the eye. She noticed that Ria took off her glasses and gave them a quick wipe and Eileen blinked. It must be the contrast with the interior of the pub.

Low-rise council blocks encircled most of the square. Towards Vauxhall, new office buildings crowded the skyline. Though just a few streets from the park, all that seemed a world away.

Ria laughed, and the others turned. "Look at the way the chain dangles from that broken crane," she said. "Like a limp penis."

"Your mind's in the gutter as usual," said Elaine.

They carried on walking. "This is a strange little park. I like it, though." Diane pointed at the rectangular stones lined up behind a brick border around the perimeter of the park. "Those look like grave stones."

Ria gave her an elbow-poke. "That's because they *are* grave stones! Didn't you read the plaque when we came in?"

"Not properly. But let's have a look at this other sign here."

Yes, the park had been a graveyard between 1703 and 1854, then a wasteground until it was turned into a public area. The plaque also said that a watch house had once overlooked the area to stop grave robbers and detain 'drunk and disorderly' persons. The watch house had been torn down in 1825.

"It's kind of creepy that we're walking among graves," Ria said as they walked past the mossy slabs. Many of them were small, as if they once marked the graves of children. Diane tried to read the inscriptions on the stones, but they had been worn to lichen-covered hieroglyphics.

"Sadly, a graveyard in a waterfront area would get a lot of business before the sewers and the embankment were built," said Eileen. "But even so, I like the idea of a graveyard that's now a park. I'd prefer it if people have fun around my grave. *Sarah* would've definitely liked it."

"Yeah, the two of you definitely had gothic tendencies back then. But this would be her kind of place, more than the organic woodland burial ground at Epping Forest where she is now. She was always a city girl."

Diane thought about Sarah as they walked. She also wondered how many people were buried here, and whether they'd left behind people who missed them as much as she missed Sarah.

Eventually they sat down on a bench built into a geometrical piazza at the centre, near a playground. Diane glanced at the council flats overlooking the park, wondering about the lights in the windows and signs of movement within. A lone palm tree spread its fronds over the fence separating the estate from the park.

She wouldn't mind living in that estate, with its own palm tree and a decent local.

She had often played this game while awaiting news on her rehousing. She would walk through streets and estates, and imagine herself living in those places. What would it be like, and what would she be like? At the time she had dreams about finding herself in strange, sometimes fabulous places. And buildings with holes for windows like the tower near the pub.

Diane leaned back on the bench, looking at the playground just behind them. Climbing ropes and frames, a slide and a tyre swing. No children played there though it was a Saturday afternoon.

She got up and walked over to the playground, stood at the low gate: *"All adults must be accompanied by a child."*

Ria and Eileen followed. "Don't think it matters if no one's here," said Eileen, pointing to the sign. "When I see playgrounds these days, I get envious and curious too. Look at the monkey bars, those shapes and colours. I would've loved them."

"I was more into swings," said Diane.

"So go on, Diane. It's your day . . . I'll push."

"I'd barely be able to get my arse onto that tyre thing. And it's for little kids, so it doesn't go very high."

But Diane opened the gate. The surface they walked on was spongy and springy, nothing like the concrete of her childhood. "We must've had more broken heads in the good old days," she observed.

No curtains twitched in the windows of the flats, but Diane felt on edge as if someone was likely to appear, tell them off and chuck them into the drunk and disorderly watch house.

Diane inserted herself between the three chains holding the swing up, wobbling before she centred herself on the tyre. She pushed herself backward and forward with her legs, then extended them in front of her. "I'm sure the swings were bigger when I was a kid."

"It only seems like that."

"No, I'm sure. They were these huge heavy clanking things. I'd swing as high as I could, then jump off onto a grassy hillside. It felt like I was flying until I hit the ground on the hill. Sometimes it hurt, but I knew how to fall."

As she spoke she found a rhythm as she swung, back and forth. Occasionally Eileen or Ria gave her a gentle push. She heard her friends' voices behind her, punctuated by laughter.

Ria was speaking. "I haven't thought about watching the sunrise on that roof in Vauxhall for years. It was important though, because that was when I decided to take up the drums. When I'm with you two, I rediscover things like that . . ."

". . . and having a drink and getting silly at children's playgrounds."

". . . in some out-of-the-way square I never knew was there."

As Diane swung backwards, the park and its fencing receded. Everything in her sight became misty and soft at the edges.

As she went forward, the scene clarified and sharpened. But each time she swung that way, elements changed. On the other side of the street, the round building that housed new luxury flats broke apart and came together as a blurred row of shops. As this scene continued to shift, she felt the first stirrings of panic, which intensified with another swing forward. *Unstuck*, she'd been thinking before.

While details of the street in front of her were still hazy, her sense of smell sharpened. There was rank water, an odour of human waste and sickness that she knows well from work. Tides of water flowing into the street reflected the dim light. Several bodies laid out on a cart, partially covered with sacking, two of them child-sized. A warm wind blew in her face and she almost gagged; when she took a backward swing the stink grew fainter.

Yet her friends carried on talking as if nothing was amiss. Diane knew she was still in the park; it was still cold and windy. Ria was talking about work again: "When I did shifts on a bank holiday in the 90s, I got paid double-time. Now it's only a pound an hour extra . . ." In her vexation, Ria gave Diane an emphatic shove forward.

The row of shops came into focus, though the tidy park entrance was now bare and rocky, crowded with broken gravestones. No foetid floodwaters or dead bodies, though. Diane was so relieved about this that she let the swing go forward again. She saw vegetables displayed in front of a grocer and a half-built boat at the entrance of a workshop; sounds of hammering drifted towards her. Whiffs of horses and horseshit, fire and ash and beer wafted towards her on the breeze. A scent of water and fish, but no sewage. *Unstuck* is better than getting stuck in the wrong place.

Lambeth High Street was now full of people. A horse drawn carriage passed, while other folks pushed handcarts. Posters on the wall near the grocery advertised defunct newspapers: *The Weekly Times, News of the World.*

Do hallucinations smell? Can you hear them? She listened to Ria and Eileen as she stared at the transformed street. She breathed deep, trying to stay calm and hold on to the presence of her friends, the sound of their voices and the occasional touch at her back.

She felt dizzy, her heart beat fast. This must be Lambeth High Street as it used to be. In the pub, Elaine had talked about uncovering "layers of time". Perhaps they were like layers of an onion; if you peel them back, you find a core of moments that are not confined by time at all. Diane shuddered, thinking about the bodies laid out to be buried and that scent of decay and disease.

But this was a *swing* into those moments. After so many period films, the street in front of her seemed bizarrely familiar. The women in long dresses and caps or bonnets. Bare-legged urchins, the variety of men's hats. But some people walked with legs bowed from rickets, other faces were pinched and gaunt. Hunger lurked amid the bustle. She glimpsed cramped alleys behind the high street.

A dark-haired woman in a cloak came out of the grocer, holding a book under her arm. It was the book that drew Diane's attention; it was not very thick but large enough to make it awkward for the woman to carry.

The dark-haired woman stopped short, looking in Diane's direction. Then she walked towards her. Her dress was a midway between green and brown, an apron smudged with dust and paint visible under her open cloak.

She stopped at the point where the waste ground turned into the park, as if hesitating to cross a threshold. She played with a fastening on the book while staring straight at Diane and her friends with wide-set brown eyes. She had an open and friendly face, the kind of face that made it easy to like someone before you've exchanged a word. A smile hovered around her lips, and her face flooded with light as if viewing a scene of unearthly beauty.

If Diane had been struggling with fear and disorientation, that changed. The wonder in this woman's face only provoked the same feelings in her.

After thinking for a moment, the young woman leaned against a tree. She opened her book, took a pencil out of her apron pocket and began drawing in it. Her hand swept back and forth over the page, circled and made adjustments.

When the artist looked up from her work Diane wished she could be close enough to see the drawing. Or at least she could speak to the stranger. Did this woman see a burial ground, a waste ground or the tree-lined paths and the playground? Did she see the palm tree swaying in a chilly spring breeze in back of the council block, see Diane swinging on a tyre with two friends egging her on?

Perhaps the woman saw something else entirely. Her expression of joy made Diane wonder. Maybe Ria had looked like that as she watched that Vauxhall sunrise in 1984.

She ought to get off her swing and have a word. She stuck her foot on the ground to stop the motion. But as she got off she lost her balance, stumbled and fell. The artist stopped drawing, then began running towards Diane to help her. She wouldn't know that the playground tarmac was soft and springy, suitable for clumsy adults as well as children.

Ria reached out first to help her up. As Diane brushed off her clothes and looked up, the young woman with the sketchpad had disappeared. The carpark was there again. So were the prominent security notices, the round block of luxury flats and the empty road.

Diane looked back at her friends. "Did you see a girl over there, drawing in a sketchbook?" *What about the high street full of shops, or the bodies and the stink of flooding water full of sewage?*

"I didn't notice anyone, but then . . . I wasn't looking," said Ria.

Eileen rubbed her hands together with an exaggerated "*brrrr*" of cold. "Isn't it time for a cuppa at your place? Why don't we watch a film, and initiate your flat properly? We can get a takeout and carry on nattering."

"Yeah, that sounds great." Diane looked again to the spot where the artist had stood. "You sure you didn't see anyone?"

"I wasn't paying attention, but maybe there was an art student wandering about," said Ria. "There's an art college over on Kennington Road, you know. I used to model there."

"Well . . ." Diane wanted to speak about what she had just seen. She should be able to talk about this with her two oldest friends.

"Well . . . Let's go," she said.

Then she saw something under a tree, a sheet of paper. "Wait, I have to get something."

Before anyone commented, she dashed over and picked up the paper. It was thick, with an old-fashioned water mark.

And it was covered with the now-familiar patterns that decorated the tiles on the nearby building, tinted with watercolour. Blues and greens and gazing eyes; stars, flowers, ivy and pinwheel patterns.

She turned the page over. Here she found a rough panorama: suggestions of flowers that wouldn't blossom this time of year, as well as the lone palm tree and stark white birch. There were hills and valleys with fruited trees, extending much further than this small piece of park.

225

And at the centre of this imagined paradise was a sketch of herself, Ria and Eileen.

Diane looked poised to fly off the swing. Though sketched in black charcoal, her boots had shadings to indicate a gleam, a colour not seen in boots of the time. Ria and Eileen flanked her. Shadings and dashed lines bracketed the three, hinting at bonds and connections that were visible in the air.

In the lower right-hand corner, she found a stylised rendering of herself and Ria and Eileen. The figures turned abstract, transformed into the arms of a star or the petals of a flower. The motion lines drawing them together were elaborated into leaves and interlocking knots.

This time, Diane's shock of recognition came as pleasure, as vindication.

"Someone was drawing *us*?" Eileen exclaimed when she saw the sketch.

Ria shrugged. "Like I told you, you get art students wandering over from that college."

"Cheeky, if you ask me. Should've asked," muttered Eileen.

"Never mind, I think that sketch is kind of nice," said Ria. "C'mon, let's go. It really is *cold* now."

Diane's thoughts stayed with the young artist in the cloak, the sketchbook she carried, and what else she could've seen when she watched them fooling about in the park.

Whatever happens, Diane thought, I'm lucky to have such great friends. I'll tell them what happened while we're 'nattering' over our takeouts, keeping in mind that the building around the corner is now the Imperial War Museum, not the Bedlam asylum it had once been. Even if I *am* seeing things, Eileen and Ria will stand by me.

She folded the paper and put it in her bag, resolving to return and look for the young woman again. "OK . . . Let's go," she said.

Then she linked arms with her friends, and they went.

The Colour of Water

This baby is much too white. Sarah wonders if she looked the same when she was little, and how her mother could have stood to hold her.

Yet the baby is strangely beautiful, with a frosting of silver fuzz on its head. A sudden spatter of sunlight through the trees gives its skin the near-transparence of milky water or the edge of a lily petal.

She's afraid to pick the infant up because it doesn't look solid enough. It begins to move its arms and fists in a way that makes her think of blind open-mouthed nestlings.

Sarah peers close enough to see tracings of pink and purple veins in the baby's cheek. Dare she touch it? She strokes the child's cheek and jerks her hand back, as if it could shatter from her touch. But no harm is done, so she lifts the baby. The weight in her arms reassures her, though heat comes through the blanket as if she cradles a tiny furnace.

Stones and twigs have been brushed from the spot where she found the child. Sarah imagines someone placing the infant under the tree by a big log, and carefully arranging the threadbare but clean white blanket into a cosy nest. Would they be fastening the bracelet that's around its wrist? A curious thing, made of a brittle ivory covered with patterns – angular, scratchy spirals. Sarah draws her finger along the raised carvings. The baby waves its arm with a flailing energy, then quiets.

Maybe the mum's just nipped into the bushes for a wee.

"Hello!" Sarah calls and looks around.

Here the woods are thick. She listens to the trees rustling above her head. You wouldn't know that they thin out soon, she thinks. You'd never suspect that you'd come to a field and a heap of rubbish as high as a four-storey block. It's full of old prams, bicycles and half-open suitcases offering glimpses of faded scraps of clothing; pieces of metal crushed and bent into shapes that leave no clue of what they'd been before. There are bottles and jars in melted shapes of thick glass in midnight blue and deep crimson.

When she was little, she would have made up stories about these things, about the people who left the suitcases. She would have tasted the thick liquids that must have been in those bottles.

But Sarah doesn't have time for that stuff now that she works in the portacabin office on the other side of the field. She only comes out at lunch to sit among the trees and the wild flowers. Though she needs to be careful in the sun, she has always loved being outside and making things grow.

That's why she 'chose' this scheme, though nothing has actually grown here except that heap of rubbish they're meant to be clearing away. She only stays in the office and puts data into a computer. Everything in little bits, cut up so no one can see what's actually going on. *Hey slug, hey ghost,* they said at school. People don't say those things to her at work, but most of the time she could very well be a ghost. She isn't really there, unless she makes a mistake or slows down.

She sits on the log, hugging the baby close to her. Whoever left this child must have cared for it too. But why leave it here? Did they know that this is where she goes to escape from work?

"Hello!" she calls again.

She hears only her own breathing – then a gasp from the bundle.

The baby opens startled eyes.

Sarah's eyes also widen as she meets their magenta gaze.

No one has eyes that colour. Not even albino people like her, with pale blue-grey eyes. Bluey-grey, *not* pink.

"I don't have pink eyes," Sarah insists out loud, as if defending herself against the schoolkid taunts all over again. *"I don't have pink* eyes. *My eyes are the colour of water!*" That remark only got her extra abuse; her head shoved in the toilet so she could see the *real* colour of water.

The baby's face twitches, as if it's about to tell her something.

"What? What are you like, eh?"

Those eyes remind her of something she encountered when she was only a kid. She might have been imagining things, or finding what she always hoped to find.

The child twists in her arms, and lets out thin mewling sounds. Grasping hands stretch out. She thinks of featherless new-born birds again, and shattered eggs on a scorched pavement.

"Oh shhh, it's alright," she tries to comfort it. "You want to see something pretty?" She rummages with her free hand and takes out an old brooch that she keeps deep in her bag. A glass flower, its clear petals infused with swirls of cloudy white, veins of purple and hints of buttered yellow. As she turns it in front of the baby's face, the pitch of the mewling drops.

"This was given to me by someone I played with one afternoon, a long time ago. Then she went away. And later, I grew flowers like this in our garden."

The baby stares at the flower, and tints of purple and yellow dance over its face. The reflections warm her own skin as they touch her arm. And she remembers the violets she once tried to plant in that same garden – the shy wild kind you find hidden in the shadiest part of the woods. Those never thrived.

The baby makes another noise, like something is broken inside. And makes it again. Sarah shoves her treasure back into her bag. This baby isn't *right*. That's why it's so hot. It needs a doctor. Looking at beautiful things won't help it.

"We'll make you better," Sarah declares to the grizzling child as she gets up and starts carrying it down the path. She'll tell them in the office what's happened, and take the kid to hospital. She doesn't give a fuck what they say. Let them cut her money.

Sarah puts on her hat before coming to the open field. The baby stops crying for a moment and gives her another big-eyed stare. I *have* seen eyes like that, Sarah thinks. Except they were closer to violet. Perhaps the colour changes when *they* get older. Ten years ago, was it? And I've seen skin as white as that, which didn't belong to me.

Sarah was eight, out for a walk in the hills with her parents. When they sat down to talk about dull adult things, she took off on her own. Her mum made her put on more sunscreen and her strongest glasses. Her dad told her not to wander off too far. Sarah said she was only going to her 'fort'. You could almost miss the remains of the old building in this place so full of stones tumbled in massive piles; stunted, warped trees struggling out from under them.

Sometimes it seemed like someone had just tossed and scattered the stones over their shoulder. And if you looked away and at them again you came close to catching their patterns, and understanding what they meant.

And if you looked *too* closely, the pattern slipped away again. Maybe that's how she found the old ruin in the first place. Her eyes didn't always focus properly, and sometimes it helped to take her glasses off and find things in her own way.

She always went to the fort when her parents took her on their rambles. It was a place that protected her. Within the walls, an old tree spread its branches and kept it dark. There was something that could have been a fireplace, a hole in one of the walls with bushes in front of it.

Sarah liked to pretend it was her house. She sat inside the space in the wall, closed her eyes and waited. If she closed her eyes, the stories would come, the stories about the place she sat in and who she really was when she lived there.

When nothing happened, she opened her eyes again.

Naked and pale and very still, another girl stood with her back to Sarah. Her paleness flared like a torch in the dim haven of the fort. She wasn't beige, but the startling white of no-colour. Like Sarah, but this girl's skin was closer to the white of pearls, a rounded white with a soft gleam. The girl's hair, that same pearl-white with a scattered highlight of gold. She held herself straight as if she didn't need clothes though she should have been cold on an autumn day.

It was the first time Sarah saw someone who looked *anything* like herself. It made her heart squeeze into itself with pleasure. She always wanted to meet someone else like her. Like her, but better.

The baby squirms and struggles in her arms, lets loose a cry with every step Sarah takes. She almost loses her grip, shocked by the wiry strength in such a small body. "Stop that! I can't help you if you do that! But wait . . ."

Some of those prams in the dump aren't in bad condition. "Look, I'll put you in a pram. I'll make it nice and comfy, it'll be easier to move you."

The delicate face scrunches into a grimace, and again lets loose a thin shriek. Without thinking, Sarah moves to cover her ears and almost drops the baby. She has to hold it tighter to make up for what she came close to committing.

No, no I won't let you go.

"S-sorry, it's not posh. But that's the best I can do now. We'll find someone who can help you." Her voice shakes as she tries to comfort the squirming thing. "I wish you could speak and tell me what's wrong! All I can do is talk useless bollocks to you! But it's better than nothing . . ."

It cries louder, and its body grows hotter. Sarah's legs aren't working; her knees seem to bend in the wrong direction as she attempts a dash towards the dump and the prams. She was always a good runner. She had to be. But panic slows her. *Faster.* Or is she getting too fast now, does it jar the little one? This baby might feel more – and hurt more.

"Sssh, *please* stop crying! I'll find a doctor, someone." A doctor? She shudders as she thinks of *someone* in a white coat bent over this baby, prodding it with gleaming instruments. Like the things they did to her, to find out why she wasn't 'achieving' at school and why she sang strange songs and kept looking for things that weren't there.

The white girl was talking to herself. It was in another language, but it wasn't French or Spanish or anything she heard before. Her voice was high and cutting, there was a twist and hiss to the words as if a different kind of mouth spoke them. It entranced Sarah, and it also grated. It was like chalk on a blackboard, but it went much deeper – a piece of chalk dragged through her insides. The sound went in her eyes and gave everything around her – the trees, the stone walls – their own fuzzy light spreading from within.

The white girl made swooping motions with her arms as if they had no bones. She stretched them above her head. Her long fingers spread to stir the air and pull the sky down, then bunched together as if she was crushing and mashing something between them. Her talking got louder until it became a kind of tuneless singing. Sarah's mouth went dry as the shivers and that glow in everything became louder.

Sarah may have moved, though she didn't think that she'd been able to move. She must have made a sound; stepped on a leaf, a twig. Something no one else would hear, but the white girl did. She gave a little jerk, her talking stopped and she turned around.

The baby screams and screams, if that noise could just be called screaming.

Sarah keeps her mouth clamped tight, to make sure she doesn't scream with it. *You need protection from the sun. I know, because I do too.* She puts the blanket over its head. The blanket muffles the screams, but they sound choked. *Am I doing the right thing? Tell me what I'm doing wrong!* She thinks of hospitals again, and what could happen there. She wonders who would leave this baby for her to find. As if she knew something.

The white girl's face twisted like she was angry or scared. She made a sound, a click in the back of her throat. Sarah couldn't do anything except think of what the girl would do to her because she got caught snooping on something important. Sarah stood up, because she knew she couldn't hide.

The girl stared at Sarah, and Sarah stared at the girl. She was just old enough to have small pointy breasts and hair below, a sparse down of the same gold-tinted white that was on her head. She took some steps closer to Sarah, still staring. The white girl's eyes were pale purple, like iris flowers. Like wild violets growing in the woods.

The child needs to be in the woods again. It wants Sarah to help. Or someone expects help from Sarah. It could be the violet-eyed girl, who would be more than a girl now. A woman, able to have babies.

"OK, white one, we're going back." Sarah turns around, clutching her bundle. Take it to the place next to the stream-bed that still smells of wet and mushrooms and ferns. This is where the baby belongs. And where she belongs too. They'll return to her fort together. She can't even remember when she stopped going there. She wanted to do other things, have boyfriends, any kind of friends.

After Sarah met the girl in the fort, she thought that she saw more of them, the white people with pearly faces peering down at her in her bed and singing to her even when she woke up. She wrote the songs down in a secret alphabet. She sang them and if she listened, sometimes she thought singing came in reply.

Where are the right tunes to sing to this baby? What will soothe it? She stopped knowing those songs long ago. She lost the alphabet.

The child no longer struggles. But it gasps, and lets loose another high sound that vibrates in Sarah's bones and draws out every pain she has known. It will drown out every other thought if she let it. Breathe. *Think.* Is the baby wet, it must need cleaning!

She unwraps the child – enough to see that it's a boy – but there's no mess in the blanket. His skin is also dry. You'd expect a sick baby to stink of poo and sick, but when she sniffs there is only an odour like woodchips after they've been swept away.

Sarah remembers her uneaten lunch and her bottle of water. She pours some water onto her sleeve and wipes it on his face and body. "There . . . that will cool you."

She looks into the magenta eyes. "Who are you," she asks, though she expects no answer. "Were you left by that girl? What can I do? Maybe you're not . . ." Sarah doesn't finish the sentence. That would be like saying she's not human herself.

Maybe she's not . . . That white girl came close. Sarah could hear her breathing and look into those pale iris-eyes. No one would dare push *her* head down a toilet! The girl moved too smoothly, like a forest creature stalking prey.

But the girl's face relaxed into a smile. She gave a jerk of her head, a nod of recognition. *She knows I'm like her. Almost.* The white girl's teeth seemed very small, but there were a lot of them. She didn't smile for long. She slipped away so quickly it took Sarah a moment to realise she was gone.

"But you're different," Sarah amends. "Very different."

The baby yawns and Sarah looks into a rose-coloured mouth. Did she ever look into a mirror and see that colour inside her own mouth? "A little like me, and like that white girl in the fort."

It's the first time she's spoken to anyone about the white girl. She didn't even tell the friend who gave her the brooch a year later – another girl as dark as Sarah was pale. Sarah still wasn't sure where her friend came from. She was the daughter of her mother's client, when she was still allowed to practise. Mum was accused of helping terrorists, finding people who 'disappeared' and letting people know where they were. Speaking about hidden things brought punishment, even for lawyers.

Speaking out loud about her own secret makes Sarah shiver the way she did when she heard the white girl singing. But saying it's real also gives her a good feeling. Maybe that will spread to the boy and make him better. Look, he quiets down – only snuffling. And she's telling him other things.

"Shall I tell you more about the white girl in the woods? Was she your mum? I kept looking for her. I'd visit the place. Sometimes I was sure that I saw something flicker, but that was all I saw. Just a flicker. That white girl . . . she was a little like me. If they left you here because I'm like you, I have to understand more about myself so I can help you. And I don't know enough!

"My dad had a bookshop and I read a lot when I was little, though I needed special glasses with the old books. My parents said that's why I made up odd things. But I didn't read the *right books.*"

The baby catches its breath, a smaller version of the sound the white girl made when she saw Sarah.

"When I come home, I pick up books from my father's old shop. It's closed now, but there's a room for them in the house. But they won't tell me how to look after you. Or where your mother has gone. How can I feed you, I don't have the right milk! I have nothing. I *am* nothing, and what will you be? It's not just my colour. I'm different *inside* and so are you. I thought those things would matter less when I grew up, but it's worse. They say I'm on 'youth empowerment" but it only gives someone else the power to make me do useless things. And they mess with my mind, like the time they made me stop singing your songs. I can't remember how they go, otherwise I'd sing them for you. Maybe they'd tell me how to make you better."

The baby is gasping again. Sarah's hands are unsteady as she wets her finger and puts it in his mouth. She tries to feed him from her mini-carton of chocolate milk, but he spits it back and it gets on her jacket. If she shows up at work with stains on her clothes there'll be another 'support session'. More marks on her report, more questions. She starts wiping off her jacket. But he makes a choked cry and up comes more, just a clear fluid. *Water has many colours. A rusty tint, staining porcelain, brown flakes drifting in and out of the cracks, filling her eyes.*

We'll show you the colour of water. Now the fluid is stained red. He *does* need a doctor.

When she dials 999 on her mobile the baby starts up a high keening. His cries are fragments of glass ground beneath a bare heel. They bring back her desolation when she realised that she'd never see the white girl again. Or when her mum said that the friend who gave her the brooch had to go home – somewhere far away – though she didn't want to.

It is like seeing the colour of water, inside a toilet.

Sarah cuts the call off. Imagine them coming here, taking him away. That's why he screams so much. And what about the others, who hide even from her? She didn't think of that before. What would they do to the white girl who sings in the woods? Put her on a 'youth-empowerment' scheme?

"You can't go to hospital, is that it? Would they put you on a table, cut you open? Shine lights in your eyes and make you fizzle?"

Like a bug under a magnifying glass, a slug covered in salt.

"Would they cut up your mum too?"

The baby's gasps quicken into a grating rhythm. If only the girl with the iris eyes could come now, and take him back to her world of pale people living in places where it is always dusk.

The movement of his arms and legs becomes jerky and spasmodic.

Where are you? Help me, help this baby, you white-haired bitch!

His skin turns even more sheer. Sarah expects to see the organs beneath it, but an opaque milkiness gathers at the child's centre and hides them.

An egg shattered on the hot pavement. Insides turning solid.

The volume of the gasps now fades, though they carry on like the ring of a phone that never gets answered. Sarah tries to give him milk again, but he doesn't even notice it. He makes an abrupt, strangled cough and all his veins flush deep red and his skin turns pink, then white again. His eyes go from magenta to washed-out pink.

"*I don't have pink eyes,*" Sarah once said. But this baby *does* have pink eyes now. He is shrinking into his blankets, translucence turning soiled and blank.

The child's heated skin is already cooling. He is no longer white, but grey all over.

Sarah catches her breath in a gasp like the baby's last cry, as his body shrivels in her hands. When Sarah wraps him in the blanket, he is like a mummy.

She can't breathe right, as if someone just punched her in the stomach and that punch has emptied her of everything. She can't do anything but sit with what is left of him and remember: the pink-veined petal of a flower, the fragile no-colour that shows wonders flowing beneath. She listens for the songs of the white girl.

She can't go back to work. Not today. She doesn't even know about tomorrow.

"I'm sorry I couldn't save him." She speaks out to the rustling between the trees. "I tried, but I had to guess. And if I guessed the other way . . . He still could have died, and the wrong people would *know.*" She is desperate for an answer. Any answer, even an angry one.

Sarah sits with the baby and waits, as the shade around her deepens.

Now it's time to go.

She has to leave this boy where he belongs, then look for a place where she belongs. How can she carry on as before, when she's just seen a tiny creature who isn't part of this world shrivel and die? She must find out where he came from, and do everything she can so she doesn't shrivel too. She must do more than wait for an answer, or *wait* again for the white girl to appear.

Sarah picks up the baby's hand, which is light and dry as a crumpled autumn leaf. She hesitates, then eases off the bracelet and holds it close to her eyes. Spirals and whirls, interlocking squares, random bumps. It's too late to help this boy, but there must be others. She can take her glasses off, look away and look again. Keep trying. Find the pattern . . .

And what will she leave in return? She thinks of the brooch given to her by the friend she played with for one afternoon. Like the white girl in the fort, she didn't speak English – but they found a way to play.

Sarah takes the glass flower out of its hiding place. She puts it within a fold of the blanket and leaves the child tucked where she found him.

When Sarah goes across the field, she sees rain clouds rolling in and the sun setting behind them. Bursts of dark gold light come from behind the clouds, slicing through the thick grey air to stream onto patches of the field and the mountain of cast-offs. An empty pram teeters on top of it, and a stray piece of sunset reflects off a piece of gleaming metal among the rusted wheels.

And as she walks into a patch of light, she feels it change her hair from white to silver, and give her skin the lustre of a pearl that glows from within.

The Peak

Dubstep throbs beneath the roar of the crowd and the thud of projectiles. At the first shattering of glass, my voice adds its own note to the tumult. I barely recognise the sound vibrating in my head. Usually my voice is soft, but resolute. Clients find it reassuring after they've confided their troubles with benefits bosses or landlords or unfair sackings. Then my job was axed and I became a 'mature' student.

Now my studies could be in peril too. So I'm joining with crowds of people half my age set on storming the Tory headquarters at Millbank Tower.

"Rise like lions from your slumber . . . rise in unvanquishable number!" A placard to my right quotes Shelley.

"They say cutback, we say fuck that!"

"Fuck that, fight back, fight fight fight back, fuck that . . ."

"There are many many more of us than of you!" People press forward, singing. Many many more of us . . . *Unvanquishable.*

"We're young! We're poor! We won't pay any more!"

From where I stand, I see that people are already inside the building, ramming stuff against the floor-to-ceiling windows as those outside do their worst too.

And the windows go through. We're all shoving forward against the police line. They push back. A protestor reels from a blow. Hands are raised, bearing phones.

"Your job is next! Your job is next!" The outnumbered police try to guard the doors as people clear the jagged remnants of glass away.

Then I join the surge into the building.

I never imagined this. Not when I set out in unseasonable November sun, expecting an amble down the road, followed by a pint. Others look just as shocked as I feel. We step inside, glass crunches underfoot.

A woman at the wedge-shaped reception desk looks the other way, as if secretly pleased we've disrupted a dull day. A portly colleague picks up the phone.

"Mask up! Mask up!"

I search in my pockets for a suitable piece of cloth, having lost my woolly scarf. Nothing. On the floor, papers. The contents of a drawer scattered.

When I look up I see that the staff have fled. People are standing on the desk, pulling down ceiling panels. A computer monitor hurtles towards the remaining glass. Someone is trying to reach a CCTV camera, but it's too high.

"Tory scum! Tory scum!"

Smoke bombs send forth pastel plumes. The whiff of burning placards from outside, a late autumn bonfire day.

I've forgotten that crowds really do *roar*. Dubstep pulses underneath the roar. And something else beneath that . . . other layers of noise. What do I hear? Silence. Can you *hear* silence? Silence echoing with the slam of a door.

I look down again. More stuff's scattered on the floor. Yes, there's a hat I can use. I pick it up. I unfold a stiff woollen cap with a long visor. It's rough and worn, threadbare in places.

"Tory scum!" Tory scum!"

"Massssk up!"

The 'visor' turns out to be a mask that covers my face, with holes for eyes and a strap that goes under my chin.

Inside the mask, the air is musty. I'm distant from the world around me, even though it's full of noise. People bump against me in the scramble. Did someone shout my name?

I can see, but only to the front. A blurred bar of fabric between my eyes divides even this in half. I try moving, going further into the lobby, away from the police line that's reformed just outside where the windows used to be.

My breath condenses on the cloth, moistening the fibres, and this releases something in turn. I'm overcome by a scent of boiled cabbage, cramped spaces and damp rope.

I remember an abandoned garden shed I broke into when I was young. I was locked there overnight after the doorknob fell off on the other side. I was terrified. And a stab of that feeling comes back to me. *Dark. Terror.* For the first time in years, I'm remembering this.

The crowd still roars around me. I listen to it again, finding single voices within it. For a moment I hear each and every voice and rejoice as the silence is driven away.

Yes, there's so much noise but it's better than too much quiet. Better than the Darks.

I'm sure someone whispered this in my ear, but when I turn around I find no one speaking directly to me.

Essie. My name is Essie.

Who? Where are you? There is more breath than voice in the words. Someone lost in the dark, finding solace is this thunderous crowd.

"To the stairs! To the stairs!"

But I'm still wedged in close to the lift, where someone has scrawled 'rise up' on the door.

I draw in another breath. Old rope in my face, bugs scuttling on the ground.

Breathe together.

This suggestion sounds softer than a whisper. Only a thought. Is it mine?

Breathe.

So I breathe again.

"To the stairs! To the stairs!"

Fire alarms whine and clamour.

"To the stairs!"

I take the thing off and put it in my pocket, and settle for pulling my hood up – a distinctive lilac colour that might as well say 'identify me'. Now I can inhale the wind that sweeps through the shattered windows of 30 Millbank, carrying the chemical scents of burning paint, wood, paper and fireworks.

A row of cops block the double doors that lead to the rest of the building, People push against them, one guy gives everyone a pained smile as he is pinned halfway up the door frame by the scrum.

"There are many more of us than of you . . . many many more of us than of you . . ." The song rises again.

And the steady pressure of the many more of us bears the cops sideways. A guy inserts himself into the half-open door and more people get through. Then we're all heading up an emergency staircase. Someone has bundled a fire hose up the stairs and turned it on, and water flows down. "It's Tory slime!"

Up a flight, then another. And another . . . I'm out of breath, but I spare a thought for the guy who's coming up with a wheelchair – with a lot of help from his friends. Nine floors, eighteen flights.

"We made it," someone ahead of me shouts. "Yay!"

The sunlight pouring through the rooftop door into the stairwell outlines a woman's grey shape.

I can't see the woman's face, only her form in a long dress. There's something Victorian in the flare of the skirt and the shape of her headgear, though the sun's reflection makes it hard to see. There've been plenty of people in fancy dress . . . the guy dressed as Cameron wielding a toy axe, people bearing papier maché models of carrots and sticks.

I'm still struggling up that last flight of stairs to the roof.

The woman in the doorway spreads her arms in an expansive gesture of freedom.

"We made it!" A girl shouts again.

Someone lends a hand to their friend in front of me, and then I'm on the roof too. A group of students from Leeds are leaning over the parapet and fastening banners, while others unfurl black and red flags.

We're on the flat part of the roof and not the top of the tower, but still I see a lot of London. The fringe of trees, the fat ribbon of the river, the big wheel across the river. The tower itself blocks the view to the west.

Below us the crowds in the courtyard are in constant motion as people keep surging against the building. Woolly-hatted heads bob up and down in a dance around a fire built from placards and newspapers. More bonfires bloom and the music gets louder.

Rooftop occupiers shout and cheer at the folks below, who cheer for us standing up here.

The sight of the dancing, celebrating crowd jammed into the courtyard of the Tory HQ makes my heart beat fast, my face flush. It's like being in love, but much better. It's like being young when we when we occupied the City of London in 1999, except this might be better too.

Can any of my old friends be down there? I lean over the parapet, trying to pick out individual faces.

Is there someone called Essie down there? Or up here?

One boy lets a fire extinguisher spritz into the air, and bottles of champagne follow suit. Word goes around: "on the Tories . . . fridges downstairs are filled with this stuff".

"Hey, Julia!" It's Debra, who shares studio space with me, a regular student rather than a grizzled mature one like me. She's calling to me from a group on an upper section of the roof. They're getting their lunch out, which seems like a good idea. Debra reaches down to help me climb up.

Up here I can see the Millbank Estate, a council estate I'd eye enviously from my own 1970s tower block. Whenever I visit the Tate or take a break from my work, I enjoy walking among those leafy squares and brick buildings graced with arches and bay windows.

And I also see the Tate itself, the main building and the annexe where the Turners and the Blakes are exhibited. My father used to take me to the Tate when I was a kid, and later I went by myself. I loved Turner's blurred landscapes and cityscapes, relished his repeated views of the burning Parliament and always peered for ages at *The Fairy Feller's Masterstroke*, Richard Dadd's miniature of a threatened fairy domain. Now the world down there seems as small and intricate as the one created by Dadd.

The approaching beat of helicopter blades nearly drowns out our conversation. There are two helicopters; one has POLICE on its side. People raise their fingers at it, which seems a futile gesture. I remember the mask in my pocket and put it on again.

"Hey, that's a cool mask," Debra says. "Much better than those Guy Fawkes masks. It's kind of scary-looking, but that's not a bad thing. Did you make it yourself?"

"I found it downstairs. It's not very comfortable."

It gets hot inside the mask, the rough material scratching me. But I'm wary of the helicopters and CCTV cameras, so I keep it on and look towards the Tate again.

Conspire. Breathe together.

But whose breath do I share?

I try to rub my eyes through the holes in the mask, and when I open them again I see something else where the Tate ought to be.

A much bigger building . . . six pentagons arranged like a star, a tower at the end of each pentagon and a central structure in the middle of this star-shape. Yellow-brown brick walls with small square windows, surrounded by a low wall. A channel of water around one side, the river borders it at the other.

Feelings wash through me at the sight. A perception of utter darkness even while I see; an awareness that I am far too familiar with what lies within the arms of that desolate star. I can make out movement within one of the pentagons, figures walking in a circle. The monotony of their motion forms a weight in my stomach.

I'm dizzy for a moment. My mouth is dry. I lift a hand to pull the mask off, but the police helicopter makes another circuit so I leave it.

Through the eye-holes the star-shaped image recedes and grows stronger with the pulse in my temples. A scent I recognise from a visit to the Wetlands Centre and hikes that encountered unexpected bogs: mud and marsh and rotting waterweed.

I move my head to see more through the eyeholes in my mask. The sight unsettles me, yet I keep looking. Then I know I must *draw* this to make sense of what I'm seeing. Let others take photos on their phones.

I take a sketch pad out of my rucksack and begin. I keep the mask on; I'm sure it's a key to what I'm seeing. And could it be a key to what I'd heard downstairs: *my name is Essie.*

"Ha! Art students! Always detached, always observing and sketching . . ." says a boy as he climbs up to join us. But he's smiling. Just teasing. Makes me feel like I belong here.

"Detachment was useful in my old job as well."

"And what was that?"

"I was an advice worker. If you let yourself get too involved with your work you'd go mad." I'm getting chatty now, up here on the roof.

"So you're a student now?"

"Yeah. I used to love art when I was a kid, so when I lost my job I decided to take the chance."

It's hard to carry on a real conversation through this mask, so I take it off. For a while though, the image of the star-shaped building is superimposed on the familiar Tate. The entrances to both buildings overlap, but the fading arms of the star extend far beyond the museum.

"You can have a look at my drawings if you want," I say to the boy. I flip the pages. "These are just rough . . ."

He does a double-take. "Is that what you see now? Or did you imagine it? *That* is Millbank prison in your drawing. They called that structure a 'panopticon', designed so someone in the middle can observe everything that goes on in the six pentagons."

He adds: "The Tate and the Chelsea School of Art stand where the prison used to be."

"I go to Chelsea now. It's just over the bridge from where I live. Strange to think that I've lived in this area so long and never knew about the prison."

"I know about this stuff because I'm studying history at UCL." The champagne bottle comes around again, along with paper cups. We both pour some and touch our cups together.

Nothing should surprise me after the takeover of Tory Towers. But this? Seeing things is one thing. Seeing things that *used* to be there is another. But finding myself on this roof is extraordinary in itself, and it makes the strangeness easier to accept.

I touch the mask in my pocket. The fabric is still damp from my breath. It really is disgusting.

But as the helicopter hovers closer I decide that the mask still has its uses. I gaze at the six-pointed star to the west again. And I also see police vans crossing Vauxhall Bridge, 21st century ones with flashing blue lights and sirens.

We breathe together, we see together too.

This mask is very old, and someone must have worn it, made this fabric wet with *their* breath.

And I am breathing it in now.

Breathe together. Conspire.

An argument breaks out near the parapet overlooking the courtyard. "That could've hit someone, anyone," someone is shouting.

The boy next to me suggests that the police are having a go-slow; even the filth are worried about the cuts.

These conversations seem distant too.

That kid was right. *Always detached, always sketching.*

I'm already wondering how to portray the revelry and riot below. A panoramic battle or a close-up as three riot vans pull up? Figures converge around them, sit down in a wave to block the vans.

The mask fractures any images. In the dark borders of my vision, colour appears in dashes and splashes. *Colour in the Darks . . . spat out by a fevered mind, but it kept me sane.*

When I look towards the east, towards Waterloo and Blackfriars, my limited vision expands to take in a different part of the river. A round-domed building. *The Rotunda.* A crowded room within, full of angry people. Then we're crossing a bridge.

"All to the West End, all for Reform!"

"Down with the police!"

"No Peel!"

"No Wellington!"

These messages come from far away, full of static, filtered through coarse cloth and memory. After the far-away chanting, quiet follows, so quiet that the static swells and grows shrill.

Then I'm back to dub-step and chants from the courtyard, the conversation of my rooftop companions. I button my coat up; as the sun sets it's getting chilly.

The noise brought me out . . . The voice in my ear is cracked and barely audible. It's the sound of someone who hasn't spoken in a long time, someone who has lost most of their words and is only just learning to use them again.

Stuck in the silent system, she tells me.

You're in the Darks. No room to move, nothing to see, just darkness.

You looked up. You looked around, when you were meant to pray in chapel. Too much looking will get you punished.

You will wear the Peak when you come out of the Darks, even in your cell. That's what they told me. They said I shouldn't look. But I will. And I will make sure someone else sees what I see. They put the Peak on me, but I will see.

The Peak?

The cap, the mask. We share it now.

It hides me. I hope. From the helicopter and the cameras.

A name forms again in my mind. *Essie.*

"Over here! We're having a meeting!" People have gathered in a corner of the roof.

Everyone in our group jumps down to join them. I push my cap back so the long visor isn't in front of my face.

They're putting together a statement. Something short and succinct about why we're occupying the roof, everyone agrees.

"We oppose all cuts and we stand in solidarity with public sector workers, and all poor, disabled, elderly and working people . . ."

"Sounds fine to me," says Debra.

"We call for direct action to oppose these cuts. This is only the beginning of the resistance to the destruction of our education system and public services."

I can't concentrate, but my cynical old heart does a flutter or two. "This is only the beginning."

Soon the statement's sent out, tweeted, posted. In celebration we pass around more food and drink. Then a phone rings, and we hear one side of a terse conversation. More riot police are in the courtyard, and others are starting to push up the stairs.

Our bunch bursts into discussion, perhaps there are more arguments than people in the group. Then Debra calls for a more orderly meeting and offers to facilitate.

Some want to stick it out, others suggest we sneak out an exit while it's still possible. "We've done what we set out to do. The whole world knows about this."

"I have no desire to get dragged down those stairs," adds Debra. "And I'm still bound over from another case."

I look at Debra, a slight dark-haired girl with a big voice. How much do I know about her, though we spend so much time working side by side and offering each other cups of tea or cans of beer?

And what do I think? I want to occupy this roof as long as possible. But as the discussion bounces back and forth, I decide it's best to leave now and try to stay free to fight another day.

We divide into two groups. One stays on the roof, the other will go. Each group plans to stick together.

There are several staircases we can use, but which one's the best?

"I heard noise from the one we came up."

"They could be sneaking up the back one right now."

"How many staircases are there?"

We take our chances and choose our escape route, which might've been the stairs the staff used to evacuate the building.

But there's graffiti here too. 'Tory scum – here we come!'

And there we *go* . . . Fast, fast, but don't push or panic.

Then I stop to stare at a relatively clean part of the wall. In my mind, words come to occupy that space like a snapshot. 'Down with Peel's gang – no Blue Devils!' I take a marker pen out of my bag and scrawl those words on the wall though I have no idea what they mean.

"Julia, what are you doing? Graffiti? Good stuff, but we got to get outta here!"

So now young Debra is the practical one and I'm just an old hooligan. I grin at her as she takes my arm.

"Come on . . . What's that about anyway? That old DJ guy and some old-fashioned kind of speed, is it?"

Then we rush down another flight of stairs. The mood is much more muted as we come back down to earth, yet the roar of the crowd grows louder and we can hear the sounds of struggle and thumps and crashes from the lobby. But our staircase of choice brings us out the back safely.

We emerge to cheers. Debra gives me a hug. People I've never met are waving at me and slapping my back. And then I see someone from years ago. She has the same bright-hennaed haircut from 2001 but it still suits her. We took a coach together to stop the IMF summit in Prague.

"Hey Julia, getting down with the kids?"

"No, going *up* with the kids is more like it!" I couldn't resist the non-joke, but we're both in the mood to laugh at it. I'm embarrassed that I don't remember her name though she still knows who I am.

Then my old comrade is gone in the crowd. Instead, I catch sight of my old boss, who waves as well. Even she seems to approve.

I have no desire to talk to her though, so I grab Debra's arm and we work our way back to the courtyard, which is still heaving with people pushing and shoving against the police line in front of the building as the party continues. The beats of dubstep compete with punk classics: "London calling to the far-away towns . . ."

But the police seem to be gaining control of the lobby, and more reinforcements are arriving. I hope those who chose to stay on the roof will be OK.

"C'mon Julia," says Debra. "Let's move on before they kettle us."

Another rinky-dink sound system is setting off with a crowd in tow. "Off to visit the Lib Dems now!"

We join them and have a dance and a less than successful push at the police line blocking the narrow street. Then we go to the pub.

I still have the mask. I turn it over, examine it. I see that it is more frayed around the edges. If I move it, the dust rising from the fabric seems to leave it lighter. It's an old thing, after all. Exposure to light must affect it. It should be in a glass case but instead it's with me.

And why did that happen?

Its slitted eyes regard me, revealing no answers. But surely some clues can be uncovered. I need to find them before the whole thing comes undone.

Debra said the mask was 'cool' when we were on top of Millbank, but when I wear it now in our studio, she says it gives her the creeps. "Must be the enclosed space," she explains.

"Well, it gives me a different perspective. And like you said, creepy and scary has its place."

I have it on now as I examine my current painting, which portrays a view from my desk at my old job. I imagined a glass bubble surrounding my desk. My clients are pressed against it, their faces mashed against the glass, desperate for the help I feel less and less able to give.

Essie . . . does this make any sense to you?

I try to listen as well as see. Is that static, or is it only the scratch of the fabric against my ears? Sometimes I hear a keening, filtered through a blanket of dark and silence. *You must wear the Peak.*

Now she's back in the Darks. Can I reach her?

I can't settle into the work. Neither can Debra, cursing as her tapestry threads break. Instead, we end up watching clips on YouTube. Scenes from the 'Battle of Millbank', celebratory hip-hop and ska anthems, singalongs with 'The Kids are Alright' and 'Forces of Victory'.

Before Millbank, Debra seemed to regard me as an auntie she found pleasant to have about, like a faded but comfortable sofa. Now she's become a friend. We go to the pub, meet each other's mates.

Together we join a group called Arts Against the Cuts, which meets in a lecture theatre at the University of the Arts in Holborn.

Someone comes from a local campaign in Lambeth, wanting to talk about disrupting the next council meeting: "Even the lollipop ladies are getting the axe! School crossings will be a lot more dangerous."

People are full of ideas; actions, graphics, art and more art. We organise teach-ins and guerrilla seminars . . . in a bank, at a supermarket, at an art auction. Insurgent lollipop ladies and lollipop guys will block traffic on the high street.

"We will turn our imagination and desires into tools of disobedience," Debra writes on a flyer for a long weekend of workshops.

While students occupy their colleges against tuition hikes, pupils and sixth-formers agitate to keep their educational allowance.

Soon we're out on a cold afternoon, following gangs of school children as they run towards Parliament Square. We're both huffing and puffing, jogging alongside orange-jacketed legal observers.

"Don't go down there . . . It's a trap. You'll get kettled," Debra calls to the youngsters.

A few girls glance at us. "We go where we want, lady," one of them shouts back.

"That's the first time anyone called me a 'lady'," Debra says. The enormity of such a thing stops her in her tracks.

"Don't worry, you get used to it."

Then we have to start running again.

We prepare for the next demonstration by making big 'books' from styrofoam, cardboard and padding, which we'll use these to protect ourselves against the police and bust our way out of kettles. We collect titles of favourite books to put on our shields: *The Dispossessed, Down and Out in Paris and London, Multitude* . . . Then I see the title that seems just right for me: *Pip Pip: A Sideways Look at Time*.

I take a sideways kind of look when I'm in the studio, peering through the mask as I begin a new painting. I've put aside painting my recent past and plan a look at the deep past. Essie's past, the foundation of the ground where I stand.

As soon as I start to think that way, I feel something stir in the side of my vision, the part that's covered by the mask.

Debra interrupts my musings. "We have to go to Arts Against the Cuts. It's an important meeting."

"I've just started on this painting. You can tell me what happens."

I was looking forward to a quiet time tonight. Time to look through the mask, find its vision again and put it on canvas.

"It's a very important meeting," insists Debra.

"Every meeting is an important meeting. Every demo is the one that's gonna topple the state. But once you go . . . you realise you could've stayed in. And there'll always be another demo."

"Did you almost stay in on the day we occupied Milbank?"

"Er . . . now that you mention it, yes. I was thinking about it." I admit. "Stay in the studio and paint, I thought. Paint what . . . I wasn't sure. I was kind of stuck."

"Looks like you worked something out now. And where did you get that idea?" She points to my canvas.

So it looks like I'm persuaded.

When we arrive, everyone's discussing a new plan – occupying the Tate Britain on the night of the Turner Awards. What will hang in the museum if no one can afford to create art, or even enjoy it? And who will have time for art if we're all forced to work longer and longer hours for less, or for nothing at all?

I think of Essie creating colour out of the darkness. She had no other choice. Essie had been an artist who never had a chance to practise her art.

So yes, let's occupy the site of the prison, raise our voices at the heart of art. Here's one in the eye of the panopticon. I love the idea, and help with a flyer. The action will start with a teach-in on 'Art and the Multitude' in front of Manet's *Execution of Maximilian*.

In the pub after the meeting, I greet the history-loving boy who chatted with me on the roof at Millbank.

"I've been meaning to ask you . . . What are the Blue Devils and who is Peel?"

He tells me that Robert Peel had founded the Metropolitan Police in 1829, and you can guess who the Blue Devils were.

Later, I get off the tube at Pimlico and walk the rest of the way home. I'm sure I can catch a whiff of the marsh as I walk along the river. There's the stink of coarse grass, weeds and mud piling up against the prison walls, acrid smoke from the potteries across the river.

Though I decided that the mask is too fragile to take on demos, I do 'mask up' when I roam the galleries at the Tate with my sketch pad. If someone stares at me, I nod and they might offer a weak smile before they look away. People think I look strange, but art students often do.

I show Essie what has become of her prison. I imagine that I'm holding her hand as we walk through the museum. The hand in mine is calloused and cut from picking oakum.

I see that red-knuckled hand writing the name on a form. She's one of the few prisoners who can read and write, which is why she's been sent to Millbank. It's where they put transportees and prisoners deemed capable of rehabilitation through silence and separation.

This building stands on the ground of your prison, I tell her. I saw it from the roof.

I guide her through the world I inhabit. It must seem an easier one. The site of Essie's prison is now dedicated to art, a college, and well-built housing for working people. The council blocks are named after artists – Turner, Rosetti, Gainsborough – and the courtyards are crowded with great pots of hydrangeas in shades of pale purple to hot pink and orange-rose. Potted trees, a picnic table.

I show her the ditch, the prison moat that was once filled with stagnant disease-bearing water. Now tenants hang clothes to dry in the paved ditch and cultivate pots of nasturtiums, squash and sunflowers.

"Looks good, Essie? But these blocks may be sold off some day . . . if we don't make changes."

I point towards Millbank Tower, though the part of the roof we occupied is hidden by the trees. *Where did your mask come from? Who gave it to me at Millbank tower?* There's no answer in words. But she shows me a mask as it drifts through the air, damp with sweat and condensed breath. And I know some of it is mine.

We walk into the Tate and stand at the bottom of the spiral staircase, gazing up at the rotunda. Essie had shown me another Rotunda down the river in Blackfriars, where radicals once met and agitated.

And I show what we hope to make happen here.

Even on a dull day, the light pours in through the glass dome. The design at its centre looks like a giant eye. We stare back at it. This mask obscures so much. But the light that does come through is much more concentrated, like sparks struck by a confined mind struggling within the Darks.

We walk through galleries bearing the names of corporations: BP, Sainsbury, sugarman Tate himself, who benefited from the labour of slaves. Perhaps these companies once profited from the work of the prisoners here, from the relentless picking of oakum and the discipline enforced in the Darks.

We pass through the twentieth-century galleries. The massive Henry Moore sculptures, abstract and detailed at once. Splashes of colour in a painting called *Azalea Garden*. We look at a black and white photo of a young woman doing a handstand in front of a grey sea, her full pleated skirt falling around her shoulders and face, bare legs and platform sandals in the air.

Essie likes that. I can feel a movement in the mask as if someone is about to nod, a whisper rustling past my ears.

Finally, I show her the Turner paintings in the Clore annexe. Time has dimmed the fabulous colours and layers created by Turner's brush and palette knife, but now I see them as new. They contain an inner light, I suggest.

If you're lucky, you will see such light in the Darks. The inner light of the mind's eye is the only light I had.

Finally, I show Essie *The Fairy Feller's Masterstroke*. I tell her that the strangely formed fairy creatures in the painting scared me as much as they fascinated me. When my father took me here, I always insisted on seeing it, but I would clutch his hand while we stood there.

He once asked: "Why are you scared of such a small thing?"

"The small things get under your skin," I told him.

Yes, that painting is like a splinter of glass under my skin.

A circle of light in the Darks, which reveals another world.

As I work on the new paintings, I anticipate 'Art and the Multitude' when we occupy the Tate. I recall the view from Millbank Tower, and the multitude laying siege to the tower above them. I paint what I see out of the two eye-holes as colour fills them. This is the most intense colour of all, invoked by an optic nerve that conjures something out of nothing.

Plunged into darkness, I have nothing to do but create my own light.

I see an image of a miner's lamp, and I paint that too.

The studio turns darker as the sun goes down. I hear Debra moving about, a door shutting. Then I'm alone in the dark. But this is another kind of darkness, the darkness that shuts out the panopticon. I pull this fertile darkness around me, gathering its depth and lustre as a weapon to blind that all-seeing eye.

Against this background, images come and go and I paint them as fast as I can.

Wild flowers raising their heads in the muck of a ditch.

Windows on a square shining through the rain and fog, a door opens spilling light into the mist. A welcoming figure at the door, whose face I can't see.

A fantasy, a dream.

In the Darks . . . In the Darks . . .

You lose the line between waking and dreaming in the Darks.

But the dark is shattered by a point of light. If you look closely at it, you see a crowd running down Whitehall. A woman lifts a stone and lets it fly. There are shouts: "Reform." "Down with the police." "No Peel."

When I paint the blue devils swinging clubs, a chuckle bubbles up from an unknown place in me.

I paint all the things I see when I'm wearing the mask, though it's wearing thin, Finally, it's coming undone.

I cut and apply the last remnants to form bars across my painting.

The mask is gone, but I continue to paint the memories it showed me. Memories enclosed in small circles on my canvas, surrounded by darkness.

Only a moment, a flare in the Darks.

And I remember sunlight in November, and the outline of a woman standing in front of the stairway door as I made my way up to the roof.

Pieces of Ourselves

Schoolkids run through the crowded street, disappearing around corners and reappearing. They are laughing, boisterous, defiant. Surely Richard doesn't remember having such a good time when he was that age.

Richard's contingent of library workers are more sedate, but still make a lot of noise. George, his assistant on the local history archive, bellows into a megaphone. A new librarian called Sally keeps blowing a horn.

The day is cold, but bright. The bare branches of trees etch patterns of dark lace against an acid-blue sky. He never realised before that branches could look like lace.

A group of art students march forward as they hoist narrow, towering black banners. Linked together, swaying . . . the banners bear splashes and bands of lavender, green and blue, a hint of grey. No slogans, only colours. How can a banner have no words? But those colours speak to him without the words, tugging at his mind. He stares as they twist and bend in the wind.

Up on some construction scaffolding, young guys cheer as they drop another banner: *"We are not your slaves . . . Austerity, up yours!"* Richard cheers along with them. That's right, up yours!

Richard usually doesn't go to demonstrations. In his student years they were usually grim affairs, populated by dour donkey-jacketed party paper sellers. He'd much rather read a book or potter about in his archive.

But this lifts him out of weeks of stress. He keeps bumping into mates he hasn't seen in years . . . people from his library course, a guy from his old hill-walking group.

They are reaching the end of the march, much too soon. On the other hand, he'll get to chat in the pub with Sally. Tall and olive-skinned with green eyes, Sally said she wanted to hear more about his oral history programme.

Richard's phone chimes with a new text message. He fumbles in his pocket for it. Ginny. *Couldn't find you. I'm with the nurses from Brighton, near the book bloc.*

The book bloc? Richard texts back.

You should know, you're a librarian.

Should he? He looks over the heads of the people around him, searching for this elusive bloc and for Ginny. He's been hoping to catch up with her. They have a lot to talk about. Richard faces the loss of his job. Ginny could lose *most* of hers if it's farmed out to a private firm. Once again, they confront similar problems. They should be here together.

He scans the crowd again. A scrawl on a home-made placard catches his eye: *"Work longer, Pay more, Get less . . . No thanks!"* Is that Ginny holding the placard?

A shove from behind cuts his search short.

One minute he's laughing, enjoying his day out. The sun still shines but everything else shifts. A roar from the crowd vies with the samba drumming and horns. Screams and shouts: "Scum, scum!"

George grabs his arm. "C'mon Richard!"

Everyone is running now. People press against him, pushing him forward. He has to run, too. But what is he running from? Where will he go? Placards and plastic crunch underfoot. Sally's horn?

Then he looks over his shoulder. A horse rearing, the bobbing helmets of mounted police. He swallows, tasting acid from his jumping stomach. He keeps running.

Up ahead, more lines of cops at the end of the road.

Demonstrators wielding improvised shields rush past him. *Our Word is Our Weapon* is the red title painted on one. A masked woman brandishes another shield in the orange, black and white of the old Penguin classics: Orwell's *Down and Out in Paris and London*.

Is this the 'book bloc'? "George, look . . ." Richard starts to say.

People are retreating, others surge forward. *Towards* the cops, to push them back? Purple smoke jets up from the ground, people dismantle the police barriers that run down the middle of the road.

Where is everyone?

"George . . ." Richard calls again. "Sally!"

But they aren't with him. None of his friends are. And in front of him . . . rows of cops.

"Fuck! We've been kettled," says someone behind Richard.

Kettled in a police cordon? Richard never thought that could happen to him.

"S'cuse me," Richard says to the closest cop. "I just need to catch up with my friends . . ." He takes a step forward, but they push him back.

"Can't go there. Exit's that way." The cop points down the road.

He stops, not sure which way to go. Other people are still trying to push against the police line. They're shoved back. Is that Ginny? He has the back view of a bobble-hat that looks like Ginny's, short black hair showing beneath it.

Two cops smack the woman-who-might-be-Ginny with their shields.

"Hey . . ." Richard tries to reach her.

"Get back, I told you!" A good push and smack for him; Richard falls and lands on his arse. The impact sends a crunch through his spine.

People help him to his feet. A piece of concrete rolls away from his foot and a gloved hand snatches that up. *"Under the pavement, the beach,"* someone says with a laugh. A familiar sentence. Is it from an advert?

Yes, he used to spend a lot of time on beaches . . . almost twenty years ago.

He repeats the phrase to himself as he rubs his back, straightening slowly. Nothing broken but damn, something hurts. He can still move enough to get up on a low wall so he can see better and search for Ginny. The crowd below him surges and pushes, others collect in groups. Stones arc towards the police line.

"Under the pavement, the beach."

That's it. A slogan from the revolt in France, 1968. He studied European history, should've known straight away.

But those stone throwers won't get anywhere near a beach. They won't even get to the end of the street, with those mounted police behind the riot cops on foot. An empty area of road, then more lines of cops. Shit. He has to get out. And if he can't get out straight away, he has to find Ginny if she's trapped in here too.

Richard jumps down from his wall, wincing as he lands, and walks towards the alleged exit. He tries to phone Ginny again, but now her phone is off. When he gets there, other cops shouts: *"No, exit's over there!"*

Richard walks away again with dragging feet. The cold starts to bite now that the sun is setting. He hunches further into his jacket, pulling his scarf higher. People are making fires from placards and huddling about them. He can join a huddle too, breathe in the chemical scent of burning paint and let the heat beat in his face.

Richard scratches his head under his woolly hat. Through his glove he feels an odd raised area, like a bump but not quite. When he takes his hand away a pale flake spots the leather of his glove, then it's off with the wind. Perhaps it's ash from the nearest fire.

Music comes from the same direction. A hundred people are dancing around a sound system pulled by a bicycle, picking up more people as they move through the crowd.

Richard falls in step. He used to love dancing. So did Ginny. When they first met, they shared regrets about their left-behind lovers; eventually they moved on to cruise bars, gigs and festivals together looking for new love. And then they found each other for a while.

Of course, he used to go dancing with Blanca back in the day . . . all the time. It was different music then, trancey stuff that evoked sunlight and warmth and the pursuit of pleasure. When they submerged into the sound and movement, time stopped; or perhaps it expanded because he was so sure they could live forever in those moments. Sound and sensation, the touch of his lover amplified by a crowd of lovers around them.

It all seems so far from now, so far from where he stands surrounded by cops on a freezing afternoon just starting to darken. Figures dancing around the sound system loom in the dwindling light, jerking about to music he doesn't know. He begins to panic again. Stuck in this kettle, away from his friends.

But soon the hoods come down, coats loosen, breath puffs in vital clouds around the dancers. Faces revealed by the streetlights show joy despite the ring of steel tightening around them. The music has changed and he doesn't know the name of it. Dubstep or grime? Slow, yet powerful.

He launches himself among the revellers. He lifts his feet, stepping with strength and purpose. No, this is nothing like that happy-clappy stuff he raved to back in Spain. Darkness pulses at the heart of this beat. It's the sound of hard times. Faster now, faster, a beat like a barrage of rocks against riot shields. It is new music to him, yet its power moves him closer to his past.

He dances on the pavement that covers the beach, and now he dances on the beach. Back to the 90s, or dancing towards a terrifying future?

Those students he saw earlier arrive with their tall banners, black splashed with colours of the sea, shades of fields and sun-baked hillsides. Richard stops in mid-step. Time contracts, expands. Twenty years of moments collide and merge.

There's Blanca, wearing shorts and a loose stripey t-shirt. She looks just as she did in 1990-something, in the summer.

He reaches back into the past . . . ready to touch its hand.

Blanca smiles and slaps his palm.

No, Blanca was never one for high-fives and palm-slapping.

He doesn't know the woman in front of him at all, though she wears a stripy top like Blanca's. She even wears shorts, along with thick woolly tights and great big boots. *Alright?* Richard nods yes to the stranger, he's alright, he *hopes*.

Does Blanca still go out dancing? What *is* she doing, where the hell is she?

They lost touch, as people did before email and Facebook. Blanca was the one who stopped writing.

She'd been talking about becoming an art teacher before he left . . . and teachers in Spain must be facing cuts now. Art teachers are doubly expendable. People are occupying city squares in Spain, taking over buildings.

Is Blanca among them?

Maybe they could be friends now. He knows that he hurt Blanca by leaving. But maybe they would've hurt or disappointed each other if he stayed. He keeps wondering about that now that the life he left her for feels so shaky.

These young people are dancing on even shakier ground. They have less to lose, though. Maybe that's why they seem so happy. He should learn from them, Join the fun. So he throws himself into more dancing, less worrying.

He doesn't notice precisely when the crowd around the sound system becomes denser and much less blissful. He can't move with his earlier abandon. Sometimes, he can barely move at all. Though he is rediscovering his enjoyment of dancing, he has no desire to revisit his moshing days.

But moshed he is getting. And isn't the police line very close? When did that happen? So many cops. Surely they must have multiplied while he danced.

The police advance, flailing and jabbing with their truncheons. He wants to shout, but suddenly he has no voice. He wants to hit back. But he can't move. He is caught in a childhood nightmare, motionless before a monster.

A wedge of horses gallop into the crowd, their hooves hitting the pavement with sparks. A mounted cop lifts his club at a boy who holds his hands in front of his face, blood showing between his fingers. Richard finally steps forward as fear blazes into anger. He stumbles on the debris left on the ground . . . rocks, heavy steel police barriers, railings. Then he tries to pick a barrier up. The cumbersome thing becomes light as someone takes the other end. *Shove it at them!*

Dodgy back be damned, he pushes it straight into the police line.

A firework falls sizzling on the ground, short of its target. He picks it up and throws it towards the cops, only hoping to get the firework out of their crowd. But a horse rears and bolts as the thing smokes and crackles, the cop barely clinging to his steed.

Richard's heart bolts too, this time with a stab of happiness. He's not sure if he's the one who frightened that horse, but even a temporary retreat thrills him.

A boy who can't be over fourteen tugs at Richard's arm. "You shouldn't throw shit at the horses. It's not the horse's fault!"

Before he can reply, he's off his feet, several cops twisting his arm behind his back.

He was arrested only once before when he was a student, for drunk and disorderly. But then he had a toilet in his cell and even a cup of tea later.

This is it, he thinks. He's nicked. It won't be so civilised now. Will they beat the shit out of him? Will he lose his job? But that's likely to go anyway.

"Stop the snatch squad!"

Other demonstrators move around them. One grabs his legs, others struggle with the cops. He's a wishbone tugged between the two sides. Will they tear him in pieces like one, and leave him to litter the ground? He squirms and flails.

A woman in an orange 'legal observer' bib takes notes. *"What's your name?"*

Suddenly he's pulled away from the cops and sent back into the crowd. Space opens up there, as if the police line has been pushed back.

Richard tries to catch his breath, then turns around to thank one of his rescuers, a bloke in a hoodie. The young man lowers the scarf covering his face.

"Hey, it's the Library Guy! You alright?"

"I'm fine, Michael," Richard says, recognising the boy. He came to a couple of oral history sessions and talked a lot about music.

Richard's legs are still shaky, but relief at the sight of a familiar face whooshes through his body and steadies him.

"I didn't expect to see *you* here . . ." Michael says.

"Why not? Libraries are getting cut, too. In fact, I came with a lot of library guys . . . and girls," said Richard.

"Look," Michael's friend interrupts. "The filth are getting ready to charge again."

"Tightening the noose." Another young guy draws his finger across his throat, smirking at Richard.

"We know a way out. Used it the last time. Come with us," said Michael.

They make their way down the road, away from the first police line. The boys greet friends, and more people join them.

"This your first demo?" Michael asks Richard. "Stick with us, we'll get you out. All that *dancing* is fun, but they won't let you dance all night. They press the crowd in tight. That's why they call it a kettle. Containing the heat . . . hey hey, they're charging now!"

People run again . . .

"Don't panic," Michael urges. "Just go this way . . . they've not blocked it yet."

They nip down an alley. This broadens into a yard enclosed by a wall, much higher than the one Richard stood on earlier. People are already scrambling over it. Richard just looks at the wall. His back is hurting from his fall and every limb aches. And he lost his hat.

"Go on, you go over first," Michael urges. "I'll give you a leg up."

Richard steps into the stirrup of Michael's hand and hoists himself up, teetering on top of the wall, then he plonks down on the other side.

Others drop down beside him, falling like autumn apples. Another gate divides this second courtyard from the street, but escapees yank it open, rattling chains and breaking padlocks. They all pour through into the street on the other side.

Richard has to bend over, trying to catch his breath again. But at least he's safe.

"We're off to Trafalgar Square, see what's happening there," Michael says.

But Richard waves goodbye and hurries to the pub to find his friends. He's had more than enough excitement for the night.

On his way, he finds a 'book' abandoned on the street. This shield had most of its stuffing knocked out – a mixture of styrofoam, newspaper and bubblewrap. He stamps on worm-like pieces of styrofoam scattered in the gutter as he picks it up.

The front cover is still there: *The Dispossessed* by Ursula K LeGuin. He picks up the shield, along with a few scuffed and tattered leaflets.

He'll take these home. He's an archivist after all, and collecting tat is what he does.

The warm air of the pub hits Richard in a welcome blast. His friends cheer and George claps him on the back.

"Did you fight your way out the kettle with *that*? Looks like it's seen some action." Sally points to his shield.

"No . . . I just found it on the street. And I really *climbed* my way out of the kettle. Now, I need a drink . . . anyone else?"

He deposits his shield in their pile of scarves, coats and rucksacks in the corner. Then he peels off his layers and heads for the bar. Out of the kettle, into the pub. It feels so good, even with all his aches and pains making themselves known. But what about Ginny? He tries to ring her while he waits at the bar, but he only hears her voicemail again.

He returns to their table with the drinks.

"Richard, what's on your head?" Sally smiles. "Ha! Did the police do that?"

"No, no, I was pushed and shoved and I fell on my arse and almost got arrested, but I'm OK now . . . outside of an aching tailbone." He decides to leave out the fireworks and the police horse, just in case Sally's another animal lover. "I even got some dancing in," he adds. "So what's wrong with my head?"

Sally touches his face just near his hairline. He finds the place too. Yes, it's that odd spot he touched before. With his gloves off, he definitely can feel that the skin is thicker, with more defined edges. A crispness at the surface.

"It's kind of red," Sally says. "It's got flaky stuff on it, looks painful."

"It doesn't hurt, though. It'll be OK," says Richard. Nothing to worry about now, not when he's out of the kettle and talking to Sally in the pub.

Friends venture out and return with reports. It's kicking off here, there, or somewhere. And people are still trapped in the kettle.

Why doesn't Ginny turn her phone on? Should he go look for her? But he'd be little use if anything truly 'kicked off'. And Sally seems happy to carry on talking.

"Richard, if your job goes, you think you'll take time out and go travelling?"

"No," he says. "I've already done that."

But what *will* he do? As he contemplates that question, his fingers go to the bumpy skin that Sally touched. He explores . . . He pulls at it. That isn't enough. He gets his fingernail just under its edge.

Then *something* comes loose.

Sally's eyes follow the path of this *something* as it settles on top of his Guinness. A thick white *flake* of skin. It almost disappears on the beige head of his pint, but not quite.

Richard excuses himself, goes to the loo and looks in the mirror. Just below his hairline, he sees that his skin is peeling in pale scales. He takes off another piece and looks.

When he was a child, he and his brother Jim used to pull off patches of skin when their sunburns began to peel. The markings on that skin had fascinated Richard. They were like maps that show the height of mountains, the shapes of valleys and plains.

This is a smaller, more compact piece. This pattern is like a blizzard of snowflakes, or the static on a TV screen.

Almost reluctantly, Richard flushes the piece of skin down the toilet.

When the lesion on his temple doesn't clear up, Richard goes to the doctor. She says he has a form of psoriasis, and prescribes a cream. He dabs it on.

While he is drinking his coffee and reading the paper the next morning, Richard reaches over to his temple . . . and tugs off another loose bit. He leaves it on the kitchen table. This piece is bigger than the one in his Guinness. It shows the tight whorls of a hill, a wider one like a valley.

When he was a kid, he stored the strips of sunburnt skin in a drawer in his bedside table. He wants to save this fragment too. It is too *interesting* to throw away. But where should he keep it? He wanders about the kitchen and living room, ending up in front of the bookcase. His gaze settles on a stone box on the top shelf. It's made of smooth grey stone, inlaid with patterns in turquoise, blue and pink and mother-of-pearl, representing flowers, butterflies and birds.

Blanca bought that box for him in a street market. There were many of them on the market tables, in different shapes and sizes.

He used to keep his dope and tobacco and pipes in the box, back when he indulged. It's empty now.

He's always been fond of this box and gives it pride of place on top of that bookshelf. Now he knows what to do with it.

He places the skin inside and closes the box with a click.

Richard and his brother had fussed over similar pieces of skin. They usually bragged about their burns after a visit to the seaside or a hike in the sun.

"Ouch, I can't lie down . . . That's nothing, I got blisters the size of eggs."

This was before people worried much about UVA and UVB, and there seemed to be many more sunny days in the year.

The real fun came when the burns began to peel. They competed to see who could take off the biggest piece. You picked at the corner of a peel, then slowly lifted the skin up, careful not to tear it. When he removed a substantial piece he'd hold it up to the light. So fine and thin, with whirls and swirls and pits where hairs had been.

"Of course we want to keep the local history archive," a councillor says in a bright and grating voice.

While pretending to listen, Richard reaches for that spot at his temple. The prescribed cream has only allowed the excess skin layers to grow thicker and more pliable. It is well worth the wait. He takes something off, about the size of his fingertip.

"We want to turn the library over to the community. We're forward-looking," insists the councillor.

Richard lets the skin drop to the table top, then places his notebook over it. No one has noticed, he's sure. Certainly none of this crowd, people who don't know the tip of their nose from their butthole. *Forward-looking*. Ugh. Time to wade in.

"The community already has the library," Richard speaks up, giving his view as the shop steward. He only became shop steward because no one else wanted to do it. No wonder, if the post involves attending meetings like this.

"You're talking in double-speak," he adds. "Double-speak! It's bad enough you're making these cuts, but do you have to abuse the English language while you hack away?"

"Is that a policy question?" one councillor asks, while the others remain stony-faced.

"Of *course* it's a policy question. Giving the library to the 'community', are you?" His voice rises. "Admit it, you're really selling it to some scabby bunch of profiteers. And how does 'the community' use a local history archive if it's moved to another city and the staff made redundant? The 'community' comes in droves to the archive now. Sometimes you can't find a seat because it's so busy."

Richard's heart pounds as if he's been running from the police again. But he's only talking to the 'Scrutiny Committee'. They're as bad as the police. Even worse. He'd love to throw a firecracker or something more lethal among this lot. How they'd squeal!

This meeting is such a far cry from his day on the streets. If he closes his eyes, he still sees the lace of black branches against a frozen sky . . . bands of blue and green from the tall banners splash across the darkness of his lids. He hears the sound systems and smells the acrid scent of smoke bombs.

If he closes his eyes again, he'll be dancing again with Blanca before she turns into a friendly stranger slapping his palm.

He sits back, sweating in the overheated room, the past filling his thoughts. The demonstration has sent memories replaying in loops, a counterpoint to his beleaguered job and evenings in stuffy council chambers.

What would Ginny say about this? She'd tell him to find Blanca.

As soon as he gets home he turns on his computer.

He looks under the two surnames Blanca uses; her professional name and her family name. He scrolls down the entries on Google, through search results on Facebook. They're both very common names. But if he keeps at it, he'll find her. Yes, dammit, he'll find her.

With a pop, the chat messenger appears. Ginny . . . asking how he fared on the demo. In the days since, they've only succeeded in talking to each others' voicemail.

"I was kettled too, I tried to find you . . ."

"My phone ran out of power . . ."

"I got out of the kettle and found the rest of the library workers in the pub."

"BASTARDS. We were stuck until the bitter end, frogmarched and squished on the bridge."

Richard pauses, then types: *"So we're bastards. And the bastards in the pub raised a glass to our friends in the kettle. I'll owe you one when we meet."*

"I'll take you up on that. So when will you visit us in Brighton?"

Richard stops to think, twisting a lock of hair. He finds a new layer of skin to peel, then he types: *"As soon as I can!"*

Meanwhile, Richard continues to scroll down the list of people who have the same names as Blanca.

As Ginny logs off, Richard lays a piece of skin on some paper.

When he drops it into the box later, it falls with a little sound. This makes him feel more substantial. The skin is *there*, while everything else is likely to evaporate into air.

He rubs the spot. Still some loose skin left. He keeps going over the patch until it's picked clean.

Before he goes to bed he looks in the mirror. The area on his temple is red, almost bleeding.

His brother once peeled a patch from his leg before it was ready. It left a raw and red area the shape of a fist. When the sun hit the exposed skin again, it erupted in new blisters. *Blisters on my blisters.* Jim was proud of this, even when the blisters began to ooze.

Blisters on my blisters. Richard looks at the damage again in the morning. He vows not to pick at the skin and give the cream more time to work.

But the longer he leaves it, the less he can resist in the end. The thick old skin just has to come off, and something else needs to be freed and revealed.

And so he drops more pieces of skin into his beautiful box.

Richard knows that many will regard his skin-peeling as a dirty and repellent little habit, like nose-picking. But they've not seen these pieces in the box, among the inlays. These are such an essential part of the outer body. They have patterns in them. How can they be ugly?

"Hey Library Guy!"

Michael, the boy who gave Richard a leg-up out of the kettle, strolls into the reference room along with a friend.

"Hey, Kettle Kids," Richard replies. They both grimace at being addressed as 'kids', but after a long look at each other plus a mutual shrug they let it go.

"Look at this . . ." Michael opens a tabloid newspaper. "It's off the Met website."

Rows of photos, alleged miscreants from the demonstration. Richard feels a punch of panic at the sight of one fellow pushing a barrier against the police line.

"Don't worry, *we're* not in it. I checked. But they show some fit girls getting stuck in. Fancy any of them?"

Richard tries to laugh. "Too young for me!"

Is Michael taking the piss? Better change the subject. "But you haven't come here to find a girlfriend for me, have you?"

"No, it's about something else, more oral history," says Michael. "A bunch of us were talking about what we're able to do when we have our educational allowance and what would happen if goes. So maybe I can interview people at my college about it. If the EMA's cut, most us won't be at college in the first place. We wouldn't be able to think about university or *anything*."

Richard wants to say that university might not be all it's cracked up to be. With his job up the spout, he is just as likely to end up with some twit at the job centre telling him to work for free at Tesco's.

Then Michael leans forward and whispers in Richard's ear. "Hey, you should've come with us. It was kicking off big time."

"I would've held you back. You saw how bad I was getting over that wall."

"But you made it! It just takes practice."

Richard chuckles. "Speaking of practice, we can have a go at recording something from you two. How about next week? I'll get the diary out."

"We could have photos," Michael adds. "My sister likes to take pictures."

"Good idea." Richard is already starting to imagine how this project might shape up.

But management would be likely to give a thumbs down on anything new.

Richard touches the patch at his temple with one hand as he leafs through diary pages with the other. They should be able to make a few recordings before the axe falls.

"What's that on your head?" Michael asks.

"Nothing," says Richard. He snatches his hand away. "It's nothing."

If people were noticing that raw patch of skin, he should be careful. Then he has another thought: would the police see it on a video and identify him with it?

Would they add him to their photo gallery?

Then he finds more peeling skin on his inner arm. The condition is spreading. What if it takes over his body? He imagines what he'll look like, covered with the stuff. It makes his stomach lurch. But when he examines this lesion, he sees its possibilities.

He can peel bigger pieces from it and no one will see it under his long sleeves.

He puts the new skin in the box. The inlay on the lid reflects light on the skin inside it, reminding him how those stone boxes stay cool to the touch even in the hot sun. He thinks about Blanca's gift to him, and the paints he bought for her just before he left.

Back then, Blanca waitressed at a seaside café. Richard taught English to young Spaniards. It was a life. Once they had enough for rent, food and Blanca's art supplies, they relaxed.

Richard spent a lot of time reading books on the beach and in cafes. He loved books so much, he thought he'd like to do work that involved them. He said this to Blanca, who agreed it was a good idea. She probably thought he wanted to be a writer, like many of the young British blokes hanging out in Spain.

Soon the English teaching began to pay less. The work was hard to find as more footloose and usually broke Brits arrived. When Richard started in the trade, he had grand ideas of teaching eager young people about English literature while he improved his Spanish. But his clients were often businessmen, and he refused to teach words like 'incentivize'.

As Blanca grew more engaged with her art, Richard wished he had a similar vocation. He watched Blanca explore new colours, while he just taught the same lessons. He wanted to do something that would enthral him, while benefiting or at least entertaining others.

He thought about what he could do with his degree in history and geography. And he imagined books, rows and rows of them. He wanted to spread their magic, and came to the conclusion he couldn't do that in Spain. It was time to go home.

When he made up his mind, Richard took Blanca out for dinner. They went for a walk on the beach afterwards and he told her about his plans.

"I have to stay here. But if you need to leave . . . I want you to be happy."

Happy, Richard wonders. Is this what we both had in mind?

Then he peels more skin from his temple, then from his arm.

When another patch comes up on his leg he goes to the doctor again. She speaks more about stress, and prescribes a holiday along with another cream.

Perhaps there is even more *stress* when he has to inform his assistant of his redundancy. *"George, this doesn't come from me. I've tried to stop it and I'll continue to campaign for your reinstatement . . ."*

"It's alright, Richard. You're only the messenger and I won't shoot you." George says, more than a few times. But is that a curl of contempt to his lip, and disgust in his eyes?

When Richard holds up a bigger piece of skin in the light, he thinks more about those criss-crossings of his surface geography, about the lines his life has taken, bringing him to this point. Perhaps the 'lifeline' runs all along a person's body, a tangle of many lines, a spaghetti junction of possibilities . . . and traps and errors.

Meanwhile, he keeps checking the police website to make sure his photo doesn't crop up in the rogues' gallery. He does recognise that young woman in the striped top, the one he mistook for Blanca. *Stay free*, he thinks.

And you stay free too, Blanca, wherever you are. Live well.

He imagines Blanca standing firm in a city square, holding her hand out to him all the way from Spain. And in her hand she offers him a piece of himself, the part he left behind.

Go on a holiday, the doctor suggested. So Richard decides to visit Ginny and her partner Bron at last.

As the train leaves London he begins to relax, looking forward to a long weekend with his friends. He gazes out the window, thinking fond thoughts. Then he realises that he left something behind. The box. It's still at home. Where will he put his pieces?

When he catches the bus from the train station, he is still thinking about that box. As he walks up the hill to Ginny's house, he continues to fret.

Though his friends live a short bus ride from the centre of Brighton, their row of houses belong to the countryside. He gazes at the rolling hills and breathes in air from the sea. Maybe that sea breeze will do his skin good.

Bron opens the door. Richard blinks. Her hair is longer, dyed bright red. But her bus-driver's jacket rings the bell of recognition.

"You're not looking good, Richard," says Bron.

This really isn't what he needs to hear, but he forgives her when she settles him in the kitchen with a mug of coffee.

Ginny comes into the kitchen and gives him a big hug. Ginny still seems the same, wiry and intense. But her black hair is now the same red as Bron's.

Bron excuses herself, saying she needs to make some phone calls. Once Bron leaves, Richard is surprised to find himself feeling shy and tongue-tied. If he's like this after a mere year, what will it be like to meet up with Blanca again after two decades?

He asks Ginny about work, just to begin with. So she frets about her health authority's plans to tender its services to a firm known for mobile phones and pop music. "Imagine the muzak we'll have to sit through when we ring up the call centre!" They both laugh, though they know it's no joke.

It's enough to put Richard at ease. "It's great to see you. Sorry I've been crap about keeping in touch."

"No problem, I've been crap too. It's a shame we didn't hook up at the demo."

"Yeah, we could've had a dance like old times. And all that raving made me think of Blanca. I even thought I saw her."

"Think she's in London?"

"No, I just got in a state thinking I saw her because of this woman's t-shirt. I don't know where she is. I need to find her."

"Go for it. I'm glad I finally contacted my ex in the States. We talk on Skype. Maybe she'll visit, since I can't go back there."

"It's different for you. I *chose* to leave Blanca. She might not want anything to do with me. But you were *forced* to leave your girlfriend when Uncle Sam gave you the boot."

"So? I could've taken steps to make my immigration status more regular. But I kept putting it off, and then . . . We all make mistakes."

Ginny is frowning, her eyes focused just above Richard's. "What's that on your temple? Near the hairline?"

"Just a bit of psoriasis," Richard explains. "Stress, the doctor said."

"It looks awful. Have you been scratching it?"

"No, if you really want to know . . ." He pauses. "I've been peeling it. A lot."

Ginny is looking at him as if she expects him to say more.

"And I've been keeping the pieces in a box. A very nice inlay box."

Ginny shrugs. "At least you don't eat the pieces. That's very common."

"Of course I don't," Richard says. "But the question is . . . what do I do before it gets worse? I'm even paranoid that the police can use it to identify me. I lost my hat in the kettle . . ."

"Identify you? Why, what did you get up to? *Wait* . . . I *don't* want to know, loose talk and all that, but good on you. As for your skin . . . worrying won't help."

Ginny adjusts her glasses and assumes an erect posture. She clears her throat. "Your problem is 'dermatillomania', and like all these things, there's a spectrum. On one end, you get self-harming behaviour. But on the other, many people bite their nails, pick scabs or peel their sunburns and it does no harm."

Ginny starts to sound so professional that Richard has to laugh.

"Sorry," she says. "I suppose I slipped into work mode. But your doctor's right that worry and stress over redundancy has triggered your skin problem. But at least you're not damaging yourself. If it still bothers you, see a counsellor."

She gives him a quick smile. "Maybe what you really need is to get out and meet more girls. When was the last time you went out with someone properly?" She nudges him.

Bron returns to the kitchen just in time for this comment. She laughs and slaps him on the back. "Yeah, you need to get out more."

"I've been too busy with work," he sighs. "None of my affairs have lasted. Still, I've stayed on good terms with *most* exes, especially the present company."

It's his turn to nudge Ginny. Bron watches them with a benign smile, which has always impressed Richard. He wouldn't have liked it if Blanca's old boyfriends had visited regularly.

"And it's not only work," Richard adds. "I'm always at meetings. Union stuff, negotiations . . . Mind you, I've met new people while fighting cuts in the library service."

"Oh yes, nothing like activism to spice up your love life," says Ginny. "And why not? No reason why changing the world should be all doom and gloom and self-sacrifice."

"Tell me about it!" Richard laughs. "But I think I blew my chances. After the demo, we went to the pub and I was chatting with this new librarian I fancied. She asked about my face, joked about my battle wound. And once she mentioned it I kept wanting to . . . dunno, kind of check it out. Then the pickings fell into my Guinness."

"Oh no . . ."

"Oh yes. Needless to say she wasn't impressed."

"Well, since your habit *is* cramping your style . . . And what do you think she'd say if she found those pieces of skin in that pretty little box?"

"Better in a box than my Guinness."

"You *both* are missing the point," says Bron. "It's not an issue of what she thinks of you, or the effects on your beer. No! The problem's much deeper than that. If you're putting those *bits* in a box, maybe you're putting *feelings* in a box."

Richard remembers that Bron completed a basic counselling course in her pre-bus driving days.

She continues. "When you go home you should open the box and dispose of the skin in a . . . excuse the expression, a ritual."

"Like, bury them and do a dance?"

"Hah! I knew you'd take the piss. Seriously though, open that box and face your fears. Then get rid of them!"

"There you go again, Bron." Ginny gets up from her chair. "I think Richard needs dinner and a few drinks more than a ritual." She opens the fridge to survey the ingredients.

Richard offers to help chop.

When Richard returns home, he's feeling better. He's even stopped missing his box, though he did drop a few flakes in the ocean when they took a walk along the beach.

But as soon as he gets in the house he has to sit down and inspect a new patch on his arm. He finds the edge, and lifts the skin up. Slow, slow, gentle.

He holds the piece up to the light and gazes at its patterns.

Cross-hatching, shadings and pits. Is there a touch of pink to its transparency as if it still lives?

He takes the box from the bookcase. The stone is usually quite cool. Now, the surface feels just a little warm in his hands. This puzzles him.

He sets the box down on the kitchen table and opens it. He glimpses *movement* within the box, along with a slick, barely audible sound. He shuts the box before he's sure of what he sees. Maybe he doesn't *want* to see it.

No, he *has* to look. Surely those aren't maggots.

He opens the box again . . .

The pieces of skin have grown. They move and twitch, blind yet searching. He puts his finger out and one piece curls around it. It is thick and waxy, and damp. He flings it back into the box.

The skin he has just removed, left on the table, is still delicate and paper-dry. Has it moved too? He drops it into the box. Then he slams the box shut and takes it to the basement. He places anything at hand on top of it . . . an oversized art book, an old computer, and finally that battered shield with *The Dispossessed* scrawled across the front.

In the following week, he considers throwing the box in the river or a rubbish bin.

But these are pieces of himself and he can't bring himself to destroy them.

When he was a kid he read Poe's *Telltale Heart*. The murdered guy's heart kept beating and pounding, loud enough to be heard, shaking the house.

But this is only skin. Skin that belongs to him, and he's very much alive.

Those pieces do create a sound, though. They send a stirring throughout the house, a shifting in the air that spreads from the basement. Those things *sing*, with a song no mouth could make.

Fortunately, his work at the library keeps him well beyond that song's range during the day. The project with the Kettle Kids is coming along.

And Richard stays out with meetings every night. His union, the fight against redundancies. He has to concentrate on that. And stop peeling and picking.

Sometimes he touches a lesion, but only a touch. Maybe the sight of that crawling, searching skin has cured his dirty habit more than counselling ever could.

And he begins to dream about opening his box.

In the first dream, the pieces begin to stir. They've grown wings and lift out of the box like horseflies clustered in the residue of a sweet drink. They fly at him, sticky with sugar. They buzz like drills and hit him in the face.

Then a *good* dream surprises him.

The bits of skin turn to fragments of glass, reminding him of the beaded curtains that tinted the light in the room he shared with Blanca. These glass pieces erupt in more hues than a Dulux paint display. He fills his hands with them and flings them upwards. They bathe him in their colours. He looks up to the cool touch of turquoise and green on his face.

After that vision of colour and light, Richard lets his guard down in his next dream.

He flings open the lid. Fleshy moths fly out of the box and fill the air. One plump insect flies straight into his face, filling his mouth and nose with dust smelling like the bottom of a birdcage.

He wakes with his heart pounding. He can't get back to sleep. He finally gets out of bed and makes himself coffee. It's already morning. He has a meeting first thing at work. He touches the back of his neck, and peels some skin.

Instead of putting it in the box, he opens the window and lets the piece fall. A breeze lifts it for a moment, then it dissolves. If it hits the ground, he certainly doesn't hear it.

But he does hear the 'singing' with no words, drifting up from the basement.

Did he imagine what he saw in that box? Does he really hear that sibilant whispering through the house, infiltrating his thoughts and dreams? Bron urged him to 'face his fears'. So maybe he should. Then he'll throw the box out.

When he brings the box up from the basement, he puts a domed cake tin next to it. If something foul comes out, he'll just clap that over. The tin was a present from Ginny. She'll be glad he's finally using it.

He puts on the TV, an everyday sound to soothe his nerves.

He just has to keep one hand on that cake tin and lift the lid off the box with the other.

It's empty.

Empty. Richard slumps, the tension leaving him.

All that fuss over an empty box, eh?

Then he sees something scrunched in the corner. A tight, contracted bundle like a ball of fine yarn. It has a clear colour, with tints of pink and purple, the delicacy of an orchid flower. Though it is quite pretty, he hesitates to touch it.

But when he does, the sensation is silken and smooth.

Feeling bolder, he lifts a strand from the ball. It comes away like a piece of string. He pulls at it more, until he holds a shining skein at arm's length. He smiles. This is not horrible at all, but strange and beautiful like the coloured glass that came out of the box in his good dream.

Curiosity blooms in his mind, spreading slow petals. He holds a mystery in his hand, and he must get to the centre of it. He pulls and pulls, letting the filaments float, swirl and settle around him. When the skein of skin touches him, it is gentle.

But the thread of matter only seeks itself, pulling together, adhering. Then it floats apart again, weaving and coalescing in a dance.

First Richard sees a hint of an arm, a leg, a torso. Then the threads swirl into formlessness again, only to define something more. A figure. A man.

This figure, this man, is naked. The TV shines a light through its chest. A photo of Richard with his hill-walking friends flickers in the figure's eyes; its mouth contains the light switch.

Yet there's density to the space within the figure. Its eyes hold the same tint as Richard's, but semi-transparent. The figure stumbles, as if trying to get its balance. It sees Richard and recoils. And it stumbles again, as if in fright.

Richard's heart is also beating fast. He feels a cold finger down his back, the jab of the unknown. But this isn't the crawling flesh he dreaded so much. Instead, gazing on this figure is like looking into an incredibly old and warped mirror.

What is this?

Fascination fights with fear. His counterpart seems terrified too.

Terrified . . . of *me*?

Richard puts his hand on the box, seeking its familiar surface. The figure sees where Richard's hand rests.

"That's Blanca's box!"

Did the figure speak? Words register in Richard's mind, carried in a voice like the creaking of a branch, the run of a river, the mellow tones of a French horn.

"Blanca?" Richard repeats the name. "You know Blanca, then?"

The figure that looks like Richard sighs. The sound is so sad, so yearning. As if . . .

Why can't he find Blanca on Facebook, or anywhere?

Where is she?

"Look . . ." Richard begins. How should he start? "Look . . . What do I call you?"

"I have the same name as you. You must know that."

No, I bloody don't.

Something in the tone annoys him. Smug, is it?

"But my Spanish friends call me Ricardo," the figure adds. "You can too, if you want."

"Ricardo . . . sure. So look, sit down, relax. Where do you come from? Do you remember how you got here?"

"Only fragments. Shimmering, like mother-of-pearl . . . a rose-blush and glimmer of green. Yes, it was the box. This box. When I found it again, I was thinking of Blanca. It's been five years. When I closed that box five years ago, it was in the hospital where I saw her for the last time."

The last time?

"You alright, Richard?" Ricardo extends a hand toward Richard, then puts it on the table. Almost, but not quite touching his.

Ricardo's hand shows the pits of pores, light hairs . . . so much like the skin Richard has stashed in the box.

But other parts of Ricardo seem fainter. His face flickers, coming into the focus and then receding.

Ricardo touches the box on the table. "Blanca gave this to me. But we shared it. I kept my dope there, and she put her bits and pieces and treasures in it . . ." He strokes the inlay on the cover. "What did *you* put in this?"

"I also kept my dope in there, years ago," says Richard. "Much later . . . several weeks ago. I put pieces of skin in there. It came off this patch of psoriasis, or whatever it is." Richard rolls up his sleeve and points to the lesion on his arm.

Ricardo reaches forward to touch the spot. Richard first wants to pull away, but he makes himself stay put. *Face your fears.*

Ricardo's fingertip feels like a breeze or a faint kiss. Richard shivers, not in an entirely bad way. The sensation reminds him of . . . reeds, sun shining off water? Still water, not the sea. He has an urge to close his eyes, as if it will help him see what he needs to see. Then Ricardo withdraws his finger.

"Does that look strange?" Richard asks. "Did *you* have trouble with your skin?"

"Not really, but I kept my sunburn peelings when I was a kid."

"So did I. Except my skin problem is now caused by stress, not sunshine. They've been cutting my department at work, you see . . . With each cut, it feels like a bit of myself is about to go missing."

Ricardo winces. "I did something like that when Blanca was ill," said Ricardo. "I took her things out of the box so she could see them on the table near her bed. I was so worried about her, I started pulling some of my hair out . . . and put that in the box."

The last time. That could mean anything.

"If Blanca was ill . . ." said Richard. "Is she OK now?"

The last time Richard saw Blanca, she was fine. They were saying goodbye at the airport.

"OK?" Ricardo is surprised at this question. "Don't you know?"

Know what?

"Blanca died five years ago. She had cancer."

Though Richard has had a sense of something deeply wrong, hearing this still knocks the wind out of him. He can't breathe. He thinks he will die too. Then air fills his lungs again in a rush.

Blanca is dead?

Don't you know, this guy asks.

"How the hell would I know?" Richard bursts out. "You should've told me!"

"Told you? And who the fuck are *you* anyway?"

Argumentative bastard. But the same could be said about himself, Richard is thinking. That's why he became shop steward. Yet he also knows how to negotiate.

"And *you* . . ." Ricardo accuses. "You left Blanca, didn't you? How could you?"

"It's not that simple," explains Richard. "There wasn't enough teaching work. I had to leave, and Blanca didn't want to come with me. I needed to do something more with myself. We kept in touch for a while, but then she stopped writing."

"So you wanted to do *what* with yourself? I managed. I found other work . . . labouring, cleaning, whatever. Sure, things were hard . . . especially since Blanca was made redundant, then rehired as a casual with no sick pay . . . But you know, we got by."

Ricardo looks like he's about to say more. But instead he just leans his head against his hands, eyes closed. Richard wonders if he's crying. He reaches over to touch Ricardo on the shoulder, then stops. "I'm so sorry," he finally mutters.

Ricardo nods. "I'm sorry too. You were close to her and you've lost her . . . *twice.*"

"I'm . . . I'm stunned. But it must've been very hard for you."

"Yes, it was . . . I lost a part of myself, as you put it. But then, I'm still here."

Barely. Richard is seeing much more through Ricardo's body. The TV . . . footage from the 'student riots', playing within Ricardo's outlines. There's that poor bloke with the police barrier again; a crate flies at a departing limo. Richard feels that familiar leap of his heart, beating with the day's exhilaration and its fear. But Ricardo is oblivious.

So *there's* a difference between them. Richard gets up to turn off the TV.

"Blanca would've been fascinated by you," says Ricardo at last. "I'm sure she'd tell us to stop bickering, or to sit still so she could paint us. And she'd want to know what you're doing. So do I. Tell me more about your job. I mean, I've had jobs and I've lost them. And I've been skint. But you're not just worried about money, are you? This involves who you are. That's still no reason to pick yourself apart over it."

So Richard talks about his archive. "It's about much more than books and paper," he tells Ricardo. "A lot of people come to our events, people who never thought of using an archive or library before."

He describes the pleasure of nurturing a project and seeing it change peoples' lives for the better. "My friend Ginny, she's a nurse, did a study on libraries and community health. Just having a warm safe place to read or think makes a big difference to many people."

Ricardo smiles when Richard tells him how he met the Kettle Kids and the work he started with them.

"But now *you* have to tell me something," Richard adds. "Tell me about Blanca. How was her art going? Just before I left, she'd been talking about doing more abstract stuff."

Ricardo describes those paintings, full of greens and blues and luminous grey mists. "She laid on layers of oil paint with a palette knife, stirred and smoothed them like plaster. She was mad for green and blue, all shades of it. With touches of lavender and grey."

Richard recalls those colours, settling over him in the dream. He remembers tall banners banded and splashed with greens, blues, pearl-grey and lavender mist.

Now he knows why those banners at the demo had provoked such feelings. They displayed the same colours Blanca splashed on canvasses he has never seen, but recognised.

"She loved her paintings," Ricardo says. "She sold a few, but in the end she hated to be parted from them. Instead of trying to live from selling her work, she trained to teach art. So I still have some paintings." Ricardo's gaze turns inward. A smile plays on his lips as memories surface.

A pang of envy and regret stabs Richard. *We would've stayed together if I hadn't left to do my course. We would've been happy after all . . . until Blanca died.*

But he can't be jealous of *himself*. And Ricardo is right to say that Blanca wouldn't have wanted them to quarrel.

"I wish I could've seen those paintings," says Richard. He moves the box so the inlays catch the light. "Blanca's favourite colours make me think of this box. Is there *something* about it? Or could it be the way we put pieces of ourselves into it . . . my skin, your hair?"

"Maybe. The box is a link, but what kind? Maybe we have other versions of ourselves hidden in our DNA . . . Or perhaps I *am* a ghost." Ricardo speaks slowly. "Maybe we don't have to be dead to haunt someone."

He is staring at the mirror behind the TV. "I don't see much of myself there." Ricardo looks at his hands, his arms, his legs. "And I think there's less than before."

"Maybe it's just the light," Richard suggests. But his voice lacks conviction.

He doesn't want Ricardo to disappear. They still have more to talk about. He's beginning to *like* Ricardo.

"If I put more skin into that box, maybe it'll make you more solid," Richard suggests. He rolls up his sleeve, and finds the patch. Since he has resisted peeling for a while, it is good and thick. "I know this is far-fetched and desperate, but what can we do?"

Ricardo nods. *What can we do?*

Richard's fingers are trembling as he peels the skin off. Then he places it in the box and closes the lid, leaving it on the table between them.

Ricardo puts his hands on the box, and Richard does the same. This box has brought them together, so it feels like the right thing to do.

Richard clasps Ricardo's hand. It's like bathing his hand in silk instead of water. The contact flicks on images in Richard's mind. They are sharp, as if lit by strip-lighting. They have the quality of a clear winter morning, though some show summer.

Blanca in hospital. Then a scene on a beach, which Richard remembers. It's the day he told Blanca he wanted to return to England for his library course.

But in *this* scene, Ricardo's scene, he doesn't talk about courses.

Richard leans closer and puts his arm across Ricardo's shoulders, resting against the chair. He sees a lake in south-eastern Europe that Ricardo and Blanca visited during a heavy damp summer. Dragonflies rise from the lake and one rests on Blanca's hand. Its wings hold tints of the water and the sky. They are as fragile as that piece of skin Richard had dropped out the window, as transparent as Ricardo himself.

Will Ricardo dissolve on the wind, or drift apart in the still air of this room? Perhaps he'll go back to Spain where the rest of him lives . . . along with Blanca's paintings.

The paintings. "Ricardo, you said you kept *some* of Blanca's work. Where's the rest?" Richard speaks as if the air expelled with his words could scatter his counterpart in pieces again.

"After Blanca died, I had to move to a smaller place, so I didn't have room for all the paintings. But I gave one to a museum, and others to the local library."

He gave Blanca's paintings to a library. Richard smiles at that, and can't stop.

Ricardo brightens as if the same idea has occurred to him. "So we have something in common."

Richard nods a passionate *yes*, for their lines of departure have finally met in a circle.

But he also hears Ricardo's voice grow faint. Richard draws him closer. A vapour like breath mingles between them, or it could be part of Ricardo himself.

He sees Blanca in the hospital again, sees her through Ricardo's eyes as he stays with her to the end.

He has to do the same for Ricardo. Stay with him as he leaves. Richard tries to tighten his grip on Ricardo. But the substance of Ricardo only slips through his hands; a puff of air, the threads of silk unravelling.

And then Richard is alone with the box.

Finally, Richard opens it. It is empty except for a ripped dragonfly wing. Or it could be a piece of his skin, a piece of himself.

Keep Them Rollin'

"You are making history," they told us at our 'Motivating the Motivators' course. "You're part of the great reformation of the British welfare system!"

But my cubicle in the open-plan office doesn't look like a history-making room. No maps with pins and flags adorn my partition, only a generic landscape painting of cliffs and waves and appropriately humble fisherfolk. It's crooked for some reason, so I put it straight just as my first 'customer' arrives.

Middle-aged lady, faded 1990s rock-chick look. Kitted out like she's off to a gig rather than an interview. Hoodie, t-shirt with an unreadable name on it. Denim skirt, black leggings, trainers. About my age and my height, but bulkier, with a battered cardboard folder under her arm. She sits down before I invite her, and places her folder on her lap.

Presentation skills need work. I make a mental note as I smile at her. "You must be Wendy Smith. I'll just get your file up on the computer."

The screen comes to life, and the desktop icons dance in front of me. I rub my eyes. I'm having trouble finding Wendy Smith's file. Could I really be hung over from last night? It was just a few drinks with Miriam from IT.

No, it's the damn system playing up again. No surprise after five years of constant overhauls, write-offs and restarts from scratch.

Whole thing's so cocked up they've just brought in another new bunch of experts, Miriam says. It's all about 'quantum computing' now.

So it's a big thing, this quantum computing. Government put millions into it. "All theoretical," Miriam said last night. She does like to bend my ear, and she likes a drink too. Must be all the stress they get in IT.

"But they're getting practical fast around here. A universal computer system for Universal Credit! Or shall we say *multiversal*, Gwen?" She downed the last of her drink with a chuckle.

I didn't quite see the humour. "Call it what you want, it sounds like gobbledygook to me." Then I went to the bar for more G&Ts.

Miriam carried on talking shop, but after a few drinks it was sounding more and more like a shop located on another planet.

At last, there's the profile for Wendy Smith, who shares my run-of-the-mill surname. Blimey. Where did she get that haircut, in a poodle parlour? I also notice the date of birth. Same as mine. Just goes to show what a crock astrology is.

I take my time before I speak. Silence makes people squirm, ready to spill.

"So Wendy, we need to talk about your Claimant Commitment, which will set out what you must do in return for our help. We have your tax records, but we need to know more since you've not been on the Job Centre system before."

"Maybe it's because I already have a job. Two of them."

Wendy speaks with a smile, so 'firm but polite'. Bet she'll talk about 'rights' next.

Expect that from working claimants, we were told at training. So now it's time to initiate a 'challenging conversation'.

I turn up my own smile. "Now we have a new system, so just having a job is not enough. We ask you to try to progress in your work and increase your earnings, and provide proof of that. To get started, why don't you tell me more about what you do?"

She looks at me like I'm an insect that's just buzzed in, and grips that thick folder on her lap as if she'd love to swat me with it.

"I'm a freelance editor and writer," she finally says.

"That must be *lovely!* But you're still not earning enough to support yourself without claiming in-work benefits. And that's what we have to tackle."

She nods. "OK, let's do that. I was fine on my income ten, even five years ago. But my rent has doubled since then. And the publishers have cut their rates."

I beam her my 'tough but sympathetic' look. This is accomplished by a steady stare, keeping eye contact but giving the lips a faint upward twitch.

"But Wendy, we have to move on. It's up to *you* to make the changes you want, and not blame anyone or anything else for shortcomings."

A burst of laughter greets that motivating morsel. "Oh yeah, and I bet 'there's no such thing as society,' like your hero Margaret Thatcher said."

"That's quite an assumption . . ." I begin. Then I see she's looking at the painting behind me.

"Those cows look like they were made by a cookie-cutter," she says. "No perspective. Where'd you get that thing?"

Cows? I look over my shoulder. The sea and the cliffs have been replaced by rolling hills and . . . badly painted cows, splotched with greasy-looking patches of purple. That picture has *changed*. Who? When? My mind refuses to accept it; my stomach lurches.

But I'm a professional and I will continue this interview.

I turn away from the painting. "You weren't invited here to comment on cows. We need to talk about your responsibilities as a claimant, and your work."

"So I have some queries, all about my work!" She takes a sheaf of papers from her folder. "These are documents produced by your office. *Universal Credit at Work, Guidance for Work Coaches* . . . available from a Freedom of Information request."

She displays a page peppered with words circled in red. "'Drive' must be used fifteen times here. *Drive earnings progression, drive the attitudes of low-earning claimants, driving a step-change in behaviours* . . . Drive, drive, drive. Are you talking about cattle or sheep? Keep those dogies rollin', rollin rollin rollin . . ."

Is she singing 'Rawhide'? Indie bands did ironic covers of that song many years ago, tending to pronounce *dogies* as *doggies*. At the time, I didn't do much work myself and spent too much time at festivals. I can hear that music now, coming from the main stage while I was waiting in a queue to use the satellite phone . . . A festival in Cornwall where everyone was off their faces and the portaloos overflowed with shit.

Wendy points at another red-circled word. "Incentivize? Spelt with 'z', no less." She visibly shudders. "Do you know what one of my editors said? Any writer using 'incentivize' should be taken out and shot." She lifts her hand in a 'stop' gesture. "Not that I'm advocating *that*. But really . . . How can an organisation that produces such bad writing and churns out such swill be entitled to tell me how to do my job? Incentivise this, incentivise that! Sounds like a bloody Dalek. *Incentivise! Incentivise!*"

Though she hasn't raised her voice, people are looking at us. Dalek-speak carries. Daleks! But last night Miriam was also talking rubbish straight out of *Doctor Who* as she rambled on about quantum computing. Qubits in many places at the same time, and people who might do that too. Parallel universes.

"*Incentivise!*" There she goes again.

Stay professional. Just remember I'm in control. Others have power over me – like that tight-arsed area manager – but I still decide what happens *here*.

I take a breath and modulate my tones to express patience and forbearance. "If you keep creating a disturbance, I'll have to ask you to leave."

The computer emits a clickety-click. I'm still afraid to look at that painting.

"But I'm being perfectly reasonable," Wendy protests. "And I have nothing against you personally. I know you have such a *tough* job." Concern knits her brows, and her face flushes with faux sympathy. Same face I put on as I pretend to 'help' while I'm really shoehorning some loser onto a scheme with a multimillion pound contract.

In fact, there are seconds when Wendy could be me . . . wearing a fright-wig. I pat my short hair for reassurance.

"You know, I almost went to work at the Job Centre myself." she says. "When I applied, I thought I'd go 'undercover' and help people get their money. But I'd already arranged to go to a festival, so I planned to ring my flatmates to find out about interviews. When I was queuing at the phone stall a friend walked by and said hey, come see a band. I thought, sod this. And when I got home a week later I found a letter saying I had an interview, but I'd missed it."

"So you missed a job interview?" I make a note.

"Yeah? So that was in 1989," she laughs. "Even if your sanctioning schtick does go retroactive, it couldn't extend that far back."

The queasy feeling returns as I remember. I'm waiting among the stalls selling overpriced veggie burgers and hippie tat. I'm anxious to make my phone call. If I have an interview I'll leave. I won't stay for the rest of the festival or join friends on a trip to St Just.

"Was . . . Was the festival in Cornwall?" My voice sounds distant in my ears. "Was there a band on the main stage playing 'Rawhide'?"

"Yes! Were you there? It was *mental*, that festival! And the loos were disgusting. But I had a good time in the end . . ."

Rollin' rollin' rollin', keep 'em rollin' rollin'. No, I told my friends. I've been waiting too long to give up on my phone call.

The receptionist comes by my partition. "Gwen! Your next customer is here."

Snap out of it, snap snap snap!

I'm tempted to wave Wendy on her way after ticking the right boxes. Why argue, when I can fulfil goals with more tractable and less mouthy individuals?

And she reminds me of times I've forgotten – or tried to forget. Moments that didn't involve shit or squalor. Finding a stage far into the woods, bands playing on it, creating music I hadn't heard before and haven't heard since.

"Customer . . ." Wendy is saying. "When I last signed on, no one called us *customers*."

Two bands jamming, creating a weave of sound that will never exist again. I could have slipped out of the queue. To hear more, I could have become like the woman in front of me. I could be living in chaos, too.

The computer's gone to sleep. I have to log on again. The document materialises, but the text has turned into hieroglyphics. A vortex forms in the middle of the screen. But it dissipates and there's Wendy Smith's profile at last. With short hair.

That's not Wendy Smith. It's me.

Or both of us. Our images are layered, mingling in the same space. Wendy, Gwen, both. My stomach starts knotting again, the ground pitching under my feet.

"Different probabilities, and a computer that can calculate them." Miriam was truly sloshed and slurring by last orders. "So quantum computing's gonna save Universal Credit. That's what they *say*. But maybe they want to influence claimant behaviour! Imagine different versions of each claimant in many universes, living out different decisions. Maybe there's one who isn't unemployed?"

I close my eyes. Open them again to look at the real and rather cross Wendy Smith.

"What are you doing? Did you really write about my missed interview in 1989? I *did* get work in publishing later."

"And look where you are now," I remind her.

"Yeah . . . it could be worse." Wendy waves, indicating the vast strip-lit room around us . . . security guards at the door, tense talk as people are interrogated. Sobbing from the reception area. That better not be my next customer

And Wendy is looking at me. *It could be worse.*

That's it. "I'm afraid our time's up," I say. "I'll write to you about our next appointment."

Wendy can't get out fast enough, papers trailing behind her. She turns to give an exaggerated salute.

Bitch. But she was right about one thing. We can't sanction claimants for actions before their claim. *Yet.* However, I *can* flag up her comments as suggesting an entrenched aversion to work. That justifies a sanction, in addition to disrupting our interview. Six months of no benefit? With her rent she'll feel the pinch.

Then I book her for a four-week programme with Grow Aspiration Success, the same organisation that ran our training. She'll enjoy the full battery of neurolinguistic programming and mind-melding techniques.

And at last I do get around to ticking the box: 'Compliance doubt'. Refer to decision-maker. *Sanctioned.*

The Lady in the Yard

Dedicated to Paul Kantner (1941-2016)

"Mutant Sue! Mutant Sue! How do you do?"

With a quick 'fuck you' gesture to the assholes, Suzy gets off the school bus.

She knows they're still watching as the bus pulls away, so she walks slowly with her head held high.

She can't bear the thought of going straight home.

"How was school?"

School was *shit*.

Instead, she takes the path through the woods that leads to the old bungalow colony. Suzy's family stayed a couple of summers in a place like this just before they left the Bronx. It used to be full of people here, but now the bungalows are falling down. Once a new highway was built, New Yorkers preferred vacations in the Catskills.

She comes to a rusting merry-go-round and a set of swings on the other end of the path. When they first moved here, Suzy used to push herself around on it, though it was slow and emitted shrieks of scraping metal. Now she gives it a kick just to hear it squeal.

Then she makes her way to the swimming pool. The fence around it is covered with morning glories that bloom and wither and bloom again, along with sumac and ivy and honeysuckle. She pushes open the rusty gate, and goes in.

Goldenrod and fireweed sprout through the cracks at the shallow end. At the deep end, rainwater collects in a pond. Old junk rusts in the stagnant water, while water lilies poke misshapen heads above it. The lilies are pale green as if their cells don't know leaf from blossom. Others are an acidic pale orange.

When they first moved in, she found tadpoles in the pool. As the summer wore on they turned to frogs and filled the night with frantic croaking.

She sits down on the skeleton of an old lounge chair and rolls a joint. She'll have one, just one joint for the day. She sometimes hangs out with the pot-smoking kids at school, but she takes care. Getting high is only a means to an end, a way to find the borderland.

The pot-head kids tolerate her though she barely says a word after a nod and muttered hello when she joins them in back of the school parking lot. It's only because she brings them good pot from a guy in Hackensack she met at the state orchestra try-outs, with just a small mark-up. She uses the bit of money she makes from selling pot to buy books.

But she won't get dope for them ever again, not after today. Did they stand up for her? No . . . just that jerk going on about his precious boring Grateful Dead. Then her *friends* joined the laughter.

Tears come to her eyes, but she *won't* cry. She's just so angry at them all. Damn. It's all because of that book. She digs into her bag, the fringed patchy suede draw-string thing that she once thought was so cool, and takes a book out. After one look at the cover and its drawing of a six-toed footprint, she flings it into the water.

She regrets it as soon as the last ripples close over it.

She *loved* that book. She'd bought it out of her hard-earned pot-selling money. It's not the book's fault. It's *her* fault things turned out so crap. She should've known. Anything to do with *toes* is bound to end badly.

She searches for a stick. She can poke about in the water and find the book, then push it to the shallow end. Then she'll take it home and dry it and clean it up.

She can't find anything long enough. Maybe she'll find a better stick at the very back of the pool enclosure.

In the beginning this area was full of thorns and prickly leaves, covered by more morning glory vines. Then she picked up her father's gardening gloves and weed clippers and hacked her way through that mess to the clearing.

It had been a lawn once, where people sat and played cards and drank their Bud. There must have been children running about, slurping lemonade and smearing ice cream on their faces.

Now it's a mini-meadow filled with yellow and orange flowers... Queen Anne's lace, buttercups and scattered stalks of mauve and pink surrounding more old lounge chairs.

She still hears bees buzzing and cars swishing by on the main road, the occasional rumble of a truck. The air is full of a rich odour that makes her dizzy. She follows the scent, and the buzzing grows louder as she approaches heavy purple blossoms hanging in grape-like clusters from vines along the fence.

She now knows that these flowers are called *wisteria*. A word like *wistful*, the way she felt when she wanted things she didn't even know about.

But their blossoms are bold and luxuriant, the scent suggestive and secret, promising intoxication.

Looking at them and smelling them calms her. School is crap, but she can always come here, to a place that is hers. She'll find a good long stick later... somewhere.

Then a loud splash from the pool makes her jump. A smaller splash follows it. *What's that?* An animal? Or what?

She is suddenly afraid, alone near the ruined pool. Her heart beats, the very blossoms in front of her seem to smirk and poke their yellow stamen tongues at her.

She rushes out of the hidden grove, looking away from the brackish pond as she closes the gate behind her.

"Can you stay in the moment between dark and light, wakefulness and dreaming? Then you can enter my world. And when you dance and sing with me, I can enter yours."

That's what the lady in the yard said to Suzy, back in the Bronx.

It's only now that she can even remember those words, or understand what they could mean. Sort of.

When Suzy saw her, she was just a kid, the winter after President Kennedy got shot.

Total dufus that she was, she'd managed to impale her wrist on the high fence in back of their apartment building.

She'd been after a stray parakeet, trying to tempt the bird to eat from her hand. It was perched in a tree in the yard next to hers. Her building's yard was all concrete, but next door had a real house with a garden and a tree that flowered with white blossoms in the spring.

The snow was coming down fast and she asked if she could go out and play in the snow. Fine, as long as she stayed in the yard where the caretakers, Alice and Don, could watch from their window. They often kept an eye on her in the yard and invited her in for cookies later.

When she arrived in the yard, Suzy looked in their window. Then she remembered that they were visiting their grandchildren in Bridgeport for Christmas.

When she glanced away from the window, she saw a green and blue parakeet sitting in the tree among a bunch of sparrows. Its colours made a bright spot against the cold white of the snow, the grey of the concrete and the outlines of the branches.

A bird like that would die out in the snow. But didn't she have a bag of nuts in her coat pocket? She'd lure the parakeet with the nuts, then take it home where it would be warm. She had called the bird Jackie after the dead president's glamorous wife.

She'd got up on Don's stepladder, but slipped while she was reaching over the fence. Her arm and then her wrist got stuck on top of the fence between her building and the house next door. The blood splashing the snow made her think of a slush cone, ground ice with raspberry syrup.

She let out a yell, but no one came, she just hung there and then maybe she fell, but she doesn't remember that. The cold soon made her numb, so she stopped feeling the cut.

Her thoughts were ticking over in circles like a tumble dryer at a laundromat, getting slower and slower too, blown by cold wind rather than hot air. But she began to feel warm, as if the sun was shining down on her through the swirling snow.

The snow turned brighter as the sky grew dark. It carried shades of blue and green and deep pink in hollows within the white. The stars winked on like the Christmas lights in the windows, guiding her through the spiralling flakes.

Was she asleep? Was she awake?

Nowadays Suzy walks around half-asleep most of the time, but she's sure that's not the kind of moment the lady in the yard spoke about.

When they moved into the house in New Jersey, Suzy asked for the room in the basement. It had been nothing more than a tiny storage room but she liked how it was away from it all.

Now she can stay up all night listening to her favourite radio shows. Her real life and learning takes place at night when she draws the covers around her, listening to dispatches from a world beyond New Jersey.

"We are deep into the night," Alison Steele would say at the start of her show on WNEW-FM.

"From this point on all sense of time ceases to exist. Only space and the sensory, that which we feel and experience, becomes the manifestation of all the cosmic waves of the universe . . . We are in space. We are above and beyond. The flutter of wings, the shadow across the moon, the sounds of the night, as the Nightbird spreads her wings and soars, above the earth, into another level of comprehension . . .

"Come fly with me, Alison Steele, the Nightbird."

Sometimes Suzy giggles at this patter. But she also loves to hover on the edge of sleep, wrapped in the intimacy of Alison's voice as she introduces a track by the Bonzo Dog Doo-dah Band. It invokes a world just beyond her sights, a secret world she enters because she is the only one awake in the house.

Other times she turns the dial to 99.5 and listens to Bob Fass on WBAI. His music is often rough and rowdy, with bands like the Fugs, Country Joe and the Fish and David Peel's Lower East Side. But when he's in the mood he'll play some quiet and doodly stuff like the Incredible String Band.

Then there's music she doesn't have any names for, because she never writes down who made the songs when she's not quite awake. Even when she falls asleep, she wakes with notes in her ears and the mystery of who might have made them.

"All sense of time ceases to exist . . ."

And when that happens, Suzy can hear what the lady in the yard used to play. Sometimes she smells her musk and hears her laugh, though she doesn't remember her laughing much.

The lady's laugh makes her shiver with a feeling that she's not in on the joke.

That time when Suzy saw the lady in the yard, she was only six. Not everything is clear, not even now since she's remembered more. She yelled, she cried, then she quieted down and her mind went *away*. She was drifting through the layers of the sky and earth. Perhaps the last layer was sleep, and she stayed suspended above it.

The music of pipes surrounded her, with notes that danced and tinted the snow. They drew together and moved in and out as if the air itself breathed . . . and a woman stood there playing an instrument that was more than a flute, but a bunch of flutes bundled together.

The cold didn't bother the woman, though she wasn't wearing many clothes. She had wings, but she was no angel. Not all her skin was bare . . . she had feathers, or perhaps it was fur. The feathers on her wings were green and blue, like the parakeet that Suzy had tried to tempt into the warmth of her hand.

The woman came closer. Suzy caught a whiff of earth, though the real earth was frozen and covered with snow. Suzy imagined a fountain covered with moss, a green layer drifting on the water. She'd seen one like that in the park.

The woman in the yard had wide-set brown eyes, a snub nose, and thick eyebrows that met in a line above her eyes. Her brown hair hung to her chin. She wasn't pretty. Maybe she was even ugly. But Suzy wanted to keep looking at her.

The woman put her face right up against Suzy's. The odour was stronger, but Suzy was getting used to it. The woman's eyes were brown, with flecks of green and an overcasting of dark blue. A friend's dog had eyes like that. Looking too much at those doggy eyes used to make her nervous, even when the dog licked her and wagged its tail.

The woman gathered Suzy in her arms. Waves of heat came off the woman's skin, and with each whirl some of that warmth seeped into Suzy. Suzy laughed, though the sudden warmth came close to pain. But Suzy knew she'd be fine. She put her arms around her new friend. It was easy to do that now that the woman no longer had wings.

Then the woman put Suzy down and began playing her music again. Suzy watched her hands on the fingerholes of the instrument. They moved fast and fluid, as if they had no joints. Then her fingers turned sharp to add a rat-tat-tat sound. The music they created made thoughts buzz about in Suzy's head.

The lady danced again and Suzy looked down. Under her feet, the snow began to melt. As her feet skipped over the pavement, the concrete broke beneath them. Sturdy shoots pushed through the cracks, and pale green flower buds unfurled to reveal berries of a deeper green.

A sad note entered the music, weaving between the snowflakes to cast a cool blue and purple light on them. It made Suzy imagine the parakeet lost in the grey and white of New York City.

Then the woman stopped playing. She put a hand to her chest, as if she was about to say the Pledge of Allegiance. But instead, she was holding it under one of her breasts.

There was a noise . . . footsteps in the snow? Someone coming to stop the music and dance? The lady licked her lips with a red tongue. It was the colour you find inside people, the colour of a cut, and the blood that had mixed with the snow.

And then Suzy woke up in a hospital. Her mother and father were sitting by her bed. She turned her head and saw her right arm, tightly bandaged from wrist to elbow.

Her brother Danny was there too, but he was more interested in his comic book.

"What are we going to do with you, Suzy?" Her mother was wiping her eyes, which often happened when Suzy did something she shouldn't.

"You're in trouble," said Danny.

However, she'd been 'lucky'. The cold had slowed down the bleeding so she only needed some stitches. But later, the skin on her two outermost toes itched and peeled, then swelled and bubbled up in black blisters.

Frostbite, they called it. It involved more visits to doctors and hospitals. *Thank goodness for Daddy's health plan.* That was one of the few good things about working for the government, they often said.

Finally, they brought Suzy in for surgery and didn't even tell her what would happen. Voila! Two toes gone. So much for those last little piggies, then.

For months after the operation she still felt those toes, itching at night.

When she went to the park in the summer, she'd want to take her shoes off and walk in the grass with the other children. She felt the grass and earth between her toes, even between the ones that were gone.

When she was little, the sight was greeted with curiosity. Later, exclamations of disgust. She stopped taking her shoes off near other people, but she can't avoid that now with phys ed. She tries to be discreet but they found her out.

When she first lost her toes, she stumbled without that bit of leverage. Now she has no trouble. When she's alone in the pool, she can do anything and not worry what people think. It's also a great place to practise her flute in the summer. Even in the winter, she'll play a little before her fingers get too cold.

She had to give up the music lessons at school because she didn't want to play in the marching band at football games. She hated that brassy bland music. And who gives a shit about football, even if her brother is on the team? All the more reason to ignore it. She just plays on her own now, with occasional sessions with Bernie the sax player from Hackensack when he deigns to meet her in Morristown, the only place her local bus will take her.

The first time she played her flute in the pool, it was a revelation. The walls of the almost-empty pool made the music loud and hollow, a sound that gave her pleasurable shivers of recognition.

The next time she went to the pool, she took her new reel-to-reel portable tape machine. She recorded herself and listened for the echo, the sound of an emptiness that she had to fill. She got up and hopped around on one leg, pretending to be the Jethro Tull flute-playing guy. She balanced on the foot with the missing toes just to make sure she could do it.

Then she played along with her recording, devising a counterpoint. The lady in the yard played a special instrument, which included seven pipes. Suzy had nothing of the sort, but she tried to get a seven-fold sound from playing against herself.

That was when she decided she wanted to become a recording engineer. When she told the guidance counsellor at school, he pursed his lips and said she had to get better at math if she wanted to become any kind of engineer.

Suzy stayed inside while she recovered from her foot operation. She drew in colouring books and watched TV. She loved films of Broadway musicals, especially *Peter Pan*. This wasn't the Walt Disney version, which she hated.

She imagined Peter Pan flying between places that you see and places that might not exist. She wished she could do that, and sometimes she did in her dreams.

She asked her parents if Peter Pan could be a real boy.

"No, of course not. He's make-believe. A man called JM Barrie made him up," her father explained. "But I think he's based on a Greek myth. He prances around and plays a flute like the Greek god Pan."

"And Suzy, it's a lady called Mary Martin who plays Peter Pan," added her mother. "So Peter's not a boy at all."

And to Suzy, that made a lot of sense.

Suzy's mind always wandered in school. She preferred watching the birds in the tree outside the classroom window to reading stories about kids with blonde hair who are always smiling with big white teeth.

She was ten when her family moved to New Jersey. She didn't do much better in the new school, though New Jersey seemed OK in the beginning. It was closer to where her father worked, so he didn't come home so tired. There were fields to roam around in, apple trees in the back of their house.

Then she started school. In the Bronx, all the kids just played together. But here the children divided into groups, and none of those groups let Suzy in. Some made fun of her New York accent, though it was no accent at all, just the way she talked.

The teachers didn't like her either, though she tried to be good. She just said the wrong things and asked the wrong questions. And the books they read here didn't interest her either.

Then a new school librarian actually asked the kids what they wanted to read. Suzy suggested a book about Greek myths, because she had always wanted to find out about the flute-playing god that Peter was based on. The librarian gave her *Bullfinch's Mythology* to try, though it wasn't really a children's book.

Perhaps those earlier lessons *had* gone in one ear, out the other. But something must have lodged in there, waiting to come out. When she read about Greek myths, she found that one letter led to the other, forming a word. The words formed pictures in her mind, then a whole movie. She could smell the air of a Greek mountaintop, feel Neptune's sea lapping at her feet.

She enjoyed these stories much more than the Jewish and Christian ones. This wasn't just about some old guy with a beard or white-robed jerks strumming on harps. Some of these gods were even *women*.

Within the pages of Bullfinch, she finally met Pan. He was the god of flocks and shepherds, which you didn't find in the Bronx or in New Jersey.

Pan is a god who loves late-night revelries and welcomes the dawn. Then he sleeps, and gets angry at anyone who disturbs him when he is resting in the day. That's kind of like Suzy, except she listens to the radio instead of cavorting with nymphs.

One nymph refused Pan's attentions and turned into a bunch of reeds. Pan blew on the reeds and a sad song came out. So he made those reeds into a musical instrument. A *syrinx*, similar to what the lady in the yard played.

Mr Bullfinch quoted a poem by Keats: *"How he did weep to find nought but a lovely sighing of the wind, along the reedy stream; a half-heard strain, full of sweet desolation, balmy pain."*

She found another book on mythology, which had illustrations. The syrinx here was a lot more basic than the one played by the lady in the yard, but she supposed even deities had to adapt. There were drawings and sculptures of Pan, which she didn't find attractive. Perhaps his syrinx expressed the nymph's anger at getting chased by some hairy guy.

So where was the lithe leaping boy? Or the woman who could become a boy?

Suzy later asked the librarian if Pan was ever a woman.

The librarian told Suzy that female deities of that sort have appeared in Roman art and in murals found under the lava in Pompeii. Here she lowered her voice.

"But I'm afraid those murals are for adults, not children. You won't find them in any books in this library."

So Pan *could* be a woman.

But Pan is just a myth, which is similar to a fairy tale.

Sometimes Suzy doubts that the woman in the yard had been real, only a hallucination spawned by her unformed hypothermic brain. But why did she live? The lady's embrace had brought warmth. Just as it raised the plants beneath the sidewalk, it kept a girl from freezing, though it didn't reach all her toes.

When Suzy went into the yard afterwards, she *did* find those cracks in the concrete. Of course, the actual plants that had grown in them would have died in the cold after the lady left.

If Suzy closes her eyes and remembers as she plays the flute, with the help of a toke or two, she comes close to finding the tune played by the lady in the yard. It came from a place where lost creatures fly . . . out of place, out of time. She still felt that way now, though the dimensions have changed.

Dimensions. That word stays in her mind, a smooth pebble she could hold in her palm.

She tries to find that common note. A sequence of notes over and over, and then stronger.

The followers of Pan worshipped him in groves and grottos. Her place in the abandoned swimming pool is as grotto-like as it gets.

But she has never *worshipped* the lady in the yard. She just wants to meet her again and talk to her. Is that so much to ask?

Suzy's parents were happy that her reading had improved and she was moving out of the 'slow' track. So they agreed to take her to the big county library and pick her up when she finished.

As she walked through the library, she felt like a new person. No one told her where to go and what to do. She could look at what she wanted, read what she wanted.

She went to the catalogue, thumbing through the thick cards for books about Roman art and books about Pompeii.

The art books were lovely to hold, their pages lustrous and smooth against her fingers. She examined a newer Pompeii book that contained art suppressed in earlier exhibitions. These pieces had been stored in a 'secret' room because they shocked the Victorians so much. But now, in the 1960s, people are all so much more open-minded.

Here she found paintings and statues of men and women tangled in many combinations. She glanced at these with mild interest and a tinge of confused disgust, which she dismissed because she considered herself an 'open-minded' 1960s person. She flipped faster through those pages as she sought an image of a female Pan.

At last, she found it – a mural from the 'Villa of Mysteries'. Two Pans, with short hair revealing pointed ears, kind of like Spock in Star Trek.

One is playing the pipes, while the other is holding *her* breast for a sleek little goat to suckle. Next to them a woman is whirling a purple cloak around as if she's in the middle of an interpretive dance.

The caption said: "A boy or young Pan plays a pipe while a Panisca offers her breast to a kid."

Panisca. So that's what a female Pan is called. Certainly not Peter.

The Panisca in this mural had shorter hair than the lady in the yard. Of course, given that these gods turned themselves into animals and what-not, a different haircut would be no big deal.

But Suzy recognised the expression on the Panisca's face, rather serious but also loving.

Another mural showed a winged woman who also reminded her of the woman in the yard. This one wore a low-slung skirt around her hips and high boots, stern as she wields a stick. Though her form was different, her face also reminded Suzy of the Panisca in the yard. Distant, not ready to forgive a mistake or slight, taking her instrument from her mouth and flicking her red tongue. If the gods change their shape, could this be the Panisca in a different mood? Maybe not the best mood.

Another woman kneels; she seems to be imploring the winged woman.

Suzy would certainly be begging to borrow those boots. She'd love a pair like that.

Suzy didn't dare take the Pompeii book out of the library. She only looked at it when she visited.

As time went by, she took more interest in the other pages. These ancient people definitely had more imagination than those hippy-looking people in her parents' *Joy of Sex* book, which Suzy had found hidden in a drawer.

When Bernie from Hackensack told her he might be gay she looked carefully at the pictures of men with men. And all that time she'd been thinking that Bernie could become her boyfriend. She cried for a couple of days, then decided it could be exciting to be friends with someone that everyone at her school would call a *fag*.

But some of it . . . *eueew*. She turned to a page with a sculpture of Pan himself doing it with a goat. And then found another book, which featured a painting of a Pan and Panisca in a sexual tangle of skin and fur, horns and hooves.

She looked around to make sure no one was watching. But what would anyone see? Just a girl reading about Roman art.

Later, her mother said: "I'm glad you're getting serious about your studies. I knew you could do so much better."

Better. She wasn't sure about that. She might read Bullfinch now, but the teachers still scolded her for not paying attention. What she loved to read and what they learned in school were two different things.

She began to branch out from mythology in her reading and discovered science fiction. She loved *The Dispossessed* by Ursula LeGuin and especially *The Chrysalids* by John Wyndham. It was the footprint with six toes on the cover that drew her attention. A girl in the book called Sophie is banished as an abomination and a mutant because she has six toes on one foot. Right. Six toes, three toes . . . in either case, you're fucked.

Meanwhile, she got in trouble for reading a science fiction book under her desk during morning home-room. It was called *England Swings SF*.

This caused more merriment in the classroom. *Suzy swings!* But she was glad she'd read that book, which included stories that had nothing to do with spaceships.

You could even set such a story in the Bronx or New Jersey.

Perhaps the radio waves dominate Suzy's night, but books rule her day. Not parents or teachers, definitely not friends. And sometimes, even those books are forbidden.

Worst are the 'High Holidays' – Rosh Hashanah and Yom Kippur – when she must attend synagogue for whole days at a time. It's especially bad when they take place on a weekend, so there isn't even the benefit of missing school.

Last year she brought a book with her, and her mother confiscated it.

"You're not meant to be reading, you're meant to be praying," said Mom.

"I don't believe in God, so why should I pray?"

Suzy had never put that thought in words before. So she didn't believe in some bearded guy who pays attention to everyone's doings and listens to their prayers. And now she wasn't sure just how a *religion* differed from a myth or fairy tale.

Yet she did believe that a Panisca, the lady in the yard, had come to her. And she is still out there, hovering about her dreams, somewhere in a world that is difficult to enter.

The Panisca is more than human, but could be fallible and lost as a human can be.

So Suzy doesn't believe in God. But there really was a lady in the yard, who might have been seen as *a* god.

"Believe or don't believe, you do what you're told and you do what is right."

This year Suzy takes care to hide a smaller book deep in the recesses of her suede-fringed bag.

At the synagogue, the little kids leave the sanctuary and run around the lobby. There's a corner of the lobby where teenagers congregate and flirt. None of them are her friends.

There is only one 'hey it's Swinging Sue' as she leaves. Sheryl Weinbaum, the bitch. Suzy ignores it as she heads outside. She has already explored the woods just in back of the parking lot, and knows a rock that's good to sit on.

Suzy rolls a joint and chuckles. These aren't called the 'High' Holidays for nothing! Then she takes out her little mythology book. Maybe she's moved on to science fiction. But it's nice to read the myths again for old times' sake.

"I sing of Pan, Nymphe-leader, darling of the Naiades, adornment of golden choruses, lord of winsome muse when he pours forth the god-inspired siren-song of the melodious syrinx, and stepping nimbly to the melody leaps down from shadowy caves, moving his all-shape body, fine dancer, fine of face, conspicuous with blond beard . . . All the earth and sea are mixed thanks to you, for you are the bulwark of all, oh Pan, Pan!"

'All-shape'. So Pan can be many shapes, any shape he or she wants. 'Pan' can refer to a pasture and it also means all, and *all* can be anything.

Since it's a warm day in September, Suzie takes off her shoes. She looks at the three toes on her deficient foot, just about visible through her panty-hose, as she wriggles them. If she could change her shape like a Greek god, would she grow those toes back?

Some scientists predict that humans could evolve to lose their little toes. Of course, in this crap school plenty of people refuse to even think about evolution. Jesus freaks . . . the school is full of them. Several in her class have taken to greeting each other by raising their index finger to the sky. There is only *one* way, it means. The way of Jesus, *my* way.

And with only a small turn of the hand, the gesture means *fuck you*. Suzy practises the transformed signal under her desk. She has a feeling it'll come in handy.

Miss Golding asks her class to do reports on a book they *love*. Not just *like*, but *love*.

Damn, thinks Suzy. Will we to have to sit through three presentations on the Bible?

So Suzy volunteers straight away to do hers. Yes, she'll do *The Chrysalids* by John Wyndham. She's read it three times. Miss Golding says she'll bring in a record player, so people can play any music that goes along with the book.

Suzy knows what will go with hers.

Miss Golding is one of the few OK people at school, but she won't be around next year. Rumour has it her contract won't be renewed because the vice principal made a pass at her and she said *no*.

But Suzy suspects it could also be down to the Jesus creeps getting together and complaining about swear words in *Catcher in the Rye*.

At her presentation, Suzy starts with a description of the book's setting – a rambling account of a conservative society, living in the shadow of the 'Tribulation', a nuclear war.

She explains that individuals who don't conform to a strict physical norm are killed or sterilised and banished to the Fringes, an area full of animal and plant mutations. The boy in the book is telepathic, and he has to hide this. Later he makes friends with a girl called Sophie and he discovers that she has six toes.

A wave of titters starts to gather, led by the Jesus creeps and amplified by the snorting of Sheryl Weinbaum. Obviously, behaving like a bigoted asshole is not an exclusively Christian affair.

Suzy squares her shoulders and carries on. "This girl who has six toes gets found out. Her family is persecuted, and they have to move."

"So how come she has six toes, then?"

"It's a mutation, caused by nuclear fall-out."

"Is that why you only have three?"

"No, that was . . ." An *accident*. No, not really. She was just stupid enough to go out and slip on a stepladder near a fence. And *that* is none of their business.

"But the book isn't about *me*. The guy who wrote it lives in England and he hasn't met any of us. The book is about letting people be different and it's an attack on religious intolerance."

Suzy doesn't look at the Jesus faction in the front of the class, but sneaks a glance at her fellow potheads in the back. No tittering comes from there, but there are definitely a few smirks. And no one helps her, or even contributes a furtive smile of support.

Mutant Sue . . . Mutant Sue . . . She knows that name will stick. She's glad that Miss Golding isn't intervening. That would only make matters worse. She clears her throat, and carries on.

"And this book inspired the Jefferson Airplane to write a song called 'Crown of Creation'. I've brought in the record." Suzy's voice rises to a shout in order to be heard.

This is worse than the time she brought in a Weavers record and the teacher said it was no good because Pete Seeger's a commie.

"Who's the Jefferson Airplane?"

"The Airplane's *crap*," says one of the potheads. "Their music's all jingly-jangly, not mellow like the Dead."

"Yeah? Well, I think the Grateful Dead are *boring*, but it's all a matter of taste." Suzy struggles to remain diplomatic about the relative merits of the Airplane and the Dead. "I'll play the song and everyone can decide. And I made dittos of the lyrics, which I'll pass out. The band actually got their words straight from the book."

Miss Golding, who had run off those dittos for her, is now looking nervous.

Suzy passes out the sheets of paper, which are met by immediate catcalls.

"Are *you* the crown of creation, Mutant Sue?"

"You've got no place to go . . . Shoulda stayed in the Bronx!"

"*You are the crown of creation* . . . that's *blasphemy*. We can't have blasphemy in our school."

Suzy can't take this any longer "Blasphemy? I'll show you some blasphemy. I'll blast out this song and blow out the shit that passes for your brain."

Miss Golding now steps in. "Suzy, there's no need for that language!"

Even the liberal Miss Golding has her limits.

The next day Suzy gets up an hour earlier to give herself time to walk to school. No getting on a bus with those idiots. At least it's the last week of school.

She goes back to the pool, this time with a nice big branch so she can get her book back. What had she been afraid of? That plop and agitation in the water could have been a frog, or something falling from a tree. Now the only thing disturbing the water's surface are swimming bugs.

She goes to the edge of the water and pokes about with her stick, trying to trawl deep enough to find the book and push it along. She only stirs up scum on the bottom. She keeps poking and poking, but stops because she doesn't want to disturb the lilies and the frogs.

She sighs with frustration and curses herself again for what she did. She misses her book. She can get another one out of the library but it won't be the same.

She sits on the steps in the pool and rolls a joint. She plays her flute tape. This time she just listens to her tape, hearing it bounce off the walls of the pool. She imagines her thoughts amplified and repeating like the echo, spiralling into the air. *Stay in that moment between wakefulness and sleep.*

Then she hears other sounds. At first it's like the usual buzz of insects. Then she realises it's singing, a song unformed by a mouth, an emanation of melody like mist. Mindless, but affecting. Shrill, but sweet. It comes from the back fence, the most hidden part of the pool area.

She goes there and finds out where the sound comes from. It's the wisteria, singing. Every blossom, calyx open and vibrating.

She puts her hand on a bunch, feeling the stirring under her fingertips. Against her ear, a multitude of tongues.

She gives a tense bark of laughter. Perhaps this is what the Panisca laughs about. Ha ha. The wisteria sings.

She decides it's time to roll another joint.

On the last day of school, Jane Whitcomb is telling everyone that her father is buying the land near to Suzy's house. The bungalow colony, the pool and the singing wisteria bower will soon be gone.

Suzy has to go there and find the Panisca. Of course, the creature once found her in the Bronx, and she can go anywhere. But she must get attached to places, to her grottos. And so does Suzy, even though there's scum on the water in this grotto and it's considered an eyesore by the township planners.

She decides to visit it at night. Then she will be closer to finding the borderland and its moment between sleep and waking, and night-time in the grotto is the best place to try.

Suzy gets in bed and turns off the lights, and plays the flute soft as she can, barely breathing into it. The sound that comes out is closer to a moan, with a tune curling its edges.

The frogs are making a racket, along with the crickets. It drifts into a rhythm, which should have lulled her. But her mind comes awake as her body slows down.

Thoughts echo and spin. The sound of a flute, many flutes, echoing among hills she's never seen. She holds her breath, then lets it go.

It's the borderland, approaching. The time between wakefulness and sleep is usually too short. Only a line of music, a shift in the room around her, a different light shining through the window.

Now she's older, she knows what she's looking for. Peter Pan was wrong. She can do more now that she's grown up, or close to it.

She's prolonging that moment, elongating it, moving within it. If she keeps her mind in the world between dreams and thought, she hears the music. She hears the wisteria singing, and the morning glories sighing in their sleep.

She changes into a t-shirt and shorts and laces up her sneakers. With her flute in a backpack, she leaves through the basement door and shuts it with barely a click.

At the pool the morning glory buds are now rolled up tight. But other living things expand and open. Suzy hears the earth exhaling, and the night-blooming plants breathing in. While the familiar green lilies have clenched their petals, a new crop of water blooms show purple and red in the moonlight.

Unseen beauty, flowering in muck amid the discards. An impulse to bow to this shabby splendour seizes her, but instead she makes her way into the tangles of the hidden lounge-lawn where she reassembles her flute.

She plays in rhythm with the frogs and crickets, adding a layer of her own to the rhythmic noise of the dark.

As the Nightbird put it: *Time ceases to exist. There is only space and the sensory . . .*

Can she be asleep and awake at the same time? As she breathes in the scent of the wisteria and night-blooming water plants, the distinction between the two states collapses.

Then a loud splash and stirring breaks the surface of the pool.

A slender and sinuous arm reaches above it, dripping with algae and surface residues.

"Don't worry. It's only a water nymph," a voice assures her.

There's a buzz to the voice, a woman's voice, which makes her think of bees making honey. Suzy takes her time to turn around and see who is talking.

The woman now wears her hair long in a dark thick braid. She still has that broad face with thick eyebrows, her eyes have that not-human cast. She carries her new-fangled syrinx, with its holes and valves and much more than seven pipes.

"You speak English . . ." Suzy begins. "I mean, I thought you'd speak Greek. Or Latin."

"I speak the language that is needed. Don't you remember when I spoke to you in the concrete yard? Your words are like tiles in a mosaic. I like the taste of them and the look of them. They can be another kind of music." She laughs and displays large white teeth.

"Are the Greek stories right, after all? We call them myths, but you're here. Are they true?"

"Myths are only symbols for things people don't understand. All stories are right, yet they are often wrong. Your scientists have their stories and symbols, which have truth too."

"What are you talking about? You sound like a goddam politician!" Suzy's heart plummets. All this fuss for a double-talking creature who seems so ordinary, even if her ears are odd. "I thought you'd be . . ."

"I can *change* if you prefer something more exotic. Do you want the goat? They loved that in Arcadia, but I'm flexible. There's some young men in California who are very keen on a mechanical element. Perhaps you'd like the wings again. It's not a big deal when the physical being is in flux. That's how it is where I live. That's how *we* are different from rocks."

"No, no, no . . . the music is enough. You played for me when I first saw you. Why did you come to me then, anyway? I'm just a girl, no one special."

"I hear music and desperation, and when they resonate I come. When more people see me and play my music, it helps me travel between worlds. The worst thing is to be trapped." She shudders, then lifts her instrument to her mouth.

"Come play with us," the Panisca invites.

Play with *us*.

The sound coming out of the Panisca's instrument assaults Suzy's ears, though it isn't very loud. She pauses. "You're a curious girl. Do you want to visit the place I come from?"

Suzy's first thought is *yes*. Then she is cautious. You don't get in a stranger's car; and you don't get in a stranger's time machine or spaceship either.

She scowls. "Maybe."

But as the Panisca continues her song, Suzy can't resist a dance. Two left feet, doing their shuffle.

The music intensifies. The warbles of songbirds weave through it. But it also condenses the caw of crows and the deep-throated signal of frogs in each note. It is the slither of snakes and worms, and the cries of mating cats. A rising sun, a dawn and a cacophony of birds.

It brings tears to Suzy's eyes, and it also makes her want to throw her head back and let her voice rise to the moon.

The Panisca whirls in a dance, leading Suzy out of the grove, around the pool. She is changing, so is the landscape. At the shallow end of the pool the cracks grow wider and plants flower.

More waterlilies raise heads above the water, which moves as if fed by a new source, deepening and swirling and advancing. It's no longer stagnant, but vital and inviting.

Suzy sits down on the side of the pool, lays down her flute and rucksack, then pulls off her sneakers and socks. And there are her feet, exposed, the space where toes should be. "The water looks so different now."

"Of course it is. This is a world of change," says the Panisca. "Life is change, as you know. That makes us different from the rocks."

"I think I've heard that line before," says Suzy as she steps in the water, which has filled most of the pool.

The Panisca holds her instrument aloft, waist-deep in the waters of the pool. Frogs leap from the water onto her shoulders.

The water is heavy satin against Suzy's skin, like a bath with fragrant oil. Its surface ripples, and something emerges from it again.

Nymphs. Three of them.

Is there such a thing as a *boy* nymph?

This one is smiling at Suzy, and he emerges from the water to extend his hand. He is dark-haired and slender, his green eyes welcome her. The two female nymphs also smile, perhaps shyly. She immediately thinks of them as the best friends she never had.

As Suzy submerges, the water flows and curls around her. She leans back upon it, then extends her legs and arms. The nymphs surround her, their touch an extension of the water. It feels good to be there. Too long she's avoided swimming for fear of exposure.

Now she swims, and *dances* in the water. She touches bottom, then floats to the top. No longer is she big and awkward. She is as graceful as her companions, who embrace her and accept her. She submerges again, holding her breath. The bottom of the pool is gone, and she doesn't miss it. It has turned into a lake, an ocean. It is another world, far better than the one she lives in. It's a world of change, of freedom.

The nymphs join her again, cushioning her descent.

She needs to breathe now. She starts a slow kick towards the surface, but her loving new friends don't realise she has to go there. They want to show her the world below, which is lit by a pearly light. It is full of caves and stunning stone grottos and flowering water plants more opulent than the lilies sprouting on the surface. They want to show her everything. She wants to see it too, but after she gets a breath.

Why are they holding her down? She struggles politely, trying to let them know that she'd love to see their abode, but first she must breathe. *Now.* She can't hold back any longer, she has to expel the old air in the lungs and take in oxygen.

Then the guy tries to kiss her. Good grief. Sure she liked the look of him and would have happily kissed him back, but not *here*.

She kicks. Even boy nymphs have balls, and she's given them a square hit. A string of bubbles eject out of his mouth and his grip loosens. She struggles and opens her mouth and more water gets in . . . and in. Her chest is burning, an incredible pressure pushes down on it. She flails the water with her hands, and then her arm brushes something wedged into a rock.

A solid square object. She picks it up, thinking to use it as a weapon against the nymphs.

And then she recognises the drawing of a six-toed foot. Her copy of *The Chrysalids*. Fat lot of good it will do her now.

But its solid square shape reassures her. So does the six-toed footprint on its cover, and the dog-ears at her favourite parts, especially where she discovered the lyrics of "Crown of Creation". She could probably find the page with the smudge of tomato sauce if she wasn't about to drown . . .

But the heaviness of the water around her is clearing, the pressure on her chest lightens. She's dizzy and her ears pop, as if she's on a plane descending into a more familiar layer of air.

Suddenly, she's crouching in three feet of water. She lifts her head up with a great gasp and cough. The water isn't so nice now, with its usual components of frog spawn and slime. There's no underground spring making it fresh, no bottomless lake full of marvels. But at least she can sit up and breathe.

And then she is staggering to sprawl at the shallow end near the steps, close to where she left her flute. Maybe she loses consciousness for a moment, but she still feels herself coughing in the dark, water and puke coming out of her mouth.

When Suzy opens her eyes the Panisca is sitting on the side of the pool, hairy legs swinging as she plays another tune. She puts down her instrument and laughs. "What a mess!"

Suzy is still clutching her book. The plastic jacket protected the cover but the pages are gummed up. She'd really love to chuck it at that pointy-eared bitch, but she's thrown that book around too much already.

"You're back sooner than I thought . . ." The Panisca winks.

Though this creature may have once saved her life, Suzy now sees that she could just as easily take it away, or let it slip away while she's playing that damned thing. Anger makes Suzy want to shout, though she can just about manage an enraged series of croaks.

"No thanks to *you*. I almost drowned. And your *friend* . . . Maybe he should have tried kissing me above the water instead of below it."

"*Kissing* you? He only wanted to help you breathe under water. That's what nymphs do if they're friendly. And these nymphs – the kind that settle in abandoned places – are friendly. They only want to bring a bit of life to the desolation and make things grow again."

"Trying to drown me is a funny way to go about it . . . Well, he should've *said* . . . you know, about the breathing. And why were you egging them on instead of helping me?"

"But you seemed so happy! I didn't want to interrupt."

"Happy as fuck!" Suzy's clothes are plastered to her skin. Though the night had been warm, the dawn is chilly. She shivers. She'll have to get home and dry off, make herself a hot drink. She hopes no one there has missed her.

And then the birds start their raucous calling and chittering as the sun starts to rise.

The Panisca yawns. "I will retire now." She picks up her syrinx and walks into the woods.

Suzy picks herself up. The water in the pool is back to its usual level and shows no signs of agitation. But new water lilies are opening their petals to bloom in the day, while the night lilies clench theirs.

One of the new lilies is dark purple, almost black. *Things always change in my world.*

As Suzy puts on her shoes and socks, she stops. Something else has changed.

Her missing toes have grown back. She touches them, wiggles them. Wee wee wee all the way home. They look so *new*. So smooth, with perfect nails. A perfect shape, unbowed by tight shoes, blisters and wear and tear.

I'll be damned, my near-fatal frolics with pointy-ears and her pals must've done some good after all!

She stashes her flute and puts her sneakers in her backpack too. She doesn't care if she encounters some rough ground. She must try out her new toes. Her excitement drives that bedraggled half-drowned shock and exhaustion away. She skips and capers.

Let me feel the grass, let me feel the mud between five that is FIVE toes on my right foot.

And just to think she was 'healed' by a swim around a pool full of rotting junk with three water nymphs. Let those Jesus creeps put that in their pipe and smoke it!

Then she stops, and thinks.

What will happen when people see that those missing toes have grown back?

People will want to understand this regeneration. They will ask questions, and more questions. Doctors will want to experiment. Kids will make fun again. *Mutant Sue, mutant Sue, got anything new? Another head, an extra boob?*

Now that she's whole, she'll be even *more* of a freak.

She'll have to hide her regrown toes from everyone. Even her family, even her parents. Even Bernie. *And you've got no place to go . . .*

Suzy halts her progress towards the house and plops down on the ground. Sneakers and socks come out of the bag, and go back on her feet.

She ties her laces tight, tighter than ever before.

Tasting the Clouds

It often begins – and ends – with a cup of coffee.

"Would you like to come in for a cuppa?"

Tim had thought things were going well when Lucy issued that invitation to him last night. Coffee, most definitely yes!

And afterwards, he'd thought everything was going even better.

Until it came to that second cup in the morning.

"It never works when you sleep together on a first date," a friend had once advised him.

But last night wasn't a first date. It wasn't really a date at all. It was the end-of-term party for their salsa dancing class, so they had actually known each other for months. Since January, they'd been throwing themselves into rounds of *cumbia, timba, bomba* and the fast two-stepping *merengue*.

It didn't take long before they became regular partners. She was dark and small, always in motion. Kind of nervy, but he liked that. It made a good counterpart to his more solid, earthbound style.

When they got to chatting in the pub after class he learned that she did office temping. She found out that he performed some task or other for the council.

But they were happy not to know too much about the daytime world that they left behind with their *merengue* and *timba*. What really mattered was the way they danced together.

They both had a hangover. But even the hang-over was pleasant in its way as they stumbled about, rubbed bleary eyes and made silly jokes about hangovers. He decided not to shave before going into work.

"It's alright for you lot," Lucy complained. "You can get away with designer stubble, or even the full facial foliage. But it's been ages since I've bothered to do my legs, and that would be unforgivable in any City office!"

She pulled on a pair of black opaque tights to hide the unforgivable – then cursed as a ladder snaked its way from mid-calf to upper-inner thigh.

She stalked defiantly into the kitchen, laddered tights and all. "But fuck 'em, fuck 'em, they shouldn't be looking at my legs anyway!"

He laughed as she beckoned to him to follow.

"But y'know . . ." She winked as she opened a cupboard to reveal a shelf packed with many kinds of tea and one large packet of coffee. "If you see a woman in an office wearing opaque tights in June, it usually means they're in *disguise*. Sort of undercover, though it gets uncomfortable on a hot day."

Then she offered him a cup of coffee.

Lucy scooped the coffee out, releasing a rich and sharp odour.

A big red star on the packet caught his eye. He took it and turned it over. *Cafe Rebelde Zapatista Organico*. "What's this? I've not seen it before."

"Oh, it's Zapatista coffee. It's produced by autonomous communities in Chiapas. You know, in southern Mexico."

"Zapatista coffee, eh?" Tim said. "I hope it's better than that old Nicaraguan piss!"

She gave him a blank look. "Nicaraguan?"

For the first time, he thought about their age difference. What year did the Sandinistas lose power – and it was no longer the righteous thing to drink Nicaraguan coffee?

"You couldn't get away from it throughout the '80s," he explained. "Especially since I shared a flat with a guy who was in the Nicaraguan Solidarity Campaign. What a loser! The high point of his social life was going to those solidarity meetings. He had his weekly bath before the meeting. And he was always at me to buy that sodding coffee. I preferred a good espresso, so what would I want with that stuff? But Ben thought it was my moral duty to drink up and do my bit for the Nicaraguan struggle against American imperialism. Autonomous communes in Chiapas, you say? Sounds too politically correct for words."

Lucy shoved the plunger down in a rather large cafetière, which erupted in a spurt of grounds.

"'Politically correct'?" If she'd been a cat, she'd be hissing. "I thought that sad banality from the 1990s got buried with Ronald Reagan! What's so 'politically-correct' about people taking control of their own land, and others giving a little support by drinking some excellent coffee?"

And Tim felt like he'd just received a vicious scratch from a purring, peaceable moggy. "Oh, erm . . . Sorry, I didn't mean to offend you. It just seemed . . . Maybe that came out wrong."

She took a deep breath and made a visible effort to smile as she mopped up the spillage. "Sorry too, for snapping at you. But you just uttered one of those little button-pushers! And do you know what it's all about? I was over there. That doesn't make me an expert, but I know something. I'll show you some pictures, though I didn't take them all myself."

She pointed out several pictures among the bills, family photos and handouts for raves and demonstrations on the household notice board. One showed masked men and women massing on the balcony of an official building. They weren't wearing the old Che Guevara olive-drab he associated with Latin American guerrilla movements, but flaunted rainbow layers of traditional clothing. Even the scarves hiding their faces were decorated with embroidered flowers and abstract designs. These flamboyant fighters did have guns though.

"So what's it all in aid of? Just another regime that lefties romanticise from afar?" Tim couldn't stop being cynical, though the embroidered face masks made him wonder a little. It must be his Inner Art Student turning him sentimental.

Lucy glared at him, then softened again. "Well, if you really want to know and you're not just taking the piss, Mexico joined an international trade agreement that privatised the common land these people lived on. The peasants had an uprising to stop it, to get rid of the big landlords and run their own communities. It's not perfect, but it's different from what you're talking about."

Tim was only half-listening, because he was examining another photo. Women stood on a mountain ridge in front of a barrier, arms crossed and linked. They were draped in flowing garments that ranged from pale green like new-grown grass, vibrant purple, golden orange and deep pink on the verge of red. A mist surrounded them, filtering and reflecting the colours of the forest behind them.

"Is that fog around those women?"

"They're really standing among the clouds. They live in a highland forest that's surrounded by constant clouds. That's where your coffee comes from!"

"And where's that?" He pointed to the Zapatistas on the balcony.

"The town hall at San Cristobal. See, they took over the Town Hall and burned all the official records. Or more likely erased them, some of those guys are good with computers."

"I can't imagine doing that at the Town Hall where I work! Well, not the bit with guns. It wouldn't be very practical." Tim had to smile, because the idea did have a certain appeal when it came to his boss.

"Well, no. But it's about freedom and we try to find it in different ways, wherever we live. And what's 'politically correct' about freedom? That vile little catchphrase should be stricken from the English language, along with 'I'm not being funny'. You'd be out the door if you said *that!*"

Lucy picked up the cafetière and held it under his nose. He took a deep breath and the fragrance that filled him made him think of the mountains where it must have grown, and a sky close enough to touch.

"Seriously Tim, you should try the coffee at least. You'd enjoy it!" She poured the fragrant liquid into two mugs.

He saw that she really didn't want things to end on a sour note. But he suspected also that she definitely wanted them to end.

I blew it. Just one word or sentence can cool the current, stop the process – even when both of you try to ignore the fact.

He made conciliatory noises too. "It wasn't all bad, with the Nicaraguan solidarity stuff. Ben took me to their fund-raising discos. They were dreadful, like school dances. But it got me listening to Latin music, so I got something out of it."

"Did you? Shut up and drink your coffee then."

So he started to drink his coffee.

It was only a sip. He licked his lips, trying to get his tongue around the flavour. Rich and smooth, yet with an edge. He had more. He could feel a freshening breeze move through the sodden layers of his mind. Alcohol-spun cobwebs wafted away and dissolved.

He closed his eyes.

Another sip, and the fuzz at the edge of his vision cleared. "Hey, this *is* good."

But the only answer was a series of purposeful picking up and packing noises from Lucy's bedroom. She emerged with her own cup at her mouth and a fatly-packed shoulder bag bumping against her hip.

"I've got to go now." She put her drained cup down with a thump.

He continued to take the smallest of draughts. He couldn't bear to rush it. The taste of the coffee was a round and ripe fruit in his mouth. His hung-over head could be a dusty dark city with lights going on one by one with each swallow. He opened his eyes wider to watch the sun slant in the kitchen window through the glass-bead curtain. Transparent blobs of colour played on the surface of the water in the washing-up bowl.

Lucy was watching him with just a hint of an amused smile. "You can take the coffee with you if you want. Despite my mishap, there's still plenty left in the pot and I've got a spare flask."

They said goodbye outside, with no exchange of phone numbers.

"I'll need to return your flask," he started, "Maybe . . ."

"Don't worry. It's just a spare one I got a jumble sale. You can keep the thing."

There goes that line.

She turned briskly and walked away.

He cradled the flask in his hand as he walked to his work at the Town Hall. Unfair, unfair to be judged so instantly. But he also knew he was just as guilty of such judgments, many times. If life was unfair, the fickleness of desire absolutely stunk.

An uncut toenail against his leg at night. That did it for him one time.

That lovely woman last year, who happened to own a horrible leg-shagging hound called Herbie.

The other one who sang Spice Girls songs in the shower. That was a real turn-off too.

So he was guilty as fuck of being unfair. He couldn't complain.

Was he being mature about this, or just a mug?

Speaking of mugs, he could do with more of that coffee.

The council's service unit where Tim worked had recently been transferred to management by a private company. This 'reframing' had been accompanied by a deluge of glossy leaflets and billboards, and a new manager came along with the shiny leaflets.

As a 'customer liaison officer', Tim used to answer questions on the phones, and spend part of the day at the front desk speaking to people. The new management got rid of the public reception space and organised the office on call centre lines.

When Tim came in and put his flask on top of his desk, his neighbour raised her eyebrows. "Not that I care, but Chatty Cathy will have a fit when she sees that."

Right. Tim thought for a moment, then put the flask on the floor under the desk. At least they still had those old desks that kept your legs and bits hidden. No one would see if you take off your shoes or scratch your balls or stash your coffee.

There was, however, talk of 'modernising' the workstations. Chatty Cathy had a catalogue passed around at one of their staff so-called meetings. CC used to run a call centre up north, but before joining the council she'd been on a managerial course in the States. So she said things like: "We need an upbeat look in the service centre that is part of the new reality we're trying to facilitate."

This meant a future of streamlined desks with no back or side panels at all. CC called these furnishings 'smart' because they were made out of a clear glass-like PVC, which would reveal the contents of every drawer and cupboard.

Chatty Cathy began her morning rounds. She was a petite woman with a dark brown bob, a naval-baring top and a nose-ring. She looked like a normal person you'd see down the shops or in a pub. It scared him to think she could have once been like him.

"Now Emily, you know you can't have any personal items at your desk," she admonished someone nearby. She snatched a newspaper away, and pulled open the drawer just to have a look there too.

"Uh . . . sorry," mumbled the sheepish Emily as she twisted a strand of hair around her finger and untwisted it. "I mean, we used to bring papers with us, no problem. It was out of habit . . ."

"I understand that everyone needs time to adjust to the new system. Even me! But we also have to work together to free ourselves from the old habits . . . Like this!" She gave a prod to a clipboard on another desk and a mobile slid out from under it. "Put it in your locker, please."

At that first meeting CC gathered everyone around her and told them: "We need *clarity* around us so we can give customers our undivided, undiminished attention. That's how we develop a real service mentality and go the extra mile we need to go."

What it really meant: no drinks at desks. No books, newspapers, no phones. Even pictures of your girlfriend or your cat were banned at workstations.

CC sailed by Tim and back into her office near his desk. Too close for comfort some might say, but at least he could listen for the opening and closing of the door . . .

Meanwhile, take advantage of those old-fashioned desks while you can.

Tim opened his flask and drank straight from it.

His phone started to ring. He had another sip before he answered. "Hello, Tim speaking. How can I help you?"

"The council hasn't paid my £10 compensation for a missed repair appointment. I sent the form in months ago!"

Tim ran a search on the name and address. "There doesn't seem to be anything on the system."

"What do you mean there's nothing on the system? It was there the last time I called. What did it do, get up and walk away? At this rate, I'll waste more than £10 ringing up the council about my compensation! If the council was incompetent before, now it's even worse!"

"I'll put a query form in for you. And I'll send you another compensation form," Tim said. "I'm sorry about the delay," he added. He made his voice almost as smooth as that coffee. "I know it must be frustrating, so I'll do what I can for you."

When he began this job, he really believed that he was performing some kind of public service. Now he was feeling like a gatekeeper at the entrance of a vast electronic moat. But at least he was polite about it.

He sensed an unclenching of a fist, a release of breath at the other end of the line. "OK."

Why didn't he talk that way to Lucy, express more feeling when he apologised? Too right she got suspicious, he must've sounded like some sad mid-90s meathead with a badly-stained copy of *Loaded* in his pocket.

Ring! Ring!

"The heating's off in my block."

"Is it communal heating? Yes? I'll check to see if anyone else has complained, and the progress of the repairs. Mind if I put you on hold while I do this, or should I ring you back?"

That one was dealt with easily enough. Repairs in progress.

"I need to speak to my rent officer. I've been threatened with eviction. Maybe I'm a few pounds in arrears, but I think there's been a mistake."

"Don't get too upset. It's just a computer-generated letter sent to frighten people. They're not *really* going to evict you just yet!"

He heard a door open, felt a stirring in the air behind him as if someone suddenly occupied it.

It was CC, frowning. Oh, so he wasn't supposed to say that? No one told him *not* to. "The best thing to do," he continued, "is to ask for a rent statement . . ."

Click! The phone went dead.

When he looked again, he saw CC striding back into her office. Maybe she had bigger fish to fry.

More coffee. Quick, under the desk, pretend to tie a shoelace. The gulp of liquid went down with a glow.

The phone rang again. And again.

Just a few more calls, and soon it should be break-time. He hid his flask under his shirt on the way to the canteen.

There was already a queue at the microwave, mostly female staff warming up their M&S diet lunches. And it was only 11.00. The poor things would be starving by 1.00.

He wondered what he'd do when the coffee ran out. There was still plenty left in the flask. He seemed to drinking from an endless well. It couldn't last forever, though.

He unscrewed the top of the flask. He usually had coffee with milk, but it was fine like this. Black. Lucy's hair was close to this colour. Dark brown rather than black, deep burnt-sugar brown. Like this coffee with just a dash of steamed milk.

He sat on the window sill and looked beyond the glass that never opened. As he drank, the coffee lifted him up with no jitter or jolt. It was such an even and calm rise, a steady glide up. The coffee-induced *clarity* in his mind cut through the dust and grime coating the windows, through to the island of grass and trees over the road from the Town Hall. There must have been even more dust on the leaves, but the green of them leapt at him.

He savoured those dark robust flavours and thought of how they had been nourished by mist and clouds. Did 'autonomy' have a taste, did it have colours?

Pieces of clear magenta flickered over the scene outside, the same colour as a dress worn by one of the women insurgents in the cloud forest.

"Alright Tim?" It was Emily. She was waving at him; the magenta came from her bracelet reflecting in the window. "Are you with us?" She seemed fully recovered from her dressing-down from CC.

Her dress was pale green and she was wearing opaque tights, dark green ones. Tim rubbed his eyes and blinked.

Emily was looking at him curiously. "Is something wrong?"

"No, I don't think so. Um, want some coffee? I got some in my flask. It's good stuff."

Emily chuckled. "You sound like you're talking about drugs!"

"Oh no, I watched my friend make this and nothing got slipped in. But you might taste clouds in it. It was grown in a cloud forest, apparently."

"Ha, you must have been partying last night too. But I might try that coffee later."

Later. Now he had to go back to work.

"Tim?" The voice was familiar. Oh, it was that pain-in-the-arse looking for his rent officer.

"Sorry about getting cut off, my cat sat on the phone! But to pick up where we left off – and it took forever to get through to you again. You said I should ask for a rent statement? I have to speak to my rent officer first. Could you put me through to him or at least give me his number?"

"Sorry, we're not allowed to give out numbers, and we can only route calls to the officers on Wednesdays. I'll send him an email and he'll get back to you."

"An email? Every time I ring it's 'I'll send an email'. Fuck emails. I want to talk to the geezer. I want to tell him what I think, and that I've paid my effing rent, and he shouldn't be wasting our money sending those stupid letters. So don't talk to me about another fucking email."

"Look, I'm sorry but I can't . . . can't put your call through. I'll send . . ."

"Talking to that tosser is like getting an audience with the Queen!"

He'd just been thinking that way, about moats and castles. But what is he defending?

"Yes, I know what you mean. Excuse me for just a moment." He reached below his desk, got out the coffee and took a quick sip he didn't bother to hide. A taste of clouds, a caffeine-fueled blast at routine.

"So," he continued, "Your Queen or King's sitting tight in the castle and it's surrounded by this electronic *moat*. In the meantime, I've got a nutcase of a boss breathing down my neck."

"Tell me about it!"

Will he be a gatekeeper any longer?

"At this moment, I'm drinking some delicious coffee. I'm not allowed to be drinking coffee in the name of 'clarity' and a 'service mentality'." said Tim. "But I'll show them some *real* service and do something else that's forbidden. I'll give you the number you need. And here's another number as well. You might want to ring that one to make a complaint."

When Tim hung up, he heard CC's door open with a grind of its ancient hinges. She was coming straight towards him. She'd left the door to her sanctum wide open, so she must be agitated.

She couldn't have heard what he just said. Maybe his earlier remark about the council's computer-generated letters had been recorded for 'quality control purposes'. And the other evidence was right there on his desk.

"Tim, we need to have some communication," she began.

Then her phone started to ring. For a moment it looked like she wouldn't answer it, then she went to pick it up.

After a while she shouted, loud enough for Tim to hear at his desk. "Who gave you this number . . . What do you mean you don't remember?"

Tim opened his flask again and poured himself a cup. The aroma drifted through the office and everyone turned their heads as if someone had shouted out to them.

"Does anyone want some coffee?"

The Turning Track

with Mat Joiner

Clutching his lover's manuscript, Edwin made his way to the train station. He dragged his feet through the piles of leaves on the empty road. When he was a kid, he loved shuffling through autumn leaves. He found it comforting now.

The crunch and swish of the leaves under his feet was the loudest thing in his ears. He was alone on this road, a half-hour walk from the terminus of the streetcar line. He'd been the only passenger by the time he arrived at that last stop.

While he walked, Edwin looked around for signs . . . of what, he couldn't say. Charles had written: "*There are verges in our world that the Train might have seeded with flowers grown in the silt of sleep.*"

He looked beneath his feet, at the roadside. There were dandelions gone to seed, lifting their heads from cracks in the concrete. He saw buddleia in all shades of purple; bindweed vines winding through rusted barbed-wire fencing, their shrivelled morning blossoms closed tight.

He searched among these common weeds for a sign of difference.

Charles had sketched some flora found beside the tracks travelled by this Train. A plump-leaved orange-flowering succulent, a spiked black thistle, white blossoms with markings that gave them clock faces, wild orchids with red lascivious tongues.

But perhaps Charles didn't only mean *flowers*. He could have meant many things. The passage of the Train would pull on the air, pull on the fabric of space and leave something behind, or change some very familiar element.

The road was deserted, but showed signs of previous use. There were buildings that could have been warehouses, with doors open and windows blank.

He looked up in the sky. What shadow had just fluttered across it?

He stopped in the forecourt of an abandoned petrol station. He wasn't sure what drew him to it. Something odd about the pumps? They were old, but . . . He walked closer and picked up a dangling nozzle.

Yes! The end of the nozzle opened into a brass flower, reminding him of an ancient gramophone. That thing wouldn't service any known vehicle.

Edwin took out his camera, fumbled with the flash and took a photo.

"I'm doing this for you, Charles," he whispered to himself. "Though it scares the bejesus out of me."

Charles, Edwin noted, would use stronger language. Charles used to swear like the proverbial sailor and gently poked fun at Edwin's more refined manners. Charles' potty-mouth didn't rule out flights of poetry, though. He had also written: *"This train is not for everyone, but its tracks stitch together many dreams."*

"OK, Charles," Edwin added. "It scares the *shit* out of me. Like you said, this train's not for everyone. I won't get on the thing, you hear? I told you I wouldn't. Of course, I wasn't expecting it would actually . . . arrive. And I won't believe that until I see it choo-chooing up the track. But if it does, I promise you I'll have a gander. A good *fucking* gander."

But you have a ticket. Edwin could imagine Charles arguing. *Someone sent you a ticket. What I wouldn't give for that!*

And Edwin answered: maybe that ticket was meant for *you*, and I don't belong on that train at all.

Edwin carried the ticket, as he had for over a year, in the money-belt tied around his waist, a relic from his grandfather's days in India when he lived in fear of getting robbed by 'natives'. Edwin never had any use for this item until the ticket arrived. He didn't really expect anyone would try to steal it from him, but he just needed to know where it was at all times. He needed to keep it safe.

The ticket came in the post at the height of summer last year. Edwin had just returned from the office, tired from a long day and a sweaty ride on the streetcar. He was feeling drained and sad, wishing things the way they once were.

Charles would break off work in his study and welcome Edwin home with a cold drink. Usually it would be beer, but on a hot day Charles might offer him home-made lemonade in a tall glass half-filled with ice. Charles used to fuss over Edwin's health, telling him to look after himself while he was young so he wouldn't end up with a dodgy heart. This meant days without drink, and without meat. Charles had some funny ideas, but Edwin went along with them.

But on that day, Charles had been dead for a month. Edwin's flat was just as he left it. The only sound was the hum of the fridge, its motor starting up and stopping with a weary gasp and heartbroken sigh. *I know how you feel,* he had thought. Then tears came to Edwin's eyes. *It's one thing to address myself to my late boyfriend. Another to start talking to a clapped out old fridge. Get a grip, Edwin.*

Edwin bent down to pick up the post without much interest. Those brown envelopes all looked like they contained bills.

As he dumped the envelopes on the table, one caught his eye. This one was brown too, but a rich brown that reminded him of fertile garden soil.

He turned it over. No return address. No postmark. But he recognised the insignia on the front of the envelope: a stylised train track twisted to form an infinity symbol or a Mobius strip. The symbol was raised and embossed, appearing three-dimensional. Edwin traced the symbol with the tip of his finger. Charles, of course, claimed that the train existed in many more dimensions than three. The same symbol – what was the word Charles used for it? *Lemniscate.* The symbol was *in* the ticket, running much deeper than mere paper should allow.

Edwin put the pump to his ear. Perhaps he heard a rushing sound, coming from a distance he couldn't imagine. Perhaps he was only hearing the wind that stirred the weeds and made a loose shutter bang.

He'd allotted time to explore the route, but he should be moving on. He started walking again, carrying on over a gentle rise. On the other side of the rise a single streetlamp shed just enough light to let him find his way. A violet moth flew in a circle around the light.

And at the end of the road: the station.

Edwin hadn't been expecting Grand Central Station, not after all his research. But the station itself didn't look like much, moss-blotched brick and smeared windows. It could have been a rural station that became stranded at the edges of a city after it expanded, then contracted for reasons involving the economy and trade. As the city receded it left behind these inbetween places, like beached flotsam after an ebb tide. The station sported those fussy flowerboxes that looked best in a cottage garden, though Edwin couldn't make out much of what grew in them.

There was a town-hall sized clock over the entrance, as if rushing commuters had once looked up there to check the time. It could have once been a landmark where people arranged to meet.

He was surprised that the big clock told the correct time, and the hands moved as they should.

Edwin opened his jacket and examined his ticket. He checked the time on the ticket and on his watch, as well as the clock. He was early. There was time to explore, and he also had a book to read while waiting. *The* book. Charles had given it a working title: *The Turning Track*. He hefted it in his hands. He'd like to think he knew it by heart, and in a sense he did. But every time he looked at it, he saw something different in the familiar sentences.

A dense grove of trees surrounded the station. *Catalpa*, Charles had called that kind of tree. They were a favourite of Charles, those big shady trees with tiers of small orchid-like blossoms. But Edwin wasn't so sure. Those exotic June blossoms always seemed dusty and wan, as if it was a struggle to flower in their city. And when the fallen flowers covered the pavement and parkland paths, their sweet scent made his eyes water.

As he came closer Edwin saw that the trees were in full flower, even as they shed their autumn leaves. As he walked beneath them, the flowers began to cast subtle light onto the station. He stopped. Charles didn't write about *this*. He chuckled at the thought that he was one up on Charles, until he remembered that he would never get to rib him or tease him. They would never even get to quarrel again. He even missed their quarrels.

The light from the flowers brought a buried memory with it: a single light on the landing at boarding school.

There was a scent of damp, a hint of musk. A steady drip of water. Before entering the station, he inspected the window box near the door. Black ivy flowed out of the window boxes and over the walls. He stroked a leaf. It had a texture like leather, thick stems like cartilage.

The station itself was deep in shadow, broken by flower-glimmer from the windows and a dim glow behind gingham curtains in the station office. He saw a flare of light from the platform, as if someone had lit a match. Then the tip of a burning cigarette.

In one way he was glad to have company, but he also bristled at the thought someone else could invade a territory that he and Charles alone had shared. And who could be in that office?

He heard the strike of a match again, and the repeated *miaow* of a cat. It reminded Edwin of Charles' cat searching the house for him and letting loose heartbreaking pleas.

He tried to avoid cats. They got to him these days, ever since he had to put Sophie down.

Miaow. Ignore the cat, move on. He had work to do.

So he left the ivy alone and stepped inside the station.

A woman in her thirties sat on the bench. She appeared wren-like and freckled in the thin light of the catalpa trees coming through the window just above her. She wore a cheap trench coat and beret. Beside her was a scuffed beige suitcase – and a carrier containing the complaining cat.

"I will *not* give you my ticket," she was saying. "I will not even sell it to you. I don't care how much money you say you have." Her voice grew shrill, then softened as she tried to soothe her pet. "Oh don't fret, you'll like it where we're going."

"You sure about that?"

A gaunt woman of about forty, black hair growing out of a severe crop, paced back and forth in front of the woman with the cat. She wore only a thin cardigan and a grey frock that might have been a fashionable party dress twenty years ago. It was a skimpy outfit for an autumn night, but she didn't appear to feel the cold.

She discarded a cigarette butt and speared it under her stiletto heel.

"That animal does like to whinge," she added with a curl of her lip. She took a gold case out of the pocket of her cardy and drew out another cigarette.

The young woman put sheltering arms around the cat carrier. "You'd complain too if you were put in a box. But it can't be helped. He'll be happy once we arrive."

"How the hell do you know? You don't even know where this train is going. Maybe they *eat* cats there."

Then she turned to Edwin. "And who are you?"

Edwin offered his hand. She ignored it. "I'm Edwin Brookes. I've been making a study of the Train, carrying on the work of Charles Bell, who died last year."

"Charles Bell? I've heard of him. Some kind of professor, been on the radio?"

"If you're referring to the anthropologist Charles Bell, that's correct."

"And if I recall, he was considered a right crackpot."

"His theories were controversial, but one person's crackpot is another person's font of knowledge." Edwin smiled, not really fazed at the woman's attitude towards his late lover. He was used to it. In this case, it was best to meet sarcasm with greater sarcasm. While he was hopeless at sport, he could certainly hold his own with a bit of verbal tussle.

And given that this woman liked the sound of her own voice, she could in fact provide some useful information. How *would* she know about the Train?

The quiet one with the cat might prove more difficult to draw out. He recognised her protective stance, how she hunched over her cat basket. She was protecting much more than her pet, perhaps some hidden core of herself. He could bet she was bullied when young. He recognised that stance because he once held himself the same way.

"I'm Carla." The gaunt woman finally flung her name at him.

Edwin sat down on the bench next to the younger woman. He nodded at her, then peered in at a long-haired black cat with a triangle of white at its chest, a large and imposing animal. The cat's orange eyes indicated Persian ancestry, but it had the robust build of a common moggie.

A far cry from Sophie, a petite shorthaired tortoise-shell.

He had nothing against cats, really. They just upset him sometimes.

Edwin poked a finger through the grate and offered the animal a tentative scratch of its head. The cat quieted, and rubbed its head against Edwin's finger.

This prompted the younger woman to introduce herself as Emily and her cat as Fintan.

"So Edwin, do you have a ticket?" Carla appraised him, head titled to one side.

"No," said Edwin, without thinking. Drat. He did have one, which he wasn't planning to use. It shouldn't go to waste, should it? Give it to this woman? But maybe he *would* want to hop on the train in the future, and he should keep hold of it.

Before he went anywhere he must publish Charles' book. And Edwin needed to add *proof*. He had to do this before he could move on. Charles would certainly want him to 'move on', but he never realised how hard it could be. The daft old bastard. Charles hadn't a clue how hard it would be to live without him.

Edwin hated deception. He'd been lied to as a child, and he vowed he wouldn't do that to other people. But that lie had just slipped over his lips before he could stop it.

"I'm studying the Train. Charles Bell started a book about that Train, which I plan to complete."

So now he *had* told the truth, more about it than he'd told anyone. "And what about you, Carla? What brings you here?"

Carla sat down on the bench, leaving a gap between herself and Edwin and Emily.

"That train took my death from me, and it left me stranded in this life," she said. "It owes me. So this time I'll get *on* it, not *under* it. You see, some years ago I was aiming to jump under the 18.05 express. But that train was late, and *this* train came along instead."

It took a while for Edwin to assimilate this last statement. Emily studiously stroked her cat through the grate. Fintan's purr swelled in the silence.

Carla scratched at her left wrist, then her right. The full sleeves of her cardy rode up, showing the trackmarks of scars on her wrist. She saw where Edwin was looking, and chuckled. "Oh yes, I tried to kill myself again, many times. Didn't work. It was that train, I tell you! Do you know my scars itch when the train is anywhere near me?"

Edwin looked down the tracks, where leaves drifted in deep piles on the sidings. There was no sign of a train, but then the indicator lit up.

Next train was due in twenty minutes. The infinity symbol appeared next to this announcement, in case there was any doubt *which* train it would be.

"But you *can't* have my ticket," interrupted Emily. "You say that train owes you, but *I* owe you nothing. That ticket came to *me*. I've grown up hearing that train. It rattled my walls as it passed, though I never lived near a railway. That ticket is mine."

"Shut up about your ticket. I'll get on anyway. Haven't you ever travelled without a ticket, miss goody two-shoes? I bet you haven't."

"But you said you had money. So what do you need to do that for?"

"For the fun of it. For the thrill. I shoplifted too. Don't anymore, because clothes don't matter now. Bet you've done nothing like that. Always dotted your i's and crossed your t's. So I'll get on without a ticket. See what happens."

A scraping sound from the station office interrupted Carla. They all turned around as the door opened and a figure emerged, holding a lantern.

"Good evening, passengers!" The man's voice rasped as if rusted and not used very often. He walked along the platform towards them, holding his lantern higher. It showed him in its flickering light, a scrawny young man with a scrubby red beard, clad in a railwayman's cap and a uniform too small for him. Despite his thin build, the faded tunic was stretched across his chest with half the buttons left undone to accommodate him.

"You . . . Do you work here?" Edwin asked.

The young man scratched his face. It brought to mind the way Carla had scratched at the scars on her wrists.

"I live here." He gave a nod towards the office. "But I intend to work for the Train, just as my grandfather did."

Edwin peered at the man's uniform in the dim light, the insignia on his cap and the badges on his jacket. *Yes.* He reached for his pouch under his shirt, so he could take out his ticket to compare the markings. Then he remembered what he'd told Carla. He couldn't reveal himself as a liar if he wanted to keep the trust of these people. But he *knew.* That insignia, that Mobius strip of train tracks, was the same as the one on the envelope and the ticket in his money-belt.

"Yeah, this uniform's pretty smart," the thin man wheezed. "I found it in my parents' attic, with a wage slip bearing the name of Stephen Henning, my grandfather. I was named after him. Seemed right to carry on his work."

Carla cleared her throat. "So what was on this wages slip? How much did your grandfather get paid?"

"That, madame, is confidential. A company secret. And the rewards of this position involve much more than money," replied Henning.

"Nothing matters more than money. If you've had it, then lost it, then no one can tell you any different," said Carla. "What do you know? You're just an old bum in an even older uniform."

Maybe the man's mad but there's no need to be cruel, Edwin thought. Carla reminded him of the kids who made his life miserable in boarding school, boys who later traded their school blazers for military khaki.

But Henning didn't seem offended by Carla's comment. He adjusted his cap and shuffled off towards his office singing to himself: *"I asked my captain for the time of day, said he throwed his watch away."*

Carla began another round of pacing, moving further down the platform. The cat was quiet now. Edwin looked in the carrier, and Fintan met his gaze with a weary dignity.

Nothing like Sophie, really. Small and sprightly, Sophie had seemed much younger than her venerable seventeen years. But after Charles died she wasted, sickened and suffered no matter what Edwin tried to do for her. Finally, the vet suggested that the most caring thing Edwin could do was put her down.

Edwin had followed the vet's instructions. And after he saw to ending Sophie's life, Edwin came close to ending his own. Then he looked at the ticket . . . again, and again. And he looked at Charles' book, which had been untouched since Charles last worked on it. Edwin couldn't leave it unfinished and unknown. He had to let others see the beauty of Charles' work, and help them understand those mysterious tracks that run like threads or veins of ore through the layers of the cosmos.

Fintan began complaining again. "Oh, I don't know what's got into him. He's travelled in that basket before without making a fuss," said Emily.

"He's picked up on our mood. He knows this isn't an ordinary train."

Emily nodded and smiled. This was the first time he saw her smile. It made him smile too.

"It's wonderful to be with someone who knows about the Train," she said. "A lot of people think I'm mad because of it. I didn't even talk about it with them, but they knew. At work, I always did my job and typed perfect letters, but they were always telling me off for my mind being 'elsewhere'. The other girls in the typing pool tried to be nice but they just didn't know what to say to me. And that Train . . . it rattled my room wherever I lived. Other people heard it and they thought I was doing something to make all the noise. I've gone through quite a few landlords."

"I used to live with Charles Bell." Damn, he'd meant to say 'used to know'! "I have his book with me. I'll show it to you if you want."

"Oh yes! Please . . . I didn't know such a thing existed."

"You won't find it in a library. It's not finished. That's my job."

The Turning Track

He opened the folder containing the manuscript and turned to a page showing sketches of the Train. He turned it so the paper would catch the tree-light.

"Oh, but this is the one I dream about," Emily exclaimed. "It's a great steam train. There are compartments where you can sleep and dream some more. I once had a dream where I dreamed I was dreaming on the train. Funny, that! The bumps of the track lulled me into sleep. I heard the names of stations being called. Some were familiar, like Horseberry. Others were Wanderstone, Mycta, Seeksome, Mercatrix, Ariantini . . ." Emily's voice rose as she recited the names of the stations.

Edwin began writing them down.

"So what are you babbling about now!" Carla exclaimed. "I could hear you from the other end of the station. Not such a quiet little mouse now, are you?"

Emily visibly quaked under Carla's gaze. And Edwin wanted to shake her as much as he wanted to punch Carla to shut her up.

Stop that, Emily! Don't you see you're worth ten of her?

Edwin had probably been just as pathetic when he was younger. Or worse. How Charles had put up with him in those early days, he'd never know.

If Charles had to deal with an obvious bully like this, he wouldn't confront them directly. He'd distract them, use their illusions of importance to his advantage. Or more to the point, to the advantage of his work.

Edwin cleared his throat. "Carla, you're the only one of us who has actually seen this train. So what are your impressions?" He made his voice calm and neutral, like a newsreader.

"You mean, I saw this train before it ran me over? Perhaps I'll take it from the bottom, sweetie. Remember, I was waiting for the ordinary express train. I was teetering on the edge of the platform, then this *thing* appeared. It was sleek, like a submarine. But it was high, like it was a double-decker, but with more levels than that. There was an open platform in that station, so I don't know how it will fit in *here*.

"It had little windows, like ship windows. There was a jolt, something like weight passing over me, a rush of darkness and ghost-light. And just before I went under, I saw two people gazing down at me from one of those windows. Who the hell were they? And where did this train come from? Perhaps I had a moment of regret that I'd never find out. There was no clue in the faces at the window. They were a blur . . . I thought it was the speed of the train or the tears in my eyes. But no, I really think those faces *were* a blur."

Carla's voice had lost its stridency. Held by her story, she'd forgotten to harass Emily.

"Tears?" Edwin prompted.

"Yes, I was a shell filled with tears. Or I was until that damned train ran me over. I looked fine on the outside. Just a few scrapes and sprains, no breaks anybody else could see. But that train flattened me in other ways. Years of weeping burst out and now I don't even have tears I can call my own."

Edwin nodded. He didn't know what to say to that. But best to keep her talking. "And what about those faces you saw?" That detail intrigued him. The train shifted, curved around the dimensions it rode. The people in it must do the same.

"What about them? Did I take a picture? No way," said Carla. "Not when a train the size of an ocean liner was barrelling down those tracks. And I was thinking: 'Take me!' So it took me, then spat me out." Her voice turned wistful, her shoulders slumped. She looked lost, the way Edwin felt after Charles' death.

This left Edwin unmoved. When he was a child, he saw school bullies, torturers in the making, break down and cry too. A relative who died, a beloved pet. He'd heard the bluster of a tough guy dissolve in the racking cry of an abandoned child. A marshmallow heart one day, a bunched fist the next; sentimentality didn't pull any punches.

"There's a hollow inside me," she said. "I wouldn't have it grow."

"Like carrying a child and losing it," Edwin murmured.

He'd only been thinking aloud. He did not expect Carla to round on him. She snapped, "It's nothing like that at all. How the hell would you know?"

Then she smiled in a toothy, dangerous way. "You ever been inside, Edwin? I know, you're a good boy. You and your Mad Professor. But even good boys get put away somewhere if they misbehave *just a little bit.* Could be the bin, could be prison. And I was basically a good girl in those days, but did that matter? They put me away, and there I stayed for many years."

"Carla, I'm sorry you had a rough time, but what's that got to do with Edwin?" Emily interrupted.

Emily was only trying to be helpful, but Edwin felt cold dread run in his veins. Had Carla guessed about him and Charles? *How did she know? Did it show?* But he was just an average-looking chap. He and Charles never went to bars, never wore pinkie-rings. They never joined a club; they only loved each other.

No, he *wouldn't* let her intimidate him. He was the one asking questions. "Carla," he began. "Why were you . . ."

"The engine passed at six o'clock, the cab passed at nine . . ." Henning was waving his lantern as he walked towards them. This time he wore tickertape looped around his neck like a silk scarf. His tunic was now buttoned up tight.

"Christ, look who's here again," muttered Carla. "Still singing. Will someone shut him up?"

"Hello passengers. I've just received word of a delay."

"Delay? That takes the biscuit. Yeah, what could possibly delay *the* Train? Leaves on the line?"

Henning touched the bill of his cap to her. "In fact . . . yes, ma'am." He peered at the tape. "Blank leaves on the rail. The Train may be delayed some time. I'll keep you updated, never fear."

"Batshit crazy," Carla scoffed. But Henning only raised his eyebrow.

"I think that's in the job description," he said mildly. "Now, if you'll excuse me." He went back to his office.

Thwarted, she began to kick through the leaves on the platform. "Leaves on the line," she muttered. "Crazy."

Pot and kettle, thought Edwin. But perhaps Carla had a point.

Emily touched his arm. "I tried to stop the Train. Maybe someone has succeeded."

"How?"

"I've heard it *everywhere* I've ever lived, in the walls, under the floor. The wheels mostly, sometimes its whistle. But always just passing through. I figured if I could find it a station, it would stop long enough for me to get on. So I went through junk shops, looking for pictures. Newspaper clippings, postcards, old books; anything that looked right. Here..."

She took out an envelope from her coat. Edwin thought she was offering him a fan of cards at first, but they turned out to be photographs of old stations, in colour, sepia, black-and-white, with pinholes at the corners. The stations themselves were as varied; some cathedrals in iron and glass and others little more than a shed at the side of the track, or brick stubs shawled with weeds. On the back of each picture she had written a name. Edwin recognised some as the dream-stations Emily had told him about.

"I stuck these up on the walls. Surely one of them would be on the Line. So I waited and waited, kept my suitcase packed under the bed. Every time the walls started shaking, I'd think, *this is it.* I watched every station to be safe. I knew how it would be, the smell of coal in my room, one of the pictures filling up with steam; I'd reach *through* somehow, and I'd be on the right side of the paper, ready to board." She laughed in embarrassment.

Edwin thought, *You don't have to laugh at yourself, not about this.*

"Sounds mad, doesn't it?"

"It's no madder than anything in here." Edwin touched the book.

Emily smiled at him. "No, but the Train never came to me. I kept moving on, room to room, putting up new pictures. I was passing through too, I suppose."

He had an image of her, in hotel rooms and bedsits, always gazing up at the unchanging stations, never giving up hope.

"Until one night, a few weeks ago," Emily said. "I came back from work and there was the ticket tucked into one of the frames. I knew at once where it had come from. The symbol in your book, the one on Henning's jacket – it's watermarked in the paper."

Edwin felt a flush of pride at that – *his* book! But honesty made him say: "It's Charles' book really. He died suddenly, and I owe it to him to finish it. I'm just following in his footsteps." He found himself wiping his eyes. *Carla complains she doesn't have any tears left*... he could certainly lend her a few of those, if not his ticket. He thought he'd finished with the tears, but they kept coming.

Emily looked him in the eye. "Charles wasn't just your *friend*, was he?"

He sagged, suddenly very tired and wondering what the hell he was doing. He could be put in prison for the wrong answer . . . in other words, the *right* answer. But if he encounters this Train with Emily, even boarding it with her, they needed to trust each other.

"No, he wasn't just my friend. Call it a labour of love, if you like. He's gone and this is the best I can do by him."

Now he felt better for telling the truth.

"Here . . ." Emily thrust her pictures at Edwin. "If they'll help with the book, you're welcome to them. I don't think I'll need them much longer." She took his hands. "I think he'd be proud of you."

Edwin smiled weakly. "I'm not so sure. I do have a ticket, but I might be scared to use it. Or I just can't decide. I keep asking myself what Charles would want me to do, and I still don't have an answer."

She pulled away. "You said you didn't have a ticket."

"I said that to Carla because I wanted to decide in the end. But really, all I want to do is *see* the Train. Charles never got the chance. But this isn't just for him. Somebody's got to stay and bear witness. How many people have seen or heard the Train and think they're mad? They didn't have anybody to help them understand. If I finish the book, then they're not alone any more. If I use the ticket, nobody speaks up for them. I thought the ticket was meant for Charles, you see, but it came too late. Hell, he'd *jump* on board if he was here. I could never do that. I'm too bloody cowardly to be passenger material."

There you go Charles – there's the truth. Hope you liked it.

"I'm scared too," Emily said. "I've spent all my life waiting. I don't even know where I'm going to end up. But I'm going to board, regardless. What will you do with the ticket?"

"Well, I could use it as evidence . . ." Edwin looked down the platform. Carla was rooting through the litter, as if she might find her stolen death under the leaves. "Or I could give it away. She needs it more than I do."

"Don't! I'm not going to share a carriage with that woman. Don't tell me you believe her?"

"I don't trust her, no. It doesn't mean I disbelieve her." Edwin thumbed through the manuscript. "There are people in here who saw the Train in the sky, made up of storm clouds and stars. You've dreamed of it as an old engine. Carla's Train was some kind of Leviathan, and God knows how I'll see it. Charles didn't know what to call it."

He closed his eyes and recited, "*How are we to classify the Train, then – ghost, god, machine, organic? Like all the old tales, it shifts shape depending on the teller. 'Train' itself seems too small a word to contain the thing; but all we have are words.*"

"That's pretty," Carla said behind him. "Maybe he could explain this, too."

She dropped a shredded glove into his lap. It might have been made of latex or lace, but it was too wrinkled to tell. It slid off him and whispered to the ground, translucent in the station lights.

"There's more like that back there." Carla nodded back at the leaf-drift. "Except most of that's not even leaves; they're goddamn *tickets*. Expired ones, of course. Rags. And this. Go on, pick it up."

"She's playing games with you," Emily said. "Don't rise to it."

"Mouse, you're boring me. Shut up. I'm talking to Mister Scholar here. What are you waiting for?"

Reluctantly, Edwin bent down. The glove was slippery and brittle to the touch, fine as an insect's wing. *Shake hands,* he thought, and wanted to be sick. "It's skin," he said.

Carla grinned. "Yeah. Look at it closely, you'll see lines and prints, probably enough to identify the poor schmuck. There was this, too." From her cardigan she brought out what looked like half a mask. She lifted the flaking thing up to her face and peered through an eyehole. Edwin heard Emily retching.

"We weren't the first passengers here," Carla went on, "and look what happened to them. There's probably a whole carriage-load of fucking *peel* back there. Anything like that in your book, sweetie?"

Through the taste of bile, Edwin said, "Nothing at all." He threw the 'glove' at Carla, who casually folded it away. "It felt old. Like snakeskin, did you notice?"

"Well, it's not. You could've read a future from that palm. Short one, obviously. We need answers." Carla pulled a razor from her sleeve; a big old-fashioned cut-throat blade. "It's time we had a proper word with the Thin Controller."

Emily plucked at Edwin's sleeve. "Don't go with her," she said in his ear.

Carla shot them a glance. "Oh, Mouse, Mouse, there's only one person I seriously tried to kill. And I had that taken from me. Keep behind me if you're that scared. I think *I'm* safe. Don't know about you."

She flicked the razor open and led them back into the station.

There was little in what Henning might have called his office; a sleeping bag and camping stove in the corner, a desk with a few books, his cap on top of them, and a mass of red-printed tape. Henning was stooped, coughing into a bandanna. When he looked up, his beard had turned darker, almost crimson.

"There's still a delay . . ."

Carla threw the skins in his face. "Update us on this one. Maybe you could give us another song. *The Butcher's Blues?*"

"Oh, *that*. Most of this accumulated before I started working here."

"But you know, don't you? Or is that another Company secret?"

Another fit of coughs shook Henning. Edwin tried to pull Carla away. "He's in no fit state to answer you."

"Fit or not, he can tell us. You can take notes, scholar-boy."

Machinery clicked somewhere in the room. Henning grew still. He wiped blood from his mouth. "Nobody dies here," he said at last. "But some people need to shed their old skins before they can board."

Like snakes, just as I said, thought Edwin. Carla snarled, "Don't fob me off with that crap."

Henning steepled his fingers. "I saw it happen once, just after I took up my place. It shook me, like it shakes you now. But I've read up on it since. The Train changes its shape for us. Seems only fair that we should return the favour."

It sounded like a quote from *The Turning Track*. There was, suddenly, something of Charles in the man behind the desk; a tattered magus surrounded by gazetteers and timetables. Edwin shivered, and Henning smiled at him.

"You're as bad as the scholar," Carla said.

"*All change here,*" Henning sang. "Doesn't have to be in the flesh." He tapped his forehead. "Here, does just as well. Nobody who ever looked upon the Train went away unmarked. Why, ma'am, you should know that yourself. Being immortal and all."

Carla turned white. "I want that back. I want my death where it belongs. Who gave you the fucking right to steal that from me?"

"Begging your pardon, but had you ever wondered if it wasn't yours to begin with? See, I'm not good with all this philosophy, I'm just a railwayman. But the Train takes freight as well as passengers."

She snarled, and the razor flickered out at Henning's face.

Edwin and Emily grabbed Carla's arms. She writhed, strong considering she was so thin. "I'll cut you as well, Mouse . . ." She rammed her elbow into Edwin's ribs. His eyes watered but he held onto her wrist until she cursed and threw down the blade.

Henning had not flinched at all. He merely got out of his chair and picked up the razor, admiring the mother-of-pearl handle before folding away the blade and offering it back to Carla.

"*Don't* give it back," said Emily. "My God, are you mad?"

Carla snatched the razor back.

"It's served its purpose, Madame."

Carla glared at him, saying nothing. She scratched at her scarred wrists.

"You carved a map you'd never lose. Good enough to follow the Train a ways, but it doesn't just use scars. There are leys and nerves; networks you and I will never see." Henning's voice was soft and sad. "I've changed too, but I won't be working the Line. It seems this is my station."

He opened his tunic and pulled up his clotted shirt. There was a machine rooted in his pigeon chest; dark metal wheels oscillating, oiled with mucus, a roll of veined paper feeding itself into the stuttering printer: destinations, lines, times stamped out in runes of blood and lymph. Cables and metallic fronds meandered through his thin skin. "Will you look at that," he said in pained awe. "I think it's taking at last. And your Train is almost due."

He tucked his shirt back in and beamed at the dumbstruck passengers. "I'm a true Company man now."

Edwin managed to speak at last. "So who is this Company? Everything I've heard about the Train, there's no mention of them." And he also wanted to ask: *Who would condemn you to that? Make that a condition of employment?*

But the simple pride in Henning's face stopped him. It was the expression of a man getting the job he had always wanted. Edwin envied him for that, despite the grisly growth on his chest. "Don't worry about the Company," said Henning. "Every effort will be made to ensure your journey is comfortable. As long as you take a certain degree of initiative, you'll be a satisfied customer."

"You should collaborate with this guy," Carla said to Edwin. "The Human Tickertape speaks your fate; make a mint at sideshows." She jammed a cigarette into her sneer; used the match-light to examine her scars. "You're welcome to each other." Still scratching, she left the office. The click of her heels was lost in echo.

"Thank God for that," said Emily, looking closely at Henning as he sat back down in his chair and glanced at the book he'd been reading.

She cleared her throat. "And what of us? Do *we* change as well?"

"I'm an employee. This . . ." He tapped his chest. "This is part of the uniform. There's still time for you to decide." He consulted a fob-watch. "A few minutes yet."

Emily bit her lip. "We'll take our chances." And when Edwin started, she quickly added, "Fintan and me."

"And you, sir?"

"I don't know. There's the manuscript . . . Who'll edit it? Who'll publish it?" Edwin raked fingers through his hair.

"These things find a way." Henning nodded. He closed his book and turned it so the spine faced them. The bronze green leather was scuffed and split; it might only have been the undependable light that made the words left on the spine come and go: *ING TRACK – BELL BROOKES GRIFFIN*.

Edwin reached out a trembling hand. The names sank into the leather. "I don't know anyone called Griffin," he whispered. "That's a fake, isn't it?" He made sure his own manuscript was under his arm.

Henning gently pushed his book just out of reach. "No, sir. It's a possibility. Best not touch it. It hasn't found all its authors yet."

A fresh coil of tape juddered out from beneath Henning's shirt. "Ah, too much talking on the job. Excuse me . . ." He reached for his cap and lantern.

Emily plucked at Edwin's sleeve. "We need to go, *now*. Can't you feel the Train? It's coming now."

"What?" But he felt the floor vibrate beneath his feet.

He let Emily drag him out to the platform, to the bench where Fintan waited.

There were too many echoes, the sense of *space* behind him. The station had begun to change. Edwin knew it, but he would not look back. This was it; he could only face forward. His heart clenched. He wondered if this was the transformation Henning spoke about.

The ground was shaking now. A wind blew down the track, making leaves, tickets, sloughed skins dance. It smelled of oil and steam and spice, fallen apples on the ground gone mushy and brown. It brought the scent of every autumn that had ever been. It made Edwin's eyes water but he stared downrail, unwilling to blink.

He hardly felt Emily's hand in his as she pulled him closer to the tracks, ready for the Train's arrival. She was laughing.

He saw Carla driven back, thrown down, her face disbelieving. She got up, fought against the wind like a bad mime. *It doesn't want you,* he thought. Carla got close enough to the platform edge to grab Emily's coat and pull her back. She shoved the younger woman against the wall.

"It won't take me," Carla said. "If I had a ticket, it wouldn't matter. C'mon, Mouse . . . you don't need it. You're young, you'll get another chance. What's a dream compared to everything I've lost?" She began to rifle through the pockets of Emily's trenchcoat.

Emily bucked against her, cursing. In a moment, Edwin knew, Carla would turn out the contents of the suitcase, going over everything, even Fintan in his box, until the ticket was in her hand. And he was back at school again, watching the bullies spill his life on the floor.

It filled him with rage. Carla believed she was *entitled* to take Emily's ticket. Despite years locked up, she still believed she could lay claim to anything and treat anyone as she pleased.

It had taken him years to learn how to stand up to people like that, years to know his worth. Charles had helped him; now he had to help Emily. Rather than wrestle with a crazy woman again, Edwin had a better idea . . .

He put his folder down on the bench and fumbled in his money-belt, then held up a ticket. "Carla!" He had to shout, straining his voice against those of the wind; they were changing all the time, modulating between whistles and horns and the call of an owl in a deep forest. The thin woman glared at him.

"Leave her alone. I've got a ticket too. You can take mine, just let her go."

Carla grinned. "You *lied*. I wouldn't have given you credit, sweetie. Alright then." She pushed Emily away.

"That's yours by right," Emily called. "Don't give it away."

"The journey's not worth this," Edwin said. He held the ticket high. Carla was snatching for it. He smiled – and let go. The wind took the ticket from his hand.

She howled and dived after it, straight onto the track. She got up, rummaging through the debris between the tracks. Then she lifted her bloodied face.

She brandished the ticket in crooked fingers, kissed it. Then she looked at it, and blanched.

"This is a fucking *streetcar* ticket!"

Edwin felt a terrible glee, but it was momentary. Whatever else Carla shouted at him was now drowned in a noise like syncopated thunder.

The indicator started flashing in a semaphore rhythm. On, off, on.

ALL STATIONS. ALL STATIONS.

There was a great darkness running down the rails towards them, studded with lights, as if the night itself was pulling into the station. And Edwin realised that Carla was making no move back to the platform.

"Get off the line, Carla! I'm sorry, I'll give you the real ticket. Just get off the line!"

Carla shot him a look of pure disgust. She stood up, dropped the streetcar ticket, and turned to face the Train. In the last moment, she spread her arms: to ward it off or embrace it.

With all the noise, he thought he heard her shriek: "Two strikes, you're out!"

Two hits by the Train, or was she screaming about his second lie?

"No, Carla, no!"

Emily glanced at Carla, shrugged, then turned her eyes towards the Train. Her face was illuminated. "It's everything I thought it would be . . . and much more."

The Train filled the station. It bellowed clouds of steam. There were whole landscapes in there, valleys, mountains, hills. The profiles of cities and forests boiled up as he watched; he could never map them all. Easier to turn his eyes downrail to ordinary land – to desolate tracks where leaves and old tickets drifted along with the discarded skins. Yet even here there was a warping and tug on the landscape.

ALL STATIONS. *Click.* ALL STATIONS.

The Train pulled in with a volley of sparks and steel. He saw many Trains, arriving as one: industrial husks with magma hearts; genteel engines of brass and enamel; chitinous bullets and shaped storms; worms with carriages wired howdah-like to their backs. He saw much more than these, layers and layers with no end or centre. After a moment he had to pull his gaze back before he was lost forever.

"I asked my captain for the time of day . . . he said he throwed his watch away."

Edwin's work on the manuscript had given him the ability to see more aspects of the Train, but the study would only ever be a scratch on the surface. How had he ever thought a camera could capture this? The thing was glorious.

And it rolled right over Carla.

She went down without a sound.

"Dear Christ," he whispered. First a liar, now he had blood on his hands. If this was the transformation wrought by the Train, he wanted no part of it.

Emily grabbed his shoulder. "Come on Edwin, she'll be alright. The bitch is immortal, isn't she?"

Bitch. That didn't sound like Emily. But the woman at his side didn't *look* like the Emily he had met such a short time ago. Her face was transfigured, eyes bright. It was hard to tell where her breath ended and the Train's began. She was totally ruthless.

Emily has already sloughed herself, he realised. Layers of mind that trapped her in fear and timidity... all gone.

"Come on Edwin, get your things. Forget about her. We have to go. The Train will stop soon." She picked up her cat and her bag.

The Train stopped in a grinding of gears that sent shivers through him. It subsided with a steamy sigh.

The doors didn't open straight away. That would give him some time to think...

"Edwin, stop dithering!" Emily scolded.

"Emily, I am a born ditherer. Literally. I was born two weeks late, as if I couldn't decide whether to stay in the womb or take a chance in the big outside. My mother had to have her labour induced. Or so she tells me. I can't remember a thing."

"Edwin!" But he saw Emily was laughing. If she had changed, at least she had retained a sense of humour.

Finally, the doors to the train slid open with a whisper and a drawn-out hiss. Light spilled out of the Train's darkness, but Edwin couldn't see who or what was inside.

Then he heard a familiar voice. "Edwin! Hop on, will you?" And when he looked up, he met the eyes of Charles peering down from an upper window.

"Charles! It's Charles! He's at a window upstairs."

Emily only nodded. Perhaps she was humouring him. Or she thought she was being kind. *But Charles is dead*, Edwin thought. *You held him as he died.*

Charles beckoned.

He didn't look like a ghost. His cheeks were ruddy with good health or perhaps a glass or two of red wine. His face had always been thin but now the hollows of illness were gone. His hair was lush again, down to the collar. Edwin had nagged him about getting it cut many times. In return Charles had gently poked Edwin in the stomach. "You should lose a few inches too, Ed." It became a long-running joke for them.

Edwin couldn't dither any longer. This time, he was pulling Emily towards the Train. "OK, I'm coming. Let's go!" And they rushed through the doors of the Train to stumble inside, with Fintan protesting at his rough ride.

A dog sitting near the luggage rack looked up. A birdcage was hooked to a passenger strap; the parrot inside squawked out a curse. Emily wasn't the only passenger to bring a pet. Edwin couldn't do anything except laugh. Oh, Charles would find this funny.

He had to find Charles. Where the hell is he?

Inside, the Train looked surprisingly normal. Passengers filled the seats. At first glance, they seemed like the passengers on any train. Perhaps many were people he didn't see about much in his town; people of African or Asian or Mediterranean origin. All ages.

But there was a shimmering to the edges of surfaces and objects, as if they masked a different state of things. And if he looked at his surroundings in another way, the right way, he would see layers unfold, surfaces invert. He thought of the Train's approach, the many shapes he saw lurking behind the first form to arrive.

"Alright, mate? Looking for anyone?" A sharp-faced little man with blond hair in rat's tails glanced up from his fiddle. The instrument was budding, breaking out into spruce needles and maple leaves.

Edwin only looked for one face. "Charles, I have to find Charles."

"Let's find seats first and get settled," said Emily. "I need to give Fintan some food and water. Then we can explore, and you can find your *friend*. I look forward to meeting him."

"You look forward to meeting Charles? You're not just humouring a madman seeing ghosts?"

"Mad? You told me nothing could be madder than anything in your book. So I'm saying . . ."

The *book*. He'd left it on the bench. He was so excited about seeing Charles in that window that he'd left *The Turning Track* behind. Charles wouldn't forgive him for that. He couldn't forgive himself.

"Emily, I forgot the book. I have to get it. The train's not left yet. I can get off and . . ."

"No, you can't. You can't get off. You may never be able to get back on. You *can't*."

"Listen to the lady, mate. She talks sense," the fiddle-player said. "You won't forgive yourself if you miss this train." He gave them a pointed glance. "And if you hold us up much longer, neither will I. I'm late enough as it is." He went back to pruning the violin, throwing foliage to the floor.

Did everyone know his business on here?

Any thought of jumping off and on was cancelled by sudden vibrations beneath Edwin's feet. The Train must be ready to go. It had rolled over Carla, and now it was rolling on.

"Edwin, we'll find seats upstairs. We're heading in the right direction. You said you saw Charles at an upstairs window."

Didn't Emily see Charles at the window? Had he been imagining it after all?

Emily led him up the spiralling stairs, stopping at the first level. They walked along a passage and found a compartment with some space. This was more opulent than the first carriage Edwin had seen, with deep velveteen seats and chandeliers with sinuous branches. An older couple sat on one side of the compartment, and a little girl sat near the window. She seemed to be on her own, though she was waving at someone on the platform. Edwin noticed a cardboard tag tied to her wrist, with felt-tip pen writing on it. She held something like a balloon on a string, but by rights it should have swam under water, undulating and shedding blue light.

The couple nodded at Emily and Edwin. They were dressed for a wedding, but perhaps the marriage had taken place in a sideshow. His morning coat had been cut to accommodate the sleeping twin fused to his shoulder; under the woman's lace dress, every inch writhed with tattoos like a kaleidoscope. The child smiled at Fintan, but ignored Emily and Edwin. Ha, when he was a boy he'd preferred animals to people too.

"Let me make more room," said the woman. She pulled something closer to her, something semi-transparent and dry. She handled it as if it was fragile, and she was very fond of it.

That couldn't be . . .

"Yes, dear, it's my old skin. Though I was glad to get it off, I still want to keep it." She held it up as if it was a dress she planned to try on. "I'll never fit back in but I can't just throw it away, can I?"

While he'd been sickened by the skin found on the tracks, this didn't bother him.

The woman smiled, then folded the skin into her handbag. "So where's yours? You didn't leave it behind, did you?"

"I *did* leave something behind," admitted Edwin. "I'm still upset about it. But . . ."

The vibration coming from the base of Train grew louder. Edwin felt it leach into his bones. It was beginning to alarm him, but Fintan began purring along with it.

Emily took him out of the box and he settled on her lap, looking twice the size that Edwin had imagined. He fluffed his fur out and slitted his eyes in feline ecstasy. His purring filled the compartment, taking on the rhythm of a powerful motor. A sound of grit and machinery, reminding Edwin of the factory where he used to work as a clerk. Fintan's sides drew in and out with the noise like a bellows. Edwin remembered the device growing out of Henning's chest; could some machine be taking root in the cat?

The juddering grew, as if spurred by Fintan's purr. Then an answering vibration and blast of static came from above.

Edwin realised this was the Train's tannoy, brass horns like the thing he'd found growing at the petrol station. Garbled tongues came through the static, an avalanche of language. Then more familiar words: "Attention passengers. We're sorry to inform you that the Train is delayed again due to leaves on the line."

"What? No body under the Train?" Edwin blurted this out. The old man raised an eyebrow.

"We had that before, bodies on the line. It doesn't take long to deal with *that*. But those leaves . . . We were stopped just down the line for that." He shook both his heads. "Leaves . . . Cause no end of trouble."

The grinding below increased rather than diminished after the announcement. Then the Train began moving backwards.

The little girl kicked the seat with exasperation.

"Why's it going backwards?" Edwin was already assuming his companions were seasoned travellers on this train bound for 'all stations'.

"Dunno. It's not done that before," said the little girl. "I've been on this train a long time and all. I'm going to see my grandma." She wriggled her fingers in the belly of her balloon. "Been promised a whole shoal of these for my birthday."

"I'll go see what's going on, and I'll see if I can find Charles," Edwin told the others.

Outside the compartment, he walked along a central aisle that led to the front of the Train. Carla had compared the Train to an ocean liner, and he saw that it was holding a shape similar to that at the moment. He could walk along the aisle to an area that broadened out like the prow of a ship. He joined others looking out of the window.

As the Train drew backwards, he saw pages from his book – Charles' book – uncovered on the tracks. He must've left the folder unfastened after he showed the manuscript to Emily.

A lump came to his throat. The centre to his life had fallen out of it once again. And if he could find Charles – what would he tell him? And if Charles was truly dead in the world of the Train as well as his own, he would still be letting him down.

Then there was a movement just on the edge of his sight, from under the train. He saw a cardigan, now in tatters with track marks and bloodstains. The grey party dress torn. Carla herself, jagged but still in one piece, crawled along on the tracks. She stood up and jerked along in an unsteady walk.

Carla picked up a page, studied it for a moment. Then she looked back at the train and a new expression crossed her face. A grin, a gleam of fascination.

Edwin had seen a similar look in the mirror when he retired after a good night's work on *The Turning Track*.

As Carla picked up stray sheets of paper, Henning came out of his office streaming more ticker-tape. He bent and extended a hand to help Carla climb back on the platform. Then she picked up the folder with the rest of the book and added the rescued pages.

As the train started to move forward again, Carla suddenly looked up and waved at Edwin, then left the station with the manuscript held to her chest.

The Train took on speed, and the world beyond the glass became a smear. Stars snail-tracked the night. Edwin thought of leaves, pages on the line, and the Train-beat sounded to him like the clatter of typewriter keys.

Then the Train shuddered under his feet. "Switchback!" came the cry from the window. He rushed back to see the night pull itself inside out and the track torque into a thousand silver lines. They were high above *everything*. Edwin's ears popped; his stomach flipped as if he was on a rollercoaster.

Paper rustled. The fiddle-player was behind him, offering a bag and a sympathetic look. "Try a lozenge," he said. "It'll help with the vertigo. That first view does it to everyone." Numb, Edwin took one; it tasted like a pear drop but left a heat like brandy.

"Where do we go now?" he said.

The fiddler shrugged. "It's all stations, matey. Your choice. But wasn't there someone you wanted to find?" He poked a thumb towards the wrought-iron staircase before he slouched off.

Edwin put his hand on the bannister. The iron was cold, his breath turned to feathers. Somewhere above him Charles was waiting: he *had* to be. A year apart, what might have passed? Perhaps Charles had changed, as they all must change. Would he still be the Charles he loved . . . and would Charles accept any changes in Edwin?

"Best foot forward," Edwin told himself. Slowly at first, then rushing like a child, he went to look for his lover.

Afterword and Dedication

Most of these stories appeared in limited edition or out-of-print anthologies between 2005 to 2016, so I'm excited to make them more widely available.

I've had an interesting time revisiting stories a good few years after they've been written. The eternal question comes up: leave them be or tweak the shit out of them some more? Well, there's that 'near-future' segment that has since become near-past. Uh-oh, got a few things wrong there . . . ever heard of a device called an I-Voice? But even in less overt cases I always see ways to improve a piece even if it's been published.

At the same time, I want to avoid the 'enormous condescension of posterity'. That phrase comes from EP Thompson, who was discussing the way historians approach radical movements of the past, such as the Luddites – or even the free-loving medieval dissidents or the student occupiers of 2010 that you've met in these pages. I try to ask myself: what was going on when I wrote this? What was I thinking when I made those writerly decisions? Then I have a drink and go to bed and see what it looks like in the morning.

On this note I need to thank David Rix from Eibonvale Press for his patience and skilful editing. And before that, the editors who originally published these stories: Mark Beech, Tom Johnstone and the late Joel Lane, Gary Couzens, Laura Hird, Lavie Tidhar and Rebecca Levene, Trevor Denyer, Andy Cox, David Gullen, David V Barrett, Sarah Crabtree, Peter Coleborn and Pauline E Dungate, Anne Perry and all the Kindred Writing Competition judges, Allyson Bird, Des Lewis, Larry Yudelson, and others. Members of the T-Party (now Gravity's Angels) and Herding Cats writers groups also provided feedback and support over the years.

I originally planned to dedicate a story to Joel Lane, who died in 2013, then found it hard to choose. His legacy animates such a large swathe of these tales – as writer, editor, comrade and critic – that it's best to do that dedicating here.

"Pieces of Ourselves" was written for an anthology he began editing with Tom Johnstone, *Horror Uncut: Tales of Economic Insecurity and Unease*. Sadly, he died before it was completed.

I started "The Peak" around the same time, but finished it much later – this is its first appearance. I'm pleased to publish them together because they're really companion pieces, both taking place within the anti-austerity resistance of 2010-11. "Survivor's Guilt", first published in *Black Static*, was reprinted by Joel along with Allyson Bird in *Never Again: Weird Fiction Against Racism and Fascism*. Joel also provided feedback on a draft of the "The Turning Track" to me and Mat.

"The Pleasure Garden" was written for *What Remains*, an anthology edited by Peter Coleborn and Pauline E Dungate. This unique collection brought together stories inspired by Joel's notes and fragments, so he's a posthumous collaborator as well.

Joel was known for his generosity to other writers. He believed that creativity doesn't flourish in isolation, but it is fed by engagement and commitment. This approach has informed the way I've tried to write, along with his fiction – a melancholic merging of social realism and the strange. He is still very much missed.

Finally, I'd like to thank Lynda E. Rucker for writing such an inspiring introduction. I'm also grateful to Birmingham writer Mat Joiner for his permission to reprint our collaboration, "The Turning Track".

If you're interested in reading more about these stories – and further writings – come visit my blog at rosannerabinowitz.wordpress.com.

Rosanne Rabinowitz
I started writing when I produced 'zines in the 1990s like *Feminaxe* and *Bad Attitude*, contributing articles, reviews and interviews. Then I began to make stuff up. My fiction has since found its way into anthologies and magazines and I completed a creative writing MA at Sheffield Hallam University. My novella *Helen's Story* was a finalist for the 2013 Shirley Jackson Award for achievement in the 'literature of the dark fantastic'. I live in South London, an area that Arthur Machen once described as "shapeless, unmeaning, dreary, dismal beyond words." In this most unshapen place I engage in a variety of occupations including care work, copywriting and freelance editing. I spend a lot of time drinking coffee and listening to loud music while looking out my tenth-floor window. Sometimes it's whisky.

Lynda E. Rucker has published numerous stories and essays in various magazines and books, as well as two short story collections, *The Moon Will Look Strange* and *You'll Know When You Get There*. She is a regular columnist for the horror and dark fiction magazine *Black Static*.

Mat Joiner lives near Birmingham, where they can be found haunting second-hand bookshops, real-ale pubs, and canal towpaths. Their stories and poetry have appeared in the likes of *Strange Horizons, Lackingtons, Uncertainties II, Something Remains*, and *Not One of Us*. They co-edit the speculative poetry webzine *Liminality*.

Lightning Source UK Ltd.
Milton Keynes UK
UKHW040952120419
340936UK00002B/812/P

9 781908 125514